CHARLOTTE FIGG
TAKES OVER PARADISE

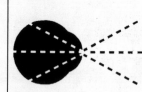

This Large Print Book carries the
Seal of Approval of N.A.V.H.

CHARLOTTE FIGG
TAKES OVER PARADISE

A NOVEL OF BRIGHT'S POND

JOYCE MAGNIN

THORNDIKE PRESS

A part of Gale, Cengage Learning

JUL   2011

GALE
CENGAGE Learning™

Detroit • New York • San Francisco • New Haven, Conn • Waterville, Maine • London

GALE
CENGAGE Learning

LIBRARY OF CONGRESS CATALOGING-IN-PUBLICATION DATA

Moccero, Joyce Magnin.
  Charlotte Figg takes over Paradise : a novel of Bright's Pond / by Joyce Magnin.
    p. cm. — (Thorndike Press large print Christian fiction)
  ISBN-13: 978-1-4104-3853-9 (hardcover)
  ISBN-10: 1-4104-3853-8 (hardcover)
  1. Widows—Fiction. 2. Trailer camps—Fiction. 3. Female friendship—Fiction. 4. Abused women—Fiction. 5. Large type books. I. Title.
  PS3601.L447C47 2011
  813'.6—dc22   2011011928

Published in 2011 by arrangement with Abingdon Press.

Printed in Mexico
1 2 3 4 5 6 7 15 14 13 12 11

To Pammy
who truly understands
the meaning of friendship

It always amazes how many
cheerleaders, experts, and editors
it takes to write a novel,
and this one is no exception.

Thank you to:

My friend, Pam Halter,
who reads every single word,
even the words that never
make it into the finished book.

My children, Emily and Adam,
who continue to understand Mama's
wacky world of writing.

The Crue — ever faithful,
ever ready to pray, advise,
and dress up in fat suits
when you need them to.

My editor, Barbara Scott,
who continues to believe and teach.

The women in my
Wednesday morning Bible study,
who laugh, pray, and listen.

Dr. Nancy Horvitz Rist,
who taught me how to deliver a baby.

All the staff and students in the
Chestnutwold Elementary
Before and After School program,
who make me smile every day.

Nick Pelka, who taught me
much about firefighting.

And, of course, my mother,
who taught me the importance
of good pie and a good dog.

1

Redemption comes to people in many ways.

— Rose Tattoo

Rewriting the rules of Paradise did not come easy. But it did come, and I even managed to have a little fun along the way — fun with a few dollops of sadness, grief, and police activity tossed into the mix.

It all started one icy January morning in 1974 when my husband, Herman, shuffled into the kitchen, sat in his chair, opened the *Philadelphia Inquirer* with a sharp flick of his wrists, and blustered. It was a horsy kind of sound that emanated from deep within his bowels, rose through his stomach and up into his throat, and came out through his lips.

"World's coming to an end, Charlotte."

The world had been coming to an end for twenty-three of the twenty-six years we had been married. It was right after the price of porterhouse steak climbed to ninety-five cents a pound that Herman had this epiphany.

"Look here, Charlotte." Herman snapped his paper. "You know the end is coming when a man can't afford a good steak without taking out a second mortgage."

"That's nonsense," I said as I refilled his cup. "The world is not coming to an end just because of the price of steak."

But I should have known better than to say anything because Herman began announcing the imminent demise of life on Earth as we know it on a daily basis. That way I was certain no one could say Herman didn't see it coming.

But the only world that ended was his. A massive brain hemorrhage knocked Herman to the floor like a two-hundred-pound sack of russets. I was busy in the powder room at the time and only heard a loud thud.

There wasn't much a fifty-one-year-old, slightly arthritic woman with only a smattering of first-aid skills could do in that situation. So I rested Herman's large and balding head in my lap and wept while I waited for the ambulance. It seemed the right thing to do.

"I didn't actually see Herman fall," I told

the driver. "But I heard a loud bang — no — more like a big thud, duller than a bang. I thought at first a hollow tree limb had fallen in the backyard. But . . ." I snuffed a tear, "it was Herman."

Unfortunately, it never occurred to Herman that he would ever actually die. I think Herman always figured he'd be around for the rapture and get taken up into heaven in a blink of an eye. As a result, Herman made no provision for his death that I knew about. I searched high and low for papers, anything that would give me a clue about what I was to do now. I didn't even know where to bury him, let alone how to pay for it.

So after they took his body to the Gideon Funeral Home, I sat on the sofa and sobbed like a lost child for almost two hours until I decided I had no choice but to figure out what to do next. I rooted through drawers and boxes hoping to find an answer. At about nine o'clock that night I discovered a wrinkled life insurance policy with the Fuller Brush Company tucked away in the bottom of his samples bag. Herman was a Fuller Brush salesman, so I suppose it was the most reasonable place for him to keep the document. I doubt he ever read it. This had been the first time I ever went through his beloved samples bag. I felt a little criminal. He protected it like it held nuclear secrets.

At least his funeral would be paid for and there would even be some cash left over for me to live on. I didn't have a career, not like Herman. He loved selling his wares door-to-door, and he was pretty good at it. I think it made him sad and even angry sometimes that I did not share his enthusiasm for brushes and cleaning supplies, although I did like to keep a clean house and bake pie. It was the one thing I was good at, and maybe if the Fuller Brush Company came out with a line of pie tins I might have been more enthusiastic.

The day after I found the policy I called that nice James Deeter at the Combined Insurance Company. James was a dear. He came over early the next morning and held my hand and served me coffee and walked me through the final arrangements. I thought that I would have liked it if I had a son like James.

He even drove me down to Gideon's so I could pick out a casket. Did you know that funeral homes have a casket showroom? I didn't. And I'm not too proud to admit that I felt a little woozy when I went inside and saw all the models. I counted fifteen different coffins and thought Herman might have been able to sell the Gideon's a boatload of lemon oil to keep those caskets gleaming the way they did.

After that chore was finished and James headed back to the insurance office, I set out to find a reverend or pastor, someone who could give Herman a proper burial. I did not want Frank Gideon to drop him in a hole without some sort of service.

I opened the yellow pages and found the number for Maple Tree Church of Faith — the church I attended as a child and into my teen years until I finally had my fill of people who said one thing on Sunday and lived another the rest of the week.

Pastor Herkmeier agreed to bury Herman. Of course, he wasn't the pastor when I attended Maple Tree. That was eons ago, and I was certain that Pastor Virgil had long since retired or died. I took the bus to see Reverend Herkmeier after taking one of Herman's suits to the funeral home — he had six gray suits, exactly alike. He only wore white shirts (long sleeve in winter, short in summer) and skinny striped ties. I wondered if I should bring undershorts. I did just in case, a freshly bleached pair.

The church stood right where it always had, down a country road and tucked away off the street in a clearing near some woods. But it was still only about a two-block walk from the bus stop. I didn't drive much. No need to really. We only had one car and Herman needed it for sales calls. He drove me pretty much everywhere I needed to go, and when he couldn't, SEPTA, the Southeast Public Transportation Authority, was happy to oblige. Riding the bus was always an adventure. You just never knew who you were going to meet or what you would see. One time I witnessed an actual purse-snatching as we drove past the Italian Market. The driver radioed the incident in, and everyone on the bus rushed to the driver's side for a better look. By then the perpetrator had bolted down Arch Street clutching the old woman's bag like a football.

Generally, the passengers on board were cordial. If there wasn't a seat, I could always count on a nice young gentleman to offer me his. It made me feel special.

Maple Tree Church was a pretty little chapel with bright red doors and a tall white steeple with a lightning rod that stood just a little taller than the trees. Seemed strange to me that God would need a lightning rod. Imagine that, zapping your own house. Of course, the building showed its age. Ivy or lichen or some such parasite greened-up the otherwise gray and silvery stone walls.

After my two-block walk from the bus stop, I took a deep breath and went inside where a young woman in a tight, blue sweater greeted me. "Can I help you?"

"My name is Charlotte Figg. I'm here to see Pastor Herkmeier."

She looked at me over the top of her pointy glasses. "Go right in. He's expecting you." The woman sat about two feet from her desk, I supposed, in order to accommodate her extra large breasts that otherwise would have continually knocked her coffee cup over.

I hesitated at the office door until Reverend Herkmeier, who stood behind a large oak desk strewn with books and papers, invited me inside.

"Mrs. Figg. Come in, come in." His voice sounded like crushed velvet. "I am indeed sorry for your loss."

He indicated a leather chair — the kind with brass buttons all around. I sat and locked my ankles around the feet of the chair just in case the temptation to run struck me. The pastor, a tall, Lincolnesque man with a ski-slope nose and a high forehead that reached clear back to his ears, twiddled his thumbs on top of the desk. I

13

made a mental note. Twiddlers, in my opinion, were the nervous sort and not to be trusted.

I imagined him in a Roman toga and wearing an ivy wreath around his bald spot. The vision relaxed me enough to speak. That was a trick I learned from my mother. She always imagined people in "alternate capacities" as she called it. She said, "Charlotte, some folks just can't be taken for who they say they are. You have to imagine their true selves and go with that." Which is why she said she always imagined my father in a tweed jacket with elbow patches. Daddy owned his own plumbing and heating company, but he wanted to write stories and live like Ernest Hemingway.

"Thank you for doing this, Pastor," I said.

"Of course, of course, Mrs. Figg." He twiddled with a tad more gusto. "I suppose the standard funeral service would be sufficient. Or did you have something special in mind?"

Special. The word stung like a mosquito. I think I might have even swatted it away with the back of my hand. There was nothing special about Herman's life, so why make his funeral into something extraordinary? Humdrum summed his life up best. Perhaps that was why Herman blustered every morning.

"No, no thank you, nothing special."

"That's fine. I can meet you at the funeral home — Gideon's, correct? — at ten o'clock on Thursday. Is that time enough to make arrangements and gather family and friends?"

I chewed my left index fingernail, still ruminating on what was special about Herman. "Unless you think it would be all right to bury him with his samples bag," I said. "I mean, Herman loved that bag. The feel of it, the smell. Kept it right near the bedside every single night. It was like his best friend." I scratched an itch above my right eye. "I think he liked that bag more than me," I whispered.

"Excuse me, Mrs. Figg. Did you say something?"

"Oh, no, no — but about that samples bag."

"Just be sure to bring it to the funeral home," Pastor Herkmeier said. "I'm certain they'll accommodate you. Frank Gideon is a good man. I once buried a woman with her cocker spaniel. They died on the same day. Can you believe that? I mean, what are the odds of —"

I coughed.

"I'm sorry, Mrs. Figg. Now, how about music? My wife, Lucinda, will be pleased to play the piano during the viewing time. She plays a lovely rendition of 'In the Garden.' She can sing it also, if you like."

I nodded. The viewing. Odd the things you don't think about when planning a funeral until you have to. Imagine that, people filing past Herman's dead body. When everything was planned, I thanked the pastor, waited for the bus, and rode home. I did all this without shedding a single tear.

But I will admit that walking into my house that afternoon was one of the most difficult things I have ever done. I stood on the stoop in the freezing air for half a minute or so before opening the front door. Maybe it was just a dream. But no.

Herman was gone, yet the house still smelled like him — a mixture of Old Spice, lemon oil, and cedar spray. I could feel his presence everywhere, especially when I stubbed my toe for the gazillionth time on his oversized La-Z-Boy recliner in the living room. It was pointed right straight toward the Magnavox TV. I had never sat in the chair — not once.

I flopped on the sofa, and the first tear of the day rolled down my cheek and splashed on my knee. "Now, why are you crying, Charlotte Figg? Tears are not going to bring Herman back." But reprimanding myself didn't make the tears stop or help me make sense of this. So there I sat in my hat and heavy coat — the one with the fuzzy collar — and cried like a baby. "Herman, you idiot. Now what am I going to do?"

The phone rang and startled the bejeebers out of me.

"Hello," I said with my palm on my thumping chest.

"Charlotte? What's the matter with you?"

"Mother," I said.

"I've been trying to reach you for hours. Where in the heck were you? I know something is wrong, Charlotte. Did that Herman finally haul off and hit you? I knew this day was coming. I knew —"

"Mother," I said with as much force as I could muster. "I have to tell you something."

I could hear her nervous breathing. "I knew it. I just knew it," she said. "And you know about my feelings, Charlotte."

I did. My mother had a feeling that JFK would be assassinated, and to this day she feels guilty for not informing the Secret Service? Right then, she made a solemn vow she would never let another feeling go by without informing the proper governmental agency or individual.

"Mother. Herman is dead."

"What? When? Oh, dear me, Charlotte did you finally lose your mind and —"

"Mother. Don't be ridiculous."

"It's a valid question, Charlotte. Now tell me what happened."

I told her the story and waited for the reply I knew would come. My mother, Lillian DeSalle, now seventy-two and living at the Cocoa Reef Retirement Village in Tampa Bay, Florida, never liked Herman.

"Well, Charlotte. I am sorry, now. I truly am. But —"

"Mother. Please don't. Not today."

"When's the funeral? Did you use Gideon? They took good care of your father, God rest his soul."

In my mind, I could see her look to the heavens, pick up his framed image, now enshrined on the telephone table next to a perpetual electric candle and a bouquet of plastic roses, and kiss his nose.

"Yes, Mother. I went to Gideon, and Pastor Herkmeier from our old church is going to do the service."

"Herkmeier? Who is Herkmeier? What happened to Pastor Virgil?"

"He's dead."

"I'll be on the next plane, Charlotte.

18

Don't bother coming to the airport; I know you can't drive —"

"I can too drive. I just —"

"Never mind that. I'll taxi out to your house."

I hung up the phone, oddly comforted that the one and only Lillian DeSalle was coming to visit.

2

Later that same day, my neighbor Midge from down the street came over with a chicken pot pie. "I thought it might help take the chill off," she said. It was in a pretty white casserole dish decorated with delicate rosebuds and smelled like celery and comfort. Midge was only a couple of years older than me but already a grandmother to three boys. She liked to wear polka dots and stripes and her blondish hair short like Doris Day's.

"Please stay," I said. "I think I still have Jell-O in the fridge for dessert."

"With fruit?"

I twisted my mouth. "Sorry, Midge, I didn't have the gumption to add fruit this time. It's just red."

"I understand. Do you have Reddi-wip?"

I shook my head no.

Midge and I ate chicken pot pie and talked about Herman and insurance policies until nearly nine o'clock. I walked her to the foyer, turned on the porch light, pulled open the door, and in tumbled my mother.

"Charlotte," she said after she regained her balance. "I had my hand on the knocker. Didn't you hear me at the door?"

"Mother, I'm sorry. I didn't know you were there. I was just seeing Midge home."

Midge peeked out from behind me and wiggled her fingers. "Hi."

"Hello," Mother said.

I raised my eyebrows at Midge. "I'll see you later. Thanks for the pot pie."

"Thanks for the Jell-O."

My mother stood there looking at me like I had deliberately tried to make her stumble.

"I wasn't expecting you until the morning," I said.

"Took an earlier flight." She stepped into the living room while I retrieved her gray Samsonite from the front porch.

My mother and I sat in the kitchen for an hour or so, nervously avoiding conversation while engaging in small talk.

"Do you need anything, Charlotte? Did that bum leave you insurance?"

There, she said it. Lillian DeSalle had come to the point.

21

"Don't call him a bum. And yes, I think I'll have plenty of money to live on. Maybe I'll get a job."

"You? What can you do? I told you you'd regret not finishing secretarial school. I told you a career should come first but no, no, you were in love." She made a dismissive, wavy motion with her hand.

"Mother."

She looked into my eyes and then reached out with her thumb and wiped a tear from my cheek. "I just wanted more for you."

My mother had been a buyer for John Wanamaker Department Store in Center City, Philadelphia. She had loved her work and thought every woman should have a career. She had worked hard and collected nearly a dozen awards for a job well done.

"Husbands are a dime a dozen, but a good career for a woman is hard to find," she had said.

"I know you always wanted my best, Mother. But did I really do that terrible?"

"Terribly," she said.

And that was pretty much how things went until the day of the funeral, which turned out mostly nice. Pastor Herkmeier did a fine job. I smiled and greeted the mourners as best I could, while my mother stood by with her long fingers intertwined in front and a practiced funeral face.

It was good to have Midge with me. She wore a navy dress with a white collar, white shoes with dark blue buckles, and a little sailor hat tipped to the left on her head. I never asked why she had felt the need to wear a sailor hat and only told her how glad I was that she came. I dressed in black except for secret pink undergarments with white lace edging that helped me feel a little less dismal. My mother made certain that I carried a small flask of cooking sherry tucked inside my purse in case I felt faint. As I remember, I might have taken three or four sips.

At one point, Gideon's viewing room was standing room only, jammed to the jalousies with Fuller Brush salesmen from all over the region. I had never seen so many gray suits, polished black shoes, and fedoras at one time.

"My goodness," Mother said after she had shaken the hand of the thirteenth salesman, "but these men all look like they popped right off some assembly line. When I was buying for Wanamaker, I met many sales-people and —"

I had to touch her shoulder. "Not here."

She took a breath and sidled near Herman's coffin.

"I'm sorry about Herman, Mrs. Figg," said a tall, skinny man who introduced himself as the regional sales manager. "He was one of our best." Then he slid an orange Fuller Brush letter opener into Herman's breast pocket. He smiled at me, plopped his gray hat on his head, and hurried out into the gray day.

By the time the funeral was over, Herman had been buried with twenty-nine letter openers in his pocket, his samples bag tucked at his left hand, and his gray fedora grasped neatly in his right hand. And there he was, Herman Quincy Figg, on his way to that final sales call in heaven. At least I hoped it was heaven.

Mother left that evening.

"My taxi is here," she said, looking out the window. "Now, you call me if you need anything. Anything at all."

"Thank you for coming, Mother. I'll be fine. I have everything I need."

She stood near the front door while the driver took her bag to the cab. She looked into my face like she was drilling for oil with her eyes. "Whatever happened to that feisty girl who climbed trees and could throw a baseball better than any boy?"

"She got married."

Mother pointed at my heart. "She might still be in there."

"Call me when you get home." I kissed her cheek.

"By the way, I couldn't help but notice your dish towels could use a splash of Clorox, and don't put chicken bones in the disposal, dear. Not good for the blades."

Once the taxi was out of sight, I went into the house, locked the door, and cried.

Three days later I met Lucky.

I opened the front door at around eight in the morning and in bounded the ugliest, hairiest mutt I had ever seen. He had wiry whiskers and eyebrows, and he looked for all the world like Nikita Khrushchev. His white paws reminded me of little girl anklets. With only a gnarled thumb — about the size of a Vienna sausage — for a tail, he went straight for Herman's chair, sniffed first, and took advantage of its cushiony comfort. He sat on his haunches, with his tongue lolled out, and panted like he had won a marathon.

My intruder barked once with a bark that seemed to emanate from deep within his bowels and then barrel through his stomach, up his throat, and out his snout. I stood there in a quasi state of shock with my hand still on the opened door. I thought Herman had come back to me in a dog's body but chalked it up to imagination.

The dog let go a second blustery bark.

"How rude," I said. "You can't just barge into a person's house like this and . . . and sit in her chair and . . . and bluster like her dead husband. Now go on home."

The dog scooted outside, but he camped in the yard for three days. Every so often I heard one of his barks and I felt sorry for him. So after some consideration, I invited him in and gave him three shampoo baths in a galvanized bucket in the backyard in the cold. I wore one of Herman's suit jackets because I didn't want to get my own clothes wet and soiled with dog grime. I dried him off with one of my good Egyptian cotton bath towels, which I subsequently dubbed Lucky's towel. About halfway through the drying I smiled when it occurred to me that if Herman had witnessed this he would have yelled something awful at me for sacrificing one of our good towels to the dog's cause.

I named him Lucky and bought him a black collar with purple rhinestones. It had been the first real financial decision, besides choosing a solid oak casket, I had made since Herman's surprising demise.

"There you go, Lucky." I clasped the collar around his skinny neck. "Guess this makes it official." He licked my face.

I found it easy to talk to Lucky, and I appreciated his affection, but I still felt like I was banging into walls with no direction. Kind of like a pinball but without all the bells and whistles and music and points.

Then one day Lucky came home with the neighbor's mail.

"Bad dog, Lucky," I said. "You mustn't steal mail. It's a federal offense, you know."

Lucky looked dejected at first but then he wagged his preposterously stubby tail and all was forgiven.

I rifled through the small stack bound with a rubber band that held the advertisements inside an RV magazine called *Road Tripper.* My eyebrows lifted. "I didn't know the Parsons had a recreational vehicle," I told Lucky. "I've never seen it, but Evie and Lewis do seem to be gone for long stretches several times a year."

Out of curiosity, I thumbed through the periodical and stopped when I saw a small block of type with bold letters pierced by a canine incisor that read:

For Sale, Nice-looking double-wide.
Contact: Fergus Wrinkel, Paradise
Trailer Park.

A small image of a light gray trailer with wide windows and awnings with hanging baskets of pink and purple trailing verbena caught my eye. The sun setting in the distance painted ribbons of orange and lilac across a sky the color of my favorite copper-bottom frying pan. I was filled with a sudden burst of wanderlust.

My heart beat as fast as the mashed potato setting on my Mixmaster. "Paradise." I said the word with a come-hither tone. Not that I had planned it. It just came out that way. "Imagine that, Lucky. We could move to" — I took another breath and exhaled the word — "Paradise." I rubbed my arms. Just the thought of living in a place called Paradise gave me goose pimples. But I closed the magazine, banded all the mail together, and dropped it on the dining room table.

"Charlotte Louise Figg," I said right out loud. "What are you saying? You can't up and move to Paradise. What would Herman think?"

I made a cup of tea, sat at the dining table, and stared at the rolled-up magazine. I kept touching it and knocking it around. Finally, I couldn't stand it anymore and opened to the page with the beautiful little trailer and nearly swooned over the verbena.

That afternoon I purchased the trailer, sight unseen, from Fergus Wrinkel, manager of The Paradise Trailer Park.

Six weeks later Lucky and I set out for our new home. I sold my house to a nice young couple — Jorge and Olivia Gonzalez. Jorge had just gotten a job as a produce supervisor at the Save-A-Lot supermarket, and Olivia was six months pregnant with their first child.

I left them the washer and dryer; all of the furniture except a Tiffany lamp, the beds, my lovely flowery sofa, and two chests of drawers; and various and sundry kitchen items like pots and pans, utensils, and my pie tins. I wanted to leave them Herman's La-Z-Boy. Jorge liked it.

"Look at this, Livie," he said as he settled the chair into its full reclining position. "I can rest here after work."

Olivia smiled. "Don't go thinking you'll be doing much resting, Jorge." She patted her bulging belly.

But no dice. Lucky wouldn't have it. He snarled and grabbed Jorge's pant leg and tried to pull him off the chair.

"Oh, my goodness gracious. I am so sorry." I rushed over and grabbed the dog by the collar. "Lucky likes the chair."

"No problem, Mrs. Figg. He didn't hurt me or nothin'," Jorge said. "I'll get a new one."

I smiled and handed him a set of house keys. "I'll leave the second set on the kitchen counter. And I also made a note with the names and numbers of the plumber, the electrician, the man who fixes my — um — your washer and dryer. Trash comes on Tuesday and Friday, and the mail is delivered by noon. If the heater goes off, just call Simon. He'll come right out. The man can fix anything, even if it's not broken. Every so often the shutters on the attic window bang against the house in a high wind, so don't get frightened and . . ." I stopped talking.

It was at that moment that I saw the reality of home ownership strike terror into the hearts of the nice young couple. Their eyes bugged out like cartoon characters.

"It is an old house," I said. "But she's a good house. And oh, I left you a pie — blueberry. And whipped cream in the fridge." Once I had gotten the agreement of sale, my baking desires returned. "And,

Jorge, make sure you check the freezer gasket. It might need replacing."

Olivia reached out and pulled me close for a hug. It surprised me a little. "Thank you, Mrs. Figg. Good luck in Paradise," she said. "I think it's wonderful, a woman your age doing such a thing."

"Why, thank you, young lady." And that was when I was suddenly filled with a sense of my own mortality, of time shifting, of the world belonging to the young. It gave me a funny feeling in my gut. There had to be something more waiting for me in Paradise. There just had to be.

That evening after supper — a TV dinner of Salisbury steak with French fries and a tiny peach cobbler — I called my mother.

"I sold the house and I'm moving to Paradise." I said the words fast because it was easier that way.

She fell silent for a good long time until she finally said, "Is this you, Charlotte?"

"Yes, Mother. It's me."

"Well, I just don't understand what the dickens you are talking about. Are you trying to tell me you're joining Herman in Paradise? Who believes that rat is even in Paradise. And —"

"Mother. Don't be ridiculous. I mean Paradise Trailer Park. I bought one."

"One what?"

"Trailer. They call it a double-wide."

She dropped the phone.

"Are you there?" I asked. "Are you all right?"

A minute later I heard her breathing again. "Yes, I'm here. I thought I heard you say the word *double-wide*. But you must have said, filled with pride, dear. You're just filled with pride over something."

"No, Mother. I said I bought a double-wide trailer."

"Oh, Charlotte. I cannot believe my ears."

And she hung up.

3

I naturally inherited Herman's Ford Galaxy convertible — candy apple red with white-wall tires. The paint shimmered in the sunlight like a bright ruby ring. He spent hours washing and polishing the thing like it truly was a precious jewel.

That nice James Deeter from the insurance company came over with two of his buddies, and they helped lug the heavy stuff and boxes to the short utility trailer named The Little Tough Guy I rented from Skip Cozy at the Texaco station. Skip told me to return it to any other Texaco close to my destination. I packed it with my most precious belongings, including two tall trophies I had stored in the attic from my softball days. I played second base for the Clifton Canaries right up until I married Herman and he told me that playing ball was for children and my trophies did not belong in the living room. I packed the trophies with newspapers and tucked them securely between two boxes of kitchen items.

Midge said she would help pack but she never showed up. Maybe Midge's gallbladder attacked her again. It usually did when there was work to be done. But that was okay. There wasn't much packing left to do after I decided she probably wasn't coming. Just clothes, some books — most of which I never read front to back — and my plate collection. My favorite came clear from Paris and had a picture of the Eiffel Tower at night on it. I forget how I came to acquire it. Herman might have gotten it on one of his business trips. Anyhoo, I packed everything I cared to pack. When we finished, I served James and his friends cherry pie and cold milk, which they ate sitting on the floor in my empty living room.

Lucky and I planned to set out for Paradise early on the morning of Tuesday, March 5.

We stopped to say good-bye to Midge at a quarter past seven that morning. I pulled the loaded-down Galaxy into Midge's driveway, but I had never pulled a trailer before and the back driver's side wheel snagged on Midge's mailbox and yanked it out of the lawn, taking a bed of roses, two cast-iron

34

garden gnomes, and six feet of lawn with it. The lamp I had shoved into the backseat, minus its shade and bulb, poked a hole through the convertible roof.

"My gnomes," Midge cried. "You killed them."

"My roof," I cried. "Herman will kill me." But then my eyebrows arched and I felt better. Even Herman's bluster could not reach me now.

I climbed under the little trailer and recovered two twelve-inch gnomes with white beards and red jerkins. "They're alive, Midge. Just a bit soiled. A good hosing will take care of it." I handed them to Midge. "I'm sorry. I'm trying to get used to driving a car again, and one with a trailer wobbling behind, for goodness sake. Not as easy as it looks when you see them whizzing past you on the highway."

"It's okay." She sniffed.

Midge and I stood in the cold for a few minutes. She clutched the gnomes to her chest. "Now, you're sure about this," she said. "Change is always hard, especially when you're used to the same."

"The same?"

"You know, the same voices, smells, the same way of doing things day to day. And now that's changing. I just thought it might be hard."

"But change can be good too, right?"

"Sometimes." She clutched her gnomes to her chest. "I only want what's best for you. Lord knows you deserve it after all you endured."

I felt the corners of my eyes crinkle as I smiled. Midge knew more than I thought she did. "It will be. I can't wait to see my new home in Paradise."

After we pulled the brass floor lamp from the backseat and sealed the hole with about six yards of duct tape, we said our final good-bye.

"I'll miss you," Midge said.

"I'll miss you too."

"You're sure you want to do this?"

"I am. It just . . . it just feels right." I took a deep breath and turned the key in the ignition.

The road to Paradise was paved with asphalt. I had written out the directions on a piece of notebook paper that I had to keep referring to in order to stay on course.

It wasn't long before I saw a sign for the Jack Frost Ski Resort. "Lucky, I am so excited. Did you see that sign? This is where we get off the turnpike. Start looking for the Paradise Trailer Park. It's supposed to be not far from the exit." I felt my spirit soar like I was riding the Wildcat Coaster on the Ocean City Boardwalk.

I had driven about thirteen miles when I saw a sign for Shoops Borough. I glanced at my directions, "This is it, Lucky. Mr. Wrinkel said I need to drive through Shoops and look for a sign to Bright's Pond and then right after that we'll see another sign for Paradise Trailer Park."

Shoops was a big small town. We passed through it quickly and only had to stop at two red lights. Then I saw a sign that read, "Welcome to Bright's Pond. Home of the World's Largest Blueberry Pie."

"Would you look at that? Home of the world's largest blueberry pie. I knew this was the right place for us. Imagine that, a town that understands the importance of pie."

Soon we were driving through the quaintest little town I had ever seen. We passed a small church across the street from a large Victorian house. There was a delightful-looking diner called the Full Moon Café. I would have stopped in for a cup of coffee and a piece of pie, but a quick glance at my watch told me I'd better head on toward Paradise. I had told Mr. Wrinkel we'd be there around noon.

Just a few minutes later I pulled The Little Tough Guy up a hill. When we reached the top I saw two spectacular and large green, orange, and yellow painted palm trees with wide leaves and coconuts on either side of a driveway on my left. A neon rainbow arch connected them. The word Paradise blinked on and off in the rainbow. I was so surprised I drove right past them and nearly crashed into a truck carrying logs.

"Goodness gracious, Lucky, did you see those palm trees?"

I slammed on the breaks and nearly jack-knifed The Little Tough Guy. But fortunately, he stayed upright. I negotiated a tricky U-turn, much to the dismay of the log driver, and headed back for the palm trees. Lucky and I drove under the rainbow into Paradise. He was so happy riding on the front seat with his tongue lolled out and wearing a wide smile. He barked twice as if to say, "We're home."

I slowed to a turtle's pace over the speed bumps. Multicolored trailer homes lined up like crayons in a box on either side of the street. In the periphery of my eye, I caught sight of another sign that read MANAGER and pointed a brown-painted finger toward a long green trailer nestled inside a grove of trees. Two tiny pink neon flamingoes flanked what I assumed to be the front door, and the word MANAGER, also in pink neon, hung over the top.

"That must be Fergus Wrinkel's office," I told Lucky. I parked on the street behind a red Datsun and heaved a huge sigh of relief that my trailer didn't capsize on the way over the speed bumps, crack open like an egg, and dump all my worldly possessions on the road.

I lingered in the car and took in the sights. The park seemed pleasant enough with groves of trees and trailers with awnings and white picket fences. Some had flower gardens with tiny gnomes like Midge's. I saw pink flamingoes standing on one leg, angel statues, and clotheslines. Other trailers looked disheveled, with weeds and overgrown grass and hanging-down, dilapidated metal roofs. Just about every single one displayed an American flag. Remnants of the last snowfall were still evident in dirty, exhaust-painted snow heaped in the shade of the trailers. Two women dodged a couple of potholes as they walked down the road. One carried grocery bags while the other pushed a stroller. When they saw me, they disappeared as quickly as snipers.

"Well they looked nice," I said. "Younger

than me, but nice enough. Just a little shy, I guess."

I draped my arm around Lucky. "Just like any old neighborhood, I suppose. Now you stay here a minute while I fetch the keys to our house from Mr. Wrinkel."

I saw no bell button, so I pulled open the rickety screen door. My knock made a tinny, hollow sound. I waited what I thought was enough time and then knocked again. The door opened slowly. One eye, one ear, and a nose peeked from the side.

"Hello," I said. "I'm looking for Mr. Wrinkel."

Nothing.

"My name is Charlotte Figg." I spoke a little louder in case the ear was hard of hearing. I couldn't tell if I spoke to a young ear or an elderly ear. "I purchased the double-wide on Mango Street. I called and told Mr. Wrinkel I'd be arriving today. About this time." I'm not sure why, but at the end of each sentence my voice rose as though I asked a question. It just came out like I wasn't very sure, and I hoped the person behind the door wouldn't think I was a crackpot.

The door opened a trifle more, and I stood eye-to-eye with a woman exactly my height who had mussed strawberry-blonde

40

hair and sad eyes. At least I thought they were sad. Dark shadows circled below their dark depths, but they also held a hint of sparkle like sunken treasure. I felt a thud in the pit of my stomach as I gazed at her in the silence. I covered my reaction with a smile.

"He ain't here," the woman said. "Gone on down to the hardware store in Shoops."

"Are you Mrs. Wrinkel?"

"Yes." She looked down at her feet or my feet, I couldn't tell which.

"Could you please give me the key? I'd like to get settled." I tried to sound more authoritative.

"Key's down there. Fergus don't keep keys in the house. Look under the mat or a rock or something. You'll find it."

I stared at the woman a moment longer before she backed away and closed the door. I heard the lock turn.

Back in the car, I spoke to Lucky. "That was an odd welcome, wasn't it? I certainly did not expect trumpeters announcing my arrival, but a considerate 'It's nice to meet you' would have been nice."

I drove slowly down the rough road. The hilly terrain forced me to keep an eye on The Little Tough Guy as we navigated over potholes and speed bumps. The trailer park gave off a summer camp vibe, complete with the odor of mold and pine.

I had no trouble finding the intersection and negotiated the right-hand turn with only the sound of what I thought was one box tumbling in the back. Stretched out between two other mobile homes, one sky blue and the other brown, sat my long double-wide trailer. It still had the scrawny FOR SALE sign stuck in a small patch of brown lawn I assumed was the front yard. I could not believe my eyes and blinked so hard I just nearly missed by a tail-length hitting a cat that darted out between two parked cars. I pulled onto a cement pad just wide and long enough to fit the Galaxy. The trailer hung out on the street like a big toe.

Lucky let loose a loud, blustery bark.

"I wish you wouldn't do that, boy," I said. "It gives me the willies."

Lucky bounded out of the car and wasted no time marking his territory. I stood near the Galaxy and stared. "Oh, dear," I said. "It's the color of the inside of an Andes Mint. This is not the trailer I saw in the magazine; that one was gray with a purple stripe and awnings and hanging baskets. This one is old and grungy." Lucky bounded over to me and rested his muddy paws on my waist. "Look at it, Lucky, it's awful."

Lucky licked my face and then dropped down. He scampered back to a small clump of trees still laden with snow around the trunks. He turned the piles from white to yellow in no time flat.

"My sentiments exactly," I murmured.

It was nearly noon. Cold and breezy air had rushed in like a cantankerous child, swirling up leaves on the ground and mussing my hair. I grabbed my handbag and heavy sweater out of the car and buttoned it all the way down. Since I wore a dress my calves were chilled like I always think chicken legs must be chilled when they run around their yards.

"This can't be it? Can it?" I checked for a trailer number. I bought number 19 and for a moment — a brief, shining moment — I thought I must be looking at the wrong trailer while I tried to locate a house number. But no, right smack dab on the front of the broken-down monstrosity was the number 19 in black paint, partially hidden by a dying yew bush. I made a mental note; cut down the ugly yew.

Lucky sniffed his way back to me. "This is it, boy. This is our new home, but something's not right. There must be a mistake. Maybe there are two Paradise Trailer Parks. Maybe we came to the wrong one. Maybe we drove into an alternate universe, you know? Like in the Twilight Zone?" Lucky shook his head and rattled his tags.

I spied an unusual rock, pitch-coal and shiny black, sitting near the cement slab like a hand had placed it there with intention. "I wonder, Lucky. You suppose our key could be hiding under that funny rock?" I kicked it over with my toe and uncovered a brass key.

A path made from splintered wood planks led to a small, square porch that looked more like an afterthought than a planned part of the trailer. It was really little more than a low deck with a slanted roof tacked onto the metal siding.

"Come on, Lucky," I called. "We might as well take a look inside." Walking down the wooden path was both odd and charming as we made clip-clop sounds reminiscent of a Western movie. The sounds echoed in the stillness of the park.

I took a breath and turned the key. I let my breath out when I heard the lock click. I turned the knob and nothing. The door stuck. I gave it a push with my hip and shoulder and when it swung open the smell that blew out nearly knocked me to the ground.

"Something must have died in there!" The

smell, a mixture of rot, mildew, and ages-
old cigarette smoke, gagged me. Lucky
scrabbled past me into the trailer to check
it out first. He barked and I nearly tumbled
feet-over-teacups off the deck when two
large, mangy beasts scampered between my
legs. "Oh, my goodness gracious. Were those
raccoons?" Lucky barked and raced off to
see what else he could find.

I stepped further inside, not far, maybe
twelve or thirteen inches, alert to the possibility of more stampeding wildlife. I felt
chilled and thought this must be what it
feels like to be a sockeye salmon in a can,
cold and totally out of my element. Linoleum the color of the inside of an eggplant
partially covered the floor. A thick, bilious
shag rug spewed over the rest of it. Someone
had paneled the walls with dark, thin paneling and covered the ceiling with white tiles,
the kind with a million tiny holes. Some of
the tiles had yellow stains and their bulging
fat bellies hung over the living room.

I walked into the small kitchen area and
noticed one of the cabinet doors had fallen
off its hinges. A tear rolled down my cheek
and into my mouth.

"Oh, Lucky. What have I done?"

4

A rickety card table stood under the kitchen bay window. An ash tray filled with old cigarette butts sat in the middle of the table. I set my purse down, pulled out the chair, brushed off the seat with my hand, and sat. The chair wobbled as though one of the legs was shorter than the others.

Lucky rested his head on my knee and looked at me from underneath his wiry eyebrows.

"It's not right, Lucky. I . . . we can't live here." And for the first time since he died, I wished Herman was there to tell me what to do. I'm not sure how long I sat there until a knock at the door startled me out of my reverie. Lucky barked and went to investigate.

"Yoo-hoo, yoo-hoo. Excuse me, yoo-hoo, excuse me. Charlotte? Charlotte Figg?"

"Hello," I called. "I'm in the kitchen." If you could call it that.

A woman wearing a heavy brown sweater with a wide collar over a long linen skirt and black boots walked toward me. She had a nice smile, twinkly eyes, and gobs of bright red, curly hair partially controlled by a long Peter Max scarf. I thought I saw an artist's paintbrush sticking out of the nest that was her head. Lucky stayed right with her, ready to defend me if necessary.

"I'm your neighbor, Rose Tattoo. Welcome to Paradise."

"Thank you," I said without really meaning it.

She looked around the trailer. "So what do you think?" She patted Lucky's head, and I thought I saw green vines tattooed on her hand. I thought to mention it but didn't in case she had some sort of weird, embarrassing physical affliction.

I averted my eyes. "It's . . . not what I expected."

Rose leaned against the small turquoise stove. "Asa — you haven't met him yet, but he takes care of things around here — thought you might be some kind of international spy looking for a place to hide out incognito. I told him he was nuts. But he insisted. Who else would buy this place except a spy needing a place to hide? That's what he said."

47

"I can assure you I am not a spy."

"Didn't think so." She gave Lucky a rub behind the ears. "He's a nice doggie. Kind of a mix, a mutt. He'll certainly fit in around here. But what in the heck happened to his tail?"

"I don't know. He came that way and we're not staying."

"What? Now, why in the world would you go to all the trouble of buying a trailer and then not stay? You sure you're not a spy or something?" She touched her hair. "Would you look at that? This is my number two brush. I was looking all morning for it and here it is in my head."

I fought back an urge to laugh. "For the last time, I am not a spy. I just . . . just . . ." I had to choke back tears. "I hate it. But I'm glad you found your brush."

"Well, what were you expecting? Didn't you know what you bought?"

I shook my head. "No, I thought I bought this." I pulled the picture of the trailer in the magazine out of my purse.

Rose looked at the image and clicked her tongue several times. "Looks like Fergus pulled a fast one." She tapped it with her brush. "What you got there is a picture of the Frost sisters' trailer."

"Frost sisters?"

"They live on the other side of Paradise."
She snorted air out her nose. "Now, that
sounds a bit ominous, doesn't it? I just
mean they have some land and live in that
trailer you got in your hand."

Rose tried to rehang the cabinet door. It
fell right back off with a slam. "It's not that
bad, Charlotte. You can fix it up. Make it
just how you want it, you know. Some new
carpet, a new ceiling, take down that awful
paneling, some new paint, appliances,
furniture. It just needs a little . . . okay, a *lot*
of TLC."

I swallowed the lump in my throat. "TLC?
TLC? But it has raccoons. Raccoons!"

Rose laughed. "Sometimes they break in
through the back windows to get out of the
cold. It happens all the time, especially in
the vacant trailers. But I'm sure they ran
away and probably won't come back now
that you're here."

All I could do was sit and stare at this
woman who seemed an eccentric combination of leftover flower child and cheerleader.

Rose brushed crumbs, or rat poison for all
I knew, from the kitchen counter. "I'll help
you, Charlotte. I'll help you fix it up." She
pushed the brush behind her ear.

For a moment I imagined the trailer with
awnings and hanging baskets of trailing ver-

bena and clean windows with pretty curtains, a sparkly new porch and shingled roof and little lights along the wooden path, pretty pink carpet and my furniture. Then I shook that stupidity from my brain.

"It would take forever to get it fixed and cleaned and painted. What it needs is some well-placed dynamite and a fur trapper." I put my head in my hands. "What would Herman say?"

"Herman?" Rose asked.

"My dead husband. I can hear him now, shouting at me from his grave. 'Caveat emptor, Charlotte. Caveat emptor.' Let the buyer beware."

Rose smiled and revealed crinkly wrinkles at the corners of her eyes. "But he's not here. And he can't say that to you, not anymore."

I looked out the window at the trees, leafless and tall with their branches reaching out to the sky and to me like giant, gnarled fingers.

"I think I need to go speak with Mr. Wrinkel and tell him I want my money back."

Rose cleared her throat. "Fergus is a tough cookie, Charlotte."

"But he sounded so nice on the phone."

"Of course he did. He just sold you a

piece of —"

I looked up. "I know. Believe me, I know about salesmen. But I have to try. Come on, Lucky."

I left Rose standing in the kitchen and backed the Galaxy onto the street, unhitched the trailer, and left it where it sat, not giving a fat patooty who it might offend.

I parked behind the red Datsun again and attempted to muster up my courage, rehearsing what I would say. It might have been ten minutes, it could have been only five, but I finally went to the door and knocked. Once, twice, three times and then I saw that same set of sad eyes peer out at me.

"I told you," she said the instant she opened the door. "Fergus ain't here. Didn't you find the key?"

"Yes, but the trailer. It's not —"

She pulled open the door a trifle more and leaned into me. "Would you please leave?" she whispered. "Fergus will be home in just a few minutes and you can talk to him yourself." Her small voice broke in places, leaving me to wonder what might have been hiding inside the cracks.

A sick feeling roiled in my stomach. It was like her outsides matched my insides. I swallowed hard. "Okay. But will you please let him know I want to speak with him?"

The woman closed the door and I left with absolutely no confidence that she would pass my message on to her husband. I sat in the Galaxy with Lucky and waited. I ran the motor to keep warm, but it had gotten so cold I could still see my breath in the car. A two-toned brown and white pickup truck pulled into the driveway.

"That must be him," I said. "Now, you stay here, Lucky. I better speak with him myself." I watched as a short, muscular man hopped out of the truck. He wore a Phillies baseball cap and a denim jacket. He turned and spotted me. I opened the door and called to him, "Mr. Wrinkel?"

"Yeah." He snagged a bag from the truck bed.

"I'm Charlotte Figg." I walked toward him. But with each step my anxiety heightened. I wished I had let Lucky out of the car. "Excuse me, but I need to speak with you."

"Did you find the key all right? Under one of them rocks up there."

"Yes, I did, but that isn't what I —"

He just kept walking toward his front door.

"Mr. Wrinkel." I raised my voice. "That trailer you sold me isn't the one in the magazine. It's not the same place."

"Never said it was. Just said I had a double-wide for sale. The picture was just a — what would you call it now —" he adjusted his cap, "a representation."

"But, Mr. Wrinkel, that trailer I bought is not livable."

He cleared his throat and spat tobacco-stained goo into a pile of snow. "Well, now, sure it is, Mrs. Figg. It's what us folks in the real estate biz like to call a fixer-upper. Just needs a little work. Now, you go on up there and I'll come by in a few and get your electric turned on and the plumbing going and show you how to work the propane tanks out back."

"Propane?"

"For cooking."

"But I . . . I . . . don't want the trailer." My chest tightened and I thought I might cry again. I imagined Fergus Wrinkel in an embarrassing clown suit with large feet. "I would like my money back, please."

"Oh, well now, Mrs. Figg, I am afraid that's not possible."

I pulled myself up to my full height. "Mr. Wrinkel, my husband was a salesman for the Fuller Brush Company, and when a customer was not one hundred percent satisfied with any product, she got her money back, no questions asked."

He cleared his throat again and took a step closer to the front door. "Well, Mrs. Figg, that's nice and all but you didn't buy some silly hairbrush. You purchased a trailer."

"But I want the one in the magazine."

"The trailer in the magazine would have cost you three times as much. Now, that ain't to say what you got ain't a classic. A real classic. A 1958 Vindar, that's what it said on the deed."

"But . . . but it has raccoons!" I took a breath. "I didn't see any mention of raccoons in the bill of sale, Mr. Wrinkel."

As he continued toward his trailer, I noticed the curtain in the bay window open and those sad, sorrowful eyes peer out at me. This time I felt a chill wriggle down my spine. "Mr. Wrinkel, I . . . I . . ."

"Caveat emptor, Mrs. Figg. Caveat emptor."

The hairs on my arms stood up. But I didn't say anything. I felt so puny next to him, like I was the one in the wrong. I looked at the ground and said, "I trusted you."

He laughed and pulled open the rickety screen door. "Like I said, I'll be down in a few to get you set up."

The woman behind the curtain disappeared like an apparition. I climbed back into the car. "Lucky, I think this is what they call the old bait and switch." I started the car and pulled away up Mango Street. "Herman always said it; I can't do anything right."

Rose Tattoo and a beanpole of a man were waiting outside the trailer when I got back. He towered over her and had short blonde hair. He wore a waist-long denim jacket and jeans with a small, frayed hole in the back pocket that opened an eye to a worn leather wallet. My dog loped over to him like he'd known him his whole life. For a moment I wondered if somehow Lucky managed to travel all the way to my front door from Paradise. He seemed to know the place pretty well and I never did learn where he came from.

Rose introduced me. "This is Asa. The man I told you about. He takes good care of us around here. He can fix just about anything that's broke."

"And some things that aren't broke," he said revealing one dimple in his right cheek.

Asa offered his left hand for me to shake, and that was when I noticed the right sleeve of his jacket was folded and held to his shoulder by a large diaper pin with a baby blue head.

"Nice to meet you, Charlotte," he said.

I smiled into his eyes to avoid contact with his infirmity.

"Did you talk to Fergus?" Rose asked.

"I did and he told me there was nothing I could do."

"He's right," Asa said. "There really isn't anything you can do now except try and sell this old bucket, and that won't be easy."

"But it's not what I bought." It surprised me how easily I talked to Rose and Asa for only knowing them a short while.

"Now, if you want," Asa said, "I can run around back and get the heat started and hook into the electric."

"I'm not staying." I chose to ignore the missing arm. "I think I'll find a hotel for the night."

"Now, why do that?" Rose asked. "Just cost you more money."

"Still, I think I'll be more comfortable until I figure out what I want to do."

"The nearest place is a B&B down in Shoops called the Bee and Bee," Rose said. "And I know for a fact that they don't take dogs. The owner is a touch persnickety about her furniture."

I leaned against the Galaxy and watched Lucky bounce around like a kindergartner at recess. "Look, I'm not saying Paradise is not completely without charm but —"

"You can fix this trailer up," Asa said. "Like brand-new."

"Maybe not brand-new," Rose said. "But new enough. We'll help you and maybe we can get some of the other women in the park to help."

"And I'll go see if Charlie Lundy will help with the moving," Asa said. "Greta, his wife, just had a baby, but he might be free. Matter of fact, he might like the notion of getting out and helping."

"What do you say, Charlotte?" Rose said. "Shame for you to drive all the way up here just to turn back around. And look at Lucky. He kind of likes it here."

I looked in time to see Lucky pee on a tree. "He does seem happy."

"Then it's settled," Asa said. "You'll stay?"

"On a trial basis. And just so long as I don't have any more raccoons."

Rose raised her hands to the sky and said, "Thank you, Jesus."

I felt my eyes widen, having never heard or seen anyone thank the Lord out loud except in church. I called Lucky over to me. I rubbed behind his ears and patted his side.

"What do you say, boy? Want to stay?"

He barked and I looked into his eyes and

saw a twinkle that outshone the dismalness of my 1958 Vindar.

5

The three of us and Lucky stood in the living room. I didn't know what they were thinking, but I felt as though I was staring down a very deep and very black hole.

"Where do we even start?" I asked. "Ordinarily, I'd offer you coffee and pie, but I don't believe I can even roll out crust on that counter or bake a decent pie in that oven."

Asa went to the kitchen and pulled open the oven door. He closed it immediately. "Yep, you need a new stove."

"It's impossible," I said. "Maybe I should just try to resell it."

Asa shook his head and looked at his feet. "You can try, but I doubt you'll find a buyer, especially this time of year, without taking a huge loss."

This time I looked to the ceiling, with tears in my eyes, and said in my head, *Oh, Herman. Tell me what to do.*

"Now, now," Rose said. "We'll take it one room at a time. Let's start in the bedroom so you have a place to sleep while we're fixing things up."

The thought made my stomach churn as I imagined my toes gnawed to bloody stumps by raccoons in the night.

"Don't worry about meals," Rose said. "I can cook and you can shower at my place."

"The bathroom," I said. "I haven't even looked —"

"Don't go near there," Asa said as he closed the bathroom door. "It's a little scary."

"Maybe it would be better if I just go to the Bee and Bee for a few nights."

Rose heaved a great sigh. "As much as I hate to say this, maybe you're right. Lucky can sleep at Asa's."

I looked around. "Where is Asa? He was just here."

"He probably went around back to turn on your electric and get you some heat in here. Once these tin cans warm up, they're pretty cozy."

I stood in the middle of the living room and started to cry again — this time angry at the tears that ran like Niagara Falls. "Do you really think we can make this dump livable?"

"Now, don't cry, Charlotte. You'll see. It'll be okay." She patted my back.

I snuffed. "Okay, but . . . but can I ask one favor?"

Rose nodded.

"I really hate this carpet. It is the ugliest darn thing I have ever seen in my life. I can live with many things, but a filthy chartreuse shag rug is not one of them."

Rose laughed. "I don't blame you one bit. That rug has definitely been beaten with an ugly stick. A big ugly stick."

I took a tissue from my purse and wiped my nose and laughed.

"Maybe the kitchen would be a better place to start," Rose said. "The floor just needs some scrubbing, and the ceiling's not half bad in there."

"No," I said. "It's all bad."

"Now, now, you just need to look for the silver lining. Every cloud has one, you know."

The kitchen, if you could call it that, seemed like it was about four feet by four feet. A single light fixture with exposed wiring, attached by two screws to the ceiling, gave the place a kind of death-row ambience. "I suppose some pretty curtains in that window would dress it up a bit and maybe some fresh paint on the cabinets and

61

a few new lighting fixtures."

"Now you're talking, honey. And I have the perfect macramé plant hanger I'll give to you. Maybe a sprawling rhododendron?"

I felt my eyes roll nearly out of their sockets but I was too distracted by the sudden odd noises, the whooshing and tapping of metal, to comment. "What's that?"

"Trailer noises," Rose said. "Asa will have the heat up any minute."

"Excuse me for asking, but what happened to Asa's arm?" I just came right out and asked.

Rose swallowed. "You mean his missing arm?"

"Mm."

"He blew it off playing with a stick of dynamite when he was about fifteen."

I cringed at the thought of his arm severing from his elbow all torn and bloody and — I stopped thinking. "My goodness" was all I could say.

"He's okay about it now, though. Most of the time anyway."

"The pain must have been excruciating," I said.

"Well, you can talk to Asa about that. Fortunately, he was knocked unconscious and claims he never felt a thing. Not a thing. At least not right off. He says he didn't feel the pain until it was all over."

"That's true with a lot of things, I suppose," I said.

Rose looked at me in a way that made me think she recognized something in what I said.

Lucky leaped up on me again and I scratched his ears. "Would it be all right if I just let him outside?"

"Sure," Rose said. "As long as you trust him not to run away."

Lucky barked and wagged his stubby tail.

"Nah, he'll stick around."

"Did you bring any cleaning supplies?" Rose asked. "If not I got —"

"Yes, I did. In the Little Big Guy — the other little trailer I used to move me here. You might need to help me lift some stuff out of the way. Not enough room in that thing for a gnat to take a breath."

At first I felt skittish letting Rose help me clean. But there was something about this woman that made me think she and I were supposed to be friends. I had never thought much about destiny. Destiny was something reserved for special people, people with a calling like Teddy Roosevelt and Susan B. Anthony. Charlotte Figg didn't deserve anything as grand as destiny. But standing next to Rose that day I had the feeling that

63

destiny belonged to all of us, even if it was a beaten up 1958 Vindar in a rundown trailer park.

The trailer warmed as the heat began to rise. It smelled like melting crayons. "You'll get used to the odor, Charlotte. It goes away after a while."

"It's the other smells that bother me," I said. "Will they ever go away?"

"Sure," Rose said. "I got some incense down at my place that I'll give you."

Later, we finished mopping the kitchen floor and discovered that it was actually the most delightful shade of sky blue. "I can live with this floor," I said.

"That's the ticket," Rose said. She wiped perspiration from her forehead. "It's getting downright hot in here now."

"Why don't you take off that heavy sweater?"

She pulled it tighter around her. "I'm okay with it on."

I gave her a funny look because it didn't make any sense to me except to think that she was hiding something under that sweater.

We carried the bucket of dirty water outside and dumped it on the yew bush. "I've been meaning to ask you," I said. "Is there something wrong with Mrs. Wrinkel?"

"Suzy?" Rose said. "Why do you ask?"

"She seems sad."

Rose nodded and grabbed the bucket. "Let's tackle the walls."

"Did I ask something off-limits?"

"No, it's just that, well, no one knows for sure. Except maybe Asa."

Asa came into the trailer before I could comment. "You're all hooked up, Charlotte. Let's take a look at your appliances now."

He pulled opened the refrigerator, and my goodness what a mess was inside. It smelled so bad that it knocked me back. I covered my nose and mouth. "Just haul it out for me, Asa," I said through my fingers. "I'll purchase new appliances tomorrow."

"Good idea. I know a guy in Shoops. He'll give you a good deal."

Rose stood near the bay window. I could almost see the gears of her mind working as she surveyed the place. I was glad hers worked because mine had about run out of grease. We worked for about another hour and then I called it quits.

"I think we've done enough for one day," I said. "I'm pooped."

"Sounds good," Rose said. "I'm hungry anyway."

"Are you heading into Shoops?" Asa asked.

"Yes. I'll stay at the Bee and Bee. Can Lucky spend the night with you?"

Lucky, who had found a comfy spot near the heat, barked.

"Sure," Asa said. "Come on, boy. It'll be fun."

I stood on the deck in the shivering cold and watched Lucky meander down the street with Asa. I missed him already. He turned around once and smiled and I knew he would be okay.

The Bee and Bee, a delightful Victorian house that sat like a queen on a corner lot, made me homesick. But I was just too tuckered out to entertain the notion for long. Sheila, the woman who owned the place, was one of the sweetest people I had ever met in my life. She served me a Yankee pot roast dinner with butter pecan ice cream for dessert. Then she brought tea to my room in a silver pot she claimed was made by Paul Revere. By nine o'clock utter exhaustion had set in and all I wanted to do was sleep. But first, I called Mother from the front desk, just to let her know I had arrived in Paradise safe and sound.

"Sweetheart," she said, "are you sure you're happy?"

"I am, Mother. The trailer is lovely." I lied.

I had to.

"If you say so, dear. I just can't understand it though. You had a perfectly nice home in Philadelphia, bought and paid for."

"So is my trailer."

"Was it money, Charlotte? Did you need money?"

"No, Mother. Just a change. A chance to do something else."

"What else? There is nothing else for you."

"What is that supposed to mean?"

"It just means that you made your bed twenty-six years ago when you married Herman and now look. You're living in a trailer — a trailer. What can you do in a trailer?" I could see her clutch her chest in anticipation of a heart attack.

"I'm not sure what I can do here yet. I just have a feeling that I'm supposed to do something."

"Feelings don't pay the bills."

"I won't have any trouble paying my bills. Good night, Mother."

Rose, Asa, and I worked like ants building a nest over the next four days, but it was the most magical experience of my life. We nailed and painted and scrubbed 'til our knuckles were raw. My furniture, pictures, dishes, and cups fell into place like they were meant to live here all along. My couch fit perfectly under the bay window in the living room. Herman's La-Z-Boy sat snug in a corner. Lucky liked it just fine. My Tiffany lamp sat perfectly on an oak table and cast just exactly the correct amount of light. Asa connected my TV to the antenna and installed my new refrigerator and stove — all with just one arm — after the delivery men set them in place. Asa was amazing and I told him so.

"I have never seen a one-armed man work before, and I've got to tell you that I am impressed. You're incredible."

"Well, thank you. I try not to let it bother me." He winked.

"That's right," Rose said. "He can do anything a man with two arms can do except tie his own shoelaces." The poignancy of that truth shot clear through my heart.

"If my Herman had lost his arm in some bizarre Fuller Brush accident, he would have taken to his bed forever."

"Really," Asa said. "Life is just as easy with one arm; just have to make some adjustments."

"That's my point," I said. "Herman was not a good adjuster."

The sweet-smelling incense that Rose

brought over masked the lingering bad odors. I set the smoldering sticks in the kitchen, living room, bathroom, and bedrooms. I thought I might have had trouble sleeping those first few nights, but I was so dog-tired at the end of the day, I climbed into my bed each night and fell instantly asleep.

Fergus Wrinkel only came around once, but he was nice enough and helped Asa and Charlie Lundy haul my mattress and sofa inside. I liked Charlie. He was one of those strong, silent types. He simply came and helped and then left without even taking me up on my offer of coffee or the Budweiser I brought from Shoops. Asa worked okay with Fergus but I detected a definite tension between them.

"How come you dislike Fergus so much?" I finally asked after the hard work was finished.

Asa clammed up tighter than a tick on Lucky's back. "I just don't like the man and that's all I can say on the subject."

"Okay, I didn't mean to pry."

"I'll be going now," he said. "If you need anything, call me."

"You won't get him to talk about it," Rose said. "Some things are better left alone."

She fell into my small rocker tired but

satisfied. "This is a job well done. It looks great in here."

It still needed a few repairs — the ceiling mostly — but all in all I had to agree. The trailer was starting to look and feel like home.

Rose fanned her face with her hands.

"Why won't you take that sweater off?" I asked. "You haven't taken it off in the five days I've been here. Are you hiding something? I mean, does it have something to do with those wispy vines on your hands?"

"Tattoos," Rose said.

"Well, I know that, Rose. I am not a dummy. Are you ashamed of them?"

"Me? No. I just wasn't sure how you'd take it, and I didn't want to rattle your nerves any more than they already were."

"Goodness gracious, Rose, I've seen bugs the size of my Galaxy crawl out from under the kitchen cabinets, had raccoons scamper between my legs, scrubbed mold that would have shocked Louis Pasteur, and you're worried a couple of little tattoos will upset me?"

Rose laughed. "You know, you're right. If this place didn't send you running back to Philly, then I guess this won't."

She removed her sweater and revealed a work of tattoo art on her arms and neck fresh from the Sistine Chapel ceiling. It looked as though she had the entire redemption story etched into her body within the curves and sinews of her wrists and forearms and biceps clear up and around her throat. I took a closer look and saw deep scars, pink and white and wrinkled, under the images of three crosses and an empty cave that looked like a tomb. I took two steps back.

"Now, you're sure they don't bother you?" she asked. "Because I can put the sweater back on."

Well, yes, as a matter of fact, they did. But I smiled. "How impressive," I said. "I don't think I've seen that many pictures on one body in my whole entire life. If my Herman was here, he'd say you were nuts, insane, probably even try to sell you some Fuller Brush Tattoo Remover if they made such a thing, but me? No, I'm fine. Curious, but fine. I mean, there must be a reason. Why in the world would you have done such a thing?"

Rose looked deep into my eyes. "It's a long story, Charlotte."

"I'm not going anywhere."

Rose lightly touched her forearm. "Now's not the time. Suffice it to say that redemption comes to people in many different ways."

6

About two weeks after I was finally settled a gunshot blast startled me out of a sound sleep — leastways I figured it was a shotgun blast, having never really heard one before. In any case, it was not a usual sound for six o'clock in the morning. Lucky barked to beat the band and nearly hauled me out of bed to see what was happening. I pulled on my robe and stayed low just in case a crazed madman was running around outside shooting up Paradise and a stray bullet might come whizzing through my bedroom window.

I heard a rap on my front door. "Is that the killer, Lucky? He's on our front stoop. I am certainly not answering that door."

Another rap, a third, and then I thought I heard Rose's yoo-hoo.

"Now, I hate to do this to you, boy, but you're going first." I took him by the collar and dragged him into the living room. I opened the door with Lucky in front of me.

"Rose, it is you." I grabbed her arm and yanked her into the trailer. "You better get inside. I heard gunshots."

She smiled like nothing was wrong. "You all right?"

"I'm fine."

Two more blasts echoed outside. "What in blue blazes is happening?"

"That's why I came over. Thought you might be a little freaked out seeing how it's your first time."

"First time?"

Rose filled the coffeepot with water. "Just Old Man Hawkins down the road. He's a trigger-happy World War II vet and every so often he goes off and starts shooting at things — usually a possum or raccoon. Sometimes he shoots up trash cans he mistakes for the enemy. One time he made a citizen's arrest on the mailman." She gave Lucky a rub behind the ears. "He'll go home in a few minutes."

"Isn't that dangerous?" I placed two cups on saucers. I liked using real china in the morning.

"I just love your little cups and saucers," Rose said. "I love the little daisies around the rim. Got any Danish?"

"Inside that cake cozy."

More blasts ricocheted outside.

I ducked. "Shouldn't he be stopped? How can you stay so calm?"

"He's harmless. Everyone takes cover. Guess folks believe that leaving him alone is the best we can do. Hate to see him go to jail — or worse, a mental hospital. Sometimes he rides that horse he keeps behind his trailer down the streets hollering that the British are coming. The British are coming."

I laughed.

"Not much Danish left," Rose said. "I'll cut this in two."

"That's fine. I'm not that hungry. But Rose, sometimes I think I moved into a crazy town. I mean, really, that man could hurt someone while he's killing phantom Nazis."

"We all have phantoms that show up now and again. Should we all go to jail?" Rose nodded toward the percolator. "Coffee's ready. Even Asa has his ghosts. With him it's pain. Even though his arm is gone, he says it still hurts some days like it was still attached."

I sipped my coffee and my mind brought up an image of Herman. Even though he was gone, some days, most days, I still felt a pain deep inside my heart and stomach and even way inside my muscles. A pain not so much of his dying, but now that he was gone and I could start to confess, pain from when he was living. But I swiped that cobweb away.

I rubbed my hands and looked out the window. "It's really a pretty little place. I'd like to meet the rest of the residents, you know."

Rose looked out the window. "You will. Folks warm up slowly around here."

A thumbnail-size chunk of white icing dropped off my Danish. I dabbed it with my index finger and ate it. "That's kind of sad. I would think a place like this would be different."

"If you mean community sing-alongs and barbecues, Paradise isn't the place." Rose looked pensive a moment. "Now, there is Marlabeth Pilkey and what she calls Marlabeth Pilkey's homegrown remedies. She's pretty friendly and likes to be sociable."

"Remedies?"

"That's right. Marlabeth has an herb or plant or seed to fix everything from headaches to menstrual cramps and liver disease. She makes teas and ointments and even old-time poultices for just about any ailment you have."

"Is she allowed to do that."

"Allowed? You mean like is she a doctor or something?"

"Well, yes, something like that."

"Nah, she doesn't claim to be one, and nobody I know ever had a problem with any of her concoctions. She's helped me." Rose rubbed her left arm. "She gives me this special cream for my scars and tattoos to keep them soft. Sometimes my skin feels tight like elastic bands are wrapped around me. Feel this." Rose took my finger and rubbed it against the inside of her forearm. It felt bumpy and tight, the skin irreparably broken, yet soft and pliable as new skin. "You might think it would bother me more than it does, but with Marlabeth's ointment, I can keep my skin supple and nice. She calls it Rose Cream, made just for me. She says it has rose hips in it, whatever they are."

I smiled. I liked the sound of Marlabeth Pilkey. "Wonder if she could help my stiff joints."

"No doubt," Rose said. "She has teas for stiff joints and arthritis, I'm sure."

We grew quiet a minute and sipped our coffee as I waited for another gunshot, but the park had quieted down so much I thought maybe Rose and I were the only ones left alive and that kook had gunned everyone else down.

Rose rubbed her arm and looked around my trailer. "This place is really starting to shape up. I like the way you decorated it. But I was meaning to ask you about that big old trophy over there. Was it Herman's?"

I burst out laughing. "Herman? That's a joke. The most athletic thing Herman ever did was shave his face. That's my trophy."

"Well, if that don't beat all. What was it from, bowling or tennis or —"

"Softball. I played softball before I was married."

"No kidding. Were you any good? Must have been, I suppose, to win a trophy that big."

I felt a warmth wash over my body. "Everyone got a trophy the year we won the regional championship. But now when I remember those days, I mostly think about how great it was to have friends like that, you know, through thick and thin, a team."

Rose's twinkly eyes grew even twinklier. "I just got a wild idea," she said. "You should start a softball team. Here. In Paradise. The women would love it. Of course, it would be all women. Asa might want to coach, and it would be a great way for you to meet everyone."

"Wait a second. Me? Start a team? I haven't played in years. Plus, how can you be sure the women around here would even want —"

"Because I know. I think it's a great idea. A softball team could be just the ticket to get Paradise out of its slump."

"I don't know."

She grabbed both my hands. "Come on, you know you want to. I saw the way your face lit up when I mentioned that trophy."

"Let me think about it." I leaned back in the chair. "I'll just think about it."

Rose finished her coffee. "Okay, you think, I'll pray, and I bet we have a team by morning."

I imagined Rose in a cheerleader uniform with pompoms and a megaphone.

"I'll do it, Rose. I mean, what's there to think about? If you think it's good idea. I'll coach the team if you help me find players and —"

"That's the ticket, Charlotte. I'll help however I can. You could start by hanging a sign on that notice board near Fergus's trailer."

"Good idea. And I could make a . . . a whatchamacallit . . . a flyer and put it in their doors."

"Yeah, just watch for dogs and guns and boiling oil when you do."

"Oil?"

78

Rose chuckled. "I'm just kidding, but some of the folks around here don't like it when strangers come to call. But not everyone. Now look, I got to get going. I need to do some serious praying today."

I missed Herman some mornings, even though for the life of me I couldn't tell you exactly what I missed. His bluster? I don't know, maybe. I guess Midge was right, folks get used to certain things in life and when they're gone it takes some doing and time to get used to the new way, or the new quiet or the new noise. Whatever the case, I would allow myself a few minutes to think about him and the way he just all of a sudden died. I mean, it came like a dynamite blast or lightning bolt. Bam! Herman's dead. I think you would have to be pretty conceited not to imagine the same thing could happen to you, so I made certain to think on it whenever the notion hit and then thank God, or whoever's concern it was, that I still had breath in me.

After a minute or so I pushed Herman's memory to the back of my brain and thought about building a softball team, something Herman would have never approved.

I found a nice black Flare pen and a pad

of lined writing paper tucked between a couple of magazines stuffed in a drawer. The paper was blank except for the Fuller Brush logo in the corner. A remnant of Herman, I thought, as I sat down to write out the flyer. But the phone rang before I could even get the first word written.

"Charlotte, it's your mother."

"Hi, Mom."

"You were supposed to call me yesterday, Charlotte. You said you would."

"I guess I've been busy getting things moved in, Mother. I was going to call you a little later." I looked around the trailer. The kitchen ceiling still had stains and bulges and needed replacement. I didn't dare tell Lillian DeSalle that I was still repairing the trailer.

"When are you going to invite me up there, Charlotte? I'd like to see where you are living. A mother's got a right to know where her child is living."

"Soon. I just need to get settled and . . . Mom, guess what?"

She fell silent a moment and I could see her grab my father's picture and hold it to her chest like I was about to give her bad news and she didn't want to take it alone.

"I'm starting a softball team. Remember after the funeral —"

"What funeral?"

"Mother. You know perfectly well. Remember, you asked me where that girl who could throw a ball like a boy was? Well, she's back. I'm going to start a softball team here in Paradise."

She laughed. "Don't be a silly goose. You can't just start a softball team."

"Sure I can. I am going to start a softball team right here in Paradise. My new friend Rose thought it would be a great idea."

"You can't be serious. You are too old to be playing games. I meant you needed a career, something to occupy your day. Something with meaning. Something like I had."

"You bought men's underwear for John Wanamaker, Mother. Not exactly the cure for cancer."

"Furnishings. I bought men's furnishings and it was full of meaning. It was something I could be proud of."

"But Mother, softball has meaning. The women around here need something like this. I think this is the reason I —"

"Charlotte, you are just talking nonsense. Now look, I just called to make sure you were still alive. I have to meet the girls for mahjong."

"Mahjong? Since when do you play mahjong?"

"Since Harriett Feinberg made me an honorary Bubba even though I don't have any grandchildren."

"Mother. Don't start."

"Fine, Charlotte, have your silly team. If that's what will make you happy. You know I only ever wanted your happiness, even when you were married."

7

Later that morning I ventured outside. The mid-March air felt crisp and cold and tickled my cheeks and the sun shone bright and happy, and for the first time in I don't know how long I felt a spring in my step. This was the first real opportunity I had had since we finished the major trailer overhaul to walk around Paradise. I went out in the Galaxy to purchase groceries and mail letters and such, but I had never taken the time to see the entire park.

Every now again I saw children running around outside, but even they didn't seem to stay out very long. Once I heard Fergus Wrinkel holler over the public address system, "Mrs. Crabtree, get your dang blame brats out of the fountain area immediately before I call the dog catcher out again."

Now, there was no fountain that I ever saw, just a circular space of cement painted blue with a pipe sticking up from the middle. I suspected that was the fountain area and figured at one time or another it actually flowed water.

Lucky and I walked down nearly every street in the park and I only saw one person, a youngish woman hanging clothes on a line strung between two poles. She was scrappy looking, wearing a spotted dress and a thick tangerine sweater. Second base, was my first thought. Scrappy is good for a second baseman.

"Hello," I called. I made sure to smile wide and even waved, but she never looked my way. "Hello," I called a second time and she turned around.

"I'm Charlotte Figg. I just moved in on Mango Street."

The woman pulled a clothespin from her mouth, turned her back to me and secured a wet tee shirt with a rip in the collar to the line.

I took a step closer. Lucky clung close to my side. "Hello," I called again. By now I was starting to feel annoyed, but persisted until she finally spoke.

"That's nice," she said. "Pleased to make your acquaintance."

I reached out my hand in a gesture of neighborliness. She took it and shook with a powerful grip. "Clara Kaninsky." But there was no real howdy-do in her voice and she went back to her laundry. Still, I took down a mental note that possibly I had found a player. The woman had big hands and strong arms — probably from carrying all that wet laundry out of her trailer.

I heaved a sigh and went back to my walk. Paradise didn't have what you would call sidewalks or pavements, only the roads that wound around the trailers like a deep, black river. Lucky and I walked down Coconut Lane until we arrived at Moonlit Bay Road — Rose's street.

"She said her trailer is the very last one," I said.

There were fewer trailers on Moonlit Bay than the other streets — fewer trailers and larger yards, more space for cars and kids. Lucky ran on ahead like he'd been there before, barking and yapping, happy that we were finally going to Rose's house. Now, I had considered Rose to be what they call eccentric and I gave her a lot of latitude by way of honoring her artistic sensibilities and not wanting to disturb the universe that was Rose's. But no amount of latitude could have prepared me for what I encountered when I stopped out in front of her trailer.

"Lucky, will you look at that? Did she

make it?"

Lucky barked and sniffed around the large sculpture in Rose's yard. A giant hand, bolted to the ground and rising about eight feet to the sky with a huge open palm, stood in her yard just as natural as any old birdbath.

"Now, I've seen some strange lawn ornaments in my day, but this . . . well, it certainly broadens the meaning of the words palm tree, Lucky."

He barked and then circled under the hand until he collapsed into a nap.

"What in the world would inspire a person to have this in their yard?"

"Charlotte," Rose called. "I saw you out the window from the kitchen. Welcome. Welcome to my home. I am so glad you finally made it up here. I know it can be a bit of a walk, but there's shortcuts I can show you. If you don't mind traipsing through Hawkin's backyard."

I couldn't take my eyes off the hand. "Rose, I . . . I . . ." I glanced over in time to see Asa come out her front door. "Rose, did you know you have a giant cement hand in your front yard?" I said without even acknowledging Asa.

She laughed and moved closer to me.

"Isn't it spectacular?" Asa said. "Rose told

me she saw it at a rundown amusement park clear over in Montvalle. Took a few days but we finally tracked down the owner and convinced him to let Rose have it. That was three years ago."

Rose chuckled. "Yes. He didn't want to just hand it over to me."

I shook my head. "How many times have you used that one?"

"It comes in handy," Rose said.

I decided to quit while Rose was ahead.

Asa, obviously bored with the many puns, continued the story. "So I drove my truck up there — me and my cousins Studebaker and Ed — and we hauled it back to Paradise. Took us nearly the whole day to get it situated. After we bolted the last bolt, Studebaker and me and Ed climbed up and ate Full Moon Pie by the light of a million stars in the hand of God."

Full Moon Pie. Now that was a curiosity what with me being a pie baker and all. "Never heard of Full Moon Pie, Asa."

Asa rubbed his belly. "Studebaker brought it from Bright's Pond. Fella named Zeb makes it — most delicious lemon meringue you'll ever sink choppers into."

I made a mental note. Learn more about Full Moon Pie.

"Well," I said. "Back to the situation at hand."

Asa cracked a smile and then peered into Rose's eyes in the way that only true friends can. "She said this hand would be her Ebenezer."

Ebenezer? The only Ebenezer I knew was Ebenezer Scrooge and that couldn't be what she meant. But I just let it go, figuring Rose or Asa would get around to explaining it to me later on.

"That's right," Rose said. "Asa helped me secure it in front of my trailer. I liked that it was a huge upturned hand, kind of like a giant offering to God. I still love the way it collects the rainwater and how the birds come and flap around and bathe."

"But that ain't all," Asa said. "Rose painted everyone's name, everyone in the park, on it. Bible says God has each and every one of us in his palm. That's why she did it. Poor Fergus about had a conniption fit when he saw it. Tried to make her remove it, but Rose won out."

"Is my name up there?"

"Not yet. Haven't gotten around to painting it on. I will though. I've been trying to decide if you are a periwinkle or more of a burnt umber. I'm leaning toward periwinkle."

Lucky couldn't help himself — he promptly peed on it as Rose spoke. "Sorry, Rose. He can't help it."

Rose smiled. "It's natural."

I shook my head, amused. "I think I found our second baseman. Woman named Clara Kaninsky."

"Pinky," Rose said.

"Pinky? She said her name was Clara."

"No, her name is written on the pinky finger."

I couldn't help but glance over and try to find it.

"How many names do you have on that thing?"

"Ninety-seven names, so far. You'll make ninety-eight."

Imagine that. My name written on God's hand. It made my knees wobble.

"You want to come inside?" Rose asked. "It's chilly out here."

"Nah, I think I'll head back. I just wanted to let you know that I'm not having much luck finding women for the team, except Clara, and she didn't even appear all that neighborly or interested."

"Don't fret," Rose said. "It will all come together."

"I hope so. I'm really starting" — my eyes darted right back to the strange hand — "to like the idea of playing softball again."

"That's the ticket," Rose said.

I continued my trek toward home, but not before I wandered past the Wrinkel trailer. I didn't see Fergus's truck, so I decided to muster a little of my newfound courage and walked right up to the front door and knocked. I knocked once, twice, a third time and still no Suzy Wrinkel. I paused a moment longer and was just about to leave when I heard the door open. My heart sped. It could have been Fergus opening the door, so I had to quell a twinge of trepidation as the door opened a smidgen.

"Yes?" Suzy's small, sad voice sneaked from the shadow.

"Suzy." I tried my best to look her straight in the eye because Lillian DeSalle always said that you learn the most about a person when you look them in the eye. I spoke quickly because there was no telling how long Suzy would allow me to stand there.

"I just wanted to say hi," I said.

"You looking for Fergus?"

"No, I just wanted to say hi to you."

Suzy pulled the door open another inch and revealed a black and purple bruise under her left eye. "Are you okay, Suzy? Maybe you should see Marlabeth. That looks like a nasty shiner."

"Fergus will be home some time after lunch," she said. Then she closed the door.

I walked away with a sick feeling in the pit of my stomach. Lucky sidled next to me and licked my hand. "I know, boy. Something's just not right."

By the end of the second week of March I had delivered a hand-written flyer to every trailer in Paradise.

Calling all Women!
Come to the first meeting of
The Paradise Trailer Park
Softball Team
To be held April 3rd at Number 19
Mango Street
7:30 PM
No experience necessary
Bring your babies and kids if need be

On the evening of April 3rd I set out a tray of cheese and crackers on the coffee table. I chose a tray with watermelon slices painted on it. I opened large bottles of soda and juice and set them on the kitchen table beside a stack of Dixie cups and small paper napkins. Rose brought a bucket of ice and a Jell-O mold with bits of fruit and a can of Reddi-wip.

I baked three apple pies that morning, the deep-dish kind with a flaky crust that melted in your mouth. I sprayed magnolia-scented Glade around the trailer because some recent rain had brought the dead animal/nicotine smell back in places and I couldn't abide that. Especially not with company coming.

Company. It was the first time in years that I expected company in my home. Rose and Asa came by, but this had the potential to be an actual party. Herman never let me have company over unless it was Midge, and she never stayed very long.

I watched the kitchen clock and waited. Seven-thirty ticked past and only Rose and Asa and I were there. By seven-forty-five I started to think that no one was coming and suggested we crack open the pie ourselves. I feared my dream of softball had struck out.

"We won't make much of a team," I said. "And you, Asa, I was hoping you'd be a coach, even if you only have the one arm. You can still coach softball, can't you? But now it doesn't look like it matters. No one is coming."

"I won't make much of batting coach since I only got the one hand to wrap around the bat but I think I could coach the pitcher well enough."

"Pitcher," I said. "We'll need a stellar pitcher. I could pitch myself but — here I go talking like we have a team."

Rose, who had been quiet for some minutes nodded toward the front door. "You'll want to answer that."

Lucky went lickety-split, slipping and sliding, and leaped up on the door like he had been expecting a long-lost friend.

"You don't suppose someone's come out for softball, do you?"

Rose turned her palms upward and said, "Thank you."

I pulled Lucky away from the door and opened it. Four women stood outside in the ankle-deep glow of my path lights.

"Oh, my goodness gracious," I said. "Welcome to my home. Come on in. I have pie and cheese and soda."

The women moved slowly, but soon they stood in my living room and my heart beat like a trip hammer. I was so excited, I had to take a breath.

"Help yourself to cheese and crackers and pie; of course, I always have pie. Rose brought plenty of ice for the soda and there's coffee in the pot."

One woman, a short, stubby lady wearing gold clam diggers and a sweatshirt with the word *Rascal* on it, stepped forward. "I need to tell you that our husbands ain't going to like this, but we came anyway so I think you better make your speech short and sweet and to the point. No time to dillydally."

"That's right," said a second woman. "I need to get back home to baby Ruth." I giggled, but when no one else joined in I figured the joke was lost.

"She's been crying for days with the colic. But I told Charlie if I didn't get out of the trailer and take a walk I couldn't be held responsible for what I might do. Charlie doesn't like it when I talk like that, even though he doesn't know if I'm serious or not. Course, I ain't."

"You must be Charlie Lundy's wife," I said. "He helped Asa carry in my furniture."

"That's right, I'm Greta. Pleased to make your acquaintance."

Asa offered crackers first, while Rose gave them each a Dixie cup. Then she plopped an ice cube into each cup as Asa poured Coke. Teamwork. It made me smile.

"I played softball in high school," said the third woman. They still stood in a row like bowling pins. "I pitched for the Macungie Sentinels. Pitched us all the way to a state championship, even though nobody cared if girls could play ball or not."

"You're a pitcher," I said. I glanced at Asa.

"Just like I said. We need a star pitcher and it looks like we got one."

She smacked a fist into her palm. "My name's Francine, but everyone calls me Frankie."

I heard a knock on the door. "That might be my Rube," Frankie said. "Wouldn't put it past the big lug to come looking for me. But you tell him I'll be home when I get there, if it is him."

Rose opened the door and in walked Clara Kaninsky. I smiled about as wide as home plate. "Second base?"

"Sure," she said. "I heard the other girls were coming so I decided to come too. Had a time getting out of the house tonight. Grady, that's my youngest, had to help him muddle through some silly science experiment — made a radio with only a potato and some wires and a five-penny nail. Imagine that."

"Imagine," I said. "Must be a bright boy."

Clara smiled. "This here is Ginger Rodgers."

I looked but I didn't see anyone until the tiniest person I ever saw up close came out from behind Clara. I did a lousy job of hiding my surprise, but I figured everyone understood, including Ginger. She laughed until I thought she'd split a gut.

"Don't fret," Ginger said as she caught her breath. She reached her hand up for me to shake. She had the nicest touch, even if it did feel like I shook the hand of a three-year-old.

"Pleased to meet you." I showed her in. She hopped up on the sofa and Lucky eyed her like she was a new chew toy. He even put his paw on her knee and watched her like he wanted me to toss her outside so he could fetch and bring her back. She pushed him away. "I am not a large bone for you to bury in the backyard."

"Lucky," I said, "go lie down."

"Nice doggie," she said.

"So glad you came." I offered her cheese and crackers.

That was when Rose sidled next to me. "Ginger wants to play."

Frankie spit soda across the room. "You, Ginger? Come on," she said. "I mean you're a sweet gal and all but softball? How?"

"I can play," Ginger said. "I'm pretty quick. Doesn't take much to propel this body around the bases, and you got to admit I have a wicked strike zone." She jumped off the sofa and held one hand at her shoulder and the other at her knees. Maybe nine inches.

She would be hard to pitch to.

"Okay," I said. "But what position?"

Ginger laughed. "Shortstop, of course."

I don't think I ever heard so much laughter in my life. There I stood with a room full of women and a one-armed man laughing and giggling. It felt fine. It felt just fine.

"Shortstop? You're serious?"

She nodded.

"Why not?" I said.

Ginger smiled. "Praise Jesus, I'm going to play softball."

I counted the women. "We need two more. Just two more to make a team."

Greta volunteered to play first base.

"No, I'm sorry," I said. "You're a little short for first base. I'm afraid we'd have balls flying over your head. But you look like a center fielder. How about center field?"

"Sure," she said. "Where's that?"

Frankie slapped Greta's shoulder. "In the center, Greta. That's why they call it center field."

"Can you throw a ball, Greta?" asked Asa.

"Throw?" said Greta. "I can throw a full beer can from the kitchen door clear out back to Charlie."

"Good enough," I said.

I offered pie to all of the women and gave out assignments at the same time. I chose

Gwendolyn, the tallest of the original three, to play first base. She seemed to like the notion well enough.

"Does that mean I get to bat first?" she asked.

"Not necessarily. We'll get to the line-up later."

Marlabeth Pilkey volunteered to play third base. "I got a wicked arm," she said. "I played ball with my brothers."

"Great." I gave her apple pie. "And I suppose you should be the team trainer also."

"Trainer?" She swallowed an apple slice whole, I thought.

"What kind of trainer?" she asked. "You mean like a dog trainer?"

"Oh, no, no. That's what we call the person who watches out for the health of the team, you know, taking care of sprains and cuts and bruises."

"Sure, I can do that. I got a remedy for whatever ails you."

Gwendolyn started to cry.

"There she goes again," Greta said. "She can turn on them waterworks whenever she wants."

"I think it's a hormone imbalance," Marlabeth said. "What she needs is some black cohosh —"

"Black cohosh," Francine said. "That's

what you gave my mama for her hot flashes."

"That's right," Marlabeth said. "And valerian root, maybe some chamomile tea. And you can use some snark weed, Greta."

"Snark weed? What in blazes is snark weed?" asked Francine.

"Keeps people from being so snarky," Marlabeth said.

"No such thing," Greta said.

"Well, there should be a tea for mean people," Marlabeth said.

"I am not snarky or mean. Gwendolyn is a crybaby and everybody knows it. I'm just the only one who says it."

"Best to leave some opinions to yourself," Rose said.

Gwendolyn blubbered and waved the air in front of her face. "It ain't hormones. It's just that I never felt so happy. I always got chosen last, you know. Most humiliating thing ever to stand there while everyone else got picked. I can still hear Donna DelTorro saying, 'Okay, I'll take Gwen-do-nothing-lynn,' like I was carrying typhoid."

Marlabeth handed Gwendolyn a box of Scotties Tissues. "Who is Donna Del-Torro?"

"It ain't important," Greta said.

It didn't take long before all the women in my trailer that evening had positions on the newly formed Paradise Women's Softball Team.

"I'm sorry, Charlotte," Greta said around nine o'clock, "but I need to get home. Ruth needs a good feeding and clean diaper — ha! So does Charlie."

The others echoed her.

"Okay, I will post another notice for the next team meeting and maybe our first practice. In the meantime, look around, we still need a left fielder and a right fielder and a couple or three alternates. And we need a name. Start thinking of some and we'll take a vote at the next meeting."

Asa and Rose hung around after the women left. Asa sat in the rocking chair with a kind of wide-eyed amazement on his face. "I wouldn't have believed it, Charlotte, if I hadn't seen it with my own two eyes."

Rose glanced skyward again. "It's a blessed day in Paradise. I do believe something powerful is happening. Charlotte, I knew the second I set eyes on you that a new day had dawned in Paradise."

I couldn't help but roll my eyes. "It's just a softball team, Rose. And it was your idea."

Asa helped himself to another slice of pie. "Now you just have to get the team organized." He laughed. "No easy task, I'm sure."

I watched him shovel a large forkful of apple crumb into his mouth and chew. "Team?" I said. "I don't have a team yet. Still need two players."

"They'll come," Rose said. "Just schedule a practice date. Steps of faith, Charlotte. Can't run all the bases in one night."

I gathered plates and napkins and started to tidy things up. At nine-thirty I was ready for Asa and Rose to go home. I was happy about the softball team, but I was also scared to death that I might have gotten myself wedged into a tight spot. It was all on me now to rally these women into a team. Women who, it was plain to see, needed and wanted to be rallied into something more than what life had pitched.

It was the more part that scared me.

8

That night I lay in bed thinking about the day and imagining what it would be like to be with this group of women on the softball field, running the bases, keeping Greta from pounding Gwendolyn into a fine powder, catching pop fly balls, hitting a home run — winning. But I also wrestled with a most intrusive thought — me sitting in Rose's giant hand of God — just sitting there like a lame duck waiting for whatever was going to happen to happen.

But I supposed Rose would have said, "Don't worry, Charlotte. You're sitting in the safest seat in the universe." And she might have been right, but I couldn't help feeling a little shaken and worried about what I had done. Me, coaching a softball team, attempting to bring community where none existed and kind of half-expecting God to work out the details. I knew it was all I had to lean on — except Rose and Asa. Herman wasn't around to tell me what to do next.

Bright and early the next morning after I let Lucky out to do his business and I made my pot of coffee and brushed my teeth, I went in search of something I thought might help inspire me. I pulled a small, red suitcase out from under my bed. I had not opened it in many years.

Packed away inside, I found my old baseball glove, a cap, a softball, and a picture of the 1942 Clifton Canaries wearing our bright yellow uniforms with green lettering and numbers. I named every player on the team. I looked a bit brighter in the picture than I did now, skinnier of course and maybe even a touch taller. I stood next to Penny Wilcox, our catcher, and Verna Gottlieb, our second baseman. These people had been the most important people in my life for a while. Together we won over fifty-two games and three championships.

I sat on the floor and lightly touched each face with the tip of my index finger.

"Penny," I said. "Where are you now? Sally Miller, the pitcher with the crazy curve ball. Would you remember me?"

The memories of these people rose and fell like a symphony. And that was when I saw the big picture. I wanted the women of

Paradise to know what I knew. In the company of women, good women, there is home. There is love, understanding, and even salvation. All of these things had somehow gotten away from me. And maybe, if I was being honest with myself, I was looking for those things also.

I placed the picture in its wobbly brown frame near the trophy. I had three trophies, but only two had survived the years. Too bad Herman never sold me any brass polish. It would certainly have come in handy. Instead, I breathed on the trophy in places and used a towel to shine it up.

Rose came by right after I put the towel and my memories away.

"I came by for pie," she said. "And I thought you could use some help."

"Help?"

"The team, Charlotte. You have a lot to decide." She noticed the picture on the table and picked it up. "Is this your old team? Which one are you? No, wait. Let me pick you out."

"Here." She pointed to Sadie Lipshutz — left field.

"Nope."

I showed her where I stood.

"You look like an entirely different person. You sure that's you?"

I nodded and set the picture down.

Rose sat with me at the kitchen table. I didn't feel much like talking. Rose was as enthusiastic as ever. But it didn't take long for her to catch on to my mood.

"What's wrong?" She asked. "You look lower than a grasshopper's knee."

"I guess I am a little sad today. Looking through old stuff, thinking about Herman."

Rose smiled into my eyes. "I understand. Grief has a way of hanging on and rearing its ugly head at the most inopportune times, Sweetie." She patted my hand.

"It does." I swiped a couple of tears away. We sipped coffee and ate pie silently until I finally said, "Rose. You said once that redemption comes in many ways. What did you mean?"

Rose took a breath and blew it out slowly. She peered out the window a moment.

"I was twenty-two years old, Charlotte, and . . . well, I killed a man."

I swallowed. "Don't be silly. I'm serious."

"So am I," she said. "I have the newspaper clippings in my trailer."

"What, like a scrapbook?"

"Kind of. There was a lot of news coverage. It was quite the talk of the town back then."

"You're joking."

"I was twenty-two, troubled and lonely. I met a man at the bus terminal. He smiled at me, bought me jelly donuts — the sugar kind, not the white powder. He bought me a Pepsi and invited me home. He kept me there for three weeks. Little food, little water." Rose looked away, out the window. "He raped me over and over again until I was bleeding and raw, sick and vomiting. He tied me to a chair while he slept and ate cheeseburgers from White Castle with ketchup dripping down his chin."

My stomach churned. "I'm sorry, Rose. You don't have to say any more." Truth was I didn't know if I wanted to hear more. I had gone from fond memories of days gone past to hearing of a friend, someone I now considered a dear friend, experience the worst that life had to offer.

"One night he got sloppy," Rose continued. "Left a cigarette lighter where I could get it while he slept off a filthy drunk. I burned through the ropes, sprinkled the mattress with the last of his whiskey and set it on fire. The flames shot up quickly in a great rushing neon wind of heat and flames, orange and red and purple, even green and yellow. I screamed and panicked, knocking flames off my arms, rolling on the floor until I finally tumbled down the steps and outside. By then my arms had been burned so badly I . . ."

"The tattoos," I said.

"Yes." Rose reached across the table and took my hand in hers. "The tattoos. They came years later, but yes, the tattoos."

I smiled into her deep, dark eyes and held her there for a second. I could not even begin to imagine the horror she must have faced. It brought tears to my eyes and I swiped them away, yet Rose didn't turn her eyes from mine. And in those few seconds she communicated more about what she had gone through than words could ever do justice. The experience had transformed her, deepened her, left her with physical scars, yet more whole than I ever dared imagine for myself.

"I have an idea," she said. "Let's go sit in the giant hand."

Now, you might think that sitting in a giant hand would feel silly. It did. At least for a few minutes, until I got my bearings. I couldn't help but giggle at the absurdity of what I was doing, having never ever sat in a giant hand before. Rose was kind and let me get it out of my system. Then she turned her own palms up, lifted them toward the now overcast sky and prayed. I listened as she trailed on about being thankful first, guilty second, and then asking for success for me and the newly formed softball team.

"Thank you, Rose," I said. "But do you think God really cares about a softball team?" I thought back to the many serious prayers I said so long ago, asking, begging God to help me get pregnant after losing my first and only baby. Seemed to me that giving life was slightly more in the world's interest than a softball team. But what did I know?

"Bible says that God has his eye on every sparrow. Not one falls without his knowledge. That every hair on your head is counted, that he calls each star by name. Seems to me a God that detail-minded would also care about the Paradise softball team."

"He named the stars? All of them?" Of course I looked up and saw none, what with it being cloudy and daytime and all. Yet I looked heavenward — truly heavenward — for the first time in many, many years.

We sat a while longer and Rose pointed out some of the names, including Suzy Wrinkel, who occupied one of the folds on the index finger.

"A Wrinkel in a wrinkle." I smiled. Payback for the previous pun fest.

Rose nodded and I assumed I wasn't the first to think of it.

Ginger Rodgers was on the thumb right next to Marlabeth Pilkey.

"Tell me about Ginger," I said.

"What's to tell? She was born that way. God made her little is all."

"I know but why is she here in Paradise?"

"Where else? What better place for her? Here she's accepted just as she is. She sews quilts and does amazing needle art stuff she sells at flea markets. Loads her car up twice every spring and makes enough to live on for the year."

"Good deal," I said.

"She's happy, Charlotte."

That was when Asa strolled by. "I've been looking for you, Charlotte."

"Me? How come?"

"You coming down or should I come up?"

Rose and I exchanged looks. "You have pie at your place?" she asked.

"Cherry."

"We'll come down," Rose called. "Charlotte has pie at her place."

We sauntered over to my house like three best friends. I couldn't remember the last time I had found myself in such good company. The thought occurred to me to say something about the odd bit of joy that

109

crept into my heart, but I winced it away on account of it might have come out sounding silly.

Lucky squeezed by me and into the trailer. For some reason that silly pooch always wanted to be the first one inside.

Asa helped himself to a ginger ale, while Rose started coffee.

"I think I found you a couple more players," Asa said.

"Really. Who?"

"The Frost sisters."

Rose put her hand on Asa's shoulders. "Really? The Frost sisters? Did you speak with them?"

"Sure did," Asa said. "They say they never got a flyer but would be happy to come out and play." Then he smiled and said, "Well, okay. I had to do some arm-twisting and they agreed to give it a try, but if they don't like it they're going to quit."

I sat next to Rose at the kitchen table. I sank into the thick polka dot cushions I had tied on to the chair. "Frost sisters? You mean the women who own the trailer I thought I was buying?"

"That's right," Asa said. "Edwina and Thomasina. They live on the other side of the woods. Lived there their whole lives. Never married. I'd say they're in their late thirties, healthy as oxen and just as strong. They own about forty acres out there. Fergus had been trying to get his grubby paws on that land —"

"But they won't sell," Rose said.

"Sisters, huh. Wonder if they'd be good at left and right field. Bookends."

Rose laughed. "I can't wait to see the whole team assembled in one place."

"Speaking of which," Asa said. "Where exactly do you think you'll practice? Fergus will never go for it anywhere in the park. And there really isn't much room."

"That is a pickle," Rose said. "Here we were so excited about the team we didn't even think about having a place to practice and play games." She paused and sipped coffee. "God will provide."

Asa snapped his fingers. "I wonder. I just wonder."

"What?" I said. "You have an idea?"

"Not sure. I'll let you know." He swigged the last of his ginger ale and scooted out the door. "I'll let you know," he called as the door slammed behind him and Lucky startled from a deep nap.

"Now where do you suppose he's off to?" I asked.

Rose shook her head. "Don't know, but he's a scrounger from way back. He might just have something up his sleeve."

My telephone rang.

"Hello?"

Nothing. Just a small breath on the other end.

"Don't tell me — people still making obscene phone calls?" I was just about to hang up when I heard a quiet female voice say, "Can you meet me at six behind my trailer?"

"Suzy? Is this Suzy?"

But she hung up without letting me know for certain.

"Really?" Rose said. Her voice rose an octave. "Was that Suzy?"

"I'm not sure. I think it was her. She said to meet her out back of her trailer at six o'clock this evening."

I watched Rose's eyes grow large. "Are you going to meet her?"

"I should. Don't you think, Rose? Don't you think I should meet her?"

She nodded, smiled, and flicked a crumb off the table. "Yes, Charlotte. I think you should. But —"

"But what?"

"Bring Lucky just in case."

"In case of what?"

"Just in case."

For the rest of the day I acted like a perfect nervous Nelly, alternately pacing around my trailer and baking pie. I decided to bring her an apple crumb and then changed it to a cherry and then decided to bring both, but I wasn't sure if I wanted to carry two pies to her trailer. After all, I wasn't even certain it was Suzy who called, and while arriving with one pie for the wrong person was embarrassing, arriving with two pies was downright silly.

At a quarter past six Lucky and I started down the street with the apple crumb covered with Saran Wrap. "I hope she likes apple crumb, Lucky. Maybe I should have brought the cherry also, just in case she likes cherries more."

Lucky barked and then moved in stride next to me. He looked proud and held his funny little head high, and if I didn't know better, I'd say he smiled.

"I hope it was Suzy on the phone," I said. "I mean, I don't know for certain. I'm just guessing it was Suzy."

We passed trailers and cars and I didn't see a soul. Not a single soul that evening. Cooking odors wafted around us, a mixture of frying onions and bacon.

I moved closer to the Wrinkel trailer and slowed my pace. I checked for the pickup truck and didn't see it and considered that a good sign.

"She said to meet her behind the trailer," I whispered.

Lucky scooted away from me and went near the trailer. He puffed around in some scraggly grass. He shot me a glance and then trotted behind the trailer. I stopped moving and sucked a deep breath.

"What if Fergus was waiting back there? What if he is upset about the team?"

I shook the thoughts from my brain. "It's a free country."

Lucky barked — not loud, more like a bluster, a grumble.

I reached the side of the trailer and stuck my head around. No one was there. Just underwear and dungarees flapping on the line.

Lucky joined me. I patted his head. "Suzy," I called but in a low voice, barely audible. "Suzy?" I raised it a little. "Suzy." I took more steps.

Nothing. Not a sound. "Guess she's not coming, Lucky."

He whimpered and we made our way to the front of the trailer, me still carrying a nine-inch apple crumb. I kept moving and headed toward home. Then I stopped, turned back, and set the pie in front of the trailer door. I gave a little rap and waited.

"Let's go home, boy. She's not answering her door."

I took a few steps and looked back in time to see the door open, a hand reach out and take the pie. A smile stretched across my face. "Apple crumb. No one can resist an apple crumb."

9

Lucky kept so close to me he knocked my knees. "So she didn't come out. At least we tried."

Lucky whimpered.

"She did take the pie, though. Hope she gets to taste it. That nasty Fergus Wrinkel will probably snatch it right away from her and eat the whole blooming thing by himself."

Lucky barked his agreement.

"But then again. Maybe she'll get a slice before he comes home tonight."

With that thought in mind I headed up the hill that was Mango Street.

The sky began to darken now and a few stars had shown up for their nightly duties. I paused a moment and remembered what Rose had said about God naming all the stars and how he calls them out at night. "Quite a job. You'd think God would delegate some of those responsibilities."

But then again, I figured if I created all the stars in the sky I'd be a bit protective of them myself.

My foot no sooner landed on the wooden path to my trailer when I heard Rose's yoo-hoo from behind.

"Charlotte," she called. "Wait up a minute. Did you see Suzy?"

I stopped and spun around. "She never showed, Rose."

"Ah, too bad. But I kind of expected that. Asa is the only one I know that's been able to get Suzy to venture more than three feet away from that trailer. And then only for a minute or two before she runs back inside. Asa calls it a dang shame, says she's a pretty woman. Says she has a nice smile and a sweet disposition hiding under all that sadness."

I pushed open the door and Rose and I settled at the kitchen table, where the cherry pie sat on a cooling rack, even though it was plenty cool by now. She picked at the crust.

"Is she sick or something? Maybe she has cancer," I said. "I hear folks with cancer can get awful depressed and she's so darn skinny. Maybe she should see Marlabeth."

"I don't think she's sick, Charlotte. This has been going on for quite some time."

My lips puckered when I chomped into a particularly sour cherry. "Every once in a while one gets through."

Rose's forehead wrinkled. "One what?"

"Sour cherry. I try to pick only the best-looking cherries, but sometimes I miss one or two and I just bit into a mighty sour one."

Rose chewed pie and looked thoughtful. "Well, I think something sour is going on in that trailer, something real sour, Charlotte. You saw her black eyes and all."

I swallowed. I didn't want to say out loud what I assumed Rose conjectured.

"You saying what I think you're saying, Rose?"

She pushed her fingers through her impossible hair. "Yeah. Sometimes, maybe on account of . . . you know, what happened to me, I get near her trailer and I get this feeling, could be the Holy Spirit, could be plain old intuition, but I get this feeling and then I get these flashbacks and, well, that's why I didn't go with you this afternoon. I try to avoid the Wrinkel trailer."

"The flashbacks?"

"Mm."

Rose and I sat silently for the next few minutes until she heaved a big sigh. "But you know what, Charlotte? I think your moving to Paradise is a sign or a signal or something. I think it's time to find out what's going on inside the Wrinkel trailer."

I didn't say anything right off. I mean, I couldn't just come right out and say, "Sure, Rose. Let's go pry into other people's business."

Rose scraped the last of the cherry filling from her plate. "I think he's sweet on her."

"Who? Who is sweet on who?"

"Asa. I think he has a kind of faraway crush on Suzy. I know he'd help us."

"But she's a married woman, Rose. You're not suggesting that Asa —"

"No, of course not, Charlotte. Asa would never do anything like that, but I think he suspects something is wrong and he cares about her is all. Cares a lot about her, you know. That's all I'm saying."

We talked for another few minutes until my eyes felt droopy and I didn't want to talk anymore about the subject. It was hard enough to think about, let alone discuss. And it made me think of Herman, and I didn't want to think about him that evening, so I made an excuse. "I'm getting tired, Rose. I think I'll read for a while, until I fall asleep."

"That's a good idea. We'll make a plan in the morning."

■ ■ ■ ■

Morning arrived in a deluge of rain and rumbles of thunder. The sky was so dark it might as well have been nighttime. Buckets of rain fell hard, pelting my metal walls with such a ruckus that I couldn't sleep past six. It was the first real storm since I had moved to Paradise. Lucky cowered under the covers next to me.

"You big old chicken. It's only thunder."

But just as the words left my mouth, a crack of thunder and a bolt of lightning filled the room and about scared me to death. "Goodness gracious, Lucky. I think that storm is sitting right over top of Paradise. It's like a weather blitzkrieg with all that booming and lightning and crackles."

I patted him. "Sorry, boy. It is pretty scary. You just hide under there as long as you need."

I climbed out of bed, shrugged on my purple robe, and made my way to the kitchen. I was just about to plug in the percolator when BAM! Another rumble of thunder echoed through the park and all the lights went out in the trailer. I stood there a second holding the plug in my hand. Herman always said not to plug things in during an electrical storm. And here I was living inside a metal house. It might have knocked me all the way to Bermuda. Still I held onto the cord, feeling a trace of shock, looked to the ceiling, and said, "That's just fine and dandy, Lord. Couldn't wait until I had my coffee made to turn off the lights, now, could you?"

I plopped into a kitchen chair. Rainwater rushed down Mango Street like a creek. The drops fell large and heavy and splattered against my bay window. It was like looking through cataracts, but I was pretty sure I saw Rose and Asa making their way down the street toward me. I rushed to my door and threw it open.

"You crazy nuts. What are you doing out in this storm?"

They made it safely inside, and I closed the door just before a bolt of lightning lit up the trailer.

"Coffee," Asa said. He removed his slicker and hung it on the coat rack near the door.

"Sorry, the power went out before I could make it."

Rose pulled a Thermos out of her slicker. "We got plenty."

I smiled and shook my head, amazed at Rose's uncanny knack for knowing things, or feeling things or suspecting things.

Whatever it was, she just had a way of being tuned into life in a way I'd never experienced before.

Asa hung Rose's rain slicker next to his. I noticed he was wearing hip-high fishing waders. I gave him a funny look and he smiled.

"I heard of it raining cats and dogs but never trout," I said.

Asa chuckled. "I like to wear them in the rain," he said. "Easier for me to slip into than tie or buckle boots when I need to slop around the park." Then he let the suspenders droop and simply stepped out of the boots.

I had to admit it made perfect sense, but that was the first time I ever had a man in waders come to my front door.

"We can ride out the storm together," Rose said.

I poured coffee from the Thermos. The aroma of the fresh-brewed coffee wafted around the small room. It was nutty and brown and smelled like dirt and rain and springtime.

"I spoke to the Frost sisters," Asa said. "They agreed to let us use some of their land to make a ball field." He reminded me of Lucky when he got all excited about going for a car ride. "A ball field, Charlotte, can you believe it? Paradise's own ball field."

"And the best part is that it isn't on Paradise land," Rose said. "Not thing one Fergus Wrinkel can do about it."

Out the corner of my eye I spotted an object flit past my trailer and then make a sharp turn down my wooden walkway. "What in tarnation was that? Looked like a dog or a great big gopher or something."

I heard a knock on the front door.

"I'll get it," Asa said.

I kept looking out the window. "What was it?"

"Just Ginger Rodgers," Asa called. "She's sopping wet."

"Ginger?" I felt a flush of embarrassment start at my toes and travel clear up to my ears. "I am so sorry. I didn't mean to imply . . . I just couldn't see . . ."

Rose touched my hand. "She didn't hear you, Charlotte. Don't fret. Even if she did, it would take a lot more than a gopher reference to upset her."

I blew air out my nose. Paradise was a little hard to get used to.

"Hello," Ginger called. She had a small-girl voice, almost as though her voice stopped growing when she did.

"Welcome," I said. "Come in. Come in." I shook the surprise from my head and went to greet her.

Asa had already draped her raincoat — tan with large purple flowers on it — over top of his on the coat rack. She kicked off her sopping wet sneakers — little white Keds with pinkish soles.

"Ginger," I said. "What a nice surprise. Truly, a nice surprise. We were just having coffee and I think I might be able to rustle up some breakfast. Maybe some bacon and eggs and I got these little tiny . . . oh I'm sorry." I could have kicked myself. "I have some mini . . ." I stopped talking.

"Oh pish," Ginger said. "There are other small things in the world besides me, Charlotte."

I nodded.

"I think she might be talking about these mini-quiche-type things I found in the freezer." Rose dropped a tray of twelve quiche Lorraines on the kitchen counter.

"That's right," I said. "You like mini-quiches."

"I like anything mini," Ginger said.

I opened the package. "Oh, dear. What am I saying? We can't cook. The power is out."

"Sure you can," Rose said. "Propane, remember? Just light your stove."

"Well, hot dog. That's wonderful."

The initial discomfort quickly wore off and pretty soon the four of us were sitting at my table — Ginger on a large book Asa set on a chair — eating breakfast and listening to the storm in the dark and extolling the virtues of cooking by propane.

"So when the rain stops later this afternoon, I'll give Studebaker a call and we'll start clearing the land out there. I figure we'll only need about an acre or less, don't you think, Charlotte?"

"I think that will do," I said. "How long do you think it will take?"

Another roll of thunder passed overhead. Ginger looked up. "That might be the last of it," she said. "The sky is starting to clear to the west."

I looked out the window. The dark clouds were moving away, leaving behind blue, cloudless sky.

"Not sure," Asa said. "We got some trees to clear, sod to lay, an infield to build."

"And who is going to pay for this?" Rose asked. She plunked a third mini-quiche on her plate.

"I will," I said matter-of-factly. "I got some money stashed away. How much you think it will cost?"

Asa scratched his head. "Don't know."

"Just do it," I said.

That was when Ginger grabbed my hand. "Thank you, Jesus, for bringing this lovely woman into our midst." Then her eyes popped open and she bit into the last of her bacon. It was like praying was an extension of breathing to her. It seemed to come so naturally and easily, like talking to a friend. I couldn't imagine God being a friend.

Asa wiped his mouth and polished off his coffee. "I got a trailer to clean out first thing and Fergus said something about Mrs. Crenshaw's toilet is leaking again. Woman needs to invest in a new pot."

"Don't think I know Mrs. Crenshaw," I said.

"Oh, she's an older woman, must be a hundred and two. She lives just over there in number 23, the trailer with all the bird-houses scattered around."

I looked out the window. "That old place? I put a flyer in her door, but I would have skipped it if I had known it was an old woman living there."

"She's just an old woman with no one but herself. Crotchety old bird," Rose said. "But she is not a hundred and two."

"She's a little cuckoo," Asa said.

"Now, Asa," Ginger said. "She has a right to her oddities, same as any old person."

Lucky must have sensed the end of the

storm. He went right for the door. "Just a sec, Lucky." I was just about to stand up, but Asa beat me to it.

"There you go, boy," Asa said. And Lucky bounded outside. "I can put a doggie door in here with no trouble at all, Charlotte."

"Like what kind of oddities?" I asked still thinking about Mrs. Crenshaw.

"How about the birdhouses for one thing," Asa said. "She's got a hundred of them over there, and then there's the hats. All them hats."

"Hats?"

Rose swallowed pie. "She must have a million of them. Puts on a new one every time she comes out to fill the birdhouses. She just sits there on that little bench waiting on the birds. I've seen Fergus go in, and of course Asa, when she has plumbing or electric issues. But she doesn't have much to say and will shoo you out after just a couple of minutes," said Rose. "Still, I painted her name on the giant hand."

"I better get on over there," Asa called. "Don't want the old bird to not be able to use her bathroom for long."

Asa pulled on his hip waders and ran across the street, jumping over two puddles.

"Charlotte tried to visit with Suzy last

night," said Rose, turning her attention to Ginger.

"Suzy?" Ginger said. "Really?"

"Well, she called me" — I nodded toward my telephone — "and said to meet her outside her trailer."

"No kidding," Ginger said. "Did she show?"

"No," I said. "But she did take the pie I left. I saw her open the door and take it inside. I do hope she enjoyed it."

"She's another odd one, and ever so shy," Rose said. "I'm glad we decided to find out what is going on inside there."

Ginger shook her head. "I think you better let things alone. Don't go stirring up the cauldron even more; never know what can bubble up."

"But I think she might be in some sort of trouble," I said.

"You can't prove it. It's her home and Fergus's. Can't just go making accusations without proof. They might be perfectly content and won't appreciate you horning in."

"But something is not right, Ginger," I said. "I can feel it in my bones."

Ginger sipped coffee and shook her head. "Mm, mm, mm. Better be careful. Pray about it. Put it in the Lord's hands."

"I did that," Rose said. She put her palms on my cheeks. "Now we have Charlotte here helping to get the folks rallied up and playing softball. I think she came express from God to us; so does Asa. Maybe we can rally for Suzy at the same time."

My stomach churned. Express from God? I did not expect to be a rabble-rouser or leader of anything but a women's softball team and only because I knew about softball. That I could do. But now all of a sudden my new friends looked at me like I was the leader of some secret mission to save Suzy Wrinkel.

"Have you tried the police?" I asked. That seemed the best thing. Let the authorities handle it. "Maybe they can at least tell us what to do." I had never called the police when Herman was out of control, and I felt a little silly even making the suggestion.

Ginger shook her head. "The cops have been out two or three times when it got especially loud over there. Never knew who called them, but they've been out and all they do is talk to Fergus outside and then leave."

"Cops always take the husband's word." Rose said. "Man's home is his castle and all that malarkey."

I knew exactly what she was saying. I had

heard those words many times before, and suddenly I wished I was back in my old house eating chicken pot pie with Midge and discussing her garden gnomes and gallbladder. I shook my head as Suzy's sad eyes surfaced in my mind like an answer on a Magic Eight Ball. "I think we should keep our eye out for her."

Rose touched my hand. "We will, Charlotte."

Ginger hopped down off the chair. "I think I'll head back home. Got some work to finish. I sold a quilt to some rich woman in Scranton and I still have a ton of sewing to do. Let me know when practice starts. I can't wait."

"I will," I said, but my mind was still on Suzy.

"Thing I don't understand," Ginger said when she got to the front door. "If Fergus is truly hurting her, why in heaven's name would she stay in a situation like that?"

Rose took a deep breath and said, "It's what happens. Women stay."

10

The next morning I heard pounding on my front door that rivaled the previous morning's thunder. Lucky leaped from a sound sleep and barreled toward the sound, skittered across the linoleum and crashed into the door. He straightened himself up and barked and even showed his teeth.

"What in the heck?" I was sitting on the couch looking over the rule book for women's softball. Of course, my copy had been tucked away with my other memorabilia and was quite old and dog-eared. I figured some of the rules must have changed.

"Who is it?" I called. I was not about to open the door. I thought Fergus might have gotten wind that I was trying to visit Suzy. The apple crumb told tales, I supposed, even if Suzy didn't. I made a mental note not to leave pie anymore.

"Who is it?" I repeated.

"Rube Felker," came the gruff answer.

Rube Felker? Then it struck me. I pulled Lucky away from the door. "Didn't Frankie, our center fielder, say her husband's name was Rube? What in the world could he want with me?"

I opened the door and there stood the biggest man I had ever seen in my life. He had long brown hair tied in a ponytail and he wore an orange coat, bright pumpkin orange, like he wanted to be seen from Mars or something.

"Hello," I said.

"You Charlotte Figg?"

"Yes, yes, I am. Can I help you?"

Lucky snarled and I had to keep him under control with my knee.

"So you're getting a softball team going with the women in Paradise."

I nodded. "That's right. Francine is going to be our pitcher. I think she'll make a fine pitcher and she looks like she can hit too. You must be so proud."

Rube stumbled over some unintelligible words, and then in a hurry he said, "Just see to it that you don't keep her out late every night. I need my dinner on the table. Kids got schoolwork."

"Of course not, Mr. Felker. Why, I just think family is the most important thing there is on earth, and I wouldn't want to interfere. Francine is sure blessed to have an understanding husband like you."

He tripped over his tongue some more, turned away, then he turned back, "You think she can play, huh?"

"Well, I need to see her on the field, but I think so. You be sure and come out to the games, now."

He walked off, and I breathed a huge sigh of relief. Somewhere along the line Herman's sales ability to sweet talk must have rubbed off. I even surprised myself.

Worried that the other husbands might be upset also, I decided to call another meeting as soon as possible to talk things over, set up a schedule and all. But first I had to get with Asa and find out what was happening with the Frost sisters and when we could expect to have a field to play on.

"Lots to do, Lucky," I said. I scratched his ears and let him outside.

I grabbed my writing pad and started to assemble my team.

Two hours later I had no more than a roster drawn up with the names of each of the women and their position alongside some silly doodles of turtles and three-D cubes, when it occurred to me that having a team isn't much good unless you have another team to play against. What is the point, other than getting out on the field and practicing for your own good? I saw the wisdom in that but decided I needed to find a league to join.

Lucky scratched at the door, so I let him in and explained my cares to him. He listened patiently as I held his muzzle and talked right into his sympathetic eyes. Lucky had become a good friend for being just a found dog. He almost never lied to me, except when he treed a squirrel and pretended he was as innocent as the new-driven snow, and I could always count on him to sidle right up next to me on a walk. Lucky was a good dog. And I was ever so glad he found me.

Later that day, after I caught up with some laundry and housework, I went to visit Rose. An aroma that reminded me of burnt sugar escaped from the trailer when she opened the front door. She still wore her heavy brown sweater.

"Charlotte, come on in." Crammed with an odd assortment of mismatched ceramics, flowers, and overstuffed furniture with stripes, her trailer had a hodgepodge museum look. A large easel with a covered canvas stood in the middle of the living room with a small table strewn with paints and brushes and a messy palate and paint-stained rags.

Tempted to lift the sheet covering the canvas, I asked Rose about it. "What are you painting?"

"Oh, it's something I was asked to do."

"Can I see it?"

"No," Rose snapped at me. "I don't show my work to anyone until it's finished. It might turn out different in the end and then you'd be disappointed."

I sat on her sofa and sank about six inches down. "Rose. We have a problem."

Rose sat on a stool near the easel and crossed one leg over the other. "Well, we all have problems. Which one are you talking about?" She wiped a brush on a rag. "I need more cerulean."

"It's the team," I said. "What good is a team with no one to play? I mean, we could go out there and toss a ball around and have batting practice, but we need to play against someone, you know, that is the point, after all — winning. Playing hard and winning."

Rose's eyes grew wide. "Really. Winning? That's what this is all about?"

Shame or embarrassment or something equally disagreeable welled in my corpuscles. "Well, not entirely. But it would be nice to find a team or two to play against and try to win, wouldn't it?"

Rose fooled with the hem of her skirt. "I guess you're right."

"But I just don't know how to go about finding one. You don't suppose there's some kind of trailer park league, do you? Or would that be asking too much?"

"Asking too much of who?" Rose flashed me a smile.

"I don't how to answer that, Rose. You keep trying to turn my attention to God, but I just don't think everything I do or say is in God's radar. Or should be."

"Maybe you could ask around in town. Go on in to Shoops and ask at the Piggly Wiggly. Someone might know something. There are quite a few trailer parks in these parts."

Thankful she avoided the discussion about how deeply God was involved with my life, I said, "I guess that's as good a place as any to start."

Then she snapped her fingers. "You don't suppose that any of those players on your old team might know something? Is there any way to get in touch with them? Who knows, unless you're the only remaining team member still holding an interest in softball and the likelihood of that is —"

"Ridiculous. How could I ever find any of them?"

Rose fell quiet a moment while she yanked at a thread on the hem of her skirt, a purple one that seemed to have been nagging her the whole time. Finally she reached down and bit it.

"I know. The library has phone books. Start there. Maybe Griselda in Bright's Pond — she's the librarian — can help you."

I shook my head. "Maybe. I think first I will venture into Shoops and poke around a little. Want to come?"

"Not today. It's Sunday."

My eyebrows arched.

"Church. A bunch of us drive into Bright's Pond. We'll be leaving in about twenty minutes. Want to come?"

"No, thank you, Rose."

Rose let go a small chuckle. "Okay. But maybe you can come next week. Bring a pie. I'm sure it will be welcome at the fellowship time after the service. They always have that Full Moon Pie, but maybe yours will be a welcome change — or not."

At noon Lucky and I headed out in the Galaxy. Unfortunately, nearly every store in Shoops was closed except for the Piggly Wiggly.

I sat in the parking lot for several minutes scanning the place. There were several cars in the lot and I watched folks go in and come out, but no one who looked like they knew diddly about softball.

"This is crazy, Lucky. How will I ever find anyone who knows anything about starting a women's softball team?"

He let go a blustery bark and settled down in the back seat.

"Well, guess this is the only game in town so. . . ." Then I saw a small restaurant on the other side of the street in my rearview mirror. Lucky must have been blocking it.

"That looks open. Let's try there."

I started the engine and found a parking spot on the street not far at all from The Pink Lady Café.

"Okay, fella, you stay here. I'll go check it out."

The Pink Lady was exactly that. Pink. Pink awning, pink tablecloths on the tables and pink lampshades on all the little lamps on the tables. Even the waitresses wore pink uniforms with white aprons. This was not shaping up to be a place where softball players would gather.

I waited a minute until I was seated at a table that gave me a good view. My eyes landed on a man wearing a baseball cap at the counter talking to one of the waitresses.

My waitress came back and poured me coffee without asking if I wanted any. "Excuse me," I said, "but would you mind if I moved to the counter?"

She looked over. "No. Got people waiting for a table now. Be my guest. But lady, if you got your eye on Cash over there, I'd —"

"Cash?" Did she think I was going to rob the place? "No, I . . . well, I just want to sit at the counter."

I set my coffee cup on a paper placemat and managed to catch the man's eye. I smiled. He smiled. The waitress moved to the other end of the counter to take an order.

"Excuse me," I said. I offered my hand. "My name is Charlotte Figg, and this might sound like a funny question, but . . . but . . ."

"Spill it," the man said. "But what?"

"You wouldn't happen to know who I could talk to about starting a women's softball team in these parts? I know it's a crazy question, but I just didn't know who or where —"

"Softball? You serious?"

"I am. I just moved into the Paradise Trailer Park and we started a team and I was wondering if there was a league. Most

139

towns have a league, don't they?"

He laughed. "You got some wild ESP," he said.

The waitress came back and dropped a plate on the counter in front of the man. "Here you go, Cash. Just the way you like it. Crispy with extra marmalade."

I looked at the man's sandwich.

"Heavens to Betsy," I said. "Is that a bacon and jelly sandwich?"

He took a bite. "Best in Shoops."

It did sound oddly tasty. So when the waitress returned, I ordered one. "Extra crispy, please."

"No problem." She scribbled on her pad, stuck the slip of paper in the silver carousel and hollered, "Another oinker dressed to kill."

I swallowed and gathered more courage. "ESP? What did you mean?"

He finished the first half of his sandwich, wiped his mouth and fingers. "My name is Cash Vangarten, and it so happens that I coach the Shoops Borough Thunder."

My heart danced a jig. "A ladies' softball team?"

A half hour later I left the Pink Lady armed with the information I needed to get my team registered with the Trailer Park League

140

and a notion to begin making bacon and marmalade sandwiches. It was indeed a tasty bite. Mr. Vangarten said I had about three days to get the team set up to play, but it meant we needed a name, a sponsor if we wanted one, uniforms, a roster, and all the league papers filled out and filed with the home office. And then we'd only be eligible to play in the summer league. That was fine by me. More time to get in shape.

Lucky was more than happy to see me and I regretted not bringing him a bacon-marmalade sandwich. "Sorry, fella. I'll make you one myself."

There was a lot of work to be done, but I was filled with enthusiasm and determination when I pulled into Paradise. At least until I noticed the mob of trailerites outside my trailer.

Lucky barked. "My goodness gracious," I said. "What's wrong?" My immediate thought was that something might have happened to Suzy. I opened the door and Lucky barked even harder. I held onto his collar. "Settle down. Settle down."

"There she is," Rube Felker called. "That's Charlotte Figg." And that was when I realized it was a mob of men. Just men.

"She's the one. She's the one that got our women all hepped up about some dang fool softball game."

A marmalade burp formed in my throat. I had never been in a riot before.

11

"What's wrong?" I called. "What happened?"

The next thing I knew, three men rushed toward me. "There ain't going to be no softball," they hollered.

Paralyzed, my mind reeled for something, anything, to say that wouldn't make me sound like a perfect blithering idiot. What I had here was potential mayhem over a women's softball team. I spotted Frankie's husband among the three.

"Rube, what's wrong? Please tell me what's wrong."

Lucky continued to bark his fool head off, but there was no way I could let him loose. I thought maybe I should put him in the car for his own safety.

That was when a tall, lanky, but mean-looking man stepped within three inches of my face. I could smell his peanut-butter-laced breath. His eyes were wide and crinkled around the edges, his teeth tanned from coffee. "Clara Kaninsky is not playing on your team. Not for one gol-darn minute she ain't."

I swallowed and stepped back. "Excuse me," I said as I pulled myself up to my full height. "I'd like to go into my home and you are in my way, you and the rest of your rabble rousers." My heart pounded in my ears. "My dog needs to go inside, Mr. Kaninsky."

I attempted to walk past him. Lucky busted loose and ran wild, barking and even nipping at a few ankles. The rest of the men formed a wall between me and the front door. I had never felt so assaulted in my life. That's exactly what it felt like — like I was being assaulted without a single one of them laying a finger on me.

My heart pounded harder. I could feel it throb in my neck and my ears. I touched my stomach as a flood of emotions rushed through me. I wanted Herman, but Herman wasn't there. He wasn't ever going to be there again. I needed to defend myself. So I pulled myself up to my full height and I waggled my finger.

"I will not stand here and let you do this," I said. "Now, I will be happy to discuss it later. Not now, later. I need to go to the bathroom, and I'm afraid if I stand here much longer I will pee my pants. Now, please step aside."

That was when Rube started to laugh. He grabbed onto Mr. Kaninsky's shoulder and pulled him aside. "Come on, Carl, let her alone. I told you this wouldn't work. Let her alone, now."

I looked into Rube's eyes. "Thank you, Rube."

The men parted and I waddled through the mob with my head high, my inner thighs tight against each other for fear I was really going to have an accident, and my mind reeling. I might have sounded strong. I might have sounded like I was not upset by their show of animosity against me, but inside I cowered like Lucky in a thunderstorm.

The trailer door needed the usual hip action. Once we were safely inside, Lucky leaped onto my waist and licked my face. "It's okay, boy. I'm okay." Then I sat down on the sofa, dropped my handbag on the floor, and cried. I sat there and blubbered with Lucky's paw on my knee and his brown eyes staring up at me as if he wanted to say, "Now where's that sandwich you promised me, Charlotte?"

■ ■ ■ ■

I only sat there a couple of minutes before I heard Rose calling, "Charlotte, Charlotte. You okay? Let us in."

I pulled open the door.

"Charlotte," Rose said. "We saw you come home and saw Charlie's motley band of vigilantes up here trying to harass you."

Ginger pushed her way into the house and hopped up on the sofa. "We were afraid they'd pull something stupid like this." She wiggled back into the couch. "But never you mind about them. This is a Holy Spirit-appointed thing you got going on. There is nothing that can or will keep us from playing ball now." She pushed her little fingers through her long hair. "We are not afraid of them bullies."

"That's right," Rose said. She had made her way into the kitchen. "You didn't give into them, did you?"

I shook my head. "Of course not, Rose."

She smiled in my direction. "Good. Because I've already seen it starting to change things around here. The women who came to church this morning seemed just a tad more self-assured, happy. Like they had something to look forward to. They yammered all about the team."

"Maybe the husbands saw it too," Ginger said. "And they don't like it."

"Phooey on them," Rose said.

My stomach sunk to my knees. "I don't want to cause a mass run to divorce court. Softball is good, but I'm not sure it's worth all this. Maybe I should rethink what I have done."

Rose laughed. "You aren't causing anyone to get divorced. This is just different for the women *and* the men. Let's give it time. Let the wives handle their husbands."

I moved into the kitchen and started a pot of coffee. "I promised Lucky a sandwich."

"A sandwich?" Rose said. "What kind of dog eats sandwiches?"

"I had the most delicious sandwich at the Pink Lady. That nice Mr. Cash Vangarten introduced me to them. Bacon and orange marmalade on toast."

"Ewww," Ginger said. "That sounds disgusting."

"But it's not," I said. I searched around in the fridge for the bacon. I kept my head inside for a few moments longer than necessary as I tried to pull myself together. It had been quite a Sunday afternoon.

The bacon sizzled in the pan before anyone said another word.

"Sounds like you have some explaining to do, Charlotte," Rose said. "What exactly happened in Shoops?"

"I went to the Pink Lady and met this nice fella named Cash Vangarten."

"Oh," Ginger said, "is that why you're all flushed?"

"Now, don't be ridiculous. If I'm flushed it's because of that mob outside."

Rose put her hand on my shoulder just as a bit of bacon grease popped onto my hand.

"Ow. I hate it when this happens. Why is bacon so darn dangerous to fry?"

"Okay, okay," Rose said. "Why don't you just tell us and we'll be quiet."

"Thank you. As it turns out, I have some good news. I mean, besides the discovery of bacon and orange marmalade on toast."

I caught the glance that passed between my friends. "You'll see. You'll try one and I guarantee you will love it."

Rose tapped her foot. "Tell us your news, Charlotte."

"Like I was saying, I met this guy named Cash Vangarten at the Pink Lady. It was the only place open besides the Piggly Wiggly, and I didn't think I'd find anyone in there who knew about women's softball." I dropped bacon onto a paper towel on a plate. "Rose, will you push that toast down?

And it turned out that, get this, he coaches a women's softball team in Shoops."

Ginger laughed. "Oh, no! What are the odds of that happening? You walk into a restaurant and just happen to meet a softball coach."

"It's true. Anyway, he told me everything we need to do to get set up in the Trailer Park Softball League."

Rose snagged the toast when it popped. "No kidding. You mean there really is such a thing?"

I slathered the toast with orange marmalade and arranged the bacon on top. "Lucky, come on, boy. I got your sandwich."

He came running. I broke off a corner, blew on the hot bread and then he gulped it like he hadn't had a meal in ten days. I put the remaining sandwich in his bowl. It was gone in two seconds and he begged for more. I patted his head. "Later. Too much bacon isn't good for you."

"Hallelujah," Ginger said. "Looks like we got a bona fide team now. And would it be too much trouble to make one of those for me?"

I put enough bacon in the pan for three sandwiches and explained what I'd learned. "Sponsor?" Rose said.

"Uniforms?" Ginger said.

"Name?" I said.

We sat at the kitchen table sipping coffee, eating our sandwiches, and ruminating on the fact that we lacked all three requirements and had precious little time to acquire them.

"Looks like we struck out before we even went to the plate," Ginger said.

"Nah," I said with all the certainty of a criminal in front of a firing squad expecting the bullet to miss. "We'll think of something."

12

It had been spring for a week and Paradise hummed with vernal activity. Early morning snow flurries gave way to warm air and bright sunshine. I entertained the notion that softball might have been the catalyst that brought the women out to tend to overgrown gardens and plant tulip bulbs. But maybe not, and I guess it didn't really matter. I was happy to see it, whatever the case might be.

I stood on the little deck watching Lucky chase squirrels when a pesky skunk that had been stinking up the place came out from behind the trailer next door. I had just instructed Lucky not to go near the skunk when I saw Francine running down the street.

"Charlotte, Charlotte," she hollered. "Get your dog inside. That sick skunk is on the loose again."

"What are you blabbering about,

Frankie?"

"Ain't you seen it?"

"Sure. That's him over there." I pointed. "I didn't know skunks grew that large."

"Get inside, Charlotte, that thing is sick. Skunks don't come out in the daylight unless they're sick and that one's got rabies sure as shootin'."

"Rabies." I pulled my robe tight around my body and called for Lucky.

Frankie's eyes darted around like two pinballs. "What should we do? I called that dang fool dogcatcher, but he ain't been out yet. Only comes if Fergus calls him out on account of the children running amok."

Lucky bounded from behind the trailer. He whooped and barked and blew right past me with his tail between his legs into the trailer. He nearly knocked me over.

"Here it comes." Frankie pointed and the skunk lumbered by. "We got to do something before he bites one of us or sprays one of us. Surprised that dog of yours hasn't gotten a cloud of stink in his face."

"What about the police?" I said. "Can you call the police?"

"Good idea." Frankie pushed past me into the trailer. She grabbed the phone and dialed. "Of course it's rabid," she said into the receiver. "I know a rabid skunk when I see one."

She hung up and we waited.

Ten full minutes later I heard the siren and looked out my kitchen bay window. A police car pulled up right in front. Two burly police officers — one male, the other female — leaped out of their car and opened fire on the skunk that was now in Hazel Crenshaw's yard.

"Oh, my goodness gracious, they killed it," I said.

"And then some," Frankie said. "Hope they remove the carcass. The dead-animal remover is even harder to get a hold of then the dog catcher."

"Dead-animal remover?"

"Sure. What? You think all them flat possums and coons and deer out on the roads get resurrected and walk away?"

I shook my head and went to the front door.

"Don't open the —" Frankie hollered. But it was too late. I opened the door, and the stink was so bad my eyes watered like I had been dicing onions all day and my chest hurt. I slammed the door.

"What do we do now?" I said.

"Just wait it out, Charlotte. It'll go away. But I wouldn't let Lucky out for a while if I were you. Dogs like to roll around in that."

Frankie grabbed one of my prettiest tea towels off the kitchen counter and made herself a little burglar-type mask. "I gotta be getting back. You stay put a while."

I found Lucky cowering under the bed. "Come on, fella. What happened?" I had to drag him out. I saw two pink stripes on his black nose. It looked like the skunk either bit him or scratched him. My heart pounded. "Oh, Lucky, we need to get you to the vet."

He was of course current on his rabies shots, but I didn't want to take a chance, and so I called the Shoops veterinary clinic right away. They were very nice and told me I could bring him right down.

The visit went well and Lucky only needed a booster shot. I think my silly pooch kind of liked Dr. Fish. I thanked her very kindly and we headed back to Paradise, but not before stopping at the Pink Lady for a take-out order. I had a hankering for a chocolate milkshake and a bacon and marmalade sandwich. And guess who was sitting at the counter, this time all dressed up in a suit and tie like he had just walked out of the window at JCPenney?

"Hello, Mr. Vangarten," I said.

He spun around on the counter stool. "Mrs. Figg. What brings you to Shoops?"

I explained about the skunk and the shooting and the vet, and he was very sympathetic and even paid for my lunch. We made eye contact at one point and I sensed a definite something pass between us, but I let it go and scolded myself when I got back to the car. "Charlotte Figg, what got into you? Why are you making eyes at Mr. Vangarten when Herman's not been dead three months?"

I got back to Paradise and parked the car. Lucky took off like a shot, like nothing had ever happened. I wondered if he was still after the skunk, but the stench should have been enough to chase him inside. I looked over at Hazel Crenshaw's and saw her pouring something red all over the ground where the unfortunate animal met his demise.

"What are you doing, Mrs. Crenshaw?" I called. It was the first time I had spoken to the woman, and Asa and Rose were correct in their assessment, I decided. She looked kind of strange and silly.

"Only way to kill the stink," she called. "And I don't have any tomato juice."

"Well, what is that you're dumping?"

"Only tomato-like stuff I could find. Spaghetti sauce."

"Why?" I felt my forehead wrinkle.

155

"Tomatoes cut the smell. Everyone knows that."

I shook my head. "If you say so."

By now it was a quarter to two and I was pretty well on my way to exhausted. I figured a cup of coffee was in order. I saw Asa out the window holding his nose as he made his way to my trailer.

I opened the front door and pulled Asa inside. "Get out of that stench," I said.

"Yeah, we heard all about the skunk."

"Yep. The police killed him, but not before he bit Lucky."

"He okay?"

I nodded, and Lucky came out of the bedroom. "Poor pooch," Asa gave him a good ear scratch.

"I was just about to make a pot of coffee."

"None for me, thanks. I came by to tell you that my cousin Studebaker and me and the Frost sisters been working like mad. We got the land cleared and ready to plant grass and build an infield and —"

I rushed to him and threw my arms around him. "Asa. Thank you."

He held onto me with his one arm for a few seconds. "Want to go see it?"

"I do," I said, stepping back. "Let's get Rose and Ginger."

■ ■ ■ ■

I had never met Edwina and Thomasina Frost until that day, and I got to tell you that they were exactly what I pictured. Bookends. Medium height with short, dirty blond hair secured at the side with a barrette. They wore denim overalls with a flannel shirt and orange work boots. The only difference between the two was that Edwina liked to keep her hands stuffed in her pockets.

"Is that them?" I saw a door open on a long, purplish grey trailer about a hundred yards ahead of us.

"Must have seen us traipsing through the woods," Asa said. "They got eyes like hawks."

"And binoculars," Ginger said.

"Are they going to shoot at us?" I asked. "I've had my fill of gunfire around here."

"Nah, we just have to raise that little yellow flag over there. That way they know we're friends."

"Flag? What flag? I don't see a flag."

"They keep it hidden so only folks who know about it will raise it."

Asa reached into a tree trunk and a little

yellow pennant zipped up a line above the trees.

Rose and Ginger laughed.

"They always laugh at the flag," Asa said. "But it really is a good idea. I mean, they are two women living alone in a trailer in the woods. Seems to me if more women had yellow flags maybe they. . . ."

He stopped talking and looked in Rose's direction.

"It's okay, Asa. I understand what you're saying."

I thought he might be talking about Rose's horrendous experience. But he was also hoping Suzy could find the courage to raise a flag and let friends inside.

Asa raised his hand. "I brought Charlotte."

Edwina and Thomasina headed toward us like we were long-lost cousins.

"Welcome," they said. "Welcome to our farm, Frosty Acres." Edwina elbowed Thomasina like she had just told the world's funniest joke. "Frosty Acres," she said. "It still slays me."

I thought a handshake would suffice. but instead I got pulled into a tight bear hug. "I'm Edwina. And this is my sister Thomasina."

"Pleased to meet you," I said.

After a few more hellos we went behind their trailer. I took a minute to admire their rig. It was gorgeous, with awnings and pink and purple trailing verbena in hanging pots. The trailer I thought I had purchased. "That creep," I said.

"Excuse me?" Thomasina said.

"That creep, Fergus Wrinkel. This is the trailer in the ad. The trailer I thought I bought when I was really buying that bucket of rust I got shystered into buying."

The whole group laughed. Ginger could hardly contain herself. "The old bait and switcheroo," she said. "The old bait and switcher—"

Rose nudged her before she could say it again.

"Not the first time he used our place to snooker some poor soul into buying a bucket of rust as you called it," Thomasina said.

I took a deep breath and just kept staring. "And look. Trailing verbena and birdhouses and it looks like those might be daffodils coming up. I. . . ."

Rose put her arm around me. "Now don't go getting all misty-eyed and sad. You bought the place you were meant to buy and we are all the richer for it."

I swiped away a tear or three. "I know.

Don't get me wrong. It's just. . . ."

"Don't fret, honey," Edwina said. "I bet one day soon you'll have that old Vindar up to snuff and looking like brand-new, like it just jumped off a page of *Trailer Times*."

They all nodded their agreement and we continued the walk out back. And then I saw it. The biggest empty field I had ever seen. Nothing but dirt and a few patches of grass and weeds. Barren and desolate yet poised to burst into new life.

"It's beautiful," I said. "It's the most beautiful field of nothing I have ever laid eyes on."

"It is rather pretty now, isn't it?" Rose said. "I might come out here with an easel one of these days."

"And soon it will be the prettiest softball field in the county, maybe the whole Pocono Region," Ginger said.

We all stared at the field. My heart raced until Rose took hold of my hand and thanked the Almighty for providing Paradise a field where bases would be run and home runs hit and strikes made and friendships found.

I saw Edwina crying in my periphery. "What's wrong?"

"It's not that anything is wrong. I'm just so happy. Been a long time since that field was used for anything. We used to grow wheat on it, but not anymore."

"Thank you for this. Thank you both." I swiped more tears.

The next thing I knew Ginger called for a group hug. We had to kneel because of Ginger being so small, and held on to each other. Rose took advantage of us all being on our knees and prayed.

That evening I went door-to-door inviting the women to our second team meeting. This was going to be an extremely important get-together as we had a lot to decide and precious little time to do it. I called the meeting for as early as possible the next day and told them to bring their kids if needed. It wasn't all that easy getting the word out. I had to make my way past a few husbands who still wanted to holler at me for "stealing their wives," as they called it.

Lucky and I walked together, well, mostly. He liked to run off ahead and sniff things out first.

"You're starting a load of trouble," Charlie Lundy, Greta's husband, said after I asked him to deliver my message. "She's got housework to do and meals to cook. That's how come all us men went to your place that day, to warn you."

Charlie was a horse of a man with thick arms and a nearly square nose. It wasn't until Greta came to the door and pushed him out of the way that I felt better.

"Go on, Charlie," she said with a shoulder hit to his waist. "Finish your dinner."

"Dinner?" I said. "The last thing I want to do is interrupt dinner. I thought it was late enough. I'm —"

She stopped me. "Don't let Charlie bother you. He had to pull a little OT at the plant and he's a mite gruff is all."

"So you can make the meeting tomorrow, my place, ten o'clock in the morning."

"Pie?"

"Plenty of it."

Greta smiled. "I'll be there."

But then Charlie bellowed from the kitchen and Greta closed the door.

That was pretty much how it went, and by eight-thirty I had everyone geared up for the meeting. Marlabeth Pilkey was last on my list. She lived close to the Wrinkels. When I saw the Wrinkel's trailer, a lump like oatmeal formed in my throat. I had to fight the urge to bang on the door and demand that Suzy come out. I can't even say why I got so flustered that night. I just stood there in the dark under the glow of a single street lamp as the smell of mold and pine and creek water filled the air and indignation rose in my belly.

I think I hoped to hear something, a fight, raised voices, anything that would give me a right, at least in my mind, to knock on the door. But it was stone cold quiet, eerie quiet. Not a peep came from their trailer. I only saw one small light in the window. It was sad, really. Sad because I envisioned Suzy sitting inside trying desperately to keep to herself, maybe knitting, maybe reading, maybe folding laundry with one eye on what she was doing and the other on Fergus. Waiting, waiting for him to start yelling or swinging.

That was something I knew all too well. Except it never occurred to me that I was unhappy. I thought sitting by myself at night reading, watching the TV, or baking pie with a knot the size of a Winesap apple in my stomach was normal married life. But since Herman died and I'd been living in Paradise, I'd started to feel the knot loosen.

Lucky whimpered and nudged my knee. I shushed him because I didn't want Fergus to hear us and come outside. "We should just go home, boy. We'll get Suzy out somehow."

I lingered a second and saw the kitchen

curtain open at the side. I saw Suzy's eyes; even in the dark I recognized them.

13

Rose and Ginger came by early the next morning. Rose was wrapped in her heavy brown sweater and Ginger was mostly hidden inside a deep blue parka. The weather had turned chilly. Rose said it was not unusual for the mountains in spring, but we were all a tad dismayed thinking that spring might have changed her mind.

"Can't believe how cold it is," Rose said. She kept her sweater on and reached for the coffeepot. "A cold front moved in over the mountains, probably bring rain later."

"Heavens to Betsy," I said. "A lot of rain? What will it do to the field? Probably turn it into a huge mud hole."

"No, no," Ginger said. She hopped onto a kitchen chair — the one with the thick book. "The dirt will get wet, but it won't wash away, least, not all of it. Besides, I saw Asa headed out that way earlier. Probably try to cover some of it."

I poured half-and-half into my coffee. I always used real cream or half-and-half in coffee. It's what makes the difference between a good, thinking cup of coffee and something you drink to jumpstart your heart. "Hope they have a tarp big enough."

"That boy has everything," Rose said. "Ever look inside that garage of his? My, my, but it's chock full of every machine, gadget, tool, auto part, and piece of wood a person could ever need. I think Asa could build his own city."

I felt a little better, but still nursed a worry. I wouldn't feel a hundred percent worry-free until the field was finished and we had proper tarps to protect the infield.

By ten o'clock we had cups and saucers and pie set up buffet-style for the team and waited for the women to arrive.

"Oh, I do hope they come," I said. "They'll come won't they, Rose?"

"Sure," she said. "Just relax. You have notes for everything you need to say?"

I grabbed my note pad from the kitchen counter. "I do. I put down my thoughts and I am not concerned about anything except the sponsor."

"Sponsor?" Ginger said. "You mean someone to take on the team and buy the uniforms and pay the fees in exchange for advertising?"

"That's right. Back in my day, Burrell's Deli sponsored The Clifton Canaries. Marty and Freda Burrell ran this little deli on High Street. My mama would buy all our groceries there, including the best fresh turkeys for Thanksgiving."

Ginger laughed. "Probably got the turkeys from us."

I squinted. "What?"

"My daddy and his daddy before him were turkey farmers just down the road about sixty miles or so. Sold to nearly every grocer outside Philadelphia."

"Amazing," I said. "It is a small world. Who knew I'd be sharing pie with the daughter of the man who provided my Thanksgiving meal?" I lifted my cup to her. "Thank you very much. They were delicious."

Ginger pushed another slice of pie in front of me. "Our pleasure."

"Now back to our latest problem. Who can sponsor our team?"

I looked at Ginger. "Your family still have a turkey farm?"

"Nah. Sold it after Daddy died."

We sipped coffee and picked at pie silently until we saw the rest of the team making their way toward the trailer.

"They're here," I said. "Maybe one of them will have a thought."

After scattered and happy greetings the women gathered in the living area with coffee and pie. I let them jabber a few minutes. Only Greta brought a child — baby Ruth. A pretty little thing with a pug nose and bright eyes, she looked a bit like Bette Davis. Greta carried her in a basket that looked to be about a hundred years old, stuffed with soft, colorful quilts. A tiny blue bunny with brown button eyes, handmade from a terry towel, hunkered down in a corner of the basket, making the whole scene that much more lovely.

"Baby Ruth is adorable," I said. Then I swallowed like I always did when I saw a new baby. It brought back all those awful feelings of longing I lived with for never having been able to bear a child. "She seems quiet now. Did the colic go away?"

Greta laughed along with the other women. "Oh, colic never goes away. It just turns into something else, like teething, stomach virus —"

"And boyfriend problems when they turn twelve," Clara said.

Greta touched baby Ruth's cheek. "Marlabeth gave me one of her tea concoctions —"

"Lemon and ginger with a skosh of fennel," Marlabeth interrupted. "Breast-fed babies eat the same thing as their mamas more or less, so I figured settling Greta's stomach would do the trick."

"And she told me to stop eating gassy foods like franks and beans."

"Now, girls," I said raising my hand. "This is all very interesting and I would love to hear more about Marlabeth's concoctions, but I think we should get to the topics at hand." I showed them my notepad. "We have three important items to discuss about our team."

"Go on, Charlotte," Ginger said. "You're the coach, after all."

"Thank you, Ginger. Well, first I want to tell you about a man I met —" and with that the women made oohs and ahs and even a whistle. I raised my hand again. "Not that kind of man."

They laughed, and then I told them about meeting Cash Vangarten.

"Do you think we can beat his team?" Carla asked.

"Sure," I said. "We're just as good as any team out there."

"I still wouldn't place any bets," Frankie

said. "Just because our hearts are in the right place doesn't mean our bats will be."

"Or gloves," added Marlabeth. "That is what they call them things we wear on our hands. I don't have one of those, but I'm a size medium."

"Don't worry, Marlabeth," Rose said. "We'll get you a glove. One that fits nice and snug."

"That's all fine and dandy," I said. "But we need a team sponsor. Now, it's not mandatory, but it sure would help. It costs a bit of money to have a team — uniforms, equipment, league fees, and such. A rich or semirich benefactor would help."

Marlabeth raised her hand. "What's a team sponsor?"

I had to wonder how a woman so smart about herbs and plants could be so ignorant on just about everything else.

Ginger explained. As she did I realized that the Frost sisters were absent. I leaned toward Rose, who sat in Lucky's chair. She was the only one he allowed. Lucky sat near the door like a chivalrous knight.

"They might still show," Rose said. "But even if they don't, that's okay. They'll most likely abide by anything that's decided to-day."

I nodded. "Thank you, Rose. Now does

anyone have a suggestion for a team sponsor?"

"What about Fergus Wrinkel?" hollered Frankie Felker.

The whole team nearly busted a gut over that one.

"Fergus?" I couldn't believe my ears. "You got to be kidding."

"Sure we are," Greta said. "Fergus would never go for it." She reached into the basket and took the baby Ruth to her breast.

And I sighed.

It never occurred to me that there would be a day in my life when I would feel jealous of a nursing mother. But there I sat in my own living area feeling about as green as a Christmas tree. Greta was all of twenty-five years old. Same age I was when I lost my first baby after trying for nearly six years. Oh, I know, like Dr. Halloway said, it might have been the good Lord's way of protecting me from a baby that wasn't quite right. But for a brief couple of minutes as Greta held her baby so close, so warm and satisfied, I wished the good Lord wasn't always so darn smart.

I busted out of my reverie when Rose poked me. "Charlotte, do you have any idea about a sponsor?"

"Well, I had thought about the Fuller

Brush Company, but I scratched it off the list. I figured they'd think sponsoring a trailer park softball team would not fit their image."

"Makes sense," she said.

"Who else you got on your list?"

I looked at my writing pad. "No one," I said, looking up.

There was a collective sigh out of the group. It seemed no one had a thought about who could take on the responsibility. All of the husbands, except Marlabeth Pilkey's, worked at the elastic factory in Shoops. And all the women were one hundred percent sure the company would never go for it. I figured their blanket dismissal had more to do with not wanting to ask their husbands.

"Well, we need a sponsor," I said. "I can't afford it all by myself."

"Why not at least ask Fergus?" called Ginger, straining to be heard over the buzz of the comparatively Amazonian women near her. "I knew you would all laugh, but who knows, maybe he'd relish the notion to advertise Paradise. Still has three or four empty trailers scattered around."

"You're crazy, Ginger," Frankie said. "That S.O.B. would never sponsor us. Doesn't even sponsor his own wife, if you know what I mean."

The room grew suddenly and ferociously silent, as though a giant cat had been let out of a bag that no one wanted to feed.

I chose to gloss over the revelation myself after Rose tossed me a knowing glance.

Gwendolyn, who sat quietly this whole time, started to cry. "We'll never find a sponsor. Never."

"Stop your yammering, Gwendolyn," Greta said. "I swear you're worse than a baby with the collywobbles sometimes."

Gwendolyn sniffed, but she stopped blubbering.

"Why don't we talk about a name for our team?" I said. "Change the subject for a bit."

That was when Marlabeth Pilkey's hand shot up so fast and so straight I thought she had a spasm. "I've been thinking," she said with her arm still raised.

"You can lower your arm, Marlabeth," Frankie said. "You got the floor."

"Oh, sorry." She rested her arm in her lap. "I've been thinking up names all night long, lying in my bed thinking of names. Why, about a thousand of them came to mind. But the one I like best — are you ready for this?"

The women all said, "Yeah, Marlabeth."

"Well, now give it some time to soak in,

but I like the name Paradise Tornados." She raised her index finger in the air and did a kind of swirly thing above her head and said, "Whoosh."

"Tornados?" Greta said. The baby lost her grip and Greta held her up for a burp. "Tornados. We are not Tornados. I was thinking something more like the Paradise Angels."

"Well, what in tarnation do Angels got to do with it?" Marlabeth said.

"What the heck reason do you have for wanting us to be called Tornados?" Greta countered.

Marlabeth bit into a piece of pie. "Simple. Trailer parks are always getting destroyed by tornados, right? Well, we'll just be the ones doing the destroying — of the other teams."

"Out west, maybe," Greta said. She returned Ruth to suckle. "But we don't get tornados around here, so nobody will get it."

"How about Destroyers?" Clara said. "I like it."

"Destroyers?" Greta said. "That's the name of a roller derby team, not a softball team."

I put my hand up. "I think Tornados is an okay name."

"Yeah," Ginger said. "When I was little
—"

"Was there ever a time you weren't?"
Clara said with a chuckle.

"Okay, okay," Ginger said. "When I was
young my father used to say I was a tornado
the way I tore around the house."

Rose, who had been looking pretty solemn
through the discussion said, "How come
you want Angels, Greta?"

Greta smiled her appreciation. "I was
thinking more about the word *paradise* and
paradise is just another word for heaven and
heaven has angels so. . . ."

"That's great," Rose said. "I vote for Angels."

Everyone but Marlabeth and Ginger
agreed, so the majority ruled.

"Tornados will be our second choice if
Angels is already taken," I said.

I wrote the name Paradise Angels on my
pad with large letters. It looked nice. But I
added the name Tornados under it, just in
case.

It didn't take nearly as much discussion
to choose our team colors. Marlabeth suggested purple and white and no one countered.

But that brought us back to the problem
of a sponsor.

Greta looked at her watch. "Where did the time go? I have to get home and take a roast out of the freezer."

"But I didn't even talk about the new field or —"

"Have to wait," Clara said. "The school bus is coming down the road with the kindergartners."

They filed out and left me and Rose and Ginger with the chore of finding a team sponsor.

"You could ask Fergus," Ginger said. She looked around my trailer. "He sort of owes you."

Rose went into the kitchen carrying plates and cups balanced high. "Maybe you could ask," she called. "It might be a good idea in the long run."

I swallowed. "Why me? By myself? You guys come too."

"Not me," Rose said.

"I'll go." Ginger hopped off the couch.

My stomach twisted into a hundred knots. Knots that I thought had started to loosen. "Guess we have no other choice. But what if he refuses?"

"Then we'll think of something else. Maybe Asa knows someone," Ginger said.

I chewed the last of my cherry pie and

contemplated the idea of Fergus Wrinkel sponsoring our women's softball team.

14

"We'll visit Fergus in the morning." I slipped Lucky a chunk of pie crust and patted his head. "You're such a good boy."

Ginger shook her head. "No, no, no, Charlotte. Let's go today. Right now, in fact." Her voice rose an octave higher. "While I have some nerve."

I took a breath. She was a feisty little thing and I had this funny image of Ginger and Fergus going a round or two in a boxing ring. I figured it would be like the elephant and the mouse. Fergus wouldn't have a chance.

"You know she's right," Rose said. "We only have a couple of days to get everything organized."

"I know, I know. Well, if you think God cares a lick about softball, you might want to toss a prayer or two. I think I'm going to need it." I could hear Herman hollering at me, "Don't put off for tomorrow what you can do today, Charlotte, that's what I always say. Better a bird in the hand than two in the bush." I shook him from my mind.

"Of course, I'll pray," Rose said. "Now go on down there and —"

"But he might not be home."

"So you go back later if he's not. But you need to go — now. It's the only idea we have."

Ginger zipped her coat. It was still odd to see her tiny hands and foreshortened arms.

"You sure you can swing a bat?" I asked.

"Sure," she said. "But you'll have to get me a small one, little league size."

I made a mental note to check on that. Softball leagues had many regulations concerning legal and illegal bats. But I didn't want to say anything to Ginger, hoping they'd make an exception considering her size.

"Think I'll bring Lucky," I said as I opened the door.

Rose went out after Lucky. "Stop by and let me know how it went. I'll be home."

I think I might have grunted. I was not looking forward to facing Fergus Wrinkel.

Lucky bounded on ahead of us and treed three squirrels in a matter of a few seconds.

"One of these days he's going to catch one and I shudder to think what he'll do."

179

"You think he'll kill it?" Ginger asked.

"No, I think the squirrel will win that battle. Bite his snout or ear. Lucky is really very sensitive and I think the emotional scars would be pretty deep. Call his manhood into question and all. Imagine being beaten up by a squirrel."

Ginger shook her head. "You're a strange woman, Charlotte Figg. But I know God loves you. I know he's got his hand on you, so I'm going to hang on for the duration just to see where he leads."

The Wrinkel trailer appeared closed up tight, just like always. Fergus's truck was parked on the cement pad. My heart palpitated. I quickly scanned the bay window for a peek at Suzy, but the curtains were drawn closed.

"Ginger, I think this is a big mistake. There is no way in the world Fergus Wrinkel will sponsor our softball team."

Ginger grabbed my hand and forced me to stop walking. "You just hold on, Charlotte. You never know anything until you try, and he likes to be in control so much he might like the chance to sponsor the team and advertise Paradise, you know? Like I said, maybe he can unload a couple of the other empties he's got scattered around."

I swallowed and started walking again. "I don't know. After the way he treated me over my trailer, the way he cheated me and I don't know how many others and the way he treats Suzy —"

"Now, hold the phone again," Ginger said. "You don't know he's treating Suzy any way. Could be she's just shy."

"Yeah, shy with black eyes? Come on, Ginger, why are you taking his side?"

"I'm not. And if that's what you think, then you can just go see him yourself."

"Aw, Ginger, I'm sorry. I —"

"Come on. Let's go talk to him. I refuse to accuse any man of any crime until I have facts. Just makes sense to me."

I looked again for any sign of Suzy at the window. None.

"So go ahead," Ginger said. "Suck it up and knock on the door. He is not going to shoot you."

I wasn't so sure.

A whiff of pine tickled my nose as I approached the door. I took one step and then another, slowly. I could feel every muscle in my body tense. Fergus Wrinkel was a bad man. I knew that sure as I knew how to peel and slice apples. But there was no way I would let the Angels down.

181

After two or three swallows I banged on the door. My knees shook. Lucky sat as close as possible as I waited a couple of minutes.

"No one is answering," I called to Ginger, who all of a sudden decided to hide behind an azalea bush.

"Knock again." Her little voice was barely audible.

I knocked. And then I waited. The door opened a crack. The smell of cigarettes rushed up my nose and down my throat. I coughed.

"What do you want?" It was Fergus's voice.

"I want to speak with you, Mr. Wrinkel."

He pulled the door open. I couldn't help but try and see past him into the trailer, hoping to get a glimpse of Suzy. Fergus stepped outside, closing the door behind him.

"If this is about the Vindar, I —"

"No. No. It's not. It's about our softball team."

He laughed. He threw his head back and laughed with a sound that seemed to come from a deep cave.

"Why are you laughing?" I asked.

"I heard about that stupid team of yours. Rube Felker told me. He couldn't stop laughing when he told me. Imagine that, bunch of trailer trash women playing ball."

Trailer trash? Never in my life had I been called such a thing. I ignored the remark but made a mental note to think about it later. "Mr. Wrinkel. I'll have you know" — I pulled myself up to my full height, which brought me just about eye-to-eye with him — "The Paradise Angels are a good team. Championship caliber, if you ask me." I imagined Fergus in a Little Lord Fauntleroy outfit with knickers and lace cuffs and that settled my nerves a little.

He lit a cigarette and let the acrid smoke linger between us.

"So why should I care?" he asked. "What's it got to do with me?"

I took a breath, even though I didn't want to suck smoke into my lungs. I had no choice.

"Well . . . I, we —" I looked around for Ginger. "Come on out, Ginger. We need to do this together."

Fergus looked in Ginger's direction. He laughed even louder. "What the — You mean that pipsqueak is on the team? Get out. She can't play ball."

"Can too," Ginger called as she made her way near us. "I can hit and run and —" she stopped talking. "Just listen to what Charlotte has to say."

"Okey dokey," Fergus said. "What does Charlotte have to say?"

I closed my eyes a second and pictured Fergus in a body cast. "Well, in order to join the league we need a sponsor and we thought you —"

He spit past my head. "No soap. I ain't laying out my hard-earned cash for some chick softball team. You're out of your minds. No way, no how."

"But, Mr. Wrinkel. It would be good for Paradise." I hoped he hadn't noticed that I kept my eyes trained on the trailer hoping to see Suzy, wishing she'd come to the door.

"Yeah. In what way?"

"Advertising," Ginger said. "The team would wear the name Paradise Trailer Park on our uniforms and everyone would know that you sponsor us. Might help sell off a couple of them buckets of nothing you got around the park."

Fergus dropped the cigarette butt on the ground and squashed it beneath his heel. "I don't know. Do I have to do anything?"

"No," I said. "Just give us money, I suppose."

"You could come to the games," Ginger added.

He laughed that evil-sounding guffaw of

his and then stopped. It was Suzy's voice that stopped him.

"Fergus," she called. "You out there?" The door opened a crack and I got a look at Suzy's whole face. She was so young and pretty. Maybe a mite thin, but her hair cascaded onto her shoulders in thick waves and made me think, goodness gracious, she can't be more than twenty years old — a babe.

Fergus turned around. "It's nothing. Just go on inside, honey buns." Fergus's voice took on a gentle tone, but there was something fake about it, placating. "I'll be right inside as soon as I —" The door closed.

"Look," he said to me. "No soap. I don't have that kind of money. But hey, if you want to use the Paradise Trailer Park name on your uniforms, go ahead. I won't mind."

"Of all the nerve, Mr. Wrinkel. No, thank you. We'll find someone else."

"That creep," I said once we were far enough away from Fergus.

"Well, we had to give it a shot. But now I'm afraid we're out of ideas. The girls are going to be so disappointed."

Lucky, who had been romping through some tall grass near the defunct fountain, scooted next to us.

"How long has it been since the fountain worked?" I asked.

Ginger glanced over. "Years. Fergus turned it off one day and it's been getting more and more run down. It was working when I moved here. I used to like the sound of the water at night. I could hear it from my trailer. It was like a concert with the water running and cicadas trilling and crickets chirping and birds singing. I miss it."

"Maybe we can get it flowing again."

"Don't count on that. Fergus doesn't care a lick about aesthetics or pleasing people. Not really. He just collects the rent."

"But he owns this land. You'd think —"

"Who told you that?"

"I assumed because —"

Then I stopped short. "Then who?"

"Nobody really knows."

"Come to think of it," I said, "when I bought my trailer I had the cashier's check made out to a company called Biddy Properties. I just figured that was him, you know."

Ginger skipped to catch up with my wide strides. "Could be, but like I said, nobody knows for certain. We just give him our rent money every month and all is well. Or nearly well. Asa does all the work around here. Fergus doesn't do diddlysquat."

"I like the idea of a fountain. The sound of flowing water. Let's talk to Asa about getting it hooked up again."

"Fergus'll just turn it off again and complain about the electric and water bill."

I paused a minute and imagined Paradise with that pretty little fountain flowing with bright, clear water. Maybe a light trained on it at night.

"Maybe someday."

The sun was about gone when we reached Rose's trailer. Ginger and I stood near the giant hand. "You think she put Fergus's name up there? I didn't see it."

"Sure she did. God loves him too, Charlotte."

Lucky circled a minute under the thumb and then curled into a hairy heap, yawned, and closed his eyes. He knew we were staying a little while.

Rose opened her door and a waft of turpentine blew out. "Well?"

"Nope," I said as we made our way inside. "He said no soap."

Rose wiped her brush and then tucked herself into her favorite rocker while Ginger and I plopped onto the sofa. "Guess that puts us back to square one," I said. "And we only have until day after tomorrow if we're going to make the summer league."

"So now what?" I asked. "What do we do now?"

"We pray," Ginger said. "God has someone in mind. It's our mission to find out who that someone is."

"If only one of the husbands would inquire at the elastic factory," I said.

Ginger chuckled. "No way. Those boys are still not sold on the idea of their wives playing ball. Most of them are just waiting for their women to fail, get tired or fed up, quit, and go back to making pot roasts on Sunday afternoons — not pop-up fly balls."

I looked out Rose's window at the woods. The ball field lay just through the trees. It saddened me to think that without a sponsor the team would never play there.

"There's just no way. I don't think. I could try but I'd hate to —"

"What are talking about, Charlotte?" Rose asked.

"Sorry. I was just prattling around in my own head again. I was wondering if I could afford to sponsor the team myself."

"You aren't a business or corporation," Ginger said. "And what if we played next year too? It's too expensive."

"I have my pies? Maybe I could —"

"Sell pies?" Rose said, the doubt in her

voice evident. "You couldn't bake enough pies to make a dent in what it will cost to keep the Angels afloat. Zeb might take some down at the Full Moon, but not enough."

"I'm just thinking, Rose. That's all."

"Listen, Charlotte," she said, "your pies are good and all, scrumptious, in fact, but you'd be baking all the time and I'm not even sure it's legal to sell pies out of a trailer home, you know?"

Another bubble burst. "I guess you're right. Maybe this wasn't such a good idea." My heart sank into my shoes. "Maybe we simply can't afford to be a team."

"Now, I won't hear any of that," Ginger said. "We can still be a team. We'll just get out there and play and see what happens."

I twisted my mouth and chewed on that a second. "No, Ginger. These women need to be a real team, playing real games and winning and losing and —"

"Then you'll find a sponsor," Rose said. She opened a jar of pink cream and slathered some on her arms and rubbed it in. "I've always found that when you really need something, I mean really need something, it has a way of coming around."

15

Hazel Crenshaw was in her front yard the next morning tending to her bird feeders. She wore a cape the color of a concord grape and a lavender felt hat with a peacock feather sticking out of it. A long, wooly scarf was wrapped around her neck. I saw her when I let Lucky out for his morning routine. That poor maple tree had been getting the worst of it all spring long.

"Lucky," I called. "Maybe you need to find another place to pee. That poor tree is getting drowned." But he only smiled.

I thought I saw Hazel look my way, but she was so covered up I couldn't really be sure. The air was still unseasonably cool. She looked like a big, purple, wooly sheep ripe for the sheering. So just to be certain, I moved down the walkway a little, pretending to check my lights along the way. I looked again and sure enough I saw Hazel wave. She appeared to be waving me over to her side of the street.

My first thought was that my imagination had gotten the best of me on account of all the stress with the team. I waved back and she waved me on, this time with a bit more assertiveness. "You stay here, Lucky."

I crept slowly across the street, looking all around. For some reason I didn't want anyone to notice me. Hazel Crenshaw had a mystique about her. I couldn't for all the tea in China figure out why she wanted me.

"Hello," I called.

She beckoned me closer. The closer I got, the easier it was to see that she was old and hunched over, and I believed that cape of hers was a feeble attempt to hide a dowager's hump the size of bowling ball.

Hazel grabbed a cane with a carved goose head on the top and started toward her door. It was a little like being beckoned into a cottage by a witch.

My goodness gracious, but the inside of her trailer defied the outside. The first thing that struck me was the overpowering smell of orange blossoms. She had some of the finest, prettiest furniture I had ever seen, all of it real wood, all of it antique, probably older than she and covered in a quarter inch of dust that itched my nose. I spied a large, tricolored cat resting on the sofa with a wide Cheshire grin.

"Don't mind Smiley," Hazel said. "You aren't allergic, are you?"

"No, I'm not allergic. I like kitty cats."

"Good, good," she said as she unwrapped herself. I helped with her cape and hung it on a solid oak coatrack carved with tiny, intricate flowers and stems and buds. I got a good look at her hump. I tried not to notice, but it was pretty pronounced.

I sneezed.

She hobbled her way to a large chair. "You're sure you're not allergic?"

"I'm sure."

"Then it's the dust." She plopped down and giggled. "You might have to help me out of this chair," she said. "Some days it takes me five minutes or more. Osteoporosis, you know." She craned her already crooked neck closer to the hump.

"Oh, I . . . I hadn't noticed."

"Don't lie, child."

"Sorry."

She coughed once, and it seemed to hurt. "Make sure you drink your milk."

"Can I get you something to drink? A glass of water or milk?"

"Water would be nice. I could drink a whole cow and it won't help me now, and while you're in the kitchen will you put the kettle on? A nice cup of tea would suit me fine, child."

As I made my way to her kitchen, I regretted not bringing her a pie. I made a mental note to bring Hazel Crenshaw a deep-dish Dutch apple sometime soon.

Hazel's trailer was about twice the size of mine. Her kitchen was almost as big as the one I left back home. She had cabinets and drawers and places to hang pots and pans and even a tall double-door pantry that made me envious. I suspected it would be full of canned vegetables, cat food, pasta, and probably the tea bags I was looking for. So I pulled open the doors, and what I saw surprised me so much I busted out laughing. She had not stuffed the shelves chock-full of food stuffs. No, Hazel had stuffed it with hats. Floor-to-ceiling hats. Hats with feathers, wide brims, fruits, veils, no veils, you name it, she had a hat to match it. I shut the doors thinking it might help contain my laughter. It didn't.

I lit the fire under the kettle and then filled two tall tumblers with cold water.

"Here you go," I said.

She took the glass and drank. "Water is good for the body and the soul."

"It is. I'll get your tea as soon as the kettle

squeals."

I helped her place the glass on the table on a rattan coaster.

"You have a beautiful home, Hazel — may I call you Hazel?"

"Thank you, Charlotte."

"Is that your husband?" I asked, pointing to a picture of a man in military uniform on the table that held her glass.

"Mm hmm. That's my Birdy. Birdy Crenshaw. Dead twenty some years now."

"I'm sorry."

"Understand you recently lost your husband."

How did she know? "That's right." I felt my eyebrows rise. "Just a couple of months ago."

"Been hard?"

I looked away from her. "Some days."

"Um. You have a story to tell, child."

The kettle squealed and I went off to make two cups of tea. "I can run back to my place and get pie," I called. "Would you like pie, Hazel?"

"Pie," she squeaked. "Store-bought or homemade?"

"Homemade." I found a TV tray stacked with magazines. I put them on the floor and set the table near her. I placed her cup and saucer, a dainty set decorated with four-leaf clovers, on the tray.

"Thank you, child. Now go on. Run and bring Hazel a hunk of that pie."

"Back in a flash."

She smiled and winced at the same time, like smiling hurt her whole body.

I dashed out the door and nearly knocked into Asa.

"Hey, what are you doing over there?" he asked.

"She invited me." I shrugged.

"No kidding?"

"Mm. Weird, but she's a lovely woman, Asa. I think folks have her all wrong. She's lovely. Just lovely. Well, the hats in the kitchen pantry is weird, but still."

"She always yells at me," Asa said. "Orders me around like I'm five years old."

"She's been nothing but nice to me. Still don't know why she wanted to see me."

Asa shook his head. "I'm sure she'll let you know. Maybe Lucky's been tearing up her yard."

"Don't think so. Now look, I'm running for pie right now. Before her tea gets cold."

"Okay, Charlotte, I came by to tell you that the sod has been laid, and we're building the infield. But I need more money."

"For what?"

Asa laughed. "Everything."

I moved closer to my front door. "Listen, I don't want to leave Hazel too long. I'll give you a check. Just get what you need."

"Given any thought to uniforms and such?"

"Not yet. But I will. We'll get them. For now just concentrate on getting equipment. You know what to get? Bats, balls. And better get some gloves. They'll need to work them in pretty quickly."

I signed a check and handed it to him.

"A blank check?"

"Get what you can." I nabbed a pie off the kitchen table.

Asa folded the check with his one hand and slipped it into his pocket. "Studebaker will help. He says he knows just where to get everything."

"Good, good. Now I better get back to Hazel."

Asa shot me a look I didn't quite understand. Almost like he was worried or jealous or both. I made a mental note to ask him about it later.

Lucky joined me this time and settled himself down under a tree in Hazel's yard. His look said nothing more than, "I love you, Charlotte." Dogs are good that way. They know everything about you and never judge.

"Hazel," I called. "I'm back. I brought deep-dish apple. Hope you like apple."

No reply. My heart skipped a beat. I looked her way and there she was, sound asleep. Or at least I hoped she was sleeping. I crept close to her. "She okay, Smiley?"

He said nothing.

"Hazel," I said. I lightly touched her cheek and her eyes popped open like two window shades. She had the greenest eyes I had ever seen. A little cloudy perhaps from cataracts or medications or just old age. Still, they were two patches of bright outfield set against stormy clouds.

"I brought the pie. Hope you like apple."

"That's fine, child. Apple is fine. Good for my bowels, you know. Never get old, Charlotte. And if you do, pray you will always get yourself to and from the toilet. It all comes down to that, you know. The minute you can't get yourself to the pot is the minute they lock you into a nursing home. Thank the good Lord I can still —"

"I understand, Hazel. Let me get you a slice."

The rest of her cabinets were chock-full of some of the finest china and porcelain I had ever seen. Some of it looked like it was fresh from the Ming Dynasty. I chose two small plates ringed with rosebuds. I pulled two

197

sterling silver forks from the drawer. Imagine using sterling for everyday. There was a lesson to be learned.

"Here you go, Hazel. Apple pie."

She blinked.

I sat on the sofa with Smiley and my pie.

Hazel chewed. "Mm-mm-mm. Why, Charlotte Figg, this is the best pie I have ever et. I mean it, child. You could sell this."

"Funny you should say that. I've been thinking I might need to."

"Need to?" She swallowed and then sipped tea.

"To raise money for the softball team I was trying to get together around here."

She put her hand up as if to stop me. "I heard there was a little trouble in Paradise."

"Trouble?"

"That's why I called you over here."

I swallowed. "But it's not trouble. The team is perfectly —"

"Hush. I got more to say."

I moved forward on the sofa an inch or so. "Is there a problem, Hazel, because if there is I can't possibly see what you can have against the team."

"I said hush."

My mother taught me to respect my elders, so I settled back and gave Smiley a scratch behind the ear. It didn't matter one iota if this woman liked the notion of a Paradise softball team. There was no way she could stop it, and why should she care? It wouldn't bother her in the least.

"I heard you were looking for a sponsor?"

My heart sped up and I all of a sudden noticed how warm it was in her trailer. "Yes, we are? Is it warm in here?"

"Open the jalousie, Charlotte."

I reached behind and cranked the slatted window open. "Old-timey," I said. "I like them."

Hazel laughed. "Everything in here is old-timey. Even Smiley. Turned seventeen just the other day."

"Wow, that's old for a cat."

"Eighty-two is old for a human. But I'm sharp as a tack." She tuned out for a second and seemed to be searching for words. "Sometimes I can't remember the day I was born. Could be August. Could be September. All I know for sure is it was the year 1892." She squinted like she was trying to see more clearly. "I think."

I shook my head and marveled. Eighteen ninety-two? My goodness gracious. My head filled with a million questions, but I was more interested to hear what she had to say.

"I'm sorry, Hazel. But I am really curious

to know why you called me over here."

She finished her tea and set the cup down with a shaky hand that clattered the china.

"You're looking for a sponsor."

"I am, but how can you —"

"I want to sponsor your team, Charlotte."

Now, I will admit that I was totally incredulous. I thought the woman's trolley had slipped its track. How in tarnation could she ever sponsor our team unless she sold off all her antiques, and I didn't think there was any chance of that happening. And besides the notion was just plain stupid.

"I don't understand, Hazel. How can —"

"Course you don't. You won't let me finish talking."

"Sorry." I scrunched back into the soft sofa.

"I can and I will if you want. Elsmere Elastic will look fine on your uniforms, don't you think?"

"Elsmere Elastic? You mean the factory where the men work? But how?"

"I own the factory," Hazel said. "Elsmere was my dead husband. Birdy's not his real name. No mama in her right mind would name a son Birdy. Nope. That there is Elsmere Crenshaw."

"How come you call him Birdy?"

"He liked birds. No big deal, huh?"

"Elsmere is a fine name."

"Now listen, child, only Fergus Wrinkel knows I own the plant. I also own Paradise. Never mind all those rumors you hear about me. Except the one about Birdy's death at the plant when he got thwacked in the head by a piece of elastic that slipped off its roller. Ironic, huh?"

I cringed. "You mean, it hit him that hard?"

"Elastic is powerful stuff, Charlotte. Folks don't realize how strong it is, and it was a pretty wide roll that slipped its gears. Hit him right upside the head." She touched her temple with the tips of three fingers. "Threw him clear across the floor."

"I'm sorry, Hazel. It must have been awful."

She pursed her thin lips as tears formed in her eyes. "You'd think you'd get over death. But you don't, not really. Grief is a strange bedfellow. Always there."

I looked around the trailer in an effort to squash my own feelings. "You have some nice things."

"Birdy took good care of me."

"But I thought Fergus owned this park."

She twisted her lips into a wrinkled prune. "He's a pip. That's just what he wants people to believe. He's nothing more than a manager."

"But I write my rent checks to Biddy Properties."

"Me," she said with another wave of her hand. "The old biddy."

"So you sold me that broken down —"

Hazel laughed. "Sorry about that." Her face fell, and I couldn't tell if she was sad or amused. "I didn't know Fergus did that 'til after it was done. But it all worked out."

"So Fergus fills you in on everything around here."

"That's right."

We talked for a few more minutes, and I told her that I would bring papers from the league for her to sign.

"Don't bring them here, for goodness sake. Take them to the factory and have Mr. Vangarten sign them."

"Vangarten? Cash Vangarten?" I said.

"You know him? He's my director of operations. He'll sign anything I tell him."

My heart fluttered and I had to will myself not to turn pippin red. "I met him the other day. He coaches a team."

"Where on earth did you meet Cash Vangarten?"

"In Shoops. At the Pink Lady. I was looking for information about joining a league.

He told me where to go and all about his team. The Thunder, I think."

Hazel chuckled and slapped her knees. " 'Spect to see some fireworks in the league this year."

"Do you sponsor his team too?"

She got off another good laugh. "No, no. That's where the fireworks will come in. He's been asking me for three years running now."

"And you keep refusing?"

"I got my reasons."

I let it go at that and we finished our pie with a few more laughs. "Thank you, Hazel," I said. "The team will be so happy . . . and grateful."

She put her finger to her lips. "Now, this is our secret. They don't need the details."

"Okay. But why?"

"I just like it that way. A girl has to have her secrets."

I kissed her cheek. It was warm and old and tasted like orange blossom dust. "Thank you, Hazel. I can't wait to tell the team."

She put a gnarled finger to her lips. "Just remember our secret. And bring me pie and win a few games, okay, Charlotte?"

She looked tired. "Maybe you should take a nap."

"I just might do that."

16

Asking me to keep a secret was a little like asking Lucky not to pee on the maple tree. But on my way across the street I decided that I would do my level best not to tell a soul about Hazel Crenshaw and the Elsmere Elastic Factory, even though I knew folks would ask how I got them to sponsor the Angels. I would have to lie or come squeaky close to lying in order to protect dear, sweet Hazel.

"Yoo-hoo, Charlotte." It was Rose's yoo-hoo. "I was looking for you all morning. Have you seen the ball field?"

"Not yet."

"Asa and Studebaker and whoever else he got to help have done a fine job. A fine job. You must go take a look."

"Okay, okay. He said he was picking up some of the equipment today."

"Well, that explains why he's gone. But let's get Ginger and go on over to Edwina and Thomasina's."

"Let me go inside and freshen up first."

"Freshen up? Where were you?"

"I was just over at — I mean, I just went for a walk."

Rose looked at me with eyes that said, "Now that's a fib, Charlotte."

My tongue had started to ache because I had to bite it so hard to keep from spilling the beans. "I'll be right out, Rose. Just need to freshen up."

I left her standing outside because I needed to catch my breath and think a minute. This was quite a morning, meeting Hazel, learning about the factory, having her agree to sponsor and all. I needed a sip of cooking sherry.

After I composed myself, I went back to Rose.

"Let's go," I said. "I can't wait to see the ball field."

"Just you wait. The Lord has come through in mighty ways. I told you he would."

"He certainly has. You have no idea."

"What are you talking about, Charlotte Figg? You look awfully suspicious, like you have a secret to tell. Now, where were you just now?"

"You'll find out with the rest of the team.

Now come on —" I grabbed her arm, "Let's go see the field."

We passed by Rose's trailer and saw Ginger standing near the giant hand. We waved. She waved.

"Come on," Rose called. "We're going over to the Frost sisters' to see the new field. It's a doozy."

I lingered near the hand a second and whispered, "Thank you."

My father took me to Phillies games when I was a kid. Lots of them. But I will never forget the very first time I saw a major league baseball park in person. My father and I weaved our way through a series of gates and around the stadium until we came up through a darkened tunnel to the stands. I stood there shaking. I had never seen anything so big and so green and so bright in my life. I couldn't breathe. Connie Mack Stadium was the prettiest thing on earth. But as incredible as that experience was, looking out over Angel Field that afternoon was even more so. Perhaps because it was ours, because it was handpicked and hand-made by friends. We all stood there staring, and I knew none of us wanted the feeling to vanish.

Rose took my hand. "That Asa. He did a fine job, Charlotte."

"It's beautiful," Ginger said.

"Connie Mack, eat your heart out," said Edwina who was wiping tears from her eyes. "Where on God's earth did he find such green, green grass?"

"You think Pa would approve?" Thomasina asked.

Edwina scratched her head. "Maybe. Can't tell. We are using his wheat field for ball playing and all that —"

"But leastways we are using it." Thomasina turned to me. "Pa always said us girls would never be able to keep the farm the way it was supposed to be kept."

"And we didn't," Edwina said.

Rose put her hand on Thomasina's shoulder. "You made it better."

I wanted to walk out on the field, but it was so new I didn't want to touch it and maybe harm the new sod. Asa would let us know when it was ready for traipsing. He knew just how much care the fledgling grass would need before we could go tromping around on it.

Ginger wasn't quite so sensitive, and she took off around the infield kicking up new dirt into small clouds and wisps.

"Ginger," I called. "Maybe we should wait."

She rounded third base and stopped. She was indeed fast.

"How come?" she called as she rounded third and headed for home.

"It's not cured or something. Might need a day or two."

She took her time getting back to us. "That was exhilarating."

I ventured closer to the outfield and knelt down. I brushed my palm lightly over the blades. "Don't know why they call them blades of grass," I said. "This is so soft. Like cotton."

"Swabs," called Rose. "They are swabs of grass."

"That's right," I said. "Swabs."

Edwina called, "Here come Asa and Stu. Looks like his truck is packed down but good."

Sure enough, Asa started off-loading bright white bases, a rubber home plate, bats, balls, a catcher's mask and pads, even a chalk machine to draw lines, and a batter's box.

"I got the chalk machine cheap," Asa

called. "It's been used quite a bit but still works great."

Next they unloaded a batting cage, wheeled it near home plate, and locked it into place. Rose and I took the bases and distributed them around the infield.

"Now, you know we'll have to measure them," Asa called.

"I know. Sixty feet."

And so it went for the next hour or so. But when all was said and done, Angel Field was just about the prettiest thing I had ever seen.

We stood on the sidelines and gazed at our masterpiece like it was a Monet. But the spell was broken when the Frost sisters, who had been supplying us with iced tea and Cokes all morning, took on a glum expression.

"What's wrong with Thomasina?" Rose asked. "She looks so sad."

"So does Edwina," I said. "What's happening to everyone?"

"What's wrong?" I asked. "Are you all just so happy that you're crying?"

I thought there might have been some kind of emotional backsplash after such hard work, but when Ginger, usually a firecracker no matter what, plopped herself on the grass and started to cry, I got really worried. Half my team was breaking down.

"Come on," I said. "Someone tell me what's wrong."

"Fine field," Edwina said. "Too bad nobody'll ever play on it. Not for real."

"What in tarnation are you jabbering about?" I asked.

"We still need a sponsor," Rose said. "I was up in God's hand nearly all night asking for it, praying for His will to be done in the life of the Angels and I suppose this is it. All dressed up, nowhere to go."

I chuckled. "Why, Rose Tattoo, I am ashamed of you."

"Me?"

"You've been saying all along that no job is too big when God is around."

Edwina snuffed back tears. "What's that got to do with Angel Field?"

"I have some very good news," I said.

They brightened up. Ginger jumped up like a jack-in-the-box. "News? Why didn't you tell us?"

"I don't know. We got so busy with the field and equipment. That reminds me, Asa, we'll need a locker or a shed of some sort to keep the bats and balls and such in. Something waterproof."

"No problem, Charlotte. Now, you better tell us your news before these ladies throw a conniption fit."

I noticed him rub his left shoulder and wince.

"You all right?"

He seemed embarrassed. "It's nothing. Just the darndest thing sometimes. After a hard day's work it aches clear down to where my fingers and wrist should be."

Phantom pain. That was what Rose called it.

"Well, maybe this will help you feel better." I took a swig of Coke. "We have a sponsor."

The small group cheered so loud I half expected the rest of the team to come running out. "Who? Who did you get? Not Fergus Wrinkel?" Rose asked.

"Now, please don't ask a boatload of questions; just accept a gift as a gift and never mind about the particulars. And no, not Fergus Wrinkel."

"Now you're just sounding mysterious," Rose said.

"But that's precisely the way God prefers to work," Thomasina said. "In mystery and might. Mystery and might."

"Can you at least tell us who?" Rose asked.

"Uh, yeah," Ginger said. "I mean we will have their name on our uniforms."

"Elsmere Elastic is our sponsor." I stood straight and tall when I said it, hoping that if I locked my knees tight I wouldn't feel so many butterflies flitting around in my stomach.

"Where the men work?" Ginger said.

"Yep. Where the men work."

"But how?" Asa said. "I can't imagine any of them going to their bosses and asking for such a favor."

"That's not how it happened," I said.

Edwina squinted at me like screwing up her eyes would help her read my mind or something.

"That's all I'm going to say. I'm driving into town this afternoon, or maybe tomorrow —" I stretched my aching back, "goodness gracious but building a ball field is hard work — and I'll get the papers signed and ready to go."

Their faces fell to a state of worriment, but I tried to buck them up. "Just accept the gift." But no one reacted the way I expected. Instead of joy and elation, I saw shock and even horror cross their faces.

"I don't think the husbands are going to cotton to this," Thomasina said finally, revealing the heart of the matter. "They aren't about to mix work with their wives; you know what I mean?"

I felt my forehead wrinkle. "Why would that matter?"

"Well, think about it, Charlotte," she said. "The husbands are none too keen on the women playing softball in the first place, and now to have their employer, the largest employer in Shoops, sponsor them?"

That was when I felt my own countenance fall. I thought they'd be whooping for joy. "I don't understand. I thought you'd be happy."

"We are, sort of," Edwina said. "It's just that the men could get pretty riled and maybe keep their wives from playing."

"They could try," Thomasina said. "They are not going to like this. No siree Bob, not one iota." She brushed her hand through her short blonde hair. "I can just hear our Pa. 'Tommy, he'd say, 'no good can from this. No good at all.' "

"It won't happen like that," I said, and I started to walk off the field like I was just ejected from the game.

"Charlotte," Rose called. "Don't be like that. You don't understand."

"I can hardly believe it," I talked right out loud to myself the whole way home. "Go through all this trouble only to have them poop on it like it was —" Just my good fortune and timing because I had just that second felt my foot stomp on what was most likely a pile of dog poo, probably from a big dog.

I emerged from the woods near the Wrinkel trailer with most of the mess scraped from my sneaker, but it still reeked. And speaking of reek, Fergus stood near his pickup. My stomach tightened. I suspected Hazel had already told him the news.

"If you have anything to say about it, Fergus, just keep it to yourself. It's none of your dang blame business."

"What are you talking about?"

"Don't play coy with me. You know perfectly —"

Suzy appeared at the front door wearing a paisley scarf on her head and an A-line shift dress with absolutely no charm. She clutched her right arm like it was hurt.

"You okay?" I called. I gave a quick glance to Fergus.

"She's fine. Just running her into town is all."

Still harboring frustration from my teammates' response to my good news and the irresponsible dog, I gave Fergus such a glare. A glare that let him know I was on to him. He backed off a step or two, and I walked away. I hid behind one of the large oaks and peeked in time to see Suzy, still holding her arm tight against her chest, climb into the truck with no help from her husband.

17

The Elsmere Elastic Factory seemed to spread out forever. I drove clear through Bright's Pond to the other side of Shoops, and then through a tall metal gate onto the main campus of Elsmere Elastic. I had never seen so many buildings scattered about with lights and stacks and garages and signs. The road wound around until I saw a sign that read: EMPLOYEES, with an arrow pointing to the right. And VISITORS, with an arrow pointing to the left. "Guess I'm a visitor," I said, and that gave me a nice feeling, like I was entering a friendly place.

At the end of the road a nice young man standing in a little building with a red roof stopped me. He handed me a clipboard. "Write your name on that line and who you are here to see on the line next to it."

I wrote, "Charlotte Figg," and then, "Cash Vangarten," on the next.

The man looked at the clipboard and then

at me. "Mr. Vangarten? Is he expecting you?"

A red blush started at my waist and traveled up to my neck and cheeks. I hadn't thought to make an appointment. Herman always figured that kind of stuff out. He would have said, "Make sure you call first, Charlotte. He might not be in. He might be busy." But my mind didn't think like that.

"Well, I don't know if he's expecting me or not. Hazel Crenshaw just told me to come see him."

"Who?"

"Hazel Crenshaw. Can I go see him?"

His back straightened. "Just a minute."

The fellow made a quick phone call. "Follow this road to the end until you come to a big old building. Go on inside and wind around through the corridors until you come to a set of double doors. Go through them doors and up the stairs. It might be noisy in there. Once you get to the top of the stairs, go through the gray door. Mr. Vangarten's office is on the left. You'll see it." He put a yellow tag under my windshield wiper.

"Thank you." I hoped I would remember all his instructions.

A yellow and white gate, the kind at railroad crossings, lifted and I drove through. I wondered if elastic was really ALL they made here. If ever a place looked like it housed some secret government projects, Elsmere was it.

I found the building easy enough and parked in a space marked VISITORS. I went inside and walked for about a mile down one corridor and around a corner into another and finally found the double doors. Once inside the sound nearly deafened me. All manner of whirrs and clanks and high-pitched sounds assaulted my ears, and I thought it was funny that elastic, generally so quiet and springy, was so darn loud to make. I walked about another half-mile and found the metal stairwell and made a mental note to ask Hazel why this place didn't have an elevator.

The walk tired me, but I figured it was good exercise for softball. When I reached the top, I waited to catch my breath and then pushed open the door, thankful the sound lessened.

A woman behind a little metal desk with a single daisy in a bud vase greeted me.

"I'd like to see Mr. Vangarten, please," I said.

"Name?"

"My name is Charlotte Figg."

She eyed me up and down and then

picked up a phone receiver and pushed a red button. "Mr. Vangarten. There's a Charlotte Figg here to see you." I had to chuckle on account of I wondered how many Charlotte Figgs there were in the world.

"Excuse me," the woman said. "Mr. Vangarten would like to know who you are with."

I looked around. "I'm not with anyone, but maybe you could tell him I'm the woman from the Pink Lady last Sunday."

Her eyebrows rose. "Really." Then she spoke into the phone. "She says you know her from the Pink Lady."

A few seconds later she ushered me into Cash Vangarten's musty-smelling office. The walls were covered with bulletin boards tacked with papers and charts. One long and tall window overlooked the plant work area. I couldn't help but look a minute at the people down below in white uniforms and red hardhats scrambling around as giant machines made miles and miles of elastic. There was probably enough elastic down there to make several billion bra straps and even more underwear bands. My goodness gracious, I would have never thought the world could use that much elastic.

His large desk was cluttered with files and

folders and miscellaneous papers and books. A coffee cup with the words "Best Grand-pop" caught my attention.

Cash was dressed in a dark suit with a pale blue shirt that day and looked far different and smelled far different from the man I met at the restaurant. Aqua Velva. I knew because it was my favorite men's cologne. I asked Herman to switch from Old Spice but he refused. "The lady customers like it," he said. "And the customer is always right." I gave him Aqua Velva for Christmas, but he never used it. I didn't mention this before, but I asked that nice Frank Gideon if he would sprinkle a little on Herman in his casket.

Mr. Vangarten offered me a chair in front of his desk. I sat with my purse on my lap.

"So, what can I do for you, Charlotte?" He sat behind his desk looking very official.

"Hazel Crenshaw sent me."

His head jerked back and he coughed. "Hazel Crenshaw? How do you know Hazel?"

I took a breath. "There's no need to be secretive. She told me everything. She lives right nearby me at the Paradise Trailer Park."

He leaned on his desk with his arms crossed. "I see. So why did she send you to see me?"

"Now, Mr. Vangarten, don't go getting yourself all worked up when I say this. She said you might get a bit miffed, but —" I had to take another breath because my nerves got the best of me. I started to shake a little, and for the first time since Herman died, I wished he hadn't.

"Well?" said Vangarten.

"You remember how we talked at the Pink Lady about me wanting to start a softball team and you gave me all the nice information, told me what I needed and where to go and who to talk to and what forms and —"

"Yes, yes, I remember, but what does this have to do with Hazel Crenshaw?"

"I'm getting to that, if you'd only give me a minute to get it all out."

"Women," he said. "Have to get yourselves all wound up before you can spill it." Then his eyes caught mine and he smiled. "I'm sorry, Mrs. Figg. Lots of headaches today." He nodded toward the giant window.

"She said you would sign sponsorship papers for my team. Elsmere Elastic is sponsoring the Paradise Angels."

He practically leaped out of his chair. "What the H—"

"Heck, Mr. Vangarten. I hope you weren't

planning on swearing at me. Hazel is my new friend and all."

He sat back down with a thud. "No, I just don't believe it."

"She said you would have some trouble with this."

"Um." He searched his desk and finally grabbed the mug. Took a sip and made a face. "I hate cold coffee." He buzzed his phone, and in a second the woman I met earlier was at his door. "Get me another cup of coffee and whatever Mrs. Figg would like."

"Nothing for me, honey. Except, well, unless you have a Tab?"

"Certainly."

"So anyway, Mr. Vangarten, I have the papers right here in my bag, and since today is the last day to get them filed so we can play in the summer league, I'd appreciate it —"

The secretary returned with a steaming mug of coffee — this one had a picture of big old bass on it — and a Tab in a glass with ice for me.

"Thank you," I said.

Vangarten didn't even acknowledge her. I cleared my throat.

He looked up. "Thank you, Claudia."

She smiled at me. I smiled at her.

I pulled the papers out of my bag and placed them on his desk. "I stopped off at the League office — didn't know it was some guy's garage — but anyhoo, he was so sweet and —"

"Fine, Mrs. Figg."

Cash Vangarten signed the sponsorship papers, with a little too much flourish, if you ask me, and even crossed his "t" with a line about an inch longer than it needed. His hostility was evident.

"Thank you," I said as I shoved the papers into my bag and stood.

He grunted.

I padded softly to the door and was just about to turn the knob when, "Mrs. Figg," he called. I turned around. "Your team? Are they any good?"

I nodded, even though I truthfully didn't know if the Angels could play or not. "Yes, Mr. Vangarten. Championship caliber, if I do say so myself." It wasn't actually a lie. They were champions, every single one of them. They just didn't know it yet.

"That's good," said Vangarten. "My team stinks. Worst in the league."

"Maybe that's why Hazel won't sponsor you."

He fiddled with a pen on his desk. "Yep, that's the reason, I'm sure."

"Good-bye, Mr. Vangarten, and thank you very much."

"Good day, Mrs. Figg."

The secretary sat at her desk sharpening a pencil.

"I don't get it," I said. "He doesn't seem like the type to take an interest in women's softball."

Claudia smiled wide. "He has no choice, Mrs. Figg —"

"Call me Charlotte."

"Let's just say he's doing time for some nasty undertakings a couple of years ago. Either he coaches the niece's team or he loses his job."

"You mean Hazel Crenshaw's niece?"

"Mm hmm, I do. Seems Mr. Vangarten got into some trouble a little while ago and, well, coaching the Thunder is his punishment."

"No fooling. Imagine that. What did he —"

The phone buzzer rang. "I better go see what he wants," Claudia said.

The sun was nearly set behind the mountains by the time I pulled into Paradise. Some low, black clouds had moved in and it looked like rain. I drove past the Wrinkel trailer, always alert for something — noise,

Suzy, anything — but all I saw was a closed-up, unfriendly trailer.

Lucky was sure glad to see me. He skittered right into my knees when I pushed open the door. "How are you, boy?" I gave him a good scratch behind his ears. Then I let him outside. Poor guy must have had to go something awful, and I was very proud that he didn't wet my floors. "Remind me to ask Asa about that doggie door."

It had been a good day. Now I just needed to turn the women of Paradise into ball players because suddenly it had become a real competition. How in the world was I going to do that? I wanted to knock the socks off of Vangarten and his team. I threw together a cherry crumb and then I stood on the front stoop ruminating and taking in the fresh smell of early spring.

I tried not to wish Herman was there to see me with the Angels. I knew he wouldn't have cared. To Herman, life pretty much revolved around selling brushes and cleaning supplies door-to-door. And he was good at that. And everyone knew it. It didn't matter if I was good at anything — except baking pies — while we were married. But still I had this whisper of a desire that Herman see me do something besides crimp crust and vacuum, even if it was impossible this side of the Jordan.

Lucky bounded back to me carrying a tennis ball. I took it from his slobbery mouth and tossed it down the street. I still had a pretty good throwing arm. Lucky sprinted after it like a proud gazelle on the African savannah. That was when I saw Hazel out by her bird feeders. She was bundled as usual, even though the air had been getting warmer. I waved. She waved me over. This time Lucky followed and I let him.

"So you got the papers signed?" she asked.

"I sure did. We're all set. Thank you, Hazel. And you were right, Cash Vangarten didn't seem too happy about it."

"He never will. Let's just say we have a score to settle." She dumped seed into a container. "Could you slip this into the feeder, dear?"

"To tell the truth, Hazel, his secretary kind of mentioned he had some trouble down the road and coaching is —"

"Yep. He was out driving drunk one night about three years ago and somehow managed to drive his car onto my front lawn and take out all my prize-winning roses. The biggest Mr. Lincolns you'd ever see."

I looked around. "You mean here? In Paradise? I don't see how —"

Hazel laughed. "No, no, dear. I have a

house, a brick house just down the road from Paradise, sits on sixteen acres with seventeen rooms. The place is much too large for me now, but I have people who keep after it. Someday I'll figure what to do with it." She took a breath and then put her finger to her lips. "Shhh, over there." She pointed toward the top of a towering pine. "Rocking on the tree branch. It's a female whistlesnook. Don't see too many of them."

I turned, but the bird must have flown off. "Whistlesnook?"

"They're very rare."

So rare I thought the whistlesnook only existed in Hazel's imagination.

"She'll be back. I got some black sunflower seed and beef suet here. She'll be back for certain."

"So you make Mr. Vangarten coach a softball team as punishment for killing your roses."

"Mm-hmm." She practically sang. "I have a niece who I love with all my heart who liked to play ball, and well that's why I asked the judge to make him do time by coaching her team."

"So she plays? What's her name?"

Hazel took my arm. "Let's go inside, dear. My legs get awful sore. That whistlesnook will come back."

Once inside, I helped Hazel with her cloak. She plopped into her rocker.

"You were telling me about your niece."

"Yes, yes, Vertabeth. She lives in Florida now. Married some rich man. Moved down there last year. She still plays softball though. But down there, of course."

"So you don't get to see her much."

"Not nearly enough. Just Christmastime now. I go down there for a couple of weeks to be with Vertabeth and Dan and the children now. I don't let on but I don't care for Dan much. Bit of a sissy, if you ask me."

I smiled and felt the corners of my eyes crinkle with laughter. Hazel was a pip. "How many more years does he have to coach?"

She slapped her knees again and laughed. "His sentence was up two years ago, but I make him do it if he wants to keep his job."

"Why, Hazel Crenshaw, you are a card. Just a wild card."

"Dearie, I could tell you stories. But right now I need to take a short nap. You go on now, keep our little secret and" — she grabbed my hand — "Beat the you-know-what out of Cash Vangarten's team, okay, dear?"

I went back to my trailer feeling satisfied, happy, and a bit sneaky. Paradise was a place of secrets, and I was the keeper of them all.

18

That Sunday I decided to see what happened at Rose's church. When I woke up around 7 a.m., which is my usual time, an odd feeling burbled in my chest. Maybe because I had that song from Sunday school running through my mind: "Do Lord, O do Lord, O do remember me." I pulled on a pretty flowered dress, then slipped into real shoes but quickly took them off and went back to my usual Keds.

"I'm going to church, Lucky." I patted his head and then I slipped him a Milk-Bone. He was appreciative and, I thought, impressed that I was even going.

Church was not on my weekly routine, and hadn't been for a long, long time. The last time I set foot inside a church building was, well, I was a young woman, unless you count my visit with Pastor Herkmeier to arrange Herman's burial, but that wasn't church. It was business. Today it felt sort of good to get gussied up and put small dabs of perfume, *Sweet Impulse,* on my wrists and behind my ears.

On my way out of the door I spotted my pad with all my notes and doodles about the Angels. I flipped through the pages thinking there might be opportunity at church to get some business done. Maybe talk to a couple of the players and schedule a full-fledged practice now that all the papers were signed and we were ready to go.

I grabbed my handbag, and a cherry crumb pie with walnuts, said goodbye to Lucky, who was looking terribly proud of me, and set off. The sun shone bright in the blue sky. Birds chirruped and called to each other. It was a perfect spring day as the trees budded with new life and I discovered yellow daffodils along my wooden walk. Funny the beauty that springs to life right under your nose sometimes. But just as I set foot off the walk, gunshots rang out. I ducked and scurried back toward my trailer, tripping on one of Lucky's bones. I nearly went head over teacups again as my pie went sailing into the sky and then SPLAT! onto the ground.

I looked out the kitchen bay window and saw my pie upside-down on the lawn in a puddle of red cherry juice. There had been no time to try and save it. It was more important to save myself, so I left it there, wounded and alone. Who said that lunatic did no harm? A perfectly fine cherry crumb gone to the crows. I heard another shot, and sure enough there was that crazy guy with his rifle shooting at some trash cans. I heard two more shots and saw a trash can go flying into the air about ten feet and a raccoon plummet to the ground in a great tumble of paws and fur and then take off across the street into Hazel Crenshaw's yard.

"That guy is nuts."

I kept low in case he pointed that rifle in my direction. But fortunately Asa met up with him and took the gun from the poor old guy. Asa tucked the gun under his armpit, and then lead Dalrympal Hawkins back toward home. I caught my breath, and fortunately a second cherry crumb was available so I took it with me. This time I made certain the coast was clear. I set the cherry crumb on the passenger's seat and kept one hand on it as I backed off the cement parking pad. I was just about at Rose's when I realized I had forgotten my notes.

A small but tidy group of Paradise residents waited by the giant hand like they were waiting to either go on a field trip or back to the asylum. I spotted Ginger and Rose, of course. Greta Lundy stood closest to the street, holding the basket with baby Ruth. Gwendolyn held hands with a very large man wearing cowboy boots, jeans, a striped shirt, and a turquoise belt buckle the size of a grapefruit.

"Charlotte," Rose said. "I'm so happy you came. The bus will be in here in a minute."

"Bus?" My stomach tightened.

"Just an old school bus. Studebaker drives around and picks folks up. We're his last stop and then we drive into Bright's Pond for church and then he drives us back. Usually we all have lunch together at my place."

"You mean we all get on a bus? I have my car. I can —"

Ginger piped up. "It's more fun to bus to church. Sometimes we sing songs."

I wasn't so sure and would have backed out of the deal if I hadn't seen the yellow school bus chugging down the road. The bus had to be fifty years old the way it chugged and rumbled to a stop.

"Bus is here," Marlabeth Pilkey called. "Everyone line up." I watched her grab a small boy by his collar. "Get in line, Warren Pilkey."

Warren did as he was told. But he was not very happy about it. I grabbed the cherry crumb from the car. "I brought this, Rose, but now I —"

"Bring it along," she said. "They'll keep it for the fellowship time after the service. But be careful, Zeb Sewickey makes his famous Full Moon Pies, so you might catch a few odd looks. Folks in Bright's Pond like their Full Moon Pie."

"Then maybe I should leave it behind."

Rose smiled. "No. Bring it along. It might be a hit, and then you can make it for their next potluck."

"Potluck? You mean one of those dinners where people bring food? I don't want to attend any potluck."

"Me neither. I don't care if I ever eat another lime Jell-O-cottage cheese-and-macaroni surprise."

I laughed.

"It's true," Rose said. "Pastor Speedwell's wife started making it just this year. She's a strange one. That's why your pies will be so welcome."

My ego swelled a tad, but I squashed it back down and said, "I suppose I could make a few and drop them off."

The bus was not exactly packed, but there were a few people on board, including an older woman in a black coat and a black hat with a black veil. Maybe she thought she'd boarded a funeral bus. She sat with her legs pressed tight together and her hands palms down on her knees and stared straight ahead with wide eyes like we were truly on our way to a funeral. There was a young couple sitting so close together they could have been sewn up the sides. The young woman looked to be about twenty years old and seven, maybe eight, months pregnant. And other sundry folks who looked like farm people and their children — well behaved for the most part — laughed and chatted.

Marlabeth Pilkey stopped on her way down the bus aisle near the pregnant woman and smiled. "How you feeling, Fleur de Lee? Still have morning sickness? Baby kicking your ribs?"

Fleur de Lee craned her neck. "Hi, Miss Marla, I'm fine and no, ma'am, that drink you gave me did the trick. I ain't vomited in two days now and you got that right, this baby sure can kick."

"He's gonna be a football player," said the young man.

Marlabeth took his chin in her hand. "That's right, Jaster. A fine, strapping football player, unless of course you have a little girl." She gave him a loving pat on the cheek. He touched the spot and smiled.

"Oh, Miss Marla, I'll love her just the same," he said. "Fact is, a little girl as pretty as Fleur de Lee would be fine. Just fine."

"I'll come by on Tuesday and check you," Marlabeth said. "Won't be long now."

"Nine weeks, three days," said Jaster.

I sat with Rose. She took the window.

"That young couple," I said, "are they —"

"Yes. They live over at Haven House — kind of a group home for folks who can't exactly be on their own but want to be independent. It's a good setup."

I looked back at them. "Don't know when I have ever seen a happier couple."

"You'll like Bright's Pond," Rose said. "The pastor is a little odd, but nice."

She rubbed her hands together like they were cold, but it certainly was not chilly that day. It was the third week of spring, and already the temperature had risen above fifty degrees two days running.

"Are you okay?"

"Not sure," she said. "I've been feeling a little achy."

Of course my mind shot directly to softball. "You'll still be able to play ball?" I wished I could have shoved the words right back into my mouth. I just couldn't understand what had gotten into me. "I'm sorry, Rose. I was just worried you might be coming down with something and we have to get as much practice in as possible."

She smiled and then pointed out the window. "Look at that." A great blue heron soared past the bus just about at eye level. It was streamlined and gorgeous like a jetliner. Silent. It flew so close I could see its eye.

"Goodness gracious," I said. "I've never seen anything like that."

"Probably on his way to Bright's Pond. Lots of wildlife there."

"It is pretty around here," I said. "Very different from back home."

"So much of God's creation to take in." Rose closed her eyes for a long second. "I mean God's creation, not that cement and steel they have in the cities. I mean just plain old nature — God's Glory."

Before I knew it, Studebaker had pulled the bus along the curb in front of a small white church. It had the ubiquitous red door and a bell tower that stood separate from the church building. A small wood sign read: BRIGHT'S POND CHAPEL OF FAITH AND GRACE. Welcome. I thought that was kind of nice — understated for a church, but nice.

We filed out of the bus, each one of us thanking Stu on our way out the door. I carried the pie in two hands, not wanting another disaster.

"Come on," Rose said. "I'll introduce you to Pastor Speedwell if I can catch him in time."

"That's okay." I had to skip a few steps to keep in stride with Rose. "Did you hear that old man shooting up the park again this morning? Scared me half out of my mind and made me drop the other pie."

Rose looked back. "I thought I heard his ricochet."

"This is the second pie. I'm sorry but I won't have one for lunch."

"That's okay," Rose said. "I have a box of Tastykakes on hand."

The church lobby was small, with a long coatrack and a doorway on one side. I could see steps through the small window. The children all ran through the door and clomped up the steps.

"Sunday school," Rose said. "The children all go to Sunday school up there while the adults have a regular service in the sanctuary."

A tall, skinny woman approached us. "Hello, Rose. See you brought a visitor."

"Hello, Edie. Yes, this is Charlotte and this" — she took the pie — "is for after the service. Best pie you'll ever eat."

"A pleasure to make your acquaintance, Charlotte. Are you just visiting?" She took my hand and patted it.

"No, well, not exactly. I mean, I am just visiting your church, but I moved permanent to the Paradise Trailer Park. Leastways I think it's permanent."

Edie smiled with tight lips. "I'll just take this to fellowship hall. Find a nice doily to set it on."

Rose pulled me away. "Let's see if he's in there. He usually likes to greet folks before the service."

She brought me through the crowd and into a large room lined with folding chairs. She dropped my hand. "Don't see him."

People filed in, taking bulletins from a woman in a yellow dress.

"It's okay, Rose. I'll meet him later." I took a bulletin and smiled.

"I guess," Rose said.

We sat in a chair toward the back along with the rest of the Paradise people. Fleur de Lee and Jaster sat up front.

A few minutes later the sanctuary quieted down as a large woman in a flowery dress and white hat released a minor key note from the organ that echoed around the small auditorium. The music swelled and carried along the rafters and a cocoon of serenity wrapped around the building. My chest felt heavy at first and then light like meringue with golden dewdrops. I sighed and reveled in the sensation.

Three men filed out of what amounted to a secret opening on the side of the room.

"That's Pastor Speedwell, the tall man with the round glasses in the middle."

Not what I imagined.

The pastor took the podium. "Good morning. Welcome. This is the day the Lord has made."

And everyone said, "We will rejoice and be glad in it."

The service continued pretty much how I remembered church services to go, with singing and money collecting and preaching and more singing. I sat and listened as best I could but found myself distracted by so many things that at one point, my brain all of a sudden became so full of Herman that I started to cry. Rose offered me a hanky, baby blue with white lace edging. I wiped my eyes.

After the benediction we all filed out and I had an opportunity to meet the pastor.

"So pleased you came today," he said. He took both my hands and held them, didn't exactly shake them like a handshake, but held them and spoke into my eyes. He was taller than me by almost four inches.

"Charlotte is a new widow," Rose said.

"I am, indeed, so sorry to hear that," he said, still holding hands. "Jesus be your comfort and your guide. Jesus fill the empty spaces in this woman's heart. Jesus." He pronounced the last syllable of Jesus — SUS — with gusto. Then he let go and I felt awash with a kind of peace that started in my ears and ended at my waist.

"Thank you," I said, fighting an almost irresistible urge to confess that I didn't actually listen to his sermon because I was preoccupied by softball and my grief for Herman, a man I was starting to think I never knew and who never knew me.

We spent a short time chatting with folks in what they called their fellowship hall, which, if you asked me, looked more like a recreation room at a women's prison — not that I ever saw one, but I could imagine. There were tables spread out with treats and paper coffee cups. A large silver urn cranked out the coffee. I was impressed that they had real cream in tiny pitchers set about. There was lemonade and fruit drinks for the children who were busy chasing each other inside and outside. But no one seemed to notice or mind. A large lime Jell-O mold with bits of pineapple and elbow macaroni on a pink plate wiggled near my nearly gone pie. I surveyed the room and spotted six people with cherry pie. It did my heart good. But I will confess I searched for women who might be ball players. That's when I spotted Fleur de Lee all by herself in a corner. She had one hand on her protruding belly and the other held a chocolate éclair.

"How are you, Fleur de Lee?" I asked. "My name is Charlotte Figg."

"I know all about you, Charlotte Figg," she said. "Miss Marlabeth told me and Jaster that you are fixin' to make a softball team. I sure wish I knew howta play softball."

I couldn't resist the urge to touch her belly. "Under the circumstances, Fleur de Lee, I think it would be best to wait until next year."

She laughed. "That's right, Miss Charlotte. I should wait but maybe . . . maybe I can come watch."

"We would love that, Fleur de Lee."

Jaster came back into the room drying his hands with a brown paper towel. "I'm sorry if I took too long, Fleur de Lee."

"That's okay, Jaster." She gave him a bite of her chocolate éclair and then wolfed the remaining quarter down.

Rose stood quietly near the door. This surprised me because I thought she would be swarmed by people. She always seemed so sociable at Paradise. She sipped coffee and took small bites from a bear claw. Folks spoke with her, but mostly she seemed disinterested, like she had other things on her mind. She wore her long-sleeve sweater with the high collar turned up, hiding her tattoos and scars, and for the first time I saw that she was hiding under that sweater. For someone who seemed so open and willing to tell it like it is, hiding didn't suit her.

"Aren't you warm, Rose?" I asked. "You should take that sweater off."

"No. It's better on." She looked me in the eye. "Not everyone will understand. Not like the friends in Paradise. It's different there."

"You mean, you never told anyone here. Not even the pastor?"

"Especially the pastor."

"Maybe you should. Maybe you should take that sweater off and let people see your suffering."

"No. Can't do that. And that's why I decided I can't play on the team, Charlotte. I'll come out and watch and cheer you all on, but I won't wear a uniform that shows my scars to the world."

I swallowed and scratched my head. "What? That's what's been on your mind? I don't understand."

She pulled me aside into a small corridor. "The bus will be leaving soon. I never told anyone outside of Paradise, and if I play ball, it will mean folks seeing my scars and the tattoos. And believe me, scars and tattoos will not —"

"So we'll get you a long-sleeve, turtle-neck uniform. And when you're in all that catcher's gear, no one will notice. Even though I think you should just —"

Marlabeth's husband, Jacob, popped his head around the corner. "Bus is loading."

"Come on," Rose said. "Don't want the bus to leave without us."

Later that same Sunday, Rose caught me up to my elbows in pie crust. I love to make pie crust when I am feeling nervous. Making good pie crust is one of those things that has to come with practice and good timing and knowing just how cold to make the water and how thick to roll out the dough. If you worry crust too much, you might as well make a pair of shoes with it. Pie truly is an art form, in my opinion, even though most people take good crust for granted. Herman always did. He loved my crust, but I don't think he ever stopped to watch me make it. To him, pie just happened. And on the few occasions when my crust didn't turn out exactly right, he scowled and blustered and said, "Not your best crust this time, Charlotte."

I don't know how many times I wanted to just tell him, "Herman, quit your blustery bellyaching and get used to the fact that good pie crust doesn't just happen. It's hard work." But I never could get my nerve up.

Rose seemed to enjoy watching me, though. She sat at the kitchen table and sipped iced tea from a tall tumbler with tiny daisies etched around the middle of it. "I could never make crust, Charlotte. Turns out like rubber."

I wiped my Crisco-ey hands on a lavender kitchen towel. My mother told me to rub the shortening into my skin. She said it's what kept her hands so young and supple. "I can teach you — maybe."

Rose snorted. "Me? No, thanks. Making pie is as much a gift as painting. That belongs to you."

I rolled out my bottom crust and fitted it into the pie plate. After crimping the edges between my index finger and thumb and pricking the bottom with a fork, I popped it into my oven to bake for a few minutes until the edges turned the most perfect shade of golden brown.

"I meant what I said. You are an artist," Rose said. "Pie artistry. Maybe you *should* open a shop. You could call it that, Charlotte's Pie Artistry."

"Herman would never allow such a —" I swallowed and rinsed my fingertips. "I plum forgot for a minute, Rose. I plum forget Herman doesn't get a say anymore. Goodness gracious."

Rose stood and put her arm around me. "Is it tough sometimes?"

I shook my head. "No, that's what's weird. I hardly ever miss him. He just comes up now and again like a cucumber or broccoli, you know? Happened at church today."

"I know. Memories are like that. Grief too. It's one of those things you carry with you, like loose change in the bottom of your purse. That's why it's so easy for it to sneak up on you — make you think dead people are still alive."

After pouring myself a glass of iced tea, I joined her at the table. "I'm a little worried about you, Rose. What gives with you and the team? We're counting on you."

"I know. I'm sorry. It's just . . . well it's just that I don't do much socializing outside of Paradise, and the notion of showing off my scars and the tattoos gives me the willies. It's hard enough at church, but I keep them hidden, you know?"

"Why? Didn't you tell me that even Jesus showed his scars? He didn't hide them, did he?"

"It's not the same."

I screwed up my mouth and thought a minute or so. "I think it is, Rose. Maybe not exactly, but you suffered and now —"

"I know. But people out there" — she nodded toward the outside — "won't understand."

The dinger on my stove went off. "I better get my crust. I'm making a lemon meringue. Not my favorite, but I thought it would make a nice change. Even though it seemed like that Zeb Whatshisname had the lemon pie market cornered. I was going to bring it to Hazel Cren —" I stopped talking.

"Hazel Crenshaw?" Rose asked. "I knew something was going on with you two." She slapped her knee. "Now spill it!"

"Goodness gracious, Rose. I might as well tell you, but you have to promise not to tell another breathing soul." I placed my crust on a cooling rack.

Rose raised three Girl Scout fingers. "I promise, Charlotte."

"Hazel Crenshaw owns the Elsmere Elastic factory, and not only that, she owns Paradise, the whole park. Fergus only works for her, and she is my contact for the team sponsorship. It was her idea." It felt like popping a pimple to tell her.

Rose swallowed, and I watched her eyes grow big. "No kidding? That's huge news, Charlotte. Really huge. The hugest news."

"But you can't tell. It's a secret. I promised her."

Rose looked out the window. "Well, I'll be darned. I knew there was more to that old woman than birds."

"Yep. But you won't tell anyone, right? Although I just don't understand why she's so concerned. Who cares if everyone knows the truth?"

"I know, I can understand Fergus wanting to keep it a secret, but Hazel? What's the big deal? You'd think she'd want people to know who she really is."

"So you agree, Rose. Secrets are just plain silly. Even for you. I think you should let your tattoos out for the whole world to see and not be ashamed of them."

I thought a minute, and then I said it. "You're a fraud, Rose. Just like so many other people who say they're all holy and forgiven and stuff. Seems to me if you really were all that stuff you wouldn't need to hide."

A small sliver of crust from my baked shell dropped off. "Darn. It's a bit crumbly. How long do you think you can hide out in Paradise, Rose?"

19

Rose Tattoo didn't speak to me for three whole days after that.

For three days I stayed home, baked, cleaned, worked on the team roster, argued with my mother on the phone, and reviewed the rule book the man in the garage gave me. Softball had changed over the years, but not much. You still couldn't steal a base and the arc of the pitch could still not be higher than six feet. I took comfort in that as I worked out batting assignments. I decided that Marlabeth Pilkey would be our leadoff batter, even though I had yet to see anyone on my team swing a bat. We had to get a practice in, and I had to start somewhere.

But mostly I missed Rose.

Lucky and I took more than a few walks in those three long days that always took us past Rose's trailer and then down to the Wrinkels's.

I saw Rose once near the giant hand, planting pansies. She never looked up. But I knew she knew I was there. It was hard to distinguish if she was refusing to look because she was mad or because she was feeling bad about her scars and tattoos and about what had happened to her so long ago.

Walking past the Wrinkel trailer filled me with a similar trepidation and concern. When I first moved to Paradise, I thought I had moved among the oddest folks on the planet, misfits and crazies. But the more I looked, the closer I became to them, the clearer it became that there was indeed trouble in Paradise.

On the second day I decided to go trailer-to-trailer and schedule our first team practice. I stopped by Greta's trailer first.

"I'm calling a practice for Thursday morning," I said, standing in the doorway.

Greta had the baby on her hip.

"She's getting big," I said. "Grown a lot in the last month."

I heard a crashing sound that seemed to come from the kitchen.

"Nuts," Greta said, "That's Charlie Junior in the pots again. Excuse me."

I stepped inside and watched her gently lay baby Ruth in her cradle then dash to the

251

kitchen area. Greta's trailer was decorated in, well, no other way to put it except to say that if you didn't know better you'd swear cowboys owned it. Lots of animal pelts scattered about, a steer horn on the wall that held two cowboy hats, and a lamp that somehow incorporated the use of a skull, a brass pipe, and turquoise.

She came back to the living area dragging a small boy by the arm. "Now sit on that couch and don't you move, Charlie Junior."

Charlie stuck his finger up his nose and obliged his mother.

"Now, what were you saying, Charlotte? Practice Thursday — in the morning. What will I do with Charlie Junior? Baby Ruth is no problem, but Junior, well, he's another story. He only goes to his preschool two days a week, Lord knows, I wish it was more but —"

She turned quickly. "Charlie Junior. Take your finger out of your nose this instant. You'll get bugs."

"I'll think of something, Greta. We have to start practicing. Games officially start on June 25th."

"I don't know, Charlotte. Maybe this wasn't such a good idea. Maybe the husbands were right."

"Nonsense. We just need someone to look

after the kiddies is all; maybe we can fence them in over at the Frost sisters' or something."

"Good one, Charlotte. A kiddy corral. Hold them dogies up."

"Dogies? Oh, right. I bet Lucky would love to help watch the tykes. Just be at the field at 10 a.m. Thursday."

Charlie Junior screamed, "I'm hungry." And that started baby Ruth crying.

I visited everyone on the team that day and was met by pretty much the same protests, but I assured them all that all the details would get worked out and that they should plan to be there, kids in tow and wearing shorts and sneakers.

Marlabeth offered me chamomile tea to soothe my nerves.

Toward evening that same day I saw Suzy out back of her trailer. Her arm was in a white plaster cast up to her elbow. She pulled laundry from the line and seemed to be getting along well enough. I waved. Lucky barked and scurried close to her and sniffed around at her ankles, but I called him back.

"It's okay," Suzy said in a hushed tone. "Your dog don't bother me."

I shot her a big smile and waved as Lucky made his way back to my side. "You play softball?"

She shrugged and went back to her under-wear and tee shirts and towels.

"We have a practice at the field Thursday morning if you'd like to join us."

Suzy didn't respond, so I took it as a no.

Thursday dawned. Asa came to my trailer bright and early and begging for coffee.

"They're calling for rain this afternoon, Charlotte," he said. "Good thing you're getting a practice in before."

I poured his coffee and gave him a bowl of oatmeal with brown sugar and raisins. "Here you go, eat up."

My own oatmeal was already on the table with a couple of tablespoons gone. Lucky had already downed his. Silly pooch liked oatmeal. But he always left the raisins behind, every single time. How he did it I'll never know, but sure enough his bowl held twelve perfectly clean raisins. Funny thing is, Herman did the same exact thing.

"Do you think the team will show up?" I asked. "I know they were worried about their kids and all."

"Not sure." Asa wiped his mouth with a cloth napkin. "Hope so. I saw most of the husbands go off to the factory this morn-ing. Carl Kaninsky drives around and picks them up in that big old Suburban of his."

"How'd they look?"

"Usual. Like a chain gang. I doubt the wives even told them about the practice."

"That's not good, Asa. I don't want to start a bunch of marital wars."

He swallowed the last of his oatmeal. "You let the wives take care of their husbands. I suspect they know what they're doing."

"What about Rose?" Even I heard the change in my voice. Suddenly lower, suddenly sad.

He shrugged. "Don't know, Charlotte. She's been feeling a little down. It's like this softball team thing all of a sudden has her scared, scared like she was when she first moved here."

"It's my fault. I started it. Well, that's not exactly true. This whole thing was her idea, for crying out loud, and now she's gone and abandoned us. We need a catcher now and —"

"Try not to worry too much," Asa said. "I'll talk to her again." He carried his bowl to the sink.

"All right, but I have an awful feeling that she's really quit on us — for good."

Asa finished his coffee and placed the cup in the sink.

"Guess we should go," I said, looking at

255

the clock. It was nearly nine and I wanted to be there early to get set up. "Did you have time to chalk the lines and —"

"Sure did. Cousin Studebaker came down yesterday and helped me. We even made a halo in the on-deck circle — you know, for Angels."

"You are something else, Asa. Thank you. The women will love it, except —"

"Except what?"

"We need a babysitter. The women can't play unless I find someone to watch their kids."

Asa and I were about to the Frost sisters' flagpole when he stopped short. "I know what we can do. I drove Marlabeth over to Fleur de Lee way early this morning because Fleur de Lee was having some contractions or something, but Marlabeth said it was nothing. She might still be over there, and maybe Fleur de Lee can come watch the youngsters."

"You think she will?"

"Sure, as long as the mothers don't mind a retard watching their children."

"Asa, that's a terrible way to put it."

Asa looked at his feet. "Ah, I don't mean any disrespect. It's just what they're called, you know?"

We arrived at the gorgeous Angel Field, and already Edwina and Thomasina were tossing a ball around. "Good morning," I called with a wave.

"Good morning, Charlotte, we just couldn't wait to get started."

I saw a large green shed with a lock on it. "Is that where you stowed all the gear, Asa?"

"Yep." He reached into his pocket and handed me the key to the padlock I saw dangling from the box. "Not that it will do any good now."

"I looked at the key and then at the box. How did they . . . ?"

Asa nodded toward the box. "Looks like Edwina shot the lock off."

I shook my head. "You people don't mess around."

"Listen," Asa said, "you want I should run by Haven House and see if Marlabeth is coming and if maybe Fleur de Lee can come watch the youngsters?"

"Yes, that's a good idea, but — well, what about Jaster? Does he work?"

"Full time at Elsmere. He's in quality control. Someone needs to make sure the elastic is stretchy enough."

I laughed. "Why is elastic so funny?"

"Because they make underwear and bra straps and jocks and stuff with it, you know, Charlotte. We all know it and it's funny, that stuff, I mean. Underwear."

Thomasina threw me the brand-new Rawlings softball. I caught it in one hand. "Go on, Asa." The softball felt so good in my hand. Still a perfect fit. I threw it back to Edwina, who stood near second base.

"Good throw," she called.

I opened the shed and was unloading bats and balls, a catcher's face mask, and shin guards when I saw the yellow flag unfurl atop the pole. The rest of the team paraded toward the field with babies and children in tow. My heart swelled as they moved closer. "They did it," I told Lucky. "They came; they all came."

Lucky barked.

"Except Rose."

Gwendolyn waved like she was conducting the Philharmonic. "Charlotte, what a beautiful day."

True. The promised rain had yet to arrive. "It is," I called back with a wave. "A great day to play ball."

The team gathered around me like I was a mother hen. I liked it. "Is everyone here?"

"Everyone who can play," Ginger said.

"Except Rose. She told me to tell you she is not playing."

"When did she tell you that?"

"Yesterday. She was sitting up in the giant hand looking like the rug got pulled out from under her. I climbed up there and sat with her a while. She hardly said a word."

"Whose gonna play catcher?" Gwendolyn whined. "Wasn't Rose the catcher?"

I nodded and took a deep breath. "Rose will change her mind," I said. "Don't worry." Even though deep inside I wasn't so sure.

That was when Charlie Lundy Junior grabbed a bat and started swinging it around, nearly conking his poor mother on the head. "Charlie Lundy, you put that bat down this instant or I'm gonna give you what for but good."

Charlie ran off toward second base with the bat and was quickly followed by four other children I hadn't met. "Someone needs to round up those kids," I said. "They'll mess up the field." I caught scowls from a couple of the moms.

Gwendolyn headed out onto the field. I watched her stamp her foot with her arms crossed against her chest. She stuck her chin out in a most menacing way as she spoke loudly to the children. I didn't know she had it in her. "Now git on over there, sit down, and be quiet!"

The children did as they were told and sat along the third-base line like ducks in a shooting gallery.

"Well," I said, "the good news is that I think Asa is coming back with Fleur de Lee to babysit the children while we have our practice."

"Fleur de Lee?" Clara Kaninsky said. "You mean that retarded girl from Haven House? She's coming to watch our kids?"

"What about it?" Ginger said. "She'll do a fine job. Be good practice for her and besides we'll keep an eye out."

"That's right," I said. "We need someone to watch the kids and keep them from running out on the field when we practice. Wouldn't want them to get hurt."

"I don't know," Clara said. "Makes me nervous, and if my Carl found out he'd throw a conniption fit."

"Let's just relax and give it try. The children will be in view the whole time."

"Yeah," Edwina said. "We'll keep an eye out. The kids will be okay."

That was when I saw Asa's truck pull onto the Frost sisters' property. "Does it look like Fleur de Lee is with him?"

The doors opened and I saw Asa and then

Marlabeth help Fleur de Lee out of the backseat.

"Looks like she's agreed to watch them."

Edwina ran toward Fleur de Lee and grabbed her hand. She pulled her toward the team. "Come on, Fleur de Lee, you come play with the little kids."

Fleur de Lee was all smiles and a big round belly. "We can go play over here," she said, taking one little girl's hand. "Let's go play."

"You be careful, Linda Sue," Clara called.

Not a single child turned to look back. Fleur de Lee was the Pied Piper leading the children around.

"Okay." I clapped my hands and brought the team to attention. "Let's get started."

But before I could give out any instructions I saw women running every which way grabbing bats and balls and gloves and shouting to each other like they had just been let loose from a zoo.

"Come on," called Greta. "Throw me a pitch." She stood on home plate swinging a bat.

I let them go for a short time until I corralled them all together again. "That was a lot of fun. But we need to get organized. I want to see how you all can swing a bat."

"I'll pitch," Asa said.

I set a bucket of balls on the pitcher's circle. "Take it easy with them. You don't want —" I stopped talking when Asa raised his hand and said, "I might have known."

"What?"

"Fergus," Asa said.

Fergus Wrinkel was making his way out of the woods. "Asa," he called in a louder-than-necessary voice. "Asa. I've been looking for you. I need you to carry them propane tanks down to the dump."

"Now?" I called. "We were just about to start our practice."

"Now," Fergus said. He was clear to the pitcher's circle and looking at Asa like a jackal staring down a rabbit. "This is a woman's team. What you want with a one-armed man anyway? Not like he can play."

Asa handed me the ball. "I'm sorry, Charlotte."

Fergus opened his mouth like he wanted to say something else, when out of the blue came a line drive hit that buzzed Fergus's head. I looked toward home plate. My whole team stood there holding bats. I needed to know which one of my players could hit a ball like that.

Asa choked back a laugh. The team was not quite so gracious and laughed like a pack of hyenas over at home plate.

"Come on, Asa," Fergus said. He sounded a tad humiliated. "Do you want to keep your job, or do you want to stay here and play sissy softball?"

Asa went off with Fergus, but I knew that Fergus had no real say in whether Asa kept his job or not. That was Hazel's call. I only wished Asa knew it also.

20

I had already decided that official practice sessions would last for an hour and a half, with one half hour dedicated to a different fundamental. The women gathered around me in a circle. Each one of their faces held a slightly different expression. I saw excitement, trepidation, questioning. Greta kept one eye peeled in Charlie Junior's direction, and Marlabeth seemed to be on an entirely different planet than the rest of us. Their hair was unkempt, and they wore clothes that looked about nine sizes too large, except Greta, who was squeezed into a pair of cutoff jeans. Clara Kaninsky looked for all the world like Lana Turner, and Thomasina insisted on wearing overalls and I wondered if I would ever get her into a uniform.

"It's always good to start a practice with some drills, so I'd like you all to run the bases two or three times," I said. "Stretch your muscles a bit."

"What?" Greta said. "You want us to run clear around them bases two or three times? I can't run that much. I'm nursing baby Ruth and I guarantee I will be leaking like a sieve by the time I make it to second base. Can't have these breasts flopping up and down all around the bases." She hoisted her burgeoning breasts in the air. I made a mental note to check with someone about what to do with the breasts of a nursing mother who wanted to play softball.

"Okay, you sit out, Greta, but the rest of you get going." I tried a more assertive voice. I heard some grumbling, in particular from Gwendolyn, who said, "When we gonna get to hit the ball? I want to hit the ball. Been wanting to hit something for about ten years now." Then she snuffed back tears.

I watched them run. Clara and Francine knew what they were doing. Marlabeth started off in the wrong direction, but Clara grabbed her hand. "This way, Marlabeth. You run the bases this way. First, second, third, home."

Ginger had already been around the bases four times before the rest of the team made their second lap. She stood next to me, huffing and puffing, with a little bit of glistening

265

sweat on her face. "That was invigorating, Charlotte. Got my heart pumping."

The team straggled onto home plate, most of them falling to their knees and gasping for oxygen. Clara, Frankie, and Greta were the only ones standing. I had my work cut out for me, and with only three weeks before our first game, my own trepidation swelled. We would have to step up practice to at least twice a week.

"I want you ladies to run whenever you can. Run through Paradise. Jogging is popular right now, everybody's doing it."

They laughed at me.

I ignored them. "Okay, let's try some batting practice."

"Edwina and Thomasina, you two head out into the outfield. Everyone else stay near the dugout."

Gwendolyn laughed. "Dugout. It ain't no dugout. It's a bench."

"It's still called a dugout," I said. "Now do what I said."

Greta ran over to Fleur de Lee to check on the baby. I heard Fleur de Lee say, "She's doing just fine, Miz Lundy. Only made a few little cooing noises."

Edwina and Thomasina stood stock-still for a second or two and then played rock, paper, scissors, with Thomasina getting right field. Wasn't sure if that made her the winner or the loser.

"Do I get to hit the ball now?" Gwendolyn said. "I want to hit a home run. I'm gonna hit that dang blame ball clear out of the park and halfway to Philadelphia." I wondered whose head she wanted to hit with that bat.

I gave out some pointers on having a proper stance and how to swing at the ball. "Now, believe it or not, it is not that hard to hit a moving object. Just time your swing correctly and BAM! It's outta here!" I got a little excited.

Clara had a nice stance and could hit with no trouble. Same for Greta and Ginger. I finally let Gwendolyn up to bat, and she looked like she was ready to rip the casing off the ball. I pitched a nice, five-foot arc and watched the ball come down right in her strike zone. She swung hard! Missed.

"Gol-dern it. Stinking, rotten ball. I'll hit ya this time."

I pitched. She swung, and another miss. This time she banged the bat on the ground. "Dagnabbit."

Clara moved close to her and helped her with her grip. "Stay low on the bat, Gwendolyn. You're gripping too high. Wait until you feel it, then swing."

"Feel what, Clara? The ball hitting my head?"

"No. When you feel it's right. Keep your eye on the ball. You'll see it."

That was when I knew I had a champion on my team. Clara knew about softball.

Gwendolyn nodded and adjusted her batting helmet. Then she ripped it off her head. "I think I'll see the ball better without that dang fool thing blocking my view." She kicked it toward the on-deck circle where Marlabeth was taking practice swings, though she looked more like a whirling dervish.

I pitched. She swung. And bam! The ball went soaring over my head like a cannon shot.

"Run," hollered the team. "Run to first base, Gwendolyn."

She took off down the first base line and I don't remember ever seeing more determination in a base runner before. She tagged first base and took off toward second. Meanwhile Edwina and Thomasina, who were in the outfield, were still running after the ball. Gwendolyn rounded second as Edwina kicked the ball further into the field.

"You moron," Thomasina hollered. "Go get the ball."

Edwina took off toward the cornfield after

the rolling ball.

"Run. Run." The team was jumping up and down by now. "Run, Gwendolyn."

Edwina grabbed the ball. Frankie pulled on her glove and ran to home base, hoping to pick Gwendolyn off. Edwina threw with all her might, but the ball barely made it to second base.

Gwendolyn had scored the first Angels home run, much to the joy of the entire team. And I do believe that it was at that very moment that this motley group of Paradise trailerites became a team.

Yet as I watched them celebrate at home plate, I couldn't help but notice the hole in the team that was Rose. I threw my glove on the ground.

"You all play ball. I'll be back in a little while."

"Where you going?" Ginger called.

"We need a catcher." I marched off toward the woods.

If there was one thing I had learned since Herman dropped dead in my kitchen, it was that I had been putting up with too much guff. A person had to stand up for herself if she was ever going to win at softball, let alone life. I walked hard, making each step count as I thought about things. Rose had a right to her secrets, but she also had a responsibility to the team. After all, she prayed for me, prayed that I would find my way to Paradise. Starting the team was her idea in the first place, and for her to all of a sudden give up on the team was wrong. I was going to tell her she had no right. No right at all, scars, tattoos, and all.

I found Rose sitting in the giant hand like Humpty Dumpty waiting to fall.

"What in the heck are you doing up there, Rose?"

"Thinking."

"About what?" I put my hands on my hips and tapped my sneaker on the ground. "What gives you the right to sit up there in God's hand and think your life away? Is that what he's telling you to do?"

"Well, he ain't telling me to play softball, either, Charlotte."

"Is too. He is too telling you to play softball."

"Is not."

"Is too."

I had to jump up and down to see her. "Rose Tattoo, you are the most infuriating woman on God's green earth, well, next to my mother." I climbed into the palm. "You come down and join the team. Nobody cares two licks about your scars or your tattoos, and you don't have to tell a soul about them if you don't want. You understand? We'll find some way to hide them."

"But you told me to tell. You said I should because Jesus did."

"I know what I said, and what I said was wrong. Your scars and your tattoos are your business. But you can't just walk away from the team. It's a team, Rose. A real team. Hiding tattoos is one thing. Letting down the team is another."

And I meant what I said.

She looked toward the field. "It is a pretty field. So green and —"

"We need a catcher something fierce over there. I'm fairly certain the Angels are running amok without me over there. They're probably tearing up the field, chasing balls, and only heaven knows what Gwendolyn is doing, probably hitting anything she can. That woman has a violent streak. I got a . . . a mentally slow girl babysitting, a nursing mother with breasts leaking all over the place, and a midget who thinks she's Mickey Mantle. Now get down and come play. I can't leave them alone too long. Only God knows what can happen. For heaven's sake, Rose, Edwina shot the lock off the equipment shed. Now I got to get back to them."

I took a huge breath and blew it out my mouth. I had never spoken so forcefully in all my days. Never. "Please, Rose. I need you."

She didn't move.

That was when I saw crystal clear what she was doing. "Rose Tattoo. You are a fraud. You've been sitting up here in the hand of God watching us practice. You want to play same as everyone else."

"I've only been here for a minute. I just got up here. I was only curious and —"

"And you want to play. Come on. I need you to help me contain the women. It's like they've been let loose from prison over there."

It was close to noon by the time Rose and I made it back to Angel Field. Already the women were complaining about needing to get their kids home for lunch, but mostly they were glad to see Rose.

"Now, look," I said. "We still could use another half hour of practice." I looked into the distance and saw dark, bottom-heavy clouds rolling toward us. "And before the rain starts."

Fleur de Lee had the children engaged in a game of ring-around-the-rosy and seemed to be doing a fine job, so I didn't worry about the children.

"Now who wants to hit?"

I should have just handed Gwendolyn the bat. "I do," she practically sang. "I love to hit that ball. Looks so pretty soaring out there over everyone's head and landing on that green, green grass."

So after a few more rounds of batting practice, I gathered the women together. Rose spoke before me. "I think it's only fitting we thank the one who made all this possible and —"

"But Asa run off to do chores with Fergus," Frankie Felker said.

"I was going to say," Rose continued, "and ask his almighty blessing on this field and —" she looked into my eyes with that sneaky smile of hers, "our team."

Frankie looked embarrassed and moved to the back of the group.

Rose raised her hands and prayed. She mentioned each woman by name and also Asa and even our mysterious sponsor. Then she said something that surprised me.

"And gracious Lord," she raised her hands higher, "If it be your will, let the Angels amount to something more, much more than softball. Something that will last and help us help Suzy Wrinkel."

As we all stood on the brand-new field, a sense of peace and calm enveloped me, like a soft, warm bathrobe.

"This is nice," Greta said. "I don't go in much for all that God talk and praying. Never works for me, but it sure does for Rose. She's got a pipeline to Heaven, don't she now."

"She sure does," Carla said. "Maybe we should make Rose our team captain."

Rose's eyes bugged out. "Captain? Sorry. Chaplain maybe, but captain? Not me."

Carla had brought up an excellent point. I never did name a team captain or give The Angels a chance to vote on it.

"Carla's right," I said. "We should have a team captain."

"Why?" Ginger asked. "How's that different from what you do, Charlotte?"

"The team captain takes care of other things and helps me keep you all happy and maybe even gives pep talks when I'm not around or when you need to talk without your coach, you know."

"Then it should be Rose," Frankie said.

But Rose kept shaking her head. "I can't. And I won't. So just count me out."

"Okay, okay." I raised my arms to quiet them and looked around at the team. Any one of them could have done it, except maybe Gwendolyn, who was so prone to crying fits I figured she'd just get everyone in a tizzy too often.

"Raise your hand," I said, "if you think you want to be captain."

Ginger, Frankie, and Clara raised their hands. I grabbed my pad and gave each member of the team a slip of paper. "Let's vote."

Two minutes later, Frankie Felker was voted in as Angels Team Captain. She stepped into the center of the circle and waved her cap. "Thank you, thank you. I will do my best to lead this team to VICTORY!"

Already she had gotten the team riled and whooping it up. And once they quieted down, the women spread out, grabbed their children, and set off through the woods chattering and laughing. It had been a good practice after all.

We practiced several more times that spring, and I'd like to say that the Angels were shaping up to be a pretty good team. But I couldn't. Marlabeth still had a habit of running the wrong direction; Ginger thought she was invisible and kept trying to steal bases, even though I told her that in softball there is no stealing; and Gwendolyn only cared about hitting the ball and couldn't catch a pop fly or a grounder if her life depended on it.

Rose was without a doubt the worst catcher I had ever seen. She couldn't throw the ball as far as second base, but she could hit. For some reason, every single time Rose got up to bat, she hit away, nearly out of the park. I think she enjoyed watching Edwina and Greta run around like Keystone Kops.

For the most part the husbands stayed well behaved. Rube and Charlie even came out to one of our late-day practices and pitched batting practice and even gave out some pointers on fielding.

"I got to tell you, Charlotte," Rube said. He towered over me like an oak over a sapling pine. "This is the motliest group of ball players I have ever seen."

"Then why don't you help?" Asa called. "Especially Rose. She's gonna lose every single game for us on pass balls if she don't learn to catch something. I gave her the biggest glove I could find and she still can't catch."

"Must have a hole in it," Rose hollered from home plate. "I keep putting it in the right place, but that dang ball just keeps going on past me."

Rube took his cap off and scratched his head a second. "Well, don't rightly know what I can do, except . . ."

He stood behind Rose and asked Frankie to pitch a few. Rose caught one out of seven. "I see what you're doing. You have to keep your eyes open, Rose. If you keep closing your eyes when Frankie pitches, you'll never catch it. This is why there are no blind catchers in professional ball."

"But I can't help it. It's not like I am consciously closing my eyes. It just happens. It's a reaction I have when a large object is hurled at my face."

"Now, Rose," Frankie said. "Rube's right. You'll never catch a thing if you don't look for it. We give you that face mask for a reason, not just because it looks so nice." Then she giggled and went back to her pitcher's circle.

Rose crouched back down in her catcher's position. "It's getting hot." Rose still wore that heavy brown sweater that covered up her tattoos.

"It would also help if you took that sweater off," Frankie said.

"Go on, Rose," I said. "I've been telling you that for days. It's got to be hard to move in that thing."

Rose stood up and began to unbutton her sweater. I took a deep breath for her and held it as she released each one — six altogether.

"Go on, Rose," I said. "You know you're safe here."

She removed the sweater and exposed her scars and tattoos.

"Holy cannolies," Rube hollered. "What you got going on there, darlin'?" He reached out to touch her arm. But she pulled it away. "Looks like you just jumped off a stage at the *Believe It or Not* museum and — those are burn scars, woman. What the —"

Rose looked at me in horror as the rest of

the team gathered around.

"I told you," she said. Tears glistened in her eyes. "Not everyone here knows about me."

"Most of us do," Frankie said. "I think they're beautiful. Why — why look at those pictures. I see Mary and Jesus and three crosses and what is that? A river?"

"The Jordan," Rose said. "It's where Jesus was baptized."

Ginger scooted into the middle. "I've been telling her all along that she is a walking work of art."

"Is this what her problem is?" Greta asked. "She's embarrassed about the tattoos and scars?"

"That's right," I said. "No one outside of Paradise has seen them."

Rose took my arm. She whispered, "No one except you and Asa knows the truth about the scars."

"Okay. I'll keep your secret."

Greta waved her hand. "Who cares, Rose? You be proud of them. They mean so much, you know."

"Don't you dare cover them up," Marlabeth said. "My goodness, woman, you got a whole art show on your arms. You just keep slathering on that cream I gave you to keep your skin smooth and supple."

Rose cried. She let the tears come that afternoon, surrounded by the Angels.

"Just one question," asked Marlabeth after a minute or two. "What happened that you have all those scars? Looks like burns to me."

"It was." Rose nodded and looked at her feet. "A fire."

A collective gasp went up in the small crowd. "Oh, my precious Lord," Frankie said. "You poor thing."

"Okay, okay," I said. "Let's get back to practice. Our first game is just three days away."

Everyone went back to their places. Frankie pitched to Ginger, and Rose caught the ball pretty much every time.

"Now, see," I heard Rube say. "If you keep your eyes open and take off the heavy stuff, it gets a lot easier."

A short while later I noticed the women were getting tired, their kids were getting cranky, and it was time to call it a day. Fleur de Lee had slowed down. She was waddling quite a bit. She waddled out onto the field and spoke with Marlabeth. "You still have two weeks, maybe more," Marlabeth said. "First babies are always late."

"I don't know about that, Miss Marla.

This baby is itching to get out into the real world."

Marlabeth touched her belly. "Two weeks, Fleur de Lee."

I blew my whistle and waved the team in for a short meeting along the third base line as Fleur de Lee made her way back to the children.

"Our first game is only three days away, and I think we're looking pretty good."

"Yes. Yes, you are," came a voice from out of the woods.

We all turned in that direction. Cash Vangarten traipsed onto the field.

"He's been spying on us, I bet," I whispered to Rose.

"Who is he?" she whispered back.

"Mr. Vangarten," I called. I moved toward him. "How long have you been here?"

"Long enough," he said. "And I got say," he snorted, "looks like the Thunder won't have a chance against you."

I introduced him. "This is Mr. Cash Vangarten. The man I told you about. The fella from the Pink Lady."

"He's our representative at Elsmere Elastic."

"I know who he is," Rube said. "He's the boss." Rube did not look thrilled to see him.

"And like I told you," I said, "Mr. Vangarten coaches the Shoops Thunder."

"So you are spying," Rose said. "You got no right —"

"You want me to run him off our property?" Edwina called. "I got my shotgun right over there."

Vangarten put his hands in the air, "Whoa, whoa, John Wayne, I come in peace. I just came to give Charlotte a receipt and let you all know that your uniforms will be ready tomorrow."

"Uniforms," Frankie said. "I can't wait. Are they purple and white?"

"With our name on them?" said Greta.

"And Elsmere Elastic on the back," Vangarten said.

"Thank you, Mr. Vangarten," I said.

His eyes grew soft again when he looked at me. "When are you going to start calling me Cash?"

"Okay, Cash," I said. "Thank you very much for bringing that receipt."

"Now get off our field, you no-good spy," Ginger said. "You didn't need to come way out here for this."

Vangarten backed off. "Testy group you got here, Mrs. Figg."

"Call me Charlotte," I said before I even had a chance to think.

"You'll be tested, all right," Ginger piped.

"Next Tuesday."

Cash put his hands in the air in an act of surrender. "I best be going before I get filled full of buckshot."

We all watched until Cash was out of sight.

Thomasina put her hands on her hips. "What gives him the right to come on our field and —"

"Don't worry about it," I said. "From what he says, the Thunder haven't got a chance against us. Now listen up. The big game is next Tuesday."

I went on to give them a pep talk, but they were really only interested in the uniforms.

"When can we get them?"

Asa chimed in, "I'll drive into Wilkes-Barre tomorrow and get them."

"Then you all come by my trailer and we'll give them out. I hope I got enough sizes to go around." I looked at Ginger. "I had to have yours special ordered, Ginger. So it might not be with the others."

"That's okay," she said. "I can still play on Tuesday without it, right?"

"Sure. Uniforms are not mandatory."

"Have you got anything purple?" Frankie asked.

"I do," Ginger said. "And I can sew some letters on a tee shirt. I can make the word *Angels* out of felt or something."

"Good idea," I said. And that was when Rube and Charlie reminded us they were still there.

"I don't like the idea of our boss being here next Tuesday," Rube said. "I ain't coming if he's here."

Frankie elbowed him in the spleen. "You will be here, Rube Felker. He ain't your boss on this field."

"That's right," said Greta. She grabbed Charlie's arm. "Leave the elastic at the factory. He's just a man like all the rest. He can't fire or hire on Angel field. And he can't boss you around."

Ginger raised her hands so we'd notice her. "You might say Cash Vangarten's authority does not *stretch* this far." Then she laughed and soon everyone laughed.

The men looked at each other. And then it was like the same idea entered their brains at the very same time.

"That's right," Rube said. "In fact, Frankie, I am going to practice with you all weekend, and you too, Greta, and all you girls if you want. We're gonna beat the snot out of the Thunder."

With that the team cheered and tossed their gloves in the air in anticipation of certain victory.

"We are the Angels," called Marlabeth.

"We won't be the second-best team on this field next week. And I have vitamin drinks for everyone too."

There were no cheers for Marlabeth's vitamin drinks. Most of us have tasted one kind or the other and they tasted pretty much like seaweed. Might be because there was seaweed mixed in the concoction. But I applauded her interest.

22

As usual on Friday evening, Rose and Asa came by for dinner. It was the first day of summer. A cool breeze blew down from the mountains and brought the smell of pine and honeysuckle with it.

When I looked in the fridge, I didn't see much to make. I would need to go grocery shopping. I did find pork chops, however, and thought they would go nicely with mashed potatoes and salad. I'd had a hankering for mashed potatoes, so I peeled and quartered six nice russets and dropped them in salted water.

Rose and Asa arrived together.

"Hey, Charlotte," Asa said. "What's for supper? I'm starved."

"Pork chops."

"Sounds good." Asa flipped on the TV and sat on the sofa. Rose helped me in the kitchen.

"I thought practice went well," I said.

"It sure did," Asa said. "There's some real talent on the team. We just have to get Marlabeth to run the right direction, and Edwina is afraid of the ball or something."

Rose set the table.

"Use the cloth napkins," I said. "The pretty ones with the daisies on the edge. It is summer, after all. We should be summery, don't you think?"

Rose's mind was still on the practice. "Except for that Cash Vangarten spying on us."

I watched her toss Asa a sideways glance. "Or should I say spy on Charlotte?"

"Me?" I tested the potatoes with a fork. "Few more minutes."

I tossed Asa a can of Coke. He placed it between his knees and popped the top. "Rose thinks he's sweet on you."

"Oh, pish. He just came by with that lame excuse about the uniforms so he could get a look at our team."

"Whatever you say," Rose said.

I drained the spuds. "Come to think of it, Rose, I did tell him we were championship caliber." I laughed and beat the potatoes with a little more gusto.

"You what?"

"Well, he was giving me such a hard time, a real chauvinist, that day at the factory about Ha—"

Rose made wide eyes at me and tilted her head toward Asa.

"Anyway," I said. "It doesn't matter, really. He was just bothering me."

"I can see why. There's just something troublesome about him."

I called Asa to the table.

"Got any applesauce, Charlotte?" Rose asked. "I always like applesauce with chops."

"I sure do. Made some yesterday."

"Made it?" Asa said. "You can make applesauce?"

"Simple," I said. "I used Pink Lady apples, so it might be a little tart."

I plopped a spoonful in a bowl and set it on the table near Asa. "Got cinnamon?" he asked, looking up at me with his quiet blue eyes.

"Pink Lady. Isn't that the name of the restaurant where you met Cash?" Rose asked, even though I knew she knew the answer.

"Aha," Asa said. "Methinks the lady of the trailer has a crush."

"I do not." I tapped the potato masher against the pot. "My husband — my late husband — has not been late for all that long. I am not interested in starting a romance." I turned my wedding ring around on my finger and wondered how long I was supposed to wear it.

"All right, Charlotte," Rose said. "We're just playing with you."

Rose tried to cut Asa's chop, but he shooed her off. "I'll just pick it up like a chicken leg, if you don't mind."

"Just don't do that in a five-star restaurant," I said.

Asa chomped off a good bit of chop. "This is good," he said with his mouth full. "What's it got on it?"

"Milk. They're called milk-fed pork chops."

Asa finished off his chop down to the bone and was just about to sneak it to Lucky, who was sitting patiently nearby waiting for scraps of any sort to reach his snout.

"Don't give him that," I said. "The vet said those little bones aren't good for dogs. They splinter and get stuck in places they shouldn't."

"How about my salad, then?" Asa said.

I shook my head. "The runs. Lettuce will give him the runs."

"So when are you going to come clean about Hazel Crenshaw?" he asked.

I looked at Rose, who looked immediately away.

"Rose, did you —"

"No, no," said Asa. "You've just been over at her place a lot, and just now, a few minutes ago, I heard you say her name."

I dropped my fork in my plate and sipped water.

"You better tell him, Charlotte," Rose said.

"Oh, all right. Hazel Crenshaw is not who you think she is. She's actually" — and I leaned closer to him — "a spy for the CIA."

"Get out, Charlotte," Asa said. "She is not."

"Okay, okay. I'll tell you, but you have to swear up and down and six ways to China that you won't breathe this to another living soul."

Asa raised his hand and then crossed his heart. "I solemnly promise never to tell —"

A slight knock on the door kept him from completing his oath.

"Now, who could that be?" I asked.

"Sounds like Ginger's knock," Rose said.

Lucky barked once and went to sniff around the door.

"One way to find out."

I pulled open the door and was just about to say, "Hi Ginger," when I saw Suzy Wrinkel standing on the stoop.

"Suzy," I said, practically choking out the word. "Suzy you —"

Rose and Asa crowded behind me. I tried

to shoo them away, but too late. Suzy stepped back and turned to leave like a case of the willies had just struck. I reached out and grabbed her arm. The one in the cast. I didn't realize I did it. "Please, Suzy. You came for a reason."

She stopped and turned back. I watched her swallow a lump the size of my Galaxy.

"Really, it's okay."

"Yeah, Suzy," said Asa. "Hi."

"Please, Suzy. Come inside. It's okay," I said.

Rose touched Suzy's cheek. "Hi, Suzy. I'm Rose, remember? We met once down near the trash heap."

Suzy twisted her mouth. "You were throwing out a lamp."

"That's right," Rose said. "Good memory."

I saw the way Asa looked at Suzy. Talk about making eyes at someone.

I still had hold of Suzy's hand. "Are you hungry? We were just having dinner. Pork chops and —"

She shook her head. "I can't stay long. Fergus will be home soon. I only wanted to come by and say thank you and return your pie plate."

"Thank you?" I said. "For what?"

"The pie. I had a slice. It was real good."

"Glad you enjoyed it."

Suzy had a nice smile. "Fergus ate the whole thing that night," she continued. "He asked me where I got it, and . . . and I lied to him." She swiped a tear. "I told him I baked it and now he's asking for another and I . . ." She started to blubber like a baby. "I don't bake pie, Charlotte. I never baked a pie in my life. I never even saw a person bake a pie. My mother never —"

I went to put my arms around her slight body, but she pulled away. "Don't you worry, Suzy. I got pie in the kitchen."

Rose's forehead wrinkled so much I thought you could slip a nickel in the folds. "You mean that husband of yours expects you to make pie with a broken arm?"

Suzy nodded. "It's not the whole arm. Just one tiny bone in my wrist. Not too serious. I've been getting along just fine. Can do pretty much everything I did before."

Asa shrugged his right shoulder and made the empty tee shirt sleeve flap like a wing. "Not so hard once you get used to it."

Suzy cracked a smile and looked into Asa's eyes. Rose and I looked at each other and smiled, but I quickly brought my attention back to Suzy.

"Come on, Suzy," I said. "You were just about to tell us how you broke your wrist."

"I fell down the trailer steps." She answered quickly, like she had been ready with that answer for days.

"When?" Rose asked.

"That morning." She looked at me. "That morning you saw me and Fergus."

"Uh-huh," was all I could say, but inside I was begging her to tell the truth. "Let me get you a pie."

"Charlotte always has pie," Rose said.

"Most of the time I do. Now you can take it home and tell Fergus you made it and I'll bake a couple more and bring them by when I don't see his truck, if that's okay, and we'll keep him up to his ears in pie."

"You would do that, Charlotte?" Suzy said. "You would make pie for Fergus?"

"I will, though Lord knows he doesn't deserve it. Now hold on. Let me get your pie. Just bring me back the tins." Maybe, just maybe, if Fergus was too busy filling his mouth with pie, he wouldn't hurt Suzy. And I didn't really care about the pie tins. I figured asking for them back was a way of getting her out of the trailer on a regular basis.

Asa looked like he was about to split a gut. His face was redder than a pomegranate. "Come on, Suzy. You can't keep saying you have accidents."

I grabbed his arm and shushed him. "Let her be, Asa."

"But . . . but, that Fergus don't deserve pie. What he deserves is a —"

"Asa," Suzy said, her voice as sweet and soft as condensed milk. "It's okay."

I took a lattice-crust cherry that was missing a slice from the kitchen counter. "You just tell him you got hungry."

She took the pie. "Thank you."

"Try serving it warmed up with a tall glass of cold milk. You be sure and get a piece for yourself, maybe two, you're so skinny, before Fergus gets to it."

Rose lifted the pie to her nose. "It smells sweet and delicious. Better than store-bought, that's for sure."

I cringed at the words *store-bought.*

"Maybe Charlotte can teach you how to make pie some day," Rose said.

"I'd like that, Suzy. I could teach you how to make pie."

"That's okay. I might be able to learn myself if I practice a while."

"Maybe," I said. "But sometimes it helps to have a friend close by when you're making crust. Proper crust can be tricky, takes some finesse."

"Thank you, Charlotte. Thank you so much. Now I better be getting back." Suzy moved to the front door. "If Fergus finds out that . . . Well, I just need to get home."

"If Fergus finds out what?" I asked.

Suzy looked into my eyes, and piercing sadness shot right out of hers into my brain. I could feel her pain. "Fergus won't know," I said.

"Does he hurt you, Suzy?" Rose asked. "Does Fergus hit —"

"Course he does," Asa said. "I just don't know why she doesn't just leave him."

"Stop talking like that, Asa," Suzy said. "If I knew you were going to be here, I wouldn't have come. Now, there isn't anything going on like that. Fergus just likes me to be home is all." She moved toward the door.

Suzy slinked out the front door. Asa and I rushed to the kitchen window, and I watched her as far as I could see her. I turned from the window. Asa kept looking outside.

"Well, if that don't beat all," Rose said slapping her knee. "I can't believe Suzy came here."

"The power of pie, Rose. It's the power of pie. But why'd you go and ask her if Fergus hit her? I don't want to scare her away. It even made me nervous. And you, Asa, why do you want to give her more pressure? What do you expect her to do?"

"She knows, Charlotte. She knows what she needs to do. She just won't do it."

"She's not ready," Rose said. "She needs to get to a place where she can stand up to him and not care what he says or does. Like when I was being held by that maniac. I never told anyone this, but there was a moment right before I set the fire that I had a second thought. He looked so pitiful and pathetic lying drunk in that bed. I almost didn't do it."

I took a deep breath, and Lucky toddled near me. I patted his head. "I understand, Rose. Having a heart capable of all that compassion is a hard thing sometimes. It makes us do the wrong thing."

Asa, who had returned to his dinner, practically had steam coming out of his ears. "He's gonna kill her one day. That's what worries me. I been telling her for months." He dug at his mashed potatoes.

"Months?" I said. "You knew about this and you never told anyone?"

"She told me not to."

I picked at my pork chop and then took a mouthful of mashed potatoes.

"Can't we help her?" Rose asked. "I've been praying that we can find a way."

Rose and Asa both looked at me like I held the answer to the Riddle of the Sphinx.

"Why are you looking at me? What can I do?"

23

I really can't remember or explain where the idea for the barbecue came from the next day. I thought of it when I pulled a package of chicken breasts out of the freezer to thaw. This after a restless night pondering Suzy Wrinkel and why I felt so responsible for her.

It was like a spontaneous combustion that ignited wildfire inside of me. I dropped the chicken on the counter, Lucky barked twice. "They do look good, don't they? Back home I would toss them on the grill with some . . ."

And that was when it struck. "Lucky, a barbecue. Why not? We can get everyone together for a giant Paradise barbecue to kick off the softball season. Kind of a pep rally. I bet Paradise never ever had a pep rally."

I got so excited about the idea that I immediately started to go door-to-door, even though it was only eight o'clock in the morning, recruiting folks to come.

Most were receptive, especially now that the men knew we were playing against their boss's team and wanted to beat the snot out of them. Carl Kaninsky, on the other hand, thought I was nuts. "A barbecue? The whole park? You're crazy, lady." He shut the door in my face. But I was undaunted and kept going, trailer-to-trailer, convincing folks to join in.

Rube and Charlie and even Jake Pilkey volunteered to man the burgers. It did my heart good to see the Paradise community start acting like one.

"What a great idea, Charlotte," Frankie Felker said. "I can't remember the last time I was at a barbecue. I'll take care of the chicken."

"A corn boil," Greta said. "Can't have a barbecue without corn on the cob. It's a tad early in the season, but I'm sure I can rustle up a few ears."

By ten o'clock that morning I had just about everyone on board. Even Edwina and Thomasina agreed to come.

"We'll get a pig slaughtered right away, Charlotte."

I gasped. "What?"

"A pig. Nothing like a whole pig for a

barbecue."

"Mm, mm, mm," Edwina rubbed her stomach. "When was the last time we ate one of our own pigs, Thomasina?"

"Daddy's funeral, I believe. You remember, don't you? We built that spit, and Uncle Carmichael kept turning it until the skin got crispy." Thomasina looked at me. "Skin turned practically orange, Charlotte. That little piggy fed us for days after Daddy died."

"So you're okay with" — I swallowed — "slaughtering a pig by yourselves?"

"Nothin' to it. Not really. Long as your knife is sharp enough," Thomasina said with a glint in her eye.

I had heard enough. If they were willing to handle it, it was fine by me. But where in the heck would they get a grill big enough to accommodate a whole hog? Edwina scratched under her John Deere cap. "Course we'll have hamburgers on the grill, but hot dogs might be a bit of a . . . a . . ."

"Redundancy," Thomasina said.

I shook my head and walked away. Thomasina was an odd combination of intellect and farm-girl tomboy.

As had become my habit when I made my journeys around Paradise, the Wrinkel trailer was my last stop. I noticed that Fergus's truck was missing. I hurried right up to the door and knocked.

Suzy pulled open the door.

"Suzy," I said. "I came to invite you to the barbecue this afternoon. The whole park is turning out. We're even roasting a pig and everything — baked beans, burgers, the whole shootin' match." I tried to make my voice as cheery as I could, but I was nervous. "And I'm going to make some pies, and Greta said something about a corn boil. It's shaping up to be a grand time. Just a grand time."

Suzy looked around like she was expecting Fergus at any second. "Thank you, Charlotte, but I don't think —"

"Nonsense. You just come. Don't you worry about Fergus. You need to just tell him, Suzy. Just tell him what you're doing. I did it. I once told my Herman, 'Herman, I don't care what you say, I am changing my hairstyle,' and I went right out that morning to the Sit and Curl and came back with the world's most embarrassing perm — they were all the rage a couple of years ago — but that wasn't the point —"

"I can't, Charlotte." She started to close the door. But I stuck my foot inside. Something I learned from Herman. "Just put your foot in the door and they can't slam it on your face," he said.

"Please, Suzy. It's just a barbecue. To celebrate summer and the softball team."

She nodded. "But I ain't on the team." She turned her profile to me and I saw a fresh bruise on her cheek.

"Is that why? You have a bruise?"

She nodded once, closed her eyes, and I saw her pain. Not just the physical pain, but what was deep down, invisible to the rest of the world. The soul damage that Fergus had done. I took a deep breath and silently asked God for courage.

"When did that happen?"

"Last night. He only hit me once last night and then stopped. It was like a miracle when he stopped this time. I thought maybe it was God's hand that stopped his. I know Rose has been praying."

"Oh, Suzy. But he shouldn't even be doing it even one time. Now, you come to the party, okay?"

"I don't want folks looking at me. And, besides, Fergus won't allow it."

"Who is going to look at you?"

"Everybody. All of them folks out there, Charlotte. They'll see what I'm hiding."

I mumbled and then said it right out loud. "You and Rose."

"What? I don't understand. What about Rose?"

"Rose has . . . her scars." A pang of guilt swept over my chest for giving away another secret. But like I said, I was no champion at secret keeping.

"She keeps them covered up. She was in a fire and —"

"But the fire wasn't her fault, I'm sure. So why would she be ashamed?"

"Exactly, Suzy. It wasn't her fault."

Suzy looked at her feet. "What about Fergus?"

"He wouldn't dare touch you if you go."

"What about later? After."

I swallowed. "I'm sorry. I guess I keep hoping —"

Lucky alerted us to Fergus's truck pulling into the drive. He didn't even bother to park it in its proper spot. He must have thrown it into park with force because the Ford lurched forward and back a couple of times before he jumped out.

"You best go, Charlotte," Suzy said.

"What are you doing here?" Fergus slammed the truck door. "Got a problem with your trailer?"

"No, no. Nothing like that. I came to invite Suzy . . . and you . . . to the barbecue this afternoon."

"Barbecue? We aren't interested in that."
He turned his attention to Suzy, and it
made me queasy. "Get on inside now,
Honey Buns. Go on." Suzy started to close
the door, but I still had my foot in the way.
And then I dropped the grenade I had been
hanging onto. "I'm sure Hazel Crenshaw
would love to see you and your pretty wife
this afternoon. You know what I mean, Fergus? Unless of course you want me to tell
the whole park your little —"

His eyes grew about as wide as half dollars. "Never mind that."

"Well, I'm sure the others would like to
know who really owns this place and who is
pulling your strings." I walked away from
the trailer and stood behind Fergus. I could
still see Suzy at the door.

Fergus kicked at some gravel and then
spun around and stared daggers at me.
"We'll come to your stupid little barbecue.
But only for a few minutes, and just to make
Hazel happy."

"Fine," I said. I glanced over his shoulder
at Suzy and gave her the thumbs-up sign.
She melted back inside the trailer.

Lucky bounded over and leaped up to my
waist. I gave him a scratch behind the ears.
"See you later, Mr. Wrinkel."

He made some kind of noise and headed

304

into the trailer. I hoped with all my heart that he wouldn't lay a hand on Suzy. I was afraid I had put her in a bad situation. But he wouldn't dare make another mark on her now. Not for the whole park to see. Not for Hazel Crenshaw to see — even though I had not invited her yet and wasn't at all certain she would even come.

I started up the hill and found Rose tending to the petunias near the Giant Hand of God.

"Hey," I called. "Did you hear?"

"I did. What gave you the idea to throw a barbecue? Everyone is talking about it."

"Just came to me like any old idea, I suppose. We have a lot to celebrate. It's summer for one and The Angels are about to play their first game and Suzy took a major step outside, asking me to make pie for Fergus."

Rose got to her feet and dropped the small trowel she was using and hugged me. "I knew you were part of God's plan for Paradise. I just knew it. You woke them up, Charlotte. You got Paradise buzzing. Just look around."

And that was when I noticed that people were out and about. Carla yanked lawn chairs from her old, rusted-out shed. Gwendolyn and her husband set up a picnic table that came from I don't know where. Asa and Jake Pilkey raised a ratty old Stars and Stripes up the flag pole. The flag probably should have been burned, but it waved proudly over Paradise.

"Oh, my goodness gracious, Rose. It's really happening." I took Rose's hand. "And you. You took that heavy sweater off. That's reason enough to celebrate."

"I was just too hot," she said and then smiled.

"Right. And get this. I blackmailed Fergus into coming and bringing Suzy. Blackmailed. I guess that's the right word."

"You what?"

I nodded and looked up at the hand. "I did. I told him if he didn't come I'd tell the whole park his little secret that he is nothing more than Hazel Crenshaw's gofer."

"Gofer?"

"You know, besides the weasel that he is, Hazel makes him go fer this and go fer that. Gofer. Herman taught me that."

I felt tears in the corners of my eyes as that nasty grief rose in my chest. Some words just trigger it for me, and all I can do is let it happen. The only difference is now I can shut it down easier. I can make it wait for a more opportune time.

"I was on my way to Hazel's. Think she'll

come out for the barbecue?"

Rose shook her head. "You know her better than anyone around here. Think I'll go back to my trailer and make up a batch of potato salad. Can't have a barbecue without it."

"Sounds good. I think we're going to have enough food for an army," I said. "A whole army."

"Hope I can remember the recipe. It's been a while since I made it last."

I nearly bubbled over with delight, but I couldn't help it. I put both my hands on Rose's shoulders. "You'll remember. Like you always say, you can do all things through Christ."

Rose's eyes glistened. "Why, Charlotte Figg, I do believe God has got his hand on you."

Lucky and I approached Hazel's trailer. It seemed quieter than usual. Almost spooky. But then again, it was still early and I thought she was a late sleeper. But then again, a woman that age, not taking the medicine her doctor prescribed, well, that could spell just about anything.

I rapped on her door and even jangled the wind chimes, five little brass sparrows all in a row. And then I waited and waited. I was just about to bust in, thinking that the poor old bird had fallen asleep last night and never woke up when the door creaked open.

"Charlotte," she said. Her voice still morning raspy. "Come in. Come in, child."

She wore a purple bathrobe that had seen better days and a pair of pink slippers that resembled flamingoes. And with no hat on her head, this was the first time I saw her hair, long and silver. Not gray, silver.

"Thank you, Hazel."

"Coffee," she said.

"No, thanks. I already had three cups this morning."

"No, not for you. Make me some coffee. Put the pot on."

"Oh, sure."

I located a can of Maxwell House and rinsed out the percolator, measured enough coffee for five or six cups, and plugged it in. "There you go, Hazel. Can I get you anything else?"

"Got some of that pecan pie you brought over the other day. It's in the fridge."

I hurried and served her a slice on a pretty yellow dish. "I have some news."

Hazel took the plate and sat in her rocker. "You know what I'm looking forward to?"

I sat next to her on the sofa. "No, Hazel. What are you looking forward to?"

"Peaches. I love peaches. Fresh. Right off the tree. There's an orchard not far from here."

"I know. Asa brings me bushels of apples for pie. I'm looking forward to the late summer also. Apples get sweeter, peaches ripen. I'll make you a fresh peach pie. But we have a whole summer to get through and —"

"Glory, child. I'll be counting the days. Rate I'm going, it could very well be my last peaches on earth."

"Now, don't go talking nonsense, Hazel."

"Oh, pshaw. I'm going to die. We all are. Or were you absent the day they taught that stuff in school?"

"I know that, Hazel. I just don't want you making a, what's it called? A self-fulfilling prophecy."

Hazel swallowed a bit of pie. "Well, aren't you all fancy talking?"

"The percolator is slowing down. I'll get your coffee."

After we chatted a few more minutes, I got back to the reason for my visit.

"Hazel, I was beginning to tell you my news."

"Oh, right, right. Go on. Spill it."

"I came to invite you to the first annual Paradise barbecue this afternoon."

"Barbecue? In Paradise? Have you been

sipping cooking sherry, Charlotte?"

"Nope. I'm serious. Everyone is coming. Looks like they're closing down the whole place to get ready. Grills are firing up, lawn chairs are getting set up in the street and I even saw two or three picnic tables. The Frost sisters even slaughtered a pig and are fixing to roast it."

"My goodness. You don't mean it?"

"I do."

She sipped her coffee and smacked her lips. "Was this your idea?"

I nodded and she smiled so hard her top partial plate slipped loose. She popped it back in place like it happened all the time.

"I knew the day I laid eyes on you when you pulled that wonky-wheeled trailer onto your property and stood there looking at that bilious green eyesore. I knew when you didn't back down from that challenge that you'd pull Paradise together."

I swallowed. "Please, Hazel. It's just a plain old barbecue. Now, how about it? How about you come out to the party? We're celebrating summer and the beginning of the softball season. All the Angels will be there."

She shook her head. "I'm too old. Barbecues are for you youngsters."

"Who says?"

"I say." She shook her head and then finished off her pie. "Sorry, Charlotte, but I'll just sit in my yard and watch from there."

"It's not like there will be fireworks in the sky for you to see. You'll need to mosey down where the action is. And besides, the team sponsor should make an appearance, even if no one knows your secret identity."

"No, no. Just bring me a plate of that roasted pork when it's ready. I'll be fine with my birdhouses."

I took a breath. "Hazel, I need you to come."

"Need?"

"Mm-hmm."

"What did you do, Charlotte? Did you tell them people about me?" Her face went marshmallow white.

"No. Well, not everyone. Rose knows."

Hazel nodded. "Figured you'd blab to someone."

"Well, I couldn't help it, and she practically guessed anyway. She saw me come out of your trailer a couple of times."

Hazel waved her hand at me. "Don't fret, child. Secret keeping can be a tough job."

"Thank you, Hazel. Now, what do you say? Come to the party?"

She clicked her tongue. "I don't know,

Charlotte."

"But I need you to come on account of Fergus and Suzy Wrinkel."

"Fergus? What's he got to do with it?"

"I can't tell you right now. Just please trust me and say you'll come. Even for a few minutes. Just show up. I'll find fresh peaches and make you a pie."

"Will you serve it a la mode?"

"You bet. Nice big plopper of vanilla ice cream on the side and —"

"And don't put it on the side, child, just drop it right on top."

24

Now, I don't suppose there was any stranger sight than the one I saw when I left Hazel's that morning. Edwina and Thomasina hauled a dead pig down Mango Street.

"How come you didn't put that thing in your truck?" I called.

"Edwina couldn't get it running," Thomasina shouted.

"I told you the battery was dead last night," Edwina said.

They looked so funny. Thomasina had the front end while Edwina lugged the back, which she dropped every couple of feet. Lucky caught a glimpse or a sniff of it and went tearing over and started puffing and snuffing all around it. I called him away, worried he might take a bite out of it. I didn't want him getting that raw pig disease — trichinosis. But he barked and followed it like it was a compact car.

"Where are you going with it?" I called.

But before they could answer, Old Man Hawkins was on them with his shotgun poised. I jumped behind a convenient oak.

"Whatcha got there, soldiers?"

"Uh-oh, must be fighting World War II," I whispered.

"Got us a Nazi prisoner, sir," Edwina said without missing a step.

Hawkins lowered his rifle. "Could be a medal in this for you," he said. "Carry on, men." Then he stood on his little makeshift porch and saluted as the pig went by.

I hurried to catch up with them because I just had to know. "Where are you taking it?"

"Down to Asa's."

"Asa?"

"He's the only one that has a roasting barbecue. Scavenged it from the old Play-town Fair years ago — same place Rose got her hand. Must be six feet long."

"Oh, now I understand."

I stayed back and watched them lug our dinner down the street.

"How long does something that big take to cook?" I hollered.

"All day," they said. "All day. Course we'll slice it down the middle and spread it out like a butterfly on the grill, and that will hasten the roasting time," Thomasina said.

I baked four pies before the festivities really got started — apple, cherry, lemon meringue, and one peach made from canned peaches, but I wouldn't tell Hazel. I would have made more, but I ran out of flour and apples and cinnamon. Not too often that I ran out of cinnamon. But I did that day, and I didn't use just any brand of cinnamon. I preferred Madagascar cinnamon that came in sticks and enjoyed scraping them and making rust-colored snow on my apples.

My kitchen smelled like heaven. At least, it was heaven to me — spicy and sugary. The citrus from the lemon gave it a clean, summer smell. I covered all the pies in Saran Wrap and went to check on Rose and her potato salad.

"Come in," she called after I rapped gently on her door.

Rose stood at her kitchen sink crying her eyes out.

"What's wrong?" I put my hand on her shoulder.

"Nothing."

"But you're crying, Rose."

"Onions. I'm crying from the onions. And

once I got started, I couldn't stop."

"Onions are like that," I said. "Great way to get a good cry going."

She nodded and blubbered. I watched the tattoos on her arms and neck wiggle and dance as she burbled and sniffed.

"You want to cry some more?"

She nodded and kept crying.

"Okay. I'll just wait over here."

I noticed she had all the fixings for potato salad ready to go. Cooked potatoes, mayonnaise, celery, onions.

"Looks like you're making good salad, Rose."

She wiped her eyes on a dish towel. "The second batch of the day. My mama's recipe. Only one she ever gave me. Only one I know."

Rose had never mentioned her mother before.

"Is your mother still alive?"

"No. She died when I was fifteen. Believe it or not, she passed away right after making potato salad for the church picnic. Now, isn't that a hoot? She just sat down and died. Doctor said it was the oddest thing he ever seen."

I wrapped my arms around Rose. "Oh, dear, no wonder you want to cry."

Rose cried and buried her face in my

shoulder. "I'll get over it, but I don't think I can make the salad myself."

"I'll help."

Rose and I made enough salad to feed fifty people. She was fine once we got to mixing and never mentioned her mother again. I didn't bring it up either. The only problem was when I suggested we put a little pickle juice into the mix.

"There is no way I am putting pickle juice in my mother's recipe, Charlotte. Besides, I hate pickles."

"Fine. No pickle juice. But did I tell you about the pig?"

Rose mixed the salad with a large spoon. "What pig?"

"The Frost sisters slaughtered and butchered a hog for today's barbecue feast. Can you stand that? Imagine killing a hog."

"Is that what I smell?" she asked.

I opened her kitchen window a bit more. The aroma of roasting pig, sweet and savory, wafted into the kitchen. "It does smell good, Rose. But I still can't get over killing an animal like that."

"Happens every day, Charlotte, and if I know Edwina and Thomasina, they did it with reverence and compassion."

Rose thanked Jesus for the pig.

"So when is this shindig scheduled to

start?" Rose asked as she lifted her head.

I picked at the salad. "Yum, it's good. I figure folks will just start showing up, you know, assembling, finding their own way." I looked out the window. Folks were already starting to mingle in the street. It kind of looked like a scene from *The Night of the Living Dead.* But I figured they'd perk up once the festivities and food got rolling.

"Looks like they're all heading toward Asa's. There goes Greta and her kids. I see Clara and her husband."

"Yeah, Asa's got the largest property — next to the Frost farm, that is."

"And that giant barbecue."

"Right. The one he took from the fair."

"Took? You mean he stole a giant barbecue?"

Rose nodded.

That was when I started to laugh.

"What is so funny?"

"Nothing. I think I'm happy," I said. "My heart feels light, and my brain doesn't feel nearly as muddled as it did before, Rose. I think this is what it feels like to do good. To do something really good that makes other people happy."

Rose looked out the window. "Here comes Ginger. She's pulling a red wagon filled with — what is all that?"

Rose ran outside and I followed. "Ginger," Rose called. "What do you have in that wagon?"

"Necessaries," she called.

Rose stopped. "I got hamburger buns, pickle relish, ketchup, mustard, gumdrops, cream soda, and more hamburger buns."

"Where did you get it all?"

"I went to the store this morning. And oh, yeah. I got a couple of new shuttlecocks for badminton."

Rose sucked enough air for the three of us. "You? You went to the store? But you never go."

"I know. Asa does all my shopping, usually, but, I don't know, this morning I got the notion to go alone, and it —"

"Wasn't so bad?" I said.

Ginger stared up at me, dropped the wagon handle, and put her tiny fists on her tiny hips. "No. It was awful. People stared at me and pointed like I had just walked out of the circus train bound for Freakville. Saw a few people snicker when I couldn't reach the pickle relish. But I ignored them, Charlotte. I ignored them, climbed up on the shelves, and got what I wanted."

Rose smiled and then started to laugh. "You really climbed the shelves?"

"Like a ladder. But then a grocery boy

came and helped me. Nice young fella. But he was freaked out, you know. I mean, how often does he see a midget in tiny blue jeans, tie-dyed shirt, and love beads?"

If I were to venture a guess, I'd say there was close to forty people gathered at the end of Mango Street. Asa's trailer was small but tidy with a lot of ground around it. He had rose bushes, pink and purple azaleas, tulips, and the greenest grass I had ever seen, besides the grass on Angel Field. But that was when I realized — that man used the leftover sod on his own property. It was fine with me.

"Asa," I said. "You have such a nice place. I've been meaning to tell you."

"Thank you. It's home."

The oversized barbecue was set off to the side on the road, which was a cul-de-sac — just perfect for entertaining.

"That pig smells delicious already," Rose said. "When can we eat it?"

"Let me check on it," Asa said as he tightened the belt on his yellow apron.

Rose, Ginger, and I followed Asa to the barbecue. It was set up alongside three small ones that were manned by Jacob Pilkey. He was flipping burgers faster than I could count them.

"Howdy, Charlotte," he said. "Burger?"

"Not just yet. I'm waiting on that roast pig."

"Yeah, me too. But the younguns like the burgers."

That was when Charlie Lundy Junior and three or four other boys popped out from behind a tree. "Eww," Charlie whined when Asa lifted the lid of the grill. "It still gots its head. No eyes but it gots a head. I ain't eating no head."

"No, not the head," Asa said. "Just its brains. In a bowl like pudding." Then he made a bugaboo noise and frightened the children off.

Asa sliced into the hog with a long, sharp knife. "Looks like another hour, hour and a half."

"Maybe you should get the sauce on it," Jacob said. "Slather that piggy down."

"You go on and do that, will you, Jake? I have to go get Mrs. Crenshaw."

"Crenshaw? You mean that crusty old bird is coming to our party?" Jake asked.

"Why not?" I said. "She lives here too."

Jacob grabbed a pail of barbecue sauce with a paintbrush in it. "I ain't saying she ain't welcome, Charlotte. I'm just saying it's weird, is all."

Asa went off to get Hazel, and I watched

Jacob paint the hog down with sauce like he was painting the side of a barn. The sauce sizzled as it hit the hot grill and charbroiled smoke wafted into the air.

"I can't wait to try it," Ginger said.

"Me neither," I said. "I never saw a whole hog cooked before."

"Well, we can thank the Frost sisters," said Rose.

"I heard," Jacob said. "Imagine them killing Beatrice for us. She was like their dog."

I swallowed. "Wait a minute. Hold on a second. You mean they slaughtered their pet? We can't eat their pet."

Jacob laughed. "No. I'm just yanking your chain. They raise pigs for market over there. I'm sure you must have smelled them when the wind blows west."

My nose wrinkled instinctively. "That's what that smell is. I was afraid to ask, thought something was wrong with the septic system."

Fortunately, the pigs were kept downwind of the ball field.

Ginger decided to go play badminton with the children, and Rose said she needed to head back to her trailer for a few minutes, so I settled down with Lucky under a large, sprawling oak tree and admired the Rockwellian picnic scene.

"I haven't seen Suzy or Fergus yet," I said. "I guess he changed his mind."

But then out the corner of my eye I spotted Suzy down the road, standing all alone. Fergus was nowhere in my line of vision. I even stood and looked, but didn't see him.

"I'm gonna go talk to her, Lucky. You better stay —" but before I could finish my thought, Lucky bounded off toward the woods.

I ventured closer to Suzy, and when I got within a few yards, Fergus popped out from behind a car.

He grabbed my elbow and led me away between two trailers where no one could see. My heart pounded like a trip hammer. "What are you doing? Take your hands off me."

I shook my way free. But he grabbed onto me again. "You listen to me," he said. "You say one word to Hazel or anyone, and I'll kill Suzy, I swear I will. Do you understand? I'll kill her sure as I'm standing here."

He let me go. I stepped back and wanted to run. But where? To who? Instead I rushed to Suzy. "You all right?"

"Do as he says, Charlotte, please?"

"Suzy, you got to do something. Go to the police."

Fergus grabbed my elbow. His eyes grew wild. "Just keep your mouth shut. You got no right telling my wife what to do."

Then he draped his arm around Suzy's shoulders. "Do we have an understanding?"

"Please," Suzy whispered.

My knees shook like two twigs in a Nor'easter. "Okay. Okay. I won't say a word."

"Just see to it that you don't," Fergus said. "And don't ever talk to my wife again." He spoke through clenched teeth.

"I won't say a word." I mustered up my courage and moved closer to Suzy. He pulled a long knife from his boot. Showed it to me and then stuffed it back inside.

I took a breath and stuck my finger in his face. "But you promise. You promise right now you will never lay another hand on Suzy."

He didn't say anything. He just glared at me.

"He . . . he already promised, Charlotte," Suzy said. "Just this morning. Said he'd never hit me again."

25

Fergus took Suzy's hand, and I watched them walk off toward the party. I had to stay right there for a minute and catch my breath. But then I headed home. I dashed into the trailer. Lucky bounded over to me. He jumped up and licked my face. It was like he knew how rattled I felt. "It's okay, boy. It's okay. I think."

I flopped onto the couch. Lucky climbed up near me. I patted his side and head. His wiry whiskers tickled my arm and let me know I was still alive. "Oh, Lucky, you won't believe what just happened. That nasty Fergus threatened me. Well, he threatened Suzy, boy. Said he'd kill her if I told Hazel. If I didn't leave Suzy alone."

Lucky whimpered. He raised his bushy eyebrows and looked at me.

"He told me to never talk to Suzy again," I said.

I pushed Lucky's paws off my lap. "I better change my clothes. I peed a little during the whole experience."

After I changed into blue jeans and a sweatshirt, I headed back to the party, even though I didn't really want to. Lucky stayed right by my side as we made our way back. The air had turned a little cooler now that the sun was nearly down. Suzy and Fergus sat next to Hazel on bright yellow lawn chairs with clamshell backs. Hazel was in her perpetual state of hunch from the hump she had covered up with a green and blue shawl. She wore an orange knit hat with a plastic daisy sticking out of the top. Fergus and Suzy laughed like there was absolutely nothing wrong. And I knew Hazel felt good because she slapped her knee two times. Fergus told Hazel how Suzy had tripped over a pair of his clodhoppers, as he called them, and went sailing down the trailer steps.

"Of course I rushed her straight to the hospital," Fergus lied. "They x-rayed it. Just a tiny fracture, but she still needs that cast."

"Hazel," I said without looking at her or Fergus or Suzy. "I'm so glad you came. Is anyone getting you some food?"

"Sit down, child. Rose already went to get me a plate."

I sat near her. "Having a good time,

Suzy?" I asked.

Suzy nodded. "Yes, Ma'am. I am." She put up a good front.

Fergus held Suzy's hand like they were the happiest married couple in Paradise. It made my skin crawl to see her smile and gush over Fergus like he was Prince Charming. Fergus stood up and Suzy followed. He smiled at me, and I knew immediately what that smile meant.

"Come on, Suzy honey," Fergus said. "Let's you and me mingle a bit. I want some of that hog I been hearing so much about."

He never let go of her hand as they walked off toward the end of the road. But I could see he tightened his grip a little.

Rose brought Hazel a plate piled high with food.

"Great jumpin' lizards, girl," Hazel said. "You don't expect me to eat all that?"

"Just eat what you can, Hazel."

Paradise folks kept wandering by for the next few minutes, talking to Hazel, introducing themselves and saying how glad they were to finally meet her. But it was clear that none of them knew any more about her than that she was an old woman who didn't come out much and wore silly hats. Just Rose and Fergus and I knew that she owned the land they stood on, that she paid their salaries that bought their groceries that fed their babies. I wanted to scream it from the top of my lungs. And I wanted to scream the truth about Fergus.

Maybe in the crowd he couldn't do anything. Maybe I could snatch Suzy away from him. Maybe the other men would do to him what he had been doing to her. But I couldn't. Fergus acted so kind and considerate. Suzy appeared so happy and normal; I was afraid they'd all take *me* for the nutcase.

Hazel grabbed hold of my sleeve and pulled me toward her. "Aren't they just the sweetest couple, Charlotte?" She nodded toward the Wrinkels. "One of the happiest couples I have ever seen. They remind me of Birdy and me years ago, always holding hands, smooching in public."

I adjusted my feet as I fought the urge to blather out the truth.

She pulled a piece of something from her mouth and tossed it on the ground. "You know something, Charlotte. I'm glad I came out today."

I nodded and my heart broke into a million pieces. I had to fight back tears.

I turned my attention to Rose, "Can I speak with you, Rose?"

She nodded but looked confused. "Sure,

I'm right here."

"No, let's go get some of that pork. I'm a bit hungry."

"Go on, you two," Hazel said. "I'll just sit here a while until I'm ready to go home."

Lucky trotted off down the road to join two other dogs chasing squirrels.

Once we were out of sight of Hazel, I pulled Rose behind the large oak. "I got to tell you something."

"What? You look like you just witnessed a murder."

"Almost." And then I told her.

She leaned against the tree. "Are you okay?"

"I think my knees will wobble for days, and I might have added a million gray hairs to my head. He showed me a big knife."

Rose raised her arms. "Oh, dear Lord. What do we do now?"

"What about Asa? Should we tell him?"

Rose shook her head. "I'm afraid of what he would do. What if he went off half-cocked and did something stupid? Took the law into his own hands — or hand, so to speak. You know how he feels about her."

I only had time to shake my head before Ginger came by. She had hold of Lucky's collar. He was pretty much dragging her along. "Charlotte," she said, "you better speak with your pooch. He's been stealing burgers and buns right off the tables. Even got his snout in a bowl of that roast pork."

"Lucky," I said, "have you been stealing food?"

He sat back on his haunches and looked about as guilty as any criminal caught red-handed — or I should say red-snouted. He had barbecue sauce all over his face.

"I think I'll just take him on home."

"You don't have to do that," Ginger said. "Nobody's mad at him. We just don't want him eating all the food."

"Okay." I couldn't help but keep looking around, afraid that Fergus might appear out of nowhere.

"Are you all right, Charlotte?" Ginger asked. "You look about as nervous as a cat in a room full of rocking chairs."

"No, no, I'm fine. I just have a splitting headache all of a sudden. Maybe I need to lie down."

"Want me to walk you home?" Rose asked.

"No, you stay here and keep an eye on the Angels. Don't let them eat too much. We have a game in a couple of days. And would you bring my pie tins back later?"

"Sure, Charlotte," Rose said. "Maybe take an aspirin or two, or better yet, find Marla-beth and ask her for a remedy for a case of nerves. I'm sure she has something."

"I will."

But I knew no amount of aspirin or tea in the world was going to get rid of this headache. As I made my way home, I thought of Herman again. "What would you tell me?"

"A man's home is his castle and his own business," that's what he would say. "You should have left well enough alone. Don't meddle in other people's business."

That thought gave me the stomps, and I stomped all the way home.

"It's not right, Lucky," I said as I pushed the door open. "How come a man can get away with this? Man's home is his castle. Pish. Then a woman's home is her castle."

Lucky went inside first, as always, to check things out. This time I was glad. Who knew what Fergus was capable of?

I sat at my kitchen table for the better part of an hour. Generally speaking, when I felt upset I would bake pies, but I had used all the ingredients and that night I felt a little too shaken up to even peel an apple.

The aroma of the roast pig and grilled burgers still drifted through my open windows. It was such a pretty night. I could see about a gazillion stars through the tree tops. I'll say this for Paradise, when it's dark, it's dark. And since most of the trailerites were still at Asa's, the usual trailer lights were still dim. I couldn't help but think again about what Rose said. "God calls each star by name, Charlotte. He puts them in their places."

That notion stuck in my throat that night. I just couldn't understand why and how a God so powerful that he commands the stars in the heavens could let a young woman suffer like that. Why in heaven's name didn't he stop Fergus?

At nine o'clock I started to feel a skosh better. My stomach rumbled, and I realized I had not had any of the hog. "Darn you, Fergus," I said out loud. "You ruined the barbecue for me."

Lucky scrambled from the kitchen floor. "I know, boy, you didn't either. Well, I'm sure there will be leftovers and maybe Rose will bring us some."

I put the tea kettle on. "Man's home is his castle, huh, well maybe if he's fit to be king."

I grabbed a cup and a tea bag and sat at the table and fiddled with my wedding ring. It had become extra noticeable lately. In all the years we were married I barely paid it any attention. But since Herman died, it became apparent, like the hole a missing tooth leaves.

"So, God," I said, looking at the night sky. "You really up there? You paying attention at all? If you are, tell me what to do."

The kettle whistled. I poured water into my cup and let the tea steep a couple of minutes. I didn't like strong tea. Dropped the bag in the trash and poured a small amount of half-and-half into the tea. But before I sat down, I slipped the gold band off my finger. It came off with a little bit of a tug at the knuckle. I put it in my palm and rolled it around. Then I slipped it back on.

"Not yet, God. Not yet."

Rose came by a little before ten.

"The party is breaking up," she said. "I brought you your tins. Not a lick of pie was left. But I managed to grab you a plate of pork and beans and potato salad."

I took the tins and set them in the sink. "Thank you. Did you see Suzy after I left?"

Rose shook her head and sat at the kitchen table. "Now, don't get yourself all worked up when I say this, but, yes, I saw her. She and Fergus looked to be having a great time."

"But you know, Rose; you know the truth?" I leaned against the kitchen counter.

"I do. I do know, Charlotte. I just wanted you to know that for the time being anyway, they seemed fine."

"It was just a show for Hazel. I have half a mind to tell her anyway."

"But can you take that chance?"

I rolled the ring around my finger again. "I guess not. She's not ready yet."

Rose didn't speak immediately. "No, she's not. But she will be. Something will happen to make her ready."

"Like what?" I sipped my tea. And then I broke off a chunk of pork. It melted in my mouth it was so tender and tasty. I slipped a chunk to Lucky. He swallowed it whole then rolled onto his back making yummy noises, begging for more.

"Don't know. But there will come a day when Suzy has had enough."

"So we wait," I said. "We just sit idly by and wait."

"Sometimes waiting is the hardest thing to do but also the best thing to do. Wait and trust, Charlotte. God has Suzy in his palm too, you know."

26

The next day was, of course, Sunday, and that meant church. Rose came by early enough to ask if I was going and, I suspected, to check on me.

"No," I said. "I think I'll stay home today."

"You sure, Charlotte?" Rose helped herself to coffee. "You had quite a scare yesterday. Church might be the best thing."

"I'm sure, Rose. You go on."

Rose sipped her coffee. "I understand, Charlotte."

"Maybe while you're there you can ask God why he's letting this happen."

"That's not the right question. I'll just ask him what we should do now."

"Yeah, Fergus has the whole ball of wax in his court. What *are* we supposed to do now?"

Rose snagged my ball and glove from the kitchen counter. She tossed the ball in the air and caught it. "Softball, Charlotte. Right now we're supposed to play softball."

Lucky, who had been resting at my feet, jumped up like he had been stung and lapped water from his bowl with loud, obnoxious laps.

"That dog thinks he's so smart. He drinks a gallon of water, then he has to run outside to pee. It's just an excuse to chase squirrels. He thinks I'm not on to his tricks."

"So are we having a practice later? We should get everyone together before the big game on Tuesday. I know I can use the practice."

"Sure, sure. I'll call a practice for tomorrow. We'll drill through the fundamentals again. That's the only way we'll win that game — back to basics. Nothing fancy."

Rose tossed me the ball and said, "Now you sound like Coach Charlotte. I'll see you later."

I dusted and then scrubbed out the tub and washed the kitchen floor just to make time fly, but I admit I felt rattled and kept Lucky nearby except when he used his doggie door to do his business. Asa had put it in for me when he patched a hole in my roof. "It'll just make it easier for Lucky and you," he said. "Won't have to get out of bed too early in the morning if you don't want to. Especially when it gets cold."

After I scrubbed the bathroom and vacuumed, I felt a trifle better and sat down with a bowl of potato chips to watch the Phillies game when the phone rang.

"Hello?"

"Charlotte, dear, this is your mother."

"I know, Mom. How are you?"

"To tell the truth, not so great. My arthritis is kicking up — you know, in my hip, and I've had just a splitting headache for days now. Doctor said it was nothing to worry about, so I got to thinking that a change of scenery might be the ticket. I've decided to come stay with you in Paradise, dear. For the summer."

I dropped the telephone into the bowl on my lap, and potato chips flew all over the place.

"Charlotte? Charlotte?" I could hear her without even putting the phone to my ear. "Did you hear me, dear? You still there? Or is it that lousy mountain phone connection again?"

I picked up the phone. "Here? With me? But why, Mother? You love it at Cocoa Reef."

"Of course, I do, but I need to get away from all of these old people down here. I am not as old as them."

337

"Yes, you are, Mother."

She snorted air into the phone. "Well, according to my driver's license I might be, but not in spirit, Charlotte. Bunch of old fogies around here. A woman can only take so much. Why, just the other day I got another flyer about a Summer Under the Stars Dance. Goodness gracious, I am not the sock hop type, Charlotte. It's embarrassing to see all the old curmudgeons shaking their booty, as the kids say these days. I hate the disco music."

"You should go. You might make a friend."

"And then on the flyer which looked like it was drawn in crayon, it said if your last name begins with A-M to bring a salad. The N-Z's get to bring dessert. Why do the A-Ms always get salad, Charlotte?"

"Salad comes before dessert, I guess."

"Precisely, dear. No one down here wants to take the chance on change. Charlotte, I'm telling you I need to get away. I need dessert before salad."

"But why here? Go to Bermuda or the South of France or Italy. You always wanted to go to Italy."

"Only if you come with me. Charlotte, come to Italy with me."

I felt my blood pressure rise. I loved my mother dearly, but the idea of traveling clear

across the globe with her gave me the willies. She'd probably think it would be fun to
go by ship, a nice, slow ship.

"I can't, Mother. I have the Angels."

"The what?"

"Angels. Softball."

I heard her mutter something to my
father's picture. "That stupid softball thing
again. Aren't you too old for softball? Come
to Italy. I'll pay for everything."

"The team is important to me." I wandered around the trailer with the phone in
my hand. Fortunately, Asa had put an extra
long cord on it for me. I could even go out
back if I wanted. "Lucky," I called. I just
that minute realized I hadn't seen him and
he always came running when Grandmom
called.

"Who?" Lillian asked.

"I'm looking for my dog."

"Now, look, Charlotte, it's all arranged. I
arrive tomorrow afternoon. I'll taxi out."

"I could come get you."

"No, no. I still can't get used to you driving that big old Herman car. I'd rather take
my chances on a cab."

"Fine. I have to go find Lucky."

I hung up the phone. "Lucky, Lucky," I
called. He didn't come and my heart
pounded. My thoughts turned to Fergus.

"No," I said. "He wouldn't."

I pulled open the front door and called. Three times, four, then tore into the yard looking for my dog. Hazel was in her front yard. "Did you see Lucky?" I hollered across the street.

She shrugged, at least I thought it was a shrug. Hard to tell with Hazel and that hump. "No, Charlotte."

I sat on my wooden walkway as tears streamed down my cheeks. "Lucky," I cried. "Where are you?"

A few moments later I heard rustling behind the trailer and went to investigate, thinking it was just some raccoons or Old Man Hawkins flushing out Nazis or Red Coats or whoever the enemy du jour was.

"Here's your dog back." Fergus held Lucky by the neck. He had him muzzled.

"You creep," I said. "How dare you?"

Fergus ripped off the muzzle, and Lucky barked to high heaven and ran to me. He snarled and growled and bared his teeth at Fergus.

"Just remember, Charlotte. This is our little secret. You tell no one about Suzy. Let this be a lesson. I mean what I say." Then he walked off like a pompous pigeon, like he hadn't a care in the world.

I took Lucky into the house, where I

checked him all over for cuts or scrapes or bruises. "Lucky, I'm so sorry. Are you all right?" He licked my face as his stubby little tail wiped the linoleum. "Did that mean old Fergus hurt you?"

After another minute or so Lucky found his water bowl. I gave him two large Milk-Bones and then I called Mother.

"Hello?" she said.

"Mother, it's me, Charlotte." My heart raced.

"I know that. What is it? If you're calling to try and —"

"No, Mother. I just called to say, I'm glad you're coming."

27

Monday arrived with bright sunshine and a slight breeze that puffed the curtains in my bedroom windows. I breathed in the fresh air that had a tinge of honeysuckle on it. "Now, this, this is what I think we came to Paradise for," I told Lucky. I plumped up my pillows behind me and closed my eyes, trying to put the events of the previous day aside and daydreamed of what it would be like when all the repairs were completed and my trailer was finally finished. I imagined yellow and white striped awnings on every window and pink and purple trailing verbena and bright red bromeliads blooming in hanging baskets. For a few short minutes I forgot about Fergus and his threats. I let my mind wander and watched the Angels score run after run until I remembered Lillian DeSalle was coming to town.

I stood on the front stoop and kept a

watchful eye on Lucky. I was not about to let him out of my sight. I also decided to put the whole Fergus incident in a different brain compartment and concentrate on the game. The way I saw it, right then there was nothing I could do that would not jeopardize Suzy's life.

Lucky sniffed around the maple tree a while, and then I called him. "Come on, boy. Time for breakfast."

I filled Lucky's bowl with kibble and then opened a can of stinky Alpo, which I dumped into his other bowl. "There you go, fella. Eat hearty. Your grandmother is coming later."

He looked at me with raised eyebrows as he slurped his Beef Banquet.

"That's right. Grandmom is coming."

Of course, she didn't bother to give me a time. But I had scheduled a practice for ten o'clock that morning. We had perfect softball weather. There was no call for rain today or tomorrow. I gathered my glove and coaching notes and headed over to the field.

All the Angels were present. Rose was already in her shin guards and Asa was pitching to her. I loved to watch him catch the ball in one hand and then pitch it back. He was like a machine.

"Good morning," I called as I waved

everyone around.

"Morning, Charlotte," Marlabeth said. "That sure was a great barbecue."

I nodded and everyone took turns exclaiming their joy at eating roast hog and burgers, pie and corn, and watching the children scramble around.

"And did you see Suzy?" Ginger said. "She and Fergus looked like two peas in a pod, happy and joyful."

I shot Rose a glance, "Okay, okay, let's get started."

Greta, who was off with the children, ran toward me. "We can't start until Fleur de Lee shows up. She's supposed to watch the little varmints again."

"She's not here? Asa, were you supposed to get her?"

"No one said anything to me, but I'll run on over to Haven House and snag her."

"Thanks."

Greta went back to the kids, who scrambled like roaches all over the Frost Sisters' property.

"Let's just run some bases," I said. "Greta won't run the bases, anyway."

"Not until she's done nursing Ruth."

I snapped my fingers. "I want you all to know that my mother, Lillian DeSalle, is coming to visit. She'll be here later, today, and I would appreciate it if you all gave her a warm welcome."

"Sure, sure, we will, Charlotte." And they took off around the bases. Ginger led the pack, as usual.

Asa arrived a short time later with Fleur de Lee, who headed straight for the children with a definitely more pronounced waddle.

"Now remember, Marlabeth," I said. "Keep your eye on the ball and swing through. Don't flinch partway."

Marlabeth swung six times without hitting the ball. Well, not really. She got a piece of one but fouled it off.

Greta stepped up to the batter's box. She slapped home plate twice with her bat and then got into her stance. "Say, Marlabeth," she said. "Fleur de Lee is looking a little uncomfortable today. She's got the penguin wobble something fierce. Maybe you should check her."

"She's not due for two weeks. Baby might have dropped, though. I'll check her before she goes back to Haven House."

Frankie pitched and Greta swung hard, hitting a line drive right over Ginger's head, which admittedly was not hard to do, and into center field where Edwina snagged it and tossed to first. Greta was safe by two strides.

I stood there and applauded. It was a tremendous effort. The Angels had become a team. We practiced for another hour before I called it quits.

"Come on in," I called. "Gather around."

The Angels formed a circle around me. "Great practice today, but let's quit now. I don't want to wear you all out or risk an injury before tomorrow."

"Ah, Charlotte," Frankie said, "can't we play a little longer?"

"Yeah, please," the others agreed.

"No, no. Let's just make this an easy day. Tomorrow will be here soon enough."

After putting away the equipment, the team scattered. Marlabeth spoke with Fleur de Lee. Rose and I watched from the sidelines.

"She is mighty pregnant," Rose said.

"And she's not even due for two weeks."

"Maybe sooner," Rose said.

Marlabeth felt her belly and shook her head. I watched her raise two fingers. "Looks like Marlabeth thinks Fleur de Lee still has some time."

That was when Asa dashed over. "I'll take her back to Haven House," he said on his way past.

Rose and I walked home together.

"So, your mother is really coming."

I sucked air and blew it out my nose. "Yep. Later today."

"That will be nice."

I laughed. "Maybe. But my mother can be such a pain in the —"

"How long is she staying?"

"Alllllll summer." I dragged out the word *all* for emphasis.

"Yikes," Rose said. "I'll pray for you."

"Thanks. But she's not all *that* bad. Not really. I try not to let her get to me."

We made our way through the woods and out onto the road.

"Oh, no," I said. "Look at that!"

Rose followed my finger with her eyes. "What? It's a taxi. So what?"

"My mother. She's here." I swallowed. "Want to meet her?"

Rose twisted her mouth and shuffled her feet. "I would love to meet your mother, but I need a shower first. I don't want to make a bad first impression."

"Listen, with my mother, any impression is most likely a bad one."

Sure enough, Lillian waited on my wooden path with six pieces of luggage, two boxes secured with string, what looked like a hatbox, and a gilded birdcage that carried her parakeet, Tweety.

I waved with a circular swipe of my hand. "Mother. I would have met you, but I didn't know what time you were arriving."

"Charlotte." She set the cage down and walked toward me. I walked toward her. "You look skinny, dear," she said. "Have you lost weight?"

I kissed her cheek and then pulled her in for a hug. "Mom, I'm glad you're here."

She pulled away from me. "Really? You're really glad? You're not just saying that?"

"No. I am truly glad."

We stood there a second eyeing each other until she turned around, stared long and hard at my trailer, and said, "You do know it is the color of the inside of an Andes Crème de Menthe Mint."

"Yes, Mother. I'm aware. I'm planning on having it painted."

Mother took the birdcage and a small bag. I pushed open the door and watched my mother take a breath like she was diving off a cliff, then walk inside. Lucky wasted no time greeting her and practically pushed her outside. She teetered on the threshold, still clutching the birdcage. I grabbed Tweety, and she grabbed the door jamb. "Lucky," I said. "Down, boy."

"That brute," Lillian said. "He almost killed me."

"You better go outside," I told the dog, and he gave me a dejected look and scampered outside.

"Well, you didn't have to banish him," Lillian said. "He just surprised me. I forgot you said you got a dog."

"He'll be fine, Mother. He'll play with the squirrels."

She looked around the trailer. "So, this is it."

"Yes. I'm still fixing it up, but it has some real charm, doesn't it, Mother?"

She moved toward the kitchen, following the natural slope of the as-yet-unleveled trailer. "Oh dear, Charlotte, is it supposed to do that?"

"You mean the slope?"

"Yes, I . . . I feel dizzy, dear. Perhaps I should sit."

I helped her to the sofa. "Just sit and let me get your stuff."

I handed off the bird to her. She sat there with the cage on her knees while I hauled her luggage inside and set it in the extra bedroom. She followed me. "Is this my room?" She stepped over the threshold still carrying the cage and set it on the dresser.

"He can't stay there, of course. You wouldn't happen to have one of those stands for cages, would you, Charlotte? You know

349

what I mean, the kind with a hook you can hang the cage from?" She opened a small case and took out my father's picture. She kissed it and then put it on the dresser.

I shook my head, wondering why she would think I would have a birdcage stand. "Sorry, but I suppose we could buy one."

"Maybe later," she said as she pushed on the mattress. "Too bad the Fuller Brush didn't sell bird supplies."

"The mattress is practically brand-new," I said.

"It's not too soft, is it? You know my back and all."

"It's fine, Mother. Now, you must have had a long day. Would you like to freshen up? Are you hungry?"

She glanced at her watch. "It's only a little before one. But I am kind of tired and a bit shaken, to tell the truth, Charlotte. That silly pilot found every air pocket in the sky. I was a perfect nervous Nellie the whole trip. Perhaps a nap would soothe my frazzled nerves. You can help me unpack later. I'll just rest in my traveling clothes."

"That's fine. The sheets are fresh and I was going to bring some flowers but you got here a little earlier than —"

"It's okay, Charlotte. Flowers just make my nose itch anymore."

"Should I wake you or —"

"I'll wake myself, dear."

"Not unless Old Man Hawkins wakes her first," I whispered.

She sat on the edge of the bed and slipped off her sensible shoes. "What did you say?"

"Nothing. Have a good rest. I'll make us a nice dinner."

"Don't go to any trouble."

I closed the door and took a deep breath, which I held until I got to the living room and flopped onto the sofa. Lucky placed a paw on my knee and looked at me as if to say, "So, how long is she staying?"

"Just until Labor Day," I said. "Not long, two months or so." I chewed a nail and spit it on the floor. "Two months . . . or so."

28

I invited Rose, Asa, and Ginger for dinner, hoping that the three of them would provide a buffer between me and my mother. I was not about to tell her about Fergus's threats, but she had a way of weaseling information out of me, which was probably why I was such a lousy secret keeper. Once, she got me to spill the beans when I discovered quite by accident that our neighbor Nathan Frye was having an affair with our other neighbor Chili Culpepper. It turned out ugly.

After Mother and I unpacked her clothes and placed them neatly in the drawers and on hangers, she set about rearranging the room to suit her taste. She placed the striped chair away from the window, saying she didn't care for too much sunlight and preferred the lamp while reading. Then she took out her own towels and arranged them in my bathroom. "I just like my yellow towels, Charlotte. All yellow, all the same."

Then she wandered into my kitchen carrying Tweety like Diogenes carried a lamp. I stood there frozen, waiting for her to rearrange my pots and pans and dishes, but fortunately she didn't. "You do have tea, Charlotte. If not, I brought along some Earl Grey." She put Tweety on the counter.

"I do, Mother. Tetley."

She waved it away. "Tetley. You mean in bags?"

"Yes. It's good."

"No, no. I like the loose leaf. I'll just get my infuser."

I turned the fire on under the kettle and finished peeling the potatoes I had started before she returned with a canister of tea, a dainty little tea cup with four-leaf clovers all around it, and a funny-looking tea ball.

She dangled it in front of me. "Do you remember this? I got it from the mayor of San Francisco during a buying trip."

"I remember, Mother."

"Delightful man. But not as delightful as your father." She clutched her chest and swooned just a tad. "I do miss that man." She sat at the table.

My father had been dead ten years.

"I invited some friends for dinner. I hope you don't mind," I said.

"No, no. Your friends are my friends."

I opened the oven door and checked my meat loaf.

"What is that, dear? A meatloaf? What is that all over it?"

"Walnuts. It's encrusted with chopped walnuts. My own recipe."

"Walnuts? Good heavens, I knew I should have sent you to cooking school. Or is that something that Herman conjured up for you to make? It sounds just wacky enough."

I ignored her and prepared broccoli. Truth was that Herman liked my walnut-encrusted meatloaf, especially around Christmastime when I made it with cranberries.

Ginger arrived first. I stood at the door looking at her for a minute before inviting her inside. In that short amount of time my mind filtered through all the possible insults my mother could muster, and all I could do was shake my head.

"Come on in, Ginger. Face my . . . I mean, meet my mother."

Lillian brought her tea into the living room. She towered over Ginger by almost four feet. Lillian DeSalle was a tall woman, nearly five feet eleven inches. She always said it made being a woman in a man's world easier. I could imagine what she would think of Ginger.

Ginger reached up her hand. "Pleased to meet you."

"Well, hello there, little gir—"

"Mother," I said, "this is Ginger Rodgers. She's on the team."

"And I'm thirty-two years old," she said. "No relation to the dancer, and I am pleased to meet you, anyway."

My mother shook her hand, nearly elevating Ginger off the floor like she was pumping a car jack. "Oh, that's right. The midget shortstop."

My heart stopped. Maybe Ginger didn't hear.

Ginger hopped up on the sofa. "Meatloaf, Charlotte? Smells good."

"Yep. Walnut-encrusted meatloaf with mashed potatoes and broccoli."

"Yum," Ginger said. "Sounds great."

My mother and Ginger continued to stare at each other in a most unnerving way. I searched my brain for something to say, something that would break the Mexican standoff. Mercifully, Asa and Rose arrived.

"Thank goodness," I said when I heard the knock.

"What did you say, dear?" Lillian asked.

"Nothing, Mother."

"She's just glad the other guests are here,"

Ginger said. "Maybe you'll stop staring at me."

Lillian turned her head toward the door. "Well, let your dinner guests in, Charlotte."

"Hello," I said. "Come on in. Meet my mother."

Rose, wearing that heavy sweater again, went in first. "Lillian," she said. "It's a pleasure to meet you."

My mother didn't stand, but offered Rose her hand.

"So nice to meet you, Rose. You're the artist, correct?"

"I am," Rose said. "But —"

"Now, don't be shy. Don't hide your light under a bushel the way Charlotte did."

Asa extended his left hand. I watched my mother notice the empty sleeve.

"Goodness gracious," she said. "What happened to your arm, young man?"

Asa laughed. "Now, that's refreshing. Most folks try to ignore it."

"A missing arm is hard to ignore even if you can't see it," Mother said.

"Kind of like little people," Ginger said. "We prefer to be called little people, not midgets."

"Now, I meant no offense, dear," Lillian said. "Kind of like little people. Some things are just too obvious to ignore."

I served dinner in the living room since my kitchen was so small. But it went well and everything turned out just right, if I said so myself. Even Mother had little to say, except that meatloaf was not her favorite food and, "Not what I would call an entrée suitable for a dinner party." She sneaked two or three bites to Lucky on the sly. He was most appreciative and enjoyed my meatloaf but left the nuts, as always.

"I mean, honestly, dear, I would love to know what went through your mind the day you decided to cover a perfectly good meatloaf with crushed walnuts."

The apple pie a la mode for dessert was a hit. Mother enjoyed ice cream. Even at her age she would eat ice cream every day if she could. The conversation drifted to the softball team, and my mother made her feelings quite clear.

"It makes no sense to me why my daughter left a perfectly nice home in the suburbs to come to a . . . a trailer land to play softball." She said this directly to Rose like I was not even in the room.

"Park," Asa said. "It's a trailer park. Not a trailer land."

"Oh, is that right?" Mother said. "Park seems a funny name for this kind of place. When I think of a park, I think of trees and grass and children on swings, not metal houses lined up like sardines."

"They call it *park* because folks park their homes here," I said.

Morning arrived with clear skies, a slight breeze, and the excitement of our first game. I woke early enough to enjoy a cup of coffee on the stoop before my mother woke. Hazel was already in her yard tending to the birds. She wore her purple shawl and a yellow knit hat.

"Morning," she called.

I raised my cup to her.

"Was that your mother I saw with all those bags?" Hazel was old, but she could holler like a woman who had been hollering out city windows her whole life.

I nodded and raised my cup again.

She waved me over.

I checked inside first and Mother was still asleep. I could hear her snore from the front door. Lucky and I walked across the street.

"Today's the big day," Hazel said. She poured seed into a red bowl and set it on a log.

"It is. We play the Thunder at seven this

evening."

"A night game."

"They all are since most of the players and coaches have day jobs."

Hazel made her way to a row of birdhouses she had nailed to the fence rail. "I just know that Whistlesnook is coming back."

"I hope he does, Hazel."

She fiddled with a little door on one of her houses constructed to look like a forest cottage. "Dang fool things. Why do they put so much nonsense on them? It's cute and all, but that Whistlesnook is looking for food, not accommodations."

I laughed. "Hazel, I'd like you to meet my mother. I could bring her by this morning."

"Oh, my, my, thanks, but not this morning; I'm feeling a little peaked. How long is she staying?"

"All summer."

"All summer? My, oh my, Charlotte, then we'll have plenty of time for a get-together."

"I better get back, Hazel. My mother will be awake soon."

"Just see to it that you beat the snot out of Vangarten's team."

"We will. Don't you worry. Are you coming to the game?"

She shook her head.

"Okay, I'll see you later." I would have tried to convince her to come but thought it might have been better that she didn't attend the first game. And maybe getting her out to the barbecue was all the excitement she wanted to handle for a while.

When I got back to the trailer, Mother was just coming out of her room.

"Morning," I said. "I made coffee."

"Charlotte," Mother said. "You'll have to get me a board."

"Aboard? Aboard what?"

"Not aboard a ship or anything. I mean a board, a piece of thin wood, for under that saggy mattress. My back feels all tight."

I smiled to myself. I knew what she meant. She placed her hand on the small of her back and limped toward the kitchen. "Think I'll sit in one of those straight backs for now."

I put a cup of coffee in front of her. "I'm sorry, Mom. I'll get Asa to bring you something."

"Asa?"

"The one-armed man."

"My goodness but this place is full of odd ducks. Already I counted a woman with tattoos. She's not hiding anything, not really. I saw them. Why in the heck any woman would want to disgrace her body like that is beyond me."

"You don't know her story."

"And then I meet a midget, a real-life midget, and a one-armed man. Charlotte. I think you lost your ever-lovin' mind. I think you blew a fuse."

I spent most of the morning trying to convince my mother that Paradise was not the loony bin she figured it to be and was getting pretty close to a breakthrough when Old Man Hawkins decided to make another mid-morning ride through Paradise shouting that the British were coming.

She ran to the window. "Holy cats, Charlotte! There is a man on a horse out there. With a gun!"

"He thinks he's Paul Revere, Mother. He's harmless."

Then I heard gunshots. Mother dropped to the floor. "Call the police, Charlotte. Call the police, or don't you have cops around here? Harmless, my eye. He's a crazy man."

Hawkins's ride did not last long. Asa and Rube took him and his horse home. It quieted down, but Mother was now on a mission to take me back to Cocoa Reef with her to live.

"You'll be safe there. Meet a nice retired gentleman, a man with sensibilities, refinement, and settle down. A man who knows

361

how to treat a woman right. Not like that salesman you married — against my wishes, you know."

"Mother, I am fifty-one years old. Old enough to make my own choices for my own life. I am not interested in romance. Herman hasn't been gone for very long, you know."

"Fifty-one is still young enough to have your fires lit, Charlotte, or don't you care about that either?"

"Mother! If we're talking about what I think we're talking about, well, it's not your business. I am not interested in romance."

"Uh-huh." She opened a loaf of raisin toast. "Scramble me an egg, please."

"Fine. And then I have to get to the ball field and make sure things are ready for the game. We play our first regulation this evening."

"That's nice, dear."

"Would you like to come and watch?"

She put her hand on the small of her back and contorted into a painful-looking position. "Oh, I don't know. All that turbulence and then sleeping on that mattress was quite enough. I don't know if I could sit on hard bleachers. I imagine that's where the spectators will sit."

"We don't have bleachers, Mother. But

someone will have an extra lawn chair, I'm sure."

"You mean one of those plastic folding things?" She waved the thought away. "I'd rather sit on hard bleachers."

Mother took her coffee and shuffled like she was a hundred and two, not seventy-two, all the way to the sofa. Lucky came in through his doggie door and leaped onto the couch next to her. Fortunately, she had just placed her cup on the end table.

"Lucky," I said, "you get down from there."

Mother grabbed onto his collar. "It's okay, Charlotte. He can stay." She patted his head. His tongue lolled out, and I swear he got the sneakiest gleam in his eye, like he had now become Grandmom's favorite boy. "It will be nice having him in Florida."

I felt my eyebrows arch. "Did you tell him you were taking him to Florida?"

She laughed. "Now, don't be silly. This dog does not understand human talk."

I was never quite so sure about that.

29

And so the time arrived for our game. The Angels had assembled, all wearing their bright new uniforms with the name *Elsmere Elastic* embroidered on the back.

Frankie was so pleased with hers that she modeled it for the team like she was Twiggy. "And see here," she said looking at her chest. "It says A-N-G-E-L-S." She spelled it out. "Angels. That's us."

Asa and Studebaker did a great job of chalking new lines and a batter's box. They even redrew the halo in the batter's circle. The grass was cut perfectly in a crisscross pattern, which gave it a real professional look. The boys had even set long purple benches along the sidelines. One for the Angels and one for the opposing team.

"You guys are amazing," I said.

"It was fun," Studebaker said. "Asa tells me you need someone to man the score-board."

I looked over at the monstrosity of a board standing over right field. "I do. I need someone to change numbers as the runs are scored."

"I can't," Asa said. "I'm coaching third base."

I looked at Studebaker. "There will be pie in it for you."

"Pie. You mean something besides Full Moon Pie?"

I nodded. "Dutch apple with raisins."

"Okay, why not?"

I sent the Angels out on the field to toss a ball around and take some batting practice. "But just have fun. Don't get tired. Don't forget, the Thunder stink."

Rose stayed with me and helped me organize everything else that needed organizing. We set extra bats against the cyclone fence that separated the field from the onlookers, put water jugs out, and orange slices and pumpkin seeds. I always liked to have orange slices and pumpkin seeds available to the team.

At six-thirty I saw a red school bus drive onto the Frost property.

"Here they come," I said. And I waved the Angels in. We all stood there and watched the Thunder get off the bus. It was not we expected.

I counted twenty players, twenty huge and husky players in pale blue uniforms. And last, but certainly not least, Cash Vangarten, also wearing a uniform.

"We've been duped."

The Angels gathered around, and we all stood there with our mouths open, including Asa and Studebaker. "I don't believe it," I said as they marched across the field like Hannibal's army across the Alps. I made eye contact with Vangarten. He smiled most nastily.

I clapped my hands and gathered my team. "Okay, Angels. Stop looking like you've already been beaten. So what if they're big?"

"Big," said Greta. "They're Amazons. They're bigger than Amazons. They're whatever comes after Amazons in the food chain, Charlotte."

"Okay, so what if they're extra-large Amazons? It doesn't mean they can play ball; probably trip over their huge, clown feet. We can take them. Just remember the fundamentals. Nothing fancy. No hotdogging, no unnecessary risks. Just hit and catch and throw. We'll do okay."

On the outside I tried to give a pep talk, but inside I shook like the last leaf of autumn on the last oak in the forest. I spied

Ginger, who looked like she had met her doom.

"And Ginger," I said. "You be extra careful. Last thing I need is a flat midget — excuse me, little person — I have to scrape off the field."

"Don't worry, Charlotte. I can run right through their legs if I have to, you know."

"We can do this!" shouted Clara. She put her hand in the circle. Greta put her hand on top of Clara's, and so on until we were all in.

"All for one," shouted Ginger, who stood in the middle under the stack of hands. We had used her head as a hand stand, so to speak.

"Knock 'em dead!" Frankie hollered.

"Let's do this," Rose said. "But first —"

And then she lifted her hands to heaven and prayed. "Almighty God, we need your mercy today. This team is large, Lord God, very large and strong. But we can go against this army. We might be a motley crew of Davids facing a team of Goliaths, but with your help and strength we can come out victorious."

"And don't let them kill any of us," said Marlabeth. "Especially Ginger Rodgers."

Just as she said those words, I had an image of their large third baseman rolling over

Ginger like a boulder.

The fans started to gather. They came with lawn chairs and blankets, coolers and picnic baskets. I was both delighted and scared to death. Here was Paradise all ready to watch their Angels win, when all I could think about was how in the world I would find enough gauze and tape to patch them all up. I thought maybe I should send the children home to roll bandages.

Fleur de Lee arrived with Jaster. I waved. I didn't think it was possible, but she appeared even more pregnant than just yesterday. She waddled like a duck to a waiting lawn chair, plopped down, and rested her hands on her belly. Jaster stood right next to her like a sentry.

"I better go speak to Fleur de Lee, Charlotte," Marlabeth said. "She looks awfully uncomfortable."

"Okay, go ahead, but get right back. We need to take the field in just a minute or two."

I looked around for my mother. I didn't see her, but I didn't really expect her. She was home making plans with Lucky to move us down to Florida.

"Okay, Angels," I called. "Take the field."

I strolled over to the Thunder's side thinking I'd shake Vangarten's hand in a display of good sportsmanship, but about halfway there I saw a couple of his players snicker and point at Ginger. She was in position at shortstop. I looked them square in the eye, shook my head, and went back to my side, but not before I heard someone say, "They got to be kidding. They got a midget on their team. This ain't the peewee league."

I raised my hands to heaven like Rose did whenever frustration set in. "Lord, help us now."

Asa was out on the pitcher's circle with Frankie, probably giving her some pointers. I wished I had done some spying of my own or at least tried to get a scouting report on the Thunder. But no, I believed Cash Vangarten when he said his team stank to the high heavens. Herman always said I was gullible, like a sponge.

Greta, Edwina, and Thomasina tossed a ball back and forth in the outfield and looked pretty good, but I knew it wouldn't take much for one of the Thunder women to sail a ball over their heads and probably into the Frost sister's cornfield.

There was precious little I could do for my team now but watch and encourage them to keep going and concede the game at first blood.

The umpire, a middle-aged man with a

paunch, called the team captains together.

Frankie came off the field and stood next to me. Cash Vangarten strutted toward us, accompanied by the largest, most square-shouldered, shortest-haired woman I had ever seen. Now, I am not saying she was a bulldog or anything, I mean she had the prettiest little face, but I got to say she could have been Paul Bunyan's kid sister.

"Okay," the ump said. "You all know the rules. No stealing. No taking leads off bases, no cussing, and if one team scores ten or more runs before the fifth inning, it is at the losing team's discretion to concede the game."

Frankie curled her lip. "Never happen."

I touched her arm, wanting her to settle and not get overconfident.

Missy — that was their team captain's name — reached out her hand and Frankie reached up and took it. "We're gonna kill you," Missy said with clenched teeth. Missy growled. She actually growled like a grizzly.

Pride filled my heart. Frankie never backed down. I shook Cash's hand and our eyes met again and I think my toes might have curled in my Keds when I noticed just how blue his eyes were — like crystal lakes.

"Play ball!" hollered the ump.

I went back to the sidelines, and on my

way I saw my mother and Hazel hobbling out of the woods. "Oh, my goodness gracious," I said to no one. "They came."

I waved until Mother found me and waved back. They marched right up to our purple bench and sat down like they belonged there. Hazel wore a dark brown shawl and a wide-brimmed straw hat with a banana, two plums, and a bunch of grapes nestled on the side. Mother had changed into a stylish pantsuit.

"Mother," I said. "You came."

"Course she did," Hazel said. "I told her we couldn't miss the first game. Now, get over there and coach this team to victory."

My mother nodded. "Go on, dear. Mother wants to see her baby girl coach the team."

I turned away and stood along the third baseline as their lead-off batter took the plate. She was mean looking, maybe not as mean as Missy, but I swear she had red eyes, red, glowing eyes that bore right through me when she looked my way. She banged dirt out of her cleats and then tapped home plate three times and took her stance. Steam puffed from her nostrils.

Frankie looked over at me as if to say, "You've got to be kidding."

Gwendolyn, on third base, had already started to cry.

I grinned and waved. "It's okay, Gwen. You can do this."

Frankie wound up. I held my breath. Frankie pitched. The ball took a nice, high arc and SMACK! I could tell by the sound it made that it was a goner. The ball sailed over Edwina's head. The batter took off like she had been shot from a cannon, blew past Marlabeth at first, became a blur as she headed for Ginger at shortstop, who leaped and dove out of the way, and by the time she rounded third and headed for home, Rose was cowering behind me.

Their player scored the first run before Edwina even snagged the ball. I let the air out of my lungs and sent my own prayer heavenward that the Angels would score at least one run today.

By the time the first half of the inning was over, the Thunder had scored five runs, Ginger had fallen over twice, Edwina had cried, and Marlabeth had threatened to quit. But now it was our turn. Clara was up first.

"Just try to hit the ball. That's all," I said. "Just make contact, don't kill it."

She struck out. The Thunder smirked and giggled when Ginger took the plate. But she stood tall, as tall as possible, and drew a walk. Unfortunately she was left stranded on first base and the inning was over. I watched my dejected team take the field, and I knew they wanted to be anywhere but there.

Cash Vangarten sat on his bench looking mighty smug with his arms folded against his chest and his long legs outstretched. I caught him looking at me every now and again. I loathed him when he made fancy hand signals. I was just happy if my team remembered to swing, let alone do some fancy hitting. By the third inning, the score was eleven to zip, and I was ready to concede according to league rules, even though the Angels wanted to finish the whole game. I just didn't want to see any more bloodshed. But Frankie spoke for the team and said, "Please, Charlotte. Let us finish the game."

Hazel called me to her side. "Don't give up, Charlotte. Just see it to the end. My Birdy always said quitters never prosper."

"Birdy?" Mother said.

"My dead husband. Wisest man to ever walk God's green earth."

I walked away before Mother had the chance to defend my father as the wisest man on God's green earth.

We had just taken the field in the top of the fourth when Fleur de Lee and Jaster made their way toward the field. Jaster had his arm around his young wife's shoulder and seemed to be pushing her toward us.

"What are they doing?" Asa asked. "They're heading toward first base by way of the infield."

"She looks sick. She's trying to get to Marlabeth."

Cash ran over to me. "What's that woman doing? She can't walk across the field like that."

Asa dashed out to Marlabeth and pointed in Fleur de Lee's direction. Marlabeth dropped her glove. I went to the home plate umpire. "Stop the game. Stop the game."

"What?" he said.

I pointed. "That woman is pregnant and she looks pretty . . ."

He raised his arms and the game stopped.

Cash Vangarten came running up to me. "What's going on? Are you ready to concede?"

"I am not conceding, Mr. Vangarten. Look."

We turned and saw Marlabeth and Jaster gently lay Fleur de Lee on the ground with her head resting on second base.

"I believe that woman is about to have a baby," I said.

"Right now? Here? On second base?"

Cash said. "She can't."

By then his Amazons had gathered around, shouting all manner of expletives and complaints. They were so loud and rambunctious that the umpire threatened to eject them from the game.

"Ever try to stop a woman from giving birth?" I said. "Just go back to your bench and sit."

"I never called a game on account of childbirth," said the umpire. "There is nothing in the rules about this. Rain, yes, darkness, yes. But childbirth?"

"Let's just treat it like a rain delay," I said.

The ump removed his black cap and scratched his bald head. "If this don't beat all."

Then all of a sudden Missy leaped from the bench and hollered, "I know that girl. She's a retard. She lives in that home. Why they let her have a baby for?"

Rose, who had been standing near home plate praying, rushed near and waggled her finger in the woman's face. "Don't you ever call my friend a retard again." Rose ripped her face-mask off and threw it on the ground. The other woman put up her fists like she wanted a fight. "I don't have time to flatten your nose," Rose said. "I need to go help my friend."

"Chicken." Missy clucked.

"Just so you know. I once killed a man." And she marched off toward the now gathering crowd at second base.

"I don't have time for this either," I said. And I headed toward Fleur de Lee. I could hear her crying and moaning. "She's in pain. What do I do now?"

That was when I felt my mother behind me. "Of course she is, dear. She's in labor."

"Do something, Mother."

"Charlotte," she put her hand on my shoulder. "Nature is a good teacher. She'll do fine, and she looks to be in good hands. Lots of them. I suppose these farm women have had a lot of experience with birth."

"Cows, Mother. Pigs. Maybe a horse, but this is a human being."

Hazel appeared next to Mother. "Calm down, child. Watch if you want. Go home and make pie if you want, but you are the team leader, the coach. You can't let them see you panic."

30

Marlabeth hollered orders like a drill sergeant.

"Asa! Run to my trailer and get my medical bag. It's just inside the front door."

"Marlabeth has a medical bag?" I said to Ginger.

"Of course she does. We're not hillbillies."

"Edwina," Marlabeth said. "You go get me some clean towels. Lots of clean towels."

Gwendolyn stood over them with her fist in her mouth, shaking like a frightened bunny rabbit. Rube put his hands on her shoulders and walked her away from the scene. "It's okay, Gwen. Fleur de Lee is going to be just fine. Just fine."

Fleur de Lee held Jaster's hand like she was hanging on for dear life. He had a look on his face that spelled fear and excitement all at the same time. "She's having the baby," he kept saying. "She's having the baby."

I noticed the Thunder still stood frozen on their side like a clump of trees.

"Maybe you should send them packing," said Clara Kaninsky. "Can't play softball with a woman giving birth on second base."

That was when the umpire strolled over. He turned his back as he spoke, like it was too much. "Should we call the game?"

I looked at him like he had just asked the stupidest question ever.

"No, Mr. Umpire. The women can just jump over the pregnant woman on their way to third base. Why don't we just give Fleur de Lee a glove so she can catch grounders?"

He slinked away.

Marlabeth spoke to Fleur de Lee in a calm, assured tone. "Just keep breathing, honey pie. You're doing fine. The baby just decided to be born a few days early."

"I told you so," Fleur de Lee said between huffs. "I told you this baby was ready."

I felt frantic. "Is that okay?" I said. "Will the baby be all right?"

Marlabeth looked up at me. "Yes. The baby will be okay. Where's Asa with my bag?"

Fleur de Lee cried. She squeezed Jasters's hand tighter. His face was as red as a pomegranate. Tears streamed down his face.

"I love you, Fleur de Lee. I love you."

She looked up at him. "The baby is coming out now, Jaster."

Marlabeth snapped her fingers in Fleur de Lee's face. "When did your water break?"

"My water?" She huffed and puffed and squirmed.

"The contractions are coming closer," Marlabeth said. She lifted Fleur de Lee's dress up and pulled off her underwear. "Where's those towels?"

"That's Elsmere underwear," Hazel said.

Cash appeared and ripped off his jersey. "Here, use this. Cover her up."

"Now, Fleur de Lee," Marlabeth said. "You remember I told you about your water breaking. Did you leak all over? Or just in dribbles?"

"We thought she just peed her pants last night," Jaster said. "We thought since the baby wasn't set to be born yet that she just peed."

"I told you it was a lot of pee," Fleur de Lee said.

"I'm sorry," Jaster said. "I just thought it was —"

"Men ain't supposed to think during childbirth," Greta said. "You did your part nine months ago. Fleur de Lee will do fine, Jaster."

"Hold on, now," Marlabeth said. She reached under the softball jersey draped across Fleur de Lee's knees. "You must have been in labor all night. You're already at ten centimeters. This baby's coming."

I stepped back a few feet and joined Rose. "You stay here," she said. "I'm going back to the trailer. I think I need to get into God's palm to pray."

I nodded and she took off with Ginger.

Asa returned with Marlabeth's medical bag, and Edwina arrived with enough clean towels to open a linen store.

Fleur de Lee cried and moaned. "It hurts. It hurts so much."

Jaster reached down and kissed her sweaty forehead. "I'm here, Fleur de Lee. I love you."

Marlabeth, who still had her hands under the jersey, instructed Greta to put the towels over her. "And keep two for the baby. We'll need to swaddle him."

She opened her bag and set it nearby where she could reach it.

Fleur de Lee screamed and then moaned. "I want to push him out," she said. "Just like you said, Miss Marla, I need to push him out."

Marlabeth stuck her hands under and then she looked. "The baby's crowning now.

Fleur de Lee, you start pushing. Jaster, you sit behind her on the ground and hold her up. Matter of fact, get me Rube back."

"Rube?" Greta said. "Why him? He don't know nothing about birthing babies."

"I need him to help support her with Jaster back there."

Greta hollered for Rube like she was calling a hog. He came running from the sidelines. "What's wrong, Greta?"

"Get behind Jaster," Greta said. "And hold her. Give her support like you're a big old couch or something."

Rube slid behind Jaster and held on to both of them with his big, strong arms.

"Shouldn't someone call an ambulance?" I asked.

"What for?" Marlabeth said. "She is not sick and she was planning to have the baby at home anyway."

"I just thought."

"It's okay," Marlabeth said. "We'll get her to the hospital after it's all over."

My mother took my hand. "Now's not the time to think, Charlotte."

"Charlotte," Marlabeth said. "You come over here and grab hold of her right knee and push back. You, Charlotte's mother, you get the other. She needs something to push against."

"Me?" Mother said.

"Just do it, Mother."

"Go on," Hazel said. "I'd do it but with my brittle bones I'm afraid she'd snap my arm."

Mother did as she was told, and there we stood with Fleur de Lee's legs in our hands, helping her give birth. For a second I felt like I might faint. But my mother locked eyes with me, and I realized this was the closest we would ever come to sharing a child.

"You can do it, Fleur de Lee," I said. "Just do what Marlabeth tells you."

Jaster, who was now sobbing like a little girl, was no help. Rube did all the bull work, holding everyone up so gravity could have a chance to do its thing.

"Okay, Fleur de Lee," Marlabeth said. "Just a couple more pushes and the baby will be out. Put your chin on your chest and push."

My mother looked down. "Jumpin' blue lizards!" she hollered. "The baby is coming out."

"You really didn't need to look, did you, Mom?" I said.

"Yes, but close up it's —"

"One more push," called Marlabeth. "One more big one and the baby will be out."

Fleur de Lee strained and pushed. Jaster continued to cry like a baby. Rube had a good hold on him and Fleur de Lee. "It's okay, Jaster buddy. Your wife is doing fine. They all look like this when they're birthing babies. Why, you shoulda seen Greta. She screamed like —"

Greta smacked the side of his head. "You shut up about that, Rube."

He smiled at her. "I love you, Sweetie."

"Push, Fleur de Lee. Push!" Marlabeth hollered. "The head is out!" And then, plop. The baby practically fell into Marlabeth's waiting hands. "Happy birthday, little girl," she said.

She held the baby by her ankles and cleared her mouth with her index finger. The baby wailed. I cried. Greta cried. Rube swiped some tears. I looked to the sidelines, and the Thunder were all sobbing like little girls. Even Cash Vangarten was moved. He reached out and hugged me. "I'm sorry I lied to you. I'm sorry I said what I said."

"This is not the time, Cash."

He nodded and backed away.

"Is that my baby?" Fleur de Lee said. "Is she mine?"

Marlabeth laid the baby on Fleur de Lee's chest. The new mommy reached for and touched her newborn. "Hi, baby," she said.

"Is it a boy or girl?"

Jaster touched the baby's forehead. "A girl. We have a little girl."

"I'm so happy," I cried.

"You can put her leg down now, Charlotte," Marlabeth said.

Mother took me aside. "Is it, you know, normal?"

"Mother, don't say such things now. I don't know if they can tell yet."

"She looks perfect," Cash said. "Just perfect."

I wrinkled my eyebrows at him. "And how would you know?"

"I just do," he said.

Marlabeth reached into her bag and pulled out two things that looked like funny, short-nosed scissors. She secured them to the umbilical cord and then cut the cord with a scissor.

"She's all yours now, Fleur de Lee."

"What should we do now?" Rube asked after Marlabeth finished.

Marlabeth pulled off her rubber gloves and wrapped them in a towel. "Now I think it would be a good idea if we get her and the baby to the hospital."

"Hospital?" Jaster said. "Why does she have to go to the hospital? Is she okay?"

"Yes, yes," Marlabeth said. "But I think

it's a good idea to let a doctor take a look at her and the baby. She'll be home tomorrow. And they'll teach her how to take care of — Do you have a name?"

Fleur de Lee kissed her baby. "Yes, Miss Marla. I got the best name now."

"You do?" Jaster said. "You do?"

"Angel. I want to call her Angel on account of she was born on Angel Field."

"Angel," Jaster said. "That's the prettiest name in the world." Then he kissed his wife. "How 'bout we call her Angel Fleur de Lee?"

"That's beautiful," I cried.

"Now I'm glad we didn't call the team The Tornados," Greta said.

"The nurses will teach Fleur de Lee how to care for Angel, bathe her, feed her, change her diapers."

Jaster snickered. "Diapers. I am not changing any poopy diapers."

"Oh yes you are," Fleur de Lee said.

Rube cradled Fleur de Lee and the baby in his arms and carried them to his waiting station wagon. "Greta and me will take them over." Rube wiped his eyes.

"I'll be right behind you," Marlabeth said. But I didn't think Fleur de Lee heard her. She was too busy admiring her Angel Fleur de Lee.

My mother took my arm.

"Charlotte Louise Figg. I never would have imagined such a thing could happen. I mean, I heard of babies being born in elevators and cabs but —"

"Isn't it wonderful, Mom? A baby was just born. Right here. On second base."

"It is wonderful, Charlotte. Just precious."

I put my arms around my mother. "It was amazing. I never experienced anything like that. Imagine that. A brand-new life."

My mother squeezed me back. "I remember when you were born," she whispered into my ear. "I screamed like a banshee."

I laughed. "I remember. I was there."

She snickered and pushed me away so she could look in my eyes. She didn't say anything. She only looked and smiled. And for the briefest moment I thought she was seeing her newborn baby.

We all watched Rube drive off with the new little family.

Cash sauntered up to me. "Guess we'll replay this game. Unless you want to concede."

"The Angels never concede, Mr. Vangarten. You get the ump. We'll be here."

I looked over at what was left of my team, and they nodded their heads like those little dolls in the backs of cars. Must be something about watching a woman give birth that spurs a team on. "And we're going to win," Edwina said. "For Angel Fleur de Lee."

Cash took his cap off and scratched his head. "You are gluttons for punishment. I'll call tomorrow and let you know when."

"We'll be ready," I said.

The Angels, minus Rose, Ginger, and Greta, stood around like they didn't have a clue what to do. Gwendolyn stood near second base sobbing. "Someone will have to clean up this mess."

There was a little blood, a little goo, but all in all it wasn't too bad. Marlabeth did a good job keeping everything in Edwina's towels.

Asa and Studebaker pushed a wheelbarrow of dirt toward us. "We'll just cover it up. Good as new."

"Well, I am not touching that base anymore," Gwendolyn said.

I shook my head. "Now, don't get yourself upset over nothing. You always do that. It's a perfectly fine base, and only Fleur de Lee's head rested on it — nothing else."

"Nothing else?"

I crossed my heart.

"I guess we'll just put the equipment

away," I told Asa. "We might pick up the game tomorrow."

"I can't wait," said Edwina. "We're gonna win, somehow."

Thomasina, who had been uncharacteristically quiet through the whole experience, spoke up. "Charlotte, I have never seen such a thing in my life. But I am so glad I did and I want you to know that I will do my best to catch every pop fly that comes my way, every line drive, every grounder. We are going to beat those no-good, lying Thunder girls."

Frankie led the team in three cheers. "Let's not lose this determination," she said. "We have to win for our littlest team member, Angel Fleur de Lee."

Thomasina put her arm around Edwina's shoulders. "It's getting dark. Let's go home."

The sun, now completely below the horizon, left behind a steel gray and plum purple sky. "What do you say, Mom. Supper?"

"This late? Charlotte."

I touched my stomach. "I couldn't eat before the game, too nervous. And now I'm famished for some reason."

"Okay, but nothing too heavy. I'm tired and need my sleep."

I looked around and noticed Hazel was gone. "Where's Hazel? Did you see her leave, Mother?"

"Yes, yes. Long time ago."

"By herself? Through the woods?"

"She's a sturdy little thing," Mother said. "Even with that hump. You'd think it would throw her balance off."

"Mother, you should have gone with her. She could have fallen on that uneven ground. It's getting dark and even darker in the woods."

I grabbed her arm. "Come on. I need to know she made it home."

"Don't worry, Charlotte. I think that one-armed man went with her."

"Why didn't you tell me?"

"I just remembered I saw them go into the forest together. There was a lot of excitement, dear."

"I'm sorry I snapped at you, and it's not a forest. Just a patch of woods."

"Trees are trees," Mother said.

I still felt relieved once we made it out of the woods without seeing Hazel splayed out on the ground with her legs tangled up in a gnarled root.

"We should stop by Rose's and let her know how it turned out. She's up in God's hand."

My mother stopped walking. "What? What are you talking about?"

"God's hand. It's sort of a statue in Rose's yard."

"You mean that monstrosity I saw when I first arrived here? As if the palm trees and neon weren't enough. The taxi driver had to drive me all over the place. Lord knows I was looking for a nice trailer, Charlotte, not that bilious thing you call a home. We drove six times around the park, and each time I swear that hand grew bigger and bigger."

"Mother, didn't we just have a nice moment? Didn't you just hug me and say you remember the day I was born?"

My mother took a couple of steps. "I just didn't know I had given birth to a child with no sense. I'll tell you that much."

We got to Rose's house, and, sure enough, she and Ginger were still up in the hand. Rose was standing like she was trying to see the ball field through the trees.

"Rose," I called. "It's all over."

"Thank you, Almighty God," Rose said. "For this safe delivery."

Ginger started down the ladder. "Thank you, Jesus," she said three times while she made her way to the ground. Then she stood next to my mother and said, "Bet that was the first time you saw a baby born on a ball field."

Mother shook her head. "This is also the first time I seen a midg— er, little person climb out of the hand of God."

"Mother, don't be rude."

"It's true," she said.

Rose came down. "So was it a boy or girl? How's Fleur de Lee?"

"She's fine. Rube took her to the hospital. She had a girl."

"I knew it," Rose said. "Asa owes me ten bucks."

"They named her Angel because she was born on Angel Field," I said. "Angel Fleur de Lee."

"That is so sweet," Rose said. "Where are they now?"

"The Lundys took her to the hospital. Marlabeth is going also."

Rose smiled at my mother. "Ever think that would happen on vacation?"

Mother didn't say anything. She was still staring at the hand.

"Mother," I said. "It's just a statue."

"But why a giant hand?" Mother asked.

Rose jumped on the opportunity to explain. "Scripture says that God holds us all in the palm of his hand. This just makes it more real to me, to us."

"Wouldn't it be simpler to just go to church?"

Rose laughed. "It is church, Lillian. Come by one day and you can sit up there. I'll paint your name as soon as I can."

"Paint my name? What are you talking about?"

"Rose painted everyone's name on the hand, well, everyone in Paradise," Ginger said.

"It's my way of lifting you all to God and asking his blessing on you."

Lillian touched the monument. "Strange. Very strange."

"Did we have to forfeit the game?" Ginger asked. "They were sure better than us."

"Cash said we might be able to pick it up tomorrow," I said. "I was going to concede, but the others wouldn't let me. So the umpire is treating it like a rain delay."

Ginger kicked at the dirt under the hand. "Ah, we should just forfeit. Ain't no way in heaven or earth we'd win."

"Let's wait until tomorrow," I said. "The others are pretty determined now, especially after Cash lied to us and all."

"Lied to you," Mother said.

"He told me his team stunk worse than rotten potatoes, Mother. And then they show up and — well, you saw them."

"That rat. You play your game, Charlotte. You knock their socks off."

"That's the spirit, Lillian," Rose said.

31

We said good-night to Rose and Ginger and headed up Mango Street. It was now dark, and the few streetlights in Paradise had come on, providing just a few circles of light as we made our way home.

"I'll bet Lucky will be glad to see us," I said. "It's been a long night."

"Now, now, Charlotte. I let him out just a few minutes before I came to see you at the ball game. Strangest thing. He was pawing at the door, and I kept telling him to go on out, that I didn't want to get up from my comfortable seat. But he wouldn't go through that teeny-weenie door; how he even fits through there is beyond me."

"He hasn't wanted to use his doggie door lately. Something spooked him the other day."

"Made me mad, he did. I had to get up and open the door. That was when I saw that Hazel Crenshaw for the first time. She

394

waved me over, and I went and we talked. She's an odd duck."

"She is. But I like her."

"I didn't say I didn't like her. We did come to your game together."

I folded my arms across my chest and rubbed my arms. "Getting chilly. The breeze has picked up. Feels like a storm might be coming over the mountains."

"I did hear something on the radio about some weather moving in."

"What would you like for supper? It's a little late, but I can whip up something."

"How about an omelet?"

"With some cheese? I think I have a few different types of cheese in the fridge."

"Two," Mother said. "I saw cheddar, Swiss, and I tossed the Muenster in the trash. It was rotting, Charlotte."

"Cheese is supposed to rot, sort of, isn't it?"

"Not like that."

My mother sat at the table while I whisked eggs. She picked at what was left of a cherry crumb pie. "You do make good pie, Charlotte. I think you get that from your grandmother. She was a chef, you know, Madame Mimieux at the famed Le Bouboule."

"I know. You've told me about a million times."

I poured the beaten eggs into the hot pan.

"Yes. In Paris, no less. Of course, that's where my family was from."

"I know. I'd like to visit some day."

"Mm." I watched her pick more crust and then plop a cherry in her mouth. "Why you didn't go to cooking school when I told you to go is beyond me. You'd be . . . be . . ."

"What, Mother?"

"Happy?" She raised her eyebrows at me like she had just said the most profound statement ever uttered by a human being.

I finished up the two-cheese omelet and slid it on a plate. "Toast?"

"No. Just some apple juice if you have it."

We ate silently for a few minutes until I heard Lucky come in through his doggie door. He ran into the kitchen and slid on the linoleum. "He comes in through the doggie door, but not out."

"Strange pooch," Mother said.

After eating our omelet, we settled in front of the TV with cups of tea and Lorna Doone cookies.

"So, Mother, your first day in Paradise was pretty exciting."

"It was that, Charlotte." She munched a cookie. "What's that over there? Something of Herman's? Some Fuller Brush doodad?"

"What?"

"That trophy-looking thing."

I laughed. "No, that's mine. You remember back when I played with the Canaries?"

"Oh, I do remember. You were so proud of that trophy."

"I was, Mother. And I think you were a little proud too."

She sipped tea and watched a few seconds of TV. "How come I never saw it at your other house, the real house made from bricks?"

I swallowed a cookie and nearly choked. "Because Herman thought it was too large to be displayed. He made me keep it in the basement."

"I don't know if you ever knew this or not, Charlotte, but I never had much regard for Herman Figg."

"No?" I said, hoping she'd catch the sarcasm in my voice.

"It's true. I wanted you to have a career and marry someone more like your father, God rest his soul." She clutched her chest.

"I was happy, Mother."

She glared at me. "Were you? Really?"

I finished my tea and turned off the television. "I think we should go to bed."

We took turns in the bathroom and then

met in the hallway.

"Goodnight, Mom." I kissed her cheek.

She patted Lucky and then kissed me. "Sleep tight, dear."

The next morning I woke to the smell of coffee brewing and the sound of birds chirping outside.

"Good morning, Mother," I said, walking into the kitchen. "Coffee smells good."

"It's from Africa," she said. "I brought you a whole pound. I still have connections with buyers all over the world and they send me stuff to try out sometimes and I rather like —"

"Mother, you're blathering. Too early for blather."

"I'm sorry, dear. I was just making conversation."

I sipped the brew. "It is good. Nutty."

"Just like me, I suppose."

"Mother, I didn't say that."

She joined me at the table. "I think you're mad at me because of what I said last night about Herman."

"What? That you didn't like him? I knew that. You and Daddy never liked him."

She sliced into the apple pie. "I have to say it again, Charlotte. Why didn't you ever open a shop?"

I shook my head. "I wanted to, but —"

"But Herman," Mother said. "Charlotte, now don't take this the wrong way, but that man never let you be who you were supposed to be."

I nodded. "Rose said I missed out on my God-intended self."

"Not too late."

I felt tears well up. "Mother, it's too early to cry."

"Tell me what happened, Charlotte. Tell Mother what that mean old Herman did to you."

And I did. We sat in the kitchen for over an hour, and I told her all about him.

"He wasn't evil, not like some men," I said in the end, meaning Fergus Wrinkel. "He just liked to be in control."

"Why didn't you tell me?" Mother asked. "I would have let you come home. You could have come to Florida with me. I mean, I suspected it all along, but you needed to make that choice. I could have talked and talked until I was blue in the face, but you had to be the one. Why did you stay?"

"I don't know. Men like Herman have a way of making you stay." I thought of Suzy.

"He brainwashed you."

"Kind of."

"I just don't get it. It's not like you had children to consider. Matter of fact, Herman is probably the reason you lost —"

"Mother, stop."

"It could be true. They're doing all kinds of studies, and they say stress early in a pregnancy has been known to cause mis—"

I stopped her again. "God just saw fit to take the baby away from me."

"And me," Mother said. "When that woman was having her baby out there on the baseball field, I couldn't help but feel sort of homesick for never holding my own grandchild."

I reached across the table and held her hand. "I know, Mother. I felt it too. But Herman never wanted to try again after that."

My mother used a paper napkin to wipe tears from her cheeks.

I looked at the clock. "Look at that, Mother, it's nearly eleven o'clock and we're not even dressed."

"I do need to use the bathroom," she said. "That African coffee irritates my bladder, I think."

"Go on. Go to the bathroom. I'm expecting Cash to call about the game today."

I cleared the table and washed the dishes and gave Lucky a bowl of Alpo. He had been listening to the whole Herman story. He whimpered a couple of times through it, almost like he knew somehow, almost like he knew he was meant to be with me now, to help get me through.

"It's okay, boy," I said. "Herman can't hurt me anymore."

Mother came out of the bedroom dressed and ready for the day. She wore blue jeans and a Penn State sweatshirt.

"Mother, you look so . . . so . . ."

"Trailer-ish?"

"No, relaxed."

The telephone rang. "I bet that's Cash."

Mother raised her eyebrows. "He has such nice eyes."

"Hello," I said.

It was him.

"I got it," I said. "Seven o'clock next Thursday. At Angel Field. We'll be ready."

Mother gave me the thumbs-up sign. I wasn't altogether certain what she meant by it.

"Fleur de Lee is fine," I said into the phone. "Thank you for asking."

I finished my conversation with Cash and then headed for the bedroom. "I'll go get changed, and then I need to go to the grocery store. I guess we can spend the day together, we aren't playing until next Thursday now."

"That's over a week away," Mother said.

"Cash said it couldn't be helped. We can't get an umpire until then because of other games being played. He was able to get the league to switch some of our games around so we can finish the Thunder game."

My mother chuckled into her hand. "I'm sorry, Charlotte, but it seems like so much fuss for a silly game. You'd think you were invading Normandy with all this planning."

"I need to get dressed," I said.

"You go ahead, and I think I will go shopping with you. I need a few things myself."

After I dressed, I told Mother I would need to let the team know not to come to the field.

"And how do you do that? Jungle drums?"

"No, not usually. I go door-to-door, but maybe I'll make calls. Better yet. I'll call the team captain and she can handle it."

"Good girl," Mother said. "Delegate."

"I'll just call Frankie, and then we can be on our way."

I pulled open the car door just in time to see Suzy and Fergus Wrinkel coming out of Hazel's door.

"Look at that," I said. "He's got Suzy right by his side. Probably won't let her leave his sight."

My mother looked in the direction I was looking. "What are you talking about? And why is she in a cast?"

"That's Fergus Wrinkel. He's been — Get in the car. I'll tell you on the way."

She climbed slowly into the passenger seat. "Now, you're certain you can drive this yacht, Charlotte? I'm old, but my life is still precious."

"Yes, Mother. I've become a good driver."

"Just go slow, okay? Nice and slow."

I pulled away from the curb and said, "Fergus Wrinkel hits his wife. Gives her black eyes. Even broke her wrist. That's why she's in the cast, and he . . ." I stopped talking and noticed my left knee was shaking.

"Are you certain, Charlotte?"

"I am, Mom. Saw the bruises myself, and then just a few days ago Suzy finally admitted it to me."

It wasn't until I had pulled onto the main road to Shoops that my mother spoke again. "What is it with you and these kind of men? It's wherever you go."

"I take out ads in newspapers, Mother. Wanted: Men who hit their wives."

"Charlotte, that's terrible. But you have to admit it's weird."

I looked at her for a long second and nearly rammed into the car ahead of me. I

403

slammed on the brakes.

"Charlotte," Mother hollered. "Take me home. You are not a fit driver."

"Too late, the shopping center is just down the road."

"Slow down. Charlotte, slow down."

The Piggly Wiggly was crowded for a Wednesday morning, but Lillian and I managed to get through it quickly. I purchased everything I needed to make pies. "I make them for Suzy," I told Mother. "Then she tells Fergus she made them."

"Why on earth would you do that?"

"Just trying to help."

My mother bought shampoo and soap because apparently the brand I used made her skin itch and her scalp tingle.

We loaded the car and headed out of the parking lot. "What's this town called?" Lillian asked.

"Shoops. It's where just about every man in Paradise works."

"Really?"

"Down at the Elastic Factory. Hazel Crenshaw owns the factory."

"She does, does she? Then why is she living in a trailer park?"

"She likes it, but she also owns a huge estate around here somewhere. Place called Willow Way. But here's what's really funny.

Cash Vangarten works for her also. He's her general manager."

"No, really?"

"And she won't sponsor his team. So he's a little miffed that she is sponsoring the Angels."

"Peyton Place," Mother said shaking her head. "Paradise is its own little soap opera."

"I guess it is. We have it all. Secrets, deception, softball."

"Softball," Mother said. "How come a woman who can bake like you plays softball?"

"I like it."

Just for kicks I drove Mother past the factory. "Elastic, huh. Now there's something you don't think about until you need it. Something mighty important though."

"Hazel says they sell it all over the world. It's used in lots and lots of products."

"That's right," Mother said. "When I was buying for Wanamaker's, I remember many conversations about the elastic quality of bras, underwear, feety pajamas."

"Hazel says Elsmere makes the best," I said.

"Come to think of it, I might remember hearing the name Elsmere Elastic before."

It was well past lunchtime when we got

home. Mother helped me unpack bags and put the groceries away, although she tried to rearrange my kitchen.

"Please, Mother. I like things where I put them."

"I'm being like Herman," she said all of a sudden as though she had been struck by lightning.

I nodded. "You kind of are."

She flopped onto the sofa. "I'm the reason you married that man."

I dropped a jar of pickles on the counter and went to her. "No, you aren't. You're nothing like Herman."

Lucky pawed at the door. "Go on, boy. Go out. Fergus isn't out there."

He looked at me warily.

"Go on, use your little door."

Lucky did as I told him, but very slowly, so slowly he got stuck about halfway and had to wiggle his body outside.

"That must be how they do it," Mother said. "Momentum pushes them through."

I looked at her. "True. Momentum helps us get through most things in life."

"So how come he's afraid? I heard you mention Fergus."

I took a huge breath and told her how Fergus had threatened me and Lucky. When I finished I was both exhausted and relieved that my mother knew.

My mother stood and put her fists on her hips. "I am going to march right over there and give that man a piece of my mind. How dare he kidnap my daughter's dog, my granddog. How dare he threaten —"

"Mother, you can't. Suzy. Remember? Her life is in danger now as it is. If you go over there all angry and Lillian-like, there's no telling what he'll do."

32

I had been awake for almost an hour when the rain started. Lucky wasn't on the floor in his usual spot. He could hear my eyelids open and always came running, ready to go out for breakfast. My heart sped the way it did since the incident with Fergus whenever I couldn't see him.

I clapped my hands and called, "Lucky. Here, boy."

And into the room he bounded and onto the bed.

"There you are, Lucky. You're all wet. Eww. Get off the bed." I gave him a push. "You've been out in the rain. I'll need to dry you off."

I hung my feet over the bed and rested a moment before getting up. The rain sounded hard. Mother appeared at the doorway in her turquoise terry robe and matching fuzzy slippers. "I couldn't sleep with all that racket the storm was making, so I got up. I let Lucky out. I made coffee." She yawned and stretched. "We have to talk."

I pulled on my robe and made my way to the bathroom first and then the kitchen.

"Thank you," I said. "This is nice, having coffee already made. It's that African coffee, isn't it?"

"Yes, Charlotte, but that's not what I want to talk about."

A huge crack of lightning split the sky as thunder rolled over Paradise. "Looks like a nasty storm," I said. "I hope Asa covered up the infield."

"The what?"

"Infield, Mother. On Angel Field. He has this huge tarp he uses to protect the dirt in the rain. Otherwise it could wash away the infield."

Mother sat at the table and warmed her hands on the coffee cup.

"Did you happen to catch the news this morning, hear the weather?" I asked. My head started to clear of its usual morning fog.

"I did," she said. "They're calling for high winds and buckets of rain. Severe storms, they said." Then she smirked.

"What's that for?"

"You Yankees," she said. "This is just a

summer shower down in Tampa. We have hurricanes down there, dear. Believe me, this is nothing."

I sipped my coffee and looked out at the dark skies and lightning. "I better check on Hazel."

Another loud boom of thunder broke just over my trailer. It sent Lucky running into the bedroom to cower under the bed. "Chicken," I called.

The lights flickered a second but stayed on. "Maybe I should get the flashlights out," I said. "And I have candles pretty much everywhere. I used them when I first moved in to help with the smell."

A crack of lightning lit up the sky. "Did you see that? It's both beautiful and frightening at the same time. Maybe I should run over to Hazel's before the lights go out."

"That's a good idea. She'd be better off here with us, but I did want to speak to you about something."

"Can it wait?"

Mother fiddled with her wedding ring. She still wore it. She couldn't bear to be without it and had no intention of ever marrying again. I rolled my band around my finger.

That was when a huge crack of lightning and thunder split all outdoors and we heard a tremendous crash that reminded me of the day Herman dropped dead. I ran to the kitchen bay window just as the lights went off. "Mother, it's Hazel's trailer. That huge oak split and half of it is on her trailer. I need to go get her."

She grabbed on to me. "You will do nothing of the kind. Let the men find her and take care of her. You can't go running outside in this storm. Besides, it looks like that tree took some wires with it. Could be dangerous."

"But I can't just sit here."

"Then go get dressed. Just in case we have to evacuate or something."

"Evacuate?"

"Could happen. Ever get floods up here?"

"I don't know, but the water is running down the street like a river."

I ran into my bedroom and pulled on jeans and a sweatshirt, socks, and Keds. I brushed my teeth, just in case we did have to leave. When I got back to the kitchen, I heard what sounded like a chainsaw starting up.

"It's Asa," I said, looking out the window. "He's over at Hazel's. I can't see real well. It's like looking through a waterfall out this window, but it looks like that tree is blocking her door."

"I hope she's all right," Mother said. She hugged Lucky around the neck.

"Of course she is. If I know Hazel Crenshaw, she's standing in the living room all dressed in her shawl and hat du jour with Smiley in her arms, waiting for the men to bust through."

"You're probably right, Charlotte. But who or what is Smiley?"

"Her cat. I hope Rose and Ginger are okay. I'm worried, Mother."

"Better turn on your emergency generator," my mother said.

I laughed. "Generator? I don't have a generator."

"Well, don't worry, Charlotte. I'm sure Rose and Ginger are just fine." She took her coffee into the living area. "This will give us time to talk."

"Talk? Now? I can't, Mother. Not until I know they're safe. Everyone's safe."

"Then come away from the window, speaking of safe. You shouldn't stand near a window in a raging storm like this."

I went about lighting candles. "Fine, now tell me what's on your mind."

Mother looked away from me for a second and then caught me square in the eye. "I've decided you are going to move to Florida. This is not a good place for you, Charlotte.

It's not safe."

I silently prayed that Rose or someone would come by. But no, I sat there and listened to my mother spout a hundred and ten reasons why I needed to move to Florida. And then she spouted another hundred and ten reasons why I should have left Herman long before he collapsed in the kitchen.

The whole lecture lasted about fifteen minutes before I finally stood up, looked my mother in the eyes, and said, "You are not the boss of me anymore. I have my own life and I like it just fine, right here in Paradise."

She argued. And then she stopped. I could see the storm raging inside her as the storm raged outside. It had not let up at all. Buckets of rain poured — lightning, thunder. The winds whipped through the trees and whistled like a train between the trailers. I saw small branches and garbage strewn around the yard and in the street. Old Man Hawkins's trash cans rolled around.

I went to the kitchen window and saw that Asa had finally made it through to Hazel's front door. I grabbed my raincoat and went tearing across the street, dodging branches and trash cans as I went.

"Get back in your trailer," Asa called.

"I will. I just want to make sure she's okay."

"Don't go near it. The tree brought down some power lines." He had to holler over the sound of the wind.

"We have to get her out."

"Where's all the men?" I called.

"Elsmere," Asa said. "They all went to work before the storm hit. They might be on the way home, but I don't know."

"What about Fergus?"

"I called, but the phone lines are out and that creep don't give a —"

"Let's get Hazel out."

Asa cleared a path. He threw his body against the front door, and on the third try it popped open. Hazel stood there in her raincoat, plastic rain scarf with daisies all over it, and yellow galoshes. She held Smiley tight to her chest. "What took you so long?" she said. "I been standing here so long I think I might have taken root."

"That's my girl," Asa said. He gently led her outside.

"I'll take her to my house."

"Good. I need to check on everyone else," Asa said. "Trees down all over."

Mother stood at the door. "Come on,

hurry." She waved her hands like a cheer-leader.

"We're coming. We're coming," Hazel said. "But my, my, your mother is a pip."

We made it inside unscathed. I helped Hazel get out of her rain gear. Mother helped her to the rocker. "No, no," Hazel said. "I want to sit on the sofa. Why do you young people always think the elderly want to sit in rockers? Makes no sense."

"Excuse me," Mother said. "I didn't mean to insult you."

"Dark in here," Hazel said. "Got any lanterns? Turn them on." She put Smiley next to her and patted his tummy. "You just stay here, darling."

I looked at the cat. He didn't move. I reached out to touch him, and Hazel slapped my hand away. "Leave him be, leave him be. He's sleeping. How a cat can sleep through this storm, I don't know."

Mother raised her eyebrows at me. "Maybe a cup of tea, Hazel?" she said.

Hazel nodded and then jumped slightly as another bolt of lightning crackled overhead. "Now you're talking. A nice cup of tea will suit me fine. And pie, of course, Charlotte."

"Wait a second," Mother said. "How can we boil water with no power?"

"Propane, Mother. I can light the stove

manually."

I followed Lillian into the kitchen. "You know the cat is dead," she whispered.

"I know."

"We can't let her sit there with a dead cat, Charlotte."

"I know. Wonder how long he's been . . . asleep."

We went back to Hazel, who was still rubbing Smiley's tummy. "That's a good kitty. You just sleep. Best thing for him during one of these storms."

Lucky came out of the bedroom.

"Well, you finally found some courage," Mother said.

He headed straight for the cat. Mother grabbed his collar. "Stay here, boy. The cat is . . . sleeping."

But she couldn't hold him, and Lucky started to sniff at the cat. Hazel tried to push him away. "Leave him alone, Lucky."

"Go on, Lucky," I said. "Go lie down."

He looked at me and let go a growl as if to say, "The cat is dead, Charlotte." And sauntered away into the kitchen.

The three of us sat in my living room until the storm started to pass. The sky out the kitchen window began to clear, revealing patches of sparkling blue, almost the color of Cash Vangarten's eyes. The thunder sounded further and further away.

"Oh, Hazel," I said, looking out the window. "Your trailer is destroyed. Thank God you're alive."

Mother echoed my sentiments.

"I heard the tree crack and I ran to the kitchen," she said. "It's furthest from the front door. I climbed under the kitchen table until it crashed down."

"You did good," Mother said. "Where was Smiley?"

"Oh, that silly old cat. He slept through the entire thing. But he's been sleeping a lot lately."

"How long?" Mother asked.

"Since a day ago, or so."

"That would explain the stiff tail," Mother whispered to me.

I went to the kitchen to make more tea. Mother followed.

"We need to tell her," I said.

"I know. But let's wait until the storm passes."

"You know she'll have to stay here. She can't go home."

Mother sucked air. "Here? You don't have the room."

I raised my eyebrows at her.

"Oh, I see what you're saying. If I left, if I went back to Cocoa Reef, then you'd have

417

room for the old biddy. Well, I see where your allegiance lies."

And she stormed off toward her bedroom.

"I'm not saying that," I called.

Actually I was, but denial is often the first defense.

I went to her room. "Mother, please don't leave. I'll give Hazel my bed, and I'm sure Asa has a cot or something for me. The man has everything anyone could need, and if not he knows where to get it."

"Good, Charlotte, because I really don't want to go without you."

I leaned against her dresser and nearly toppled Tweety to the ground. "He doesn't seem to mind the storm."

"Nah, Tweety likes the rain, I think. Reminds him of life in the rain forest."

Rain forest. "Mother, Tweety has never been in a rain forest."

"I meant that in a more romantic sense, dear. You know — ancestral connections."

"Anyway, I am not moving to Florida with you. I have responsibilities here now, and I kind of like it. I like coaching the women and sitting with Rose in the hand, and, Mother, I even went back to church."

"You can lay down roots as easily in Cocoa Reef. We got churches, Charlotte."

I heard Hazel cough.

"I'm not old enough for Cocoa Reef," I said.

"So I'll sneak you in."

What could I do? I pulled Mother close for a hug. "I love you, Mother, you sneaky old woman. But I need to get back to Hazel and Smiley. We need to get him out of the house."

"I saw some of those large trash bags under your sink."

"Mother. I'll get Asa to dig a hole and we'll bury him."

By one o'clock the rain had stopped. The sun shone high in the sky, and all that remained of the storm was downed trees and a few wispy clouds that skirted around like little girl pinafores in the sky. Steam rose off the asphalt as the humidity and temperature rose.

"Hot for early summer," Hazel said. She had not moved off the sofa.

"It is." And that of course made it all the more imperative that we remove the dead cat.

At twelve-fifteen Rose and Ginger came by. Mother still sulked in her bedroom with Tweety. Probably telling him what a terrible daughter I am. Funny thing is that just a few months ago, before Herman died, I would have been inclined to agree.

"Come on in," I said. "I'm glad you didn't try and get here while the storm was still going on."

"I tried," Ginger said. "But Rose stopped me."

"Good idea, Rose."

"It was some storm." I saw her notice Hazel. Rose leaned into me and whispered, "Why's she here?"

I took her by the arm and showed her Hazel's trailer through the window.

"My stars! I didn't even notice it on my way over."

Asa and Jake Pilkey were already there with chain saws, clearing what was left of the oak. "I heard that the men are coming home early from Elsmere."

"Sure are," Hazel said. "I called Cash Vangarten just before that dang-fool tree fell on my house and told him to let those people go as soon as he could. They need to get home and help out."

That was when Ginger leaped onto a kitchen chair. She stood on it to make herself as tall as possible. "Hazel called? What does Hazel have to do with Elsmere Elastic? I knew there was something fishy going on around here. So spill it."

Rose and I exchanged looks. "Better tell

her," Rose said.

"Ginger," I whispered. "Hazel owns the factory."

"And Paradise," Rose added directly into Ginger's ear.

"Stop whispering," Hazel hollered. "I hate whispers. If you can't say it in front of me, don't say it at all."

"Hazel," I said, walking toward her. "Ginger knows your secret."

"Course she does. I just told her. Now, what's happening with my trailer?"

Rose sat on the other side of Smiley. I watched her touch the cat, and I tried to avert her with my eyes but it was too late.

"This cat is dead," Rose said.

My heart stopped.

"He is not," Hazel said. "He's just been sleeping a lot. Might have gotten a hairball caught in his tummy and he's sleeping it off. Poor thing. Imagine that. You'd sleep too if you had wadded up hair in your guts."

Ginger made her way to the cat.

"Hazel. How about if I take the kitty into the kitchen for some water?" she said. "Maybe he needs a drink."

Hazel patted the cat. "Well, okay. But not too much. I don't want him throwing up all over Charlotte's floor."

"I don't think we have to worry about

that," Ginger said. And she gently lifted the stiff (and getting stiffer) cat off the couch.

I followed her into the kitchen.

"What do we do now?" I asked.

"I say we take it outside and bury it," Ginger said. "Have a service. Do something. The woman can't live with a dead cat."

Lucky got up from his spot in the kitchen and sniffed the cat again. Then he lay back down.

Just making sure, I supposed.

"We have to make her understand."

I looked back and saw Rose holding Hazel's hands.

"I think Rose is doing that."

Ginger and I stayed in the kitchen a couple of more minutes until we heard Hazel whimper, "Smiley is . . . is gone?"

33

Mother came out of the bedroom dressed in her traveling dress and holding Tweety's cage.

"I'll call a cab, Charlotte."

"Mother. What are you doing?"

"I can tell I'm no longer wanted here."

I sucked air and blew it out my nose.

"Mother. Don't leave like this."

"How should I leave, through the window? Do you expect me to sprout wings and fly, Charlotte? Should I pirouette out the door?"

"Mother."

"Well, you made it very clear. There is not enough room in this decrepit little trailer house for me and your good friend Hazel and her dead cat."

Hazel, who was wiping her nose on a pink tissue, spoke up. "What in the heck are you yammering about? I am not staying here. Who said I would stay here?"

"Well, I just thought —"

"You just thought? I hate it when people think. Didn't I tell you I have a whole big house down the road a piece? I'll stay there until I replace the trailer."

I felt like an idiot. "I didn't think about that."

"Of course, you didn't. I'll just have Fergus drive me over there. He can open the house and get the electricity turned on and the gas. I'll be fine."

"There, now. See, Mother, you can stay."

"I still think I should go, Charlotte."

"Oh, Lillian," Rose chimed in. "At least stay until we win a game."

"Yeah, stick around," Ginger said.

"No. I'll call a cab."

"Let her go," Hazel said. "She's just being a martyr. I hate martyrs."

Mother harrumphed toward the telephone. "I am not a martyr."

"You can't call a cab. The phones are out."

"Okay, fine. You want me to stay. I'll stay."

Lucky jumped up and ran to the door and barked.

"What is it?" Rose asked. "What is it, boy?"

We heard a loud bang on the door.

"Well, open it," Hazel said. "See who's there."

Fergus stood on the stoop. "The storm

has trees down all over. The only road in or out of the park is closed. You all just stay put."

"Where's Suzy?" I asked.

He glared at me. "She's fine. Don't you worry about her, Charlotte." And he dashed away from the door.

I didn't appreciate his tone. "I just hate the thought of Suzy all alone in a dark trailer. She should be here, with us."

"Ah, don't fret," Hazel said. "We've weathered storms like this before. She will be fine down there."

"But, Hazel, you don't un —"

My mother piped up. "Maybe we should try and listen to a weather report. Do you have a battery-operated radio, Charlotte?"

"Rose," I said, "reach into that drawer next to you. I have a transistor radio."

She flipped it on and set it on the coffee table.

"Keep an ear tuned to it and see if they have any more information. I wonder if the men can get through from Elsmere."

"Oh, pshaw," Hazel said. "Some of them will climb over branches and the rest will pitch in to help clear the roads. They'll get here sooner or later."

"Then I guess we just sit and wait," I said. "Anyone want coffee or tea?"

Ginger grabbed her raincoat and pulled on her boots.

"Where the devil do you think you're going, little missy?" Hazel asked.

"I'll be back. I just want to make the rounds and make sure everyone else is okay. You know, the rest of the team."

I snapped my fingers. "The team. Good idea. And tell anyone who can, to come to my place."

"A party," Hazel said. "Reminds me of the olden days when the power went out and the neighbors would gather and we'd roast hot dogs in the fireplace and pop corn."

"I remember times like that," Mother said. She sat next to Hazel. "Why, my Henry, that was my husband's name, would get a fire roaring and . . ."

A smile as wide as the Thunder's first baseman's behind stretched across my face, and I went to the kitchen to make coffee and serve pie. Rose and Ginger ventured out to check on the Angels. "If you can, would you check on Suzy?" I asked them before they left. "Just knock on her door. She'll answer."

I brought tea to the living room and heard the weather report coming on the radio. "Shh, listen," I said. I turned the transistor up. "The storm has left quite a path of destruction," the announcer said. "The weather bureau has now declared that a tornado did set down in Cranston, just a half mile east of Shoops. We have a reporter on the scene at Haven House, where there is a report that the roof has blown off the group home there."

"Haven House," I said. "Fleur de Lee and the baby."

Mother grew quiet, and I saw her take Hazel's hand.

"Is that the little girl who had the baby on the field?" Hazel asked.

"Yes," Mother said. "Shhh."

Hazel snarled but kept quiet.

"Thanks, Dave," the reporter said. "I'm standing here with Jaster Cook, a resident of Haven House. Mr. Cook, it looks like the twister destroyed the place."

Jaster breathed hard. "Yes, it was mighty scary. I grabbed my wife and baby and we got to the basement before the roof tore off. It was like a train . . . like a big old train come rumbling right through our house. Fleur de Lee cried, but she done all right until we got the all clear."

Hazel gasped. "Jaster works for me. I hope he's okay. And the baby."

"But we're okay," he said. "My Fleur de

Lee and tiny Angel Fleur de Lee are A-OK."

"Thank you, Lord," I said. A remark that garnered a strange look from Mother. I turned off the radio. "They'll need a place to stay," I said.

"You're not suggesting here?" Mother said.

I shook my head. "No, Mother, but if I had the room."

Hazel slapped her knee. "They can stay at Willow Way. I got plenty of bedrooms in Willow Way. They'll just stay there."

"Willow Way?" Mother said. "Charlotte told me about your mansion."

"Birdy named it that because of all the willow trees on the way up the long, long driveway."

"Well, why in the world do you live here? In a trailer?"

Hazel chuckled. "I like it in Paradise and just as soon as they get my trailer fixed or I can arrange for a new one, I'll be back."

I watched my mother turn her mouth into a puckered hole.

"Once you get to know the folks, you'll understand, Mother."

She shook her head. "Well, I never will. I mean —" She turned toward Hazel, "You obviously have money, so why not spend it?"

Hazel slapped her knee. "Money isn't everything. I couldn't get used to knocking around that big old house all by my lonesome. And I spend plenty of money, just how I see fit. Who do you think paid for all those uniforms and equipment? That reminds me, Charlotte, I had Mr. Vangarten deposit enough money in your bank account to more than cover whatever you took out to get the ball rolling."

"That is so sweet of you. Thank you."

I watched her yawn and settle back into the sofa. "Where is Fergus? I need him to drive me to Willow Way. This has been quite a day."

"He'll come get you when the roads are clear," I said.

Lucky whimpered and hid his eyes under his paws. Mother gave him a quick pat and a scratch behind the ears. "That's a good doggie. The storm will be over soon, and you'll be back to chasing squirrels."

For a second I wasn't sure which storm she referred to. The door opened, and in came Rose and Ginger with a happy report.

"The Angels are fine, all snug with their children, and the men are making their way home. Fergus just learned the roads are clear."

"Praise Jesus," Ginger said. "It could have

429

been so much worse."

"Did anyone check on Suzy?" I had settled into the rocking chair. "I've been worried sick about her."

"She's with Fergus," Rose said. "She's been following him around while he checks on things."

"That's crazy," Hazel said. "Why would he cart his wife with the broken arm all around?"

No one answered.

Hazel stood up for the first time since the morning. "This is turning into a regular donnybrook fair. Cats are dying, and people are either going off the deep end or getting their houses blown away by a nasty wind. What's next?"

"Hopefully nothing," I said. "I'll go over to your house and see if you can get in to pack a few things."

"I don't need anything from there. What I don't have at Willow Way I'll send Fergus for. Where is that fool? And what did you do with Smiley?"

"He's outside," I said. "You dozed off a few minutes and Lillian and me put him in a bag and set him outside."

"You did what? My Smiley in a plastic bag? Outside in the rain?"

"Well, it's stopped now, and we just

thought it would be best to put him out."

"The raccoons will eat his liver, or the buzzards — nasty dang birds — will pick him clean."

"Hopefully not," Mother said. "Maybe we can bury him before you leave."

"Capital idea, Lillian," Hazel said. "We'll let Rose do the service."

Rose, who was drying her hair on a towel, said, "It will be an honor to send Smiley off to kitty heaven."

There was a knock at the door. Lucky bounded over and barked his head off. I grabbed his collar. "Come on, boy. Just sit and behave."

"What's wrong with him?" Hazel asked.

"He doesn't care much for Fergus." I pulled open the door. Lucky snarled and bared his teeth.

"Get that mutt away from me," Fergus said. Then he let Suzy inside first. "You go on."

Hazel got to the door with Rose's help. I moved back and joined Rose. "I don't think he's let her out of his sight since the barbecue."

"He's afraid," she said.

"We could say something now."

"No. Let him get Hazel to her house."

"Yeah."

"Got any stuff to take, Hazel?" Fergus said.

I looked at Suzy and smiled. She looked away and stood there shivering like a drowned rat.

"Now, look," Hazel said. "Suzy doesn't need to take the ride to Willow Way. She can stay here with Charlotte and Rose and —" she looked around. "Where's Ginger?"

Ginger came out of the bathroom. "I'm right here."

"You girls stay put. Fergus won't be long."

Suzy stepped away from Fergus. "Is it all right, Fergus?"

"Why you asking his permission?" Hazel said. "Course you can stay."

I smiled at Fergus. He glared at me, and I knew exactly what he was thinking. He was scared to death I would talk Suzy into doing something while he was gone. He was in a pickle now.

"Come on, Hazel," he said. "Let's get you home."

"I'm coming, I'm coming, but we got to bury Smiley first."

I watched Fergus's shoulders rise and fall in exasperation.

"Fine, fine. Let's get it over with."

We paraded to Hazel's yard. I carried Smiley. The men had cleared most of the tree.

Hazel found a lovely spot near her sitting bench. "This is good. Fergus, dig a hole."

He ran to his truck and retrieved a shovel. By then Asa and Rube came walking down the street. I waved them over.

"I think we're pretty secure," Asa said. "Looks like Hazel got the worst of it." Then he looked at us like we had all sprouted petunias out of our heads. "What's going on? What's in that bag?"

Hazel sat on the bench. "Smiley."

"Smiley? You mean he's . . ."

I nodded. "We're here to bury him."

Fergus started digging, and I must admit that I enjoyed watching him dig. I only wished he was doing it in a prison camp.

"My dear friends, neighbors, sisters and brothers," Rose said. "We are here to see our feline, furry friend Smiley off to heaven's gate. He was a good cat, a fine companion, and he will be sorely —"

"Hold on, hold on," Hazel said. "Don't be so dang-blame solemn."

"Would you care to speak?" Rose asked.

Hazel shook her head, and then she nodded. "It's too hard. I just want to say that I'll miss him. He was my best friend for a long, long time. My only friend until Charlotte came to town and opened my eyes to more — opened up all our eyes to joy and softball and friendship."

My heart raced. Mother and I made eye contact, but she turned away.

"Rest in peace, my friend." Hazel closed her eyes and then popped them open. "Shh. Listen. Over there. It's that Whistlesnook."

We all turned in the direction she pointed, toward a big maple in the corner. And sure enough, there was a bird that kind of resembled a woodpecker with odd blue wings, perched on the trunk.

"He came to say goodbye," Hazel said. "Animals have a way of knowing. He must have cleared out before the storm, and now he's back to say goodbye to Smiley. They were friends, you know, even though nature told them to be archenemies."

The little crowd exchanged glances, and then Fergus dropped the bag in the hole.

"Pull me a daisy over there, will you, Asa?"

She dropped it on top of Smiley. "Go on, Fergus. Bury him."

We waited until Fergus tamped the wet dirt on the grave.

"I'm going over to Haven House," Asa said. "See if I can help out."

"You can bring Jaster and his wife and baby and whoever else wants to come over to Willow Way," Hazel said. "They'll need a place to stay."

Hazel took Fergus's arm. "C'mon, we'll need to stop at the Rexall," Hazel said. "I need a toothbrush, you know."

"You mean, there isn't one toothbrush in that whole big house?"

"And I want to stop at the pound."

"The pound?"

"Need a new cat."

His complaining voice trailed off as he got her to his truck. Rose and Suzy and Ginger and I watched him pick the old girl up and sit her in the truck cab.

Suzy took a huge breath and fainted dead away.

34

After we revived Suzy, we helped her back to my trailer, where I got her a change of clothes. She had fallen into the mud in Hazel's yard, so I tossed her dress in the wash. We gathered in the living room, and I supposed it couldn't have been helped, but we all circled around Suzy like cowboys circle their wagons when Indians attack. It was a little hard to tell if she minded or not. She was on the shy side.

"Are you all right?" Ginger asked. "Maybe you should go see a doctor. Did you hurt that arm?"

"No, no," Suzy said. "I don't need a doctor. I don't know why that happened. Maybe I just need to eat."

"You look skinny," my mother said. "When was the last time you ate anything?"

She shook her head. "A day or so ago. I just haven't been hungry."

"Well, that's understandable," Mother

said. "Look at what you're going through. Charlotte, get this girl some food."

Suzy pulled her fingers through her scraggly hair. "But that's what's weird. He hasn't hit me since the day before the barbecue. He says he's changed. But it's making me even more nervous. I haven't had much of an appetite."

I went into the kitchen to warm some chicken noodle soup. I chose a pretty bowl with purple flowers on it and my prettiest tumbler, the one with the ivy vines trailing around it.

Ginger clicked her tongue. I could hear her clear to the kitchen. "You mean, it's true, Suzy? Fergus hits you?"

She nodded. "But not lately, like I said. Lately he's been real nice. Calm, you know." Her eyes glistened with tears. "Too calm."

"There's always calm before a storm and it is not to be trusted," Mother said in only the way my mother could. "Yesterday was a grand day and now look."

Suzy's body language told me she was feeling uncomfortable. She wiggled her backside into the sofa and folded her arms — cast and all — across her chest.

"Why is he making you stick so close to him then?" Rose asked.

Suzy shrugged and sipped a glass of water.

"He just is. Says he can't let me out of his sight right now until things blow over a bit. Says he's worried about his job."

"You realize it's only a matter of time," I said. "I remember when Herman would —" I stopped talking. "It's nothing."

"What were you going to say?" Rose said.

"Yes, Charlotte," Mother said. "What were you going to say?"

Tears pooled in my eyes.

"You're crying," Suzy said.

"Herman used to hit me too," I said. "Not as much as Fergus, but . . ."

Rose put her hand over her mouth and then pulled it away. "I had a feeling. I had a feeling there was something you were hiding."

"Like your tattoos," Mother said. "And those scars. Why are you hiding?"

"Can't anymore," she said. She stood up and removed her sweater. "See that, Charlotte? You're the one who said I shouldn't hide my scars. Same goes for you."

Tears came a little harder as my mother wrapped her arms around me. "Oh, honey, I knew. I always knew something wasn't right, but I thought he just yelled a lot and ordered you around like you were some buck private in his army. If I had —"

"It's . . . it's okay, Mother. I wanted to tell

you. But it's hard, and just so you know, I think sometimes the yelling and name-calling hurts as much as the hitting — maybe even more. Bruises heal, but some words just linger forever."

I watched Suzy nod her head so hard I thought it would jump right off her shoulders. "That's true. That's true. Fergus can say just terrible things. Things that would hurt in a way his fist doesn't, hurt way down deep."

"He has no right," Rose said.

Suzy looked away and sighed. "But sometimes I think I deserve it when I do dumb things. Like the time I accidentally knocked some of his stamps off the table."

"Stamps?" I said.

She nodded. "Oh, yeah, Fergus has a very valuable stamp collection. He's always fiddling with it. Staring at those little pictures under a magnifier. He buys them and sells them and even goes to stamp shows. He hates it when I make fun of them."

She cracked a smile. "Sometimes I do it just 'cause I know it makes him mad. See how I am? It's my fault."

"It is not. He never has a right to hit you. Ever!" Mother said. "No matter how mad you make him."

"But he says he's helping me not be so

stubborn."

I wiped my eyes and nose, and then Rose grabbed my hands. "Really? Herman hit you? I thought he just yelled a lot."

I shook my head. "Yes. Especially if a sales call didn't go well. Somehow it was my fault and . . ."

"The Lord dealt with him but good," Ginger said.

"Let's not say that," I said. "Herman just ate too much butter and ice cream."

I looked at Suzy and took her hands in mine. "But it is better. I feel like a real person now."

Suzy started to cry. "But I love him. I don't know why, but I do. Still sometimes I feel like I don't. Like I want him to just go away."

"I know. I know," I said. "It's crazy. We love men who hurt us."

Lucky sidled near Suzy and put his head in her lap and whimpered. Suzy patted his side.

"Lucky knows," I said.

We talked for a good long while until Fergus came back. He leaned on his horn. I opened the door. He stood near his truck with his hand through the window poised to blow it again.

He seemed nervous. "Where's Suzy?" he called.

Rose whispered to her. "You don't have to go."

She nodded. "I'll be okay. Don't worry."

"Why's she wearing that?" Fergus hollered. "Where's her dress?"

"She fell," I said, "in Hazel's yard. She's wearing one of my dresses. I'll wash hers and bring it by."

He waved his hand. "No, no. Just keep it."

Suzy turned back and looked at us just before she climbed into the truck. "Don't worry," she mouthed.

It had been a difficult day, and time flew by at breakneck speed. It was already nearly four o'clock when Suzy left.

The phone rang.

"Hey," Ginger said. "They got the phones back up."

"Hello," I said bracing myself for anything. But it was only Cash Vangarten.

"We're all okay," I said. "Hang on." I put my hand over the mouthpiece. "He just wants to see how we made out in the storm."

"Oh," Rose said. "He's checking on you."

"Now, stop that. He's just concerned. His boss does live in Paradise."

I went back to Cash and listened while he asked about Hazel and the men.

"She's fine. A tree fell on her trailer but never touched her. She's at Willow Way. Most of the men came home and were out helping clear trees and branches."

Cash expressed his relief and then changed the subject.

"Yes. We'll still be able to play next week. Don't see why not."

After I hung up, Rose said, "That man likes you, Charlotte."

"He does not. And I don't care if he does like me. I am not ready for any relationship."

My mother whispered to Rose. They laughed. But I didn't dignify it by asking what was so funny, even if it did help relieve some tension in the room. For the next few hours we stayed close to home and made light of the storm and played Scrabble. By nine o'clock the power was still not restored, so we went to bed.

My watch read midnight, and I still had not fallen asleep. I could hear Lillian's nose whistle through the wall. It was so loud that I thought it was what kept me awake. But, no, the truth was that I had a hundred and one thoughts leapfrogging in my brain.

Thoughts about Herman, the game, Suzy, moving to Florida, all manner of worries.

At one o'clock I went to the bathroom, got a drink of water, and sat at the kitchen table in the glow of two candles and cried as quietly as I could. I thought it was monster grief again rearing its ugly head, but it didn't feel the same as before. I rolled my wedding band around on my finger. "Why am I keeping you? Maybe it's time."

It stuck a little at the knuckle and I twisted and pulled so hard I thought I might dislocate my finger, but it came off and I held it in my palm.

"Herman," I whispered, "it needs to be over now. I can't hang on to you anymore. This ring was supposed to be a symbol of unending love, but it never really was. So, like the reverend said, till death do us part."

At that moment the power came on, and the two lights over my stove came on and cast a glow in the kitchen. I took the ring to my bedroom, opened my jewelry box, and dropped it inside. "Goodbye, Herman. I did love you. Too bad you never knew it."

Lucky, who was lying in a circle on the floor near my bed, suddenly perked up like he heard something strange.

"Oh, no! Don't tell me that maniac is making another midnight ride through

Paradise." I waited, but I didn't hear any hoof beats or gunshots.

Lucky still seemed alarmed. "What's wrong?"

He took hold of my pajama pant leg and pulled.

"What? You need to go out?"

He barked.

"All right, all right. Can't sleep, anyway."

I pulled on my robe and slippers and took Lucky to the door. I opened it. He grabbed my sleeve and pulled.

"I don't want to go out, you do. Now go on. I'll make some cocoa."

Mother must have heard us. "What's happening?" she called from the hallway.

"It's just Lucky. I thought he needed to go out, but he won't go."

He ran to Mother and pulled the hem of her nightgown.

"He's upset about something," she said. "He wants us to go with him."

"Okay, Lucky. Show us."

He bounded out the door. We followed with my flashlight.

The moon was full and high in the sky, so it cast a generous light on the street. Lucky moved fast. I tried to keep up. He'd run out ahead. Stop. Turn back to make sure we were still there and then run. It looked like he was heading for the Wrinkels's.

"Where are you going?"

Then he veered off and headed toward Angel Field. I followed as fast as my legs could carry me. My slippers kept coming off until I finally just left them in the woods and went barefoot over the rough ground and twigs and leaves. But then, just at the edge of the woods before the grass started, I saw Suzy lying in a heap.

Lucky licked her face and whimpered.

"Suzy. Suzy." I ran to her. "She's still alive."

"But she's badly beaten," Mother said. "I'll stay with her. Go get Asa."

I looked toward the Frost Sisters' house. No lights.

I patted Suzy's cheek. "Wake up. Wake up, Suzy. Suzy."

She opened her eyes as much as she could. They were nearly swollen shut.

"Oh, Suzy. I'm so sorry. I should have made you stay."

"Not now, Charlotte," Mother said. "Go get Asa so he can help carry her home."

I took Lucky's head in my hands and spoke directly into his eyes. "Asa. Go get Asa."

He took off like a bullet through the woods.

Tears streamed down Suzy's face. "I ran. I ran out the door, only I didn't know where to go."

"It's okay," I said. "You just stay quiet." I dabbed at the blood running from her lip with my robe.

She tried to get up.

"No. Just stay. We should get you to the hospital."

She shook her head. "No. No. Please."

"Okay. But at least let me get Marlabeth," I said.

She nodded and closed her eyes.

"Don't let her fall asleep," Mother said. "She might have a concussion. She could go into shock or something. Keep her talking." She patted Suzy's hand and rubbed her arm and brushed her hair out of her face.

We didn't wait long before we heard Asa and Lucky tramping through the woods.

"Asa, look what he did," I cried. "He really hurt her this time."

Asa knelt near Suzy. He scooped her up with his one arm. "Come on, let's get you out of here. Can you walk?"

She nodded.

"Take her to my place," I said. "I'm going to get Marlabeth and Rose."

35

Marlabeth treated Suzy's wounds with a variety of ointments and tea. She bandaged the cut on her cheek and even stitched a gash in her forehead. Then she checked the cast on her arm, all without saying a word.

When she finished, she said, "You can't go home now, Suzy. I'm going to send Jacob over there with Rube and Charlie Lundy. They'll fix his wagon."

"No. Don't," she said. "They'll kill him."

Marlabeth patted her hand. "Right now you need rest and chamomile tea. Let the men handle it."

"She's right," Mother said. "It's high time that man got his just deserts."

"But don't be like him. I don't want the others to be like him."

"Then call the police," Mother said.

Marlabeth dropped gauze and tape in her medical bag. "They won't do nothing for her. Up here police believe a man has a right to do this. Maybe not in the big city. But up here."

"That tears it," Mother said. "Charlotte, you're coming home with me for certain now."

"Mother. It's not the time."

I could tell Rose was trying to keep from talking, but she couldn't help it. "What? Are you moving away, Charlotte?"

"No. At least" — I looked at my mother — "I don't know. Now is not the time."

Lucky and Asa stayed at Suzy's side as she lay in my bed until she fell asleep. I didn't know what Marlabeth gave her, but it did the trick.

"Valerian root," she said. "It'll knock an elephant out. She'll sleep for a good long while."

I walked her to the door. "Thank you." I kissed her cheek.

"Call me if you need me. But I'll come by and check on her in a few hours."

Rose and I sat at the kitchen table. "It's my fault," Rose said. "I should have done something. I knew what was going on long before you got here."

"Don't do that. What we need to do now is convince her not to go back."

"She will, you know," Rose said.

"I know." I patted her arm — the one with

three crosses etched into it in purple ink.

We talked until dawn, when Rose decided to go home and try and sleep. I watched her walk down the street, and when I went inside, I found her heavy brown sweater on the sofa.

I grabbed it and ran after her. "Rose. You forgot —"

"Don't need it anymore. Suzy can't hide, you can't hide, and I'm not hiding anymore. Jesus paid the price for us all — me, you, Suzy, Fergus, even Herman. Who am I to think my sin or my brand of suffering is worse than anyone else's?"

I swallowed and choked back tears.

"Hardest thing in the world is to forgive your enemies," Rose said. "Second hardest is to share it with those who need sharing. Third hardest is leaving them behind."

When I went inside, Asa was filling the coffeepot with water and Mother was slicing apple pie.

"How is she?" I asked.

"Sleeping still," Asa said.

"What now?"

"I'll need to go over there," Asa said. "I need to see if the boys did anything to Fergus."

"Do you think they did?"

"Pretty sure they might have beaten the

tar out of him. If not last night, then soon. Marlabeth will tell them to."

I got cups from the cupboard. "Funny. When I first moved here, I didn't think anyone cared about anyone else around here."

"We take care of our own. We might not talk a lot, or have lots of barbecues, but we care about each other."

"I see that now. I'm going to go peek at Suzy."

She was still asleep. Her eyes were so swollen I figured she wouldn't be able to open them when she woke up. Lucky still sat at her side. I patted his head. "Good boy. You are our hero, you know. Who knows what might have happened if you didn't find her."

I started to walk out the door, but first I took Herman's picture and dropped it in the trash can. Then I turned back to Lucky. "Only, how did you know?"

He smiled and blustered.

I reached into the trash can and got the picture. "Hardest thing in the world is to forgive." I put the picture in my top drawer. "Maybe someday I'll be able to look you in the eye again."

It turned out that the men did visit Fergus. The next time I saw him, later the next day, he had two very shiny black eyes. It was also the day Suzy decided to go home. Mother and I tried to talk her out of it. But she was determined. Maybe I shouldn't have told her I saw Fergus.

"He'll be good for now. And as long as I don't do nothing to make him upset —"

I shook my head. "This is wrong, Suzy. Very, very wrong. At least wait until the swelling goes down."

"Or until he comes looking for you," Mother said. "Do you think he's even been looking for you?"

Suzy lightly touched her cheek. "I . . . I don't know. I reckon he might have looked. Maybe Asa or one of the other guys told him I was here."

"Please think about it," I said. "You can stay here as long as you need."

She took my hand. "Thank you, Charlotte. But don't worry. I have a feeling it's all going to be okay."

Mother and I walked her to her trailer. We stopped at Rose's on the way. She was under the hand tending to her petunias.

"Suzy," she said. "I was just up in the palm praying for you. How are you feeling?"

"I'm okay," she said. I could see that she was looking up at the hand, even through swollen eyes. "I don't understand about the hand. Fergus says he hates it. Says it gives him the creeps. Says he's gonna take a sledgehammer to it one of these days."

"That's because he doesn't believe," Rose said. "But imagine it, Suzy. Imagine that God has you, Suzy Wrinkel, in his hand, right now, today."

I looked up at the statue. The afternoon sun filtered through the trees with a beam landing right smack dab in the middle.

"God doesn't have hands," Suzy said, and she started on her way down the street. Mother and I had to hurry to catch up with her, the determination evident on her face.

That was when we saw Fergus. He met up with us, took Suzy by the hand, and led her home without saying a word. Not a single word. My stomach tightened. "Mom, he's gonna kill her."

"Let's call the police," she said. "At least we can talk to them. Beg them to arrest him. Surely they will do something."

"Okay, let's go call. But I have a feeling the others are right. I think they're just going to blow it off, like that big wind the other day. Just leave more destruction."

The Angels waited at the trailer.

"What gives, Charlotte?" Clara said. "We ever playing ball again?"

"Yeah. I feel like I need to slaughter that ball," Gwendolyn said.

"You bet. We're playing the Thunder again next week. It's all arranged. Right here on Angel Field. Seven o'clock, Tuesday." I tried my best to sound upbeat.

"What about some practice time?" Frankie asked.

"Tomorrow. One o'clock. That okay?"

"What about a babysitter? Fleur de Lee can't do it now."

"I'll think of something."

The team wandered off, and I grabbed my mother's sleeve. "Come on, let's go make that call."

Lucky met us at the door but ran right past us. He had other things on his mind.

I dialed the police and spoke with Officer Flegel. He pretty much gave me the brush-off. "Sorry, Ma'am, but unless the victim makes the call, there is nothing we can do."

"Hear that, Mom? They don't even care. It's like getting a marriage license gives the husband the license to kill. It isn't right."

Mother hugged me. "No, Charlotte. It's not. Maybe that will change someday."

After dinner I started to think about the game again and drew up a new batting order. "I think I'll let Rose lead off this time," I said. "She can be a powerhouse. Maybe she'll knock one into the cornfield."

"That could give your team some gusto," Mother said. "And then maybe Ginger, put the Thunder off their guard, and then Gwendolyn."

"Mother," I said. "You do care."

"You were right, Charlotte. There's just something about Paradise."

"Who are we going to get to watch the children for practice now that Fleur de Lee is busy with her own Angel?"

Lillian flipped through a copy of the *TV Guide.* "Don't look at me. I'm too old to watch a bunch of kids. I'm afraid I couldn't keep up. I don't move as quickly as I once did."

"I wonder if Asa's cousin will come down again," I said. "He's such a nice man. Claims he was the recipient of a miracle. Got cured of cancer."

"Oh, that's rubbish," Mother said.

Rubbish or not, Asa managed to talk Studebaker into watching the children.

I arrived with Rose and Ginger around one o'clock. The others were already there, including Marlabeth, who had a great report on Fleur de Lee and our littlest Angel.

"They are all resting at Willow Way," she said. "Hazel Crenshaw is keeping watch.

Have you ever seen that mansion? It's got fifteen rooms; five bathrooms; the biggest kitchen I ever saw, with copper-bottom pots hanging from the ceiling; and, get this, there's a bowling alley in the basement — if you can call it something as ordinary as a basement."

"A bowling alley?" Greta said. "I knew it was huge, but —"

"I heard it burned down," Clara Kaninsky said. "And that's why Hazel came to live here. We heard it burned down right after Birdy died. He left the factory to her, you know."

"No, it didn't burn down," I said. "It's still out there on — wait a minute, you know about Hazel Crenshaw?"

They cracked up. "Of course we do, Charlotte. The husbands don't know. But we all do." She pointed with her thumb around the circle.

"I didn't," said Ginger.

"That's because she don't sign your paycheck."

They laughed. "She's a good old bird. We're going to miss her around here."

"She'll be back," Marlabeth said. "I was talking to her just a little while ago. She bought a new trailer. It's going to be delivered in a couple of weeks."

"Good," Frankie said. "We need her around here."

"But that's not all," Marlabeth said. "She gave Willow Way to Haven House. They all moved in. The whole group. I think there were six others besides Jaster and Fleur de Lee. She just needs someone to take charge, you know, run the place."

I sighed. "I wish I could get her to help Suzy."

The team grew quiet and thoughtful. Rose raised her hands like she was about to pray.

Frankie pushed her arm down. "Hold on. If she won't, maybe we can. Maybe this bunch of kooky ball players can get Suzy to leave that rat fink of a husband."

They all started talking at once. Tossing ideas out. Clara suggested they sneak her out under cover of darkness and take her to the new Haven House to live. "She can take care of them. Lord knows she'd fit in."

"I could send her to my cousin in Idaho," Greta suggested. "She could help out on the farm."

The ideas sputtered out until I quieted them down.

"Those are all good ideas, but we can't make Suzy leave until she's ready. We have to help her make the decision herself."

I tossed a softball in the air and caught it.

"But right now, we have a game to get ready for. Cash Vangarten and the Thunder pulled a fast one on us. But we're going to get them this time," I said. My voice rose a little.

"You really think we can beat them?" Edwina said.

"Why not?" Thomasina said. "Some of us just have to remember to catch the ball." She glared at her sister.

"And some of us need to hit the ball." Gwendolyn said.

"Okay, okay. Let's get started with some batting practice."

I waved to Greta, who had run to check on the kids in the Frost Sisters' yard. She held Baby Ruth and spoke with Studebaker a minute. He took the baby and shooed her away.

I waved everyone around again and tried my best to convince them that they were better than the Thunder. "They may be big, but you all have something they don't."

"Yeah," Marlabeth said. "The stinks. We got the stinks real bad."

"I won't listen to that. I was going to say you all have heart and soul. Think about it. Who rushed to Fleur de Lee's side when she was having the baby? The Thunder just stood there like oxen in headlights. Look at the way we pitched together through the storm. We are a real team."

"We are," Rose said. "One for all and all for one."

"That's the spirit. Keep talking and let's get out there and beat the socks off 'em. We have four days before the game. Gwendolyn, you bat first. Frankie, you pitch her some hard ones. Don't let up. Ginger, you get over there at shortstop and start thinking about some trick plays you can pull — you know you're dying to."

She scampered off like a munchkin. I expected her to burst into song, she seemed so elated to have permission to be sneaky.

Rose plopped her catcher's mask on. "And Rose, you just concentrate on where you throw the ball. Take your time. Get it to the correct player and you'll do fine."

"I can do all things. I can do all things," she repeated on her way to home plate.

I raised my hands to heaven. "Lord, if you're listening, ignite a fire in these women that won't blow out."

36

The Angels had their best practice ever. Studebaker Kowalski was a natural with the children, and Asa managed to get Edwina to keep her eyes open when a pop fly came her way. Gwendolyn just kept getting better at hitting, Thomasina could catch pretty much anything, and Frankie controlled her pitches like the pro I knew was inside her. The Angels were shaping up, and I was very proud.

Afterwards, I invited Rose and Ginger back to my trailer. As much as I hated to admit it, I needed a buffer between myself and my mother again, and they always did the job so well.

"I'm hungry," I said as I pushed open the door. "How about you guys?"

"Sure," Ginger said. "I could eat."

Lucky greeted me with his usual enthusiasm. I patted his head and then reached for the Milk-Bones on the counter. "Here you go, boy."

He slid under the kitchen table and gnawed on his treat.

"How'd that crazy dog know she was hurt and lying in the woods?" Ginger asked. She hopped up on her chair.

"Dogs have a kind of ESP," Rose said.

"Get out," Ginger said. "ESP."

"I said a *kind* of ESP. They're very tuned into their surroundings, and when something isn't right, they know it. And they do their best to tell you."

"Where's my mother?" I said.

"She wouldn't just leave, would she?" Rose asked.

"She's done crazier stuff. Once she had an argument with my father and ran off to France for dinner by herself."

"France?"

"Yep. Got on a plane and ZOOM! Off she went for escargot."

"Eww, snails," Ginger said.

"Don't knock them till you tried them," Mother said as she walked down the hallway.

"Mother. I was worried you left."

"No, Charlotte. I just took a nap. And don't forget I brought you back that lovely perfume from Paris that time I ran away as you called it and that dish you were so crazy about."

I pulled some burger out of the freezer. "Darn. I should have gotten this out this morning. Had my mouth all ready for a juicy cheeseburger."

"Let's go out," Ginger said. "Let's drive into Shoops and go to the Pink Lady Restaurant. I hear you can get a mighty fine burger there."

"Pink Lady, oooohhh," Rose said. "That's where Charlotte met Cash Vangarten." She said it with a sing-song lilt to her voice.

"Sounds like a plan," I said. "How about it, Mom? Want to come?"

Mother's body language spoke volumes. "No, no. That's all right. I'll stay here. Don't take this wrong, dear, but I could use a little space tonight."

"Come on, Rose, let's go. When was the last time you went out to eat?"

"Years."

"We'll get Asa for protection and go," I said.

I pushed the burger back into the freezer next to some spaghetti sauce I was saving.

"I don't know," Rose said.

"Come on, Rose," I said. "It'll be fun. Girl's night out . . . well, except for Asa."

Rose heaved a sigh. "Okay. Let's go."

461

I called Asa, and he jumped at the chance. I invited Studebaker also, but he had already gone back to Bright's Pond.

So there we were, piled into the bright red Galaxy headed into town — the widow, the midget, the one-armed man, and the tattooed woman.

The Pink Lady was crowded, but we got a table pretty quickly. Probably because I went in first, secured the table, and then the others followed. The crowd eyed them like a traveling freak show had just come to town. I could feel Rose's anxiety in my chest. Ginger walked across the crowded room with her head held as high as she could. Even though I heard someone whistling the "Heigh Ho" song from *Snow White and the Seven Dwarves.*

"I miss my sweater," Rose said. "You should have let me wear a jacket." She slid into the booth.

Ginger sat next. But not before someone in the restaurant said, "Hey, she needs a booster seat."

I watched Asa make eye contact with the creep.

The waitress brought us waters and slopped them on the table. "I'll be back for your order." She snapped her gum.

"That's disgusting," Rose said.

"Shh. Just enjoy being out."

Now, I would never say this to anyone, but I will admit that as I sat there with my friends, I felt a little like the nurse taking the patients out of the asylum on a trial run.

Rose sipped her water. Her hand shook as she drank.

"I know what I want," I said. "Cheeseburger, fries, and a chocolate milkshake. I haven't had a good cheeseburger since I left home. Left home. Listen to me, I make it sound like I ran away."

"You did," Asa said.

The waitress, wearing a pink uniform with white lace on the collar and sleeves and a white apron smeared with grease and ketchup, came back. She dropped four menus on the table. "I'll be back for your order."

Ginger sneezed twice. *Not now!* I thought.

"Hey Sneezy," hollered the creep. "Where are the other six dwarfs?" Then he let out a belly laugh that shook the tiny restaurant.

That was all Asa could take. Ginger tried to settle him down. But Asa, being the protective sort, leaped to his feet and marched toward the creep. The creep stood, all six feet of him, with shoulders just about as wide and a pulsing tattoo of a scantily clad girl on his bicep. I could smell his onion breath from where we sat.

"You got something to say?" Asa said. "You say it outside."

"Oh yeah?" the creep said. And he balled up his fist. "What's a one-armed freak gonna do?"

Asa decked him. Just like that. Asa reared back and SMACK! Home run.

That was when the cook came running out of the back wielding a spatula. "Get out of my restaurant. Take it to the alley."

Asa brushed his jeans and extended his hand to the creep, who was still on the floor rubbing his jaw.

The creep pushed his hand away. "Ah, go back to the circus."

"Better to have one arm than no brains," Asa said.

The waitress congratulated Asa. "Glad somebody finally decked that moron. He's been asking for it for a long time." She gave Asa extra fries.

My burger was exactly what I wanted. Asa ate two — one was on the house — and Ginger and Rose enjoyed their first restaurant meal in a very long time.

It was nearly nine o'clock by the time we got back to Paradise. I dropped off Rose and Ginger and then drove up the hill and parked the Galaxy. Asa was slow to move and fidgeted with the buckle on his boot.

"You okay?" I put my hand on his shoulder. I was always glad when I could touch his left arm. There was still something creepy about touching what was left of his right.

"I haven't seen Suzy in a couple of days," he said before opening the car door. "I hope she's okay."

"Do you really see her that much? I mean, she does stay inside her trailer most of the time. And I'm sure Fergus has a tight leash on her now."

Asa smiled. "Yeah. I see her. Used to anyway. We had a signal. She knew when I was coming by the trailer, and if Fergus wasn't around she'd meet me in the back. Just to say hi. It wasn't like we —"

"I understand. I worry too, but let's pray she's all right."

"I hope," Asa said. "But I got to admit that I'm afraid Fergus is gonna kill her one of these days. Maybe not on purpose, but —"

"Have you ever talked to Suzy about it?"

"I tried. Once or twice. She just keeps going back to him. Heck, I even told her she could leave him and marry me. I'd never,

ever treat her like that."

"I know, Asa. You're in love with her."

He nodded. "Think I should try and talk to her again?"

"I do, Asa. I think you need to tell her how you feel."

He reached over and kissed my cheek. "I'm glad you found Paradise, even if it isn't what you wanted."

"Oh, Asa, let's just say it's not what I expected, but as it turns out, it's exactly what I needed. I just didn't know it."

I waited until he was out of sight. I looked toward Hazel's trailer. It was still there, with the bent roof. "Hurry home, Hazel. I miss you."

Mother was asleep on the couch with Lucky's head in her lap. That explained why he didn't greet me. He didn't want to disturb her. I patted his head and rubbed behind his ears. "Good dog," I whispered.

Mother woke. "You're home. Have a good time?"

"We did." I held up a pink bag. "I brought you a doggie bag."

Lucky barked. "Not for you, silly. A people doggie bag."

She looked inside it. "Cheese fries. I haven't had them in a long time."

I made tea, and we watched TV for another hour or so before turning in for the night. "Tomorrow's a big day," I said. "I hope the Angels play well. I'm a little nervous."

"Don't let them know," Mother said. "If you're nervous, they'll all be nervous. You be strong, they'll be strong."

"Thanks, Mom." I kissed her cheek. "Good night." I patted her cheek and she caught my hand.

"Charlotte. I still think you should come to Florida. We'll wait until after softball, but please, would you at least consider it? You deserve more than a run-down trailer."

"Mother, look, I'll think about it."

37

Game day arrived, and I woke with a headache the size of Mount Rushmore after a
third in a row of restless nights. Mother had
coffee brewing, and I thought I even heard
bacon sizzling. Lucky sat near the bedroom
door waiting for me.

"Today's the day," I said. "Do you think
we can do it?"

He barked and then lay down and hid his
eyes with his paws.

"Some cheerleader you are."

I took a quick shower and dressed. Mother
looked as though she had been up for hours.
The trailer was clean, dusted, and organized. Breakfast waited for me on the
kitchen table.

"Thank you, Mom, this is so sweet," I said
as I sat at the table.

She filled my cup — even remembering
that I preferred morning coffee in an actual
cup and saucer. "I'm happy to help, Char-

lotte. This is what it will be like when you come to Cocoa Reef."

"Mother. I have a headache. I don't want to discuss this now. I like it here."

"Here? But, Charlotte, that maniac who thinks he's Paul Revere was out riding through the place again this morning. Woke me from a sound sleep at five a.m."

I laughed. "Boy, I must have been tired. I didn't hear a thing."

"See, see, that's what's worrying me. You've gotten so used to the . . ."

"Zaniness?"

"Okay, zaniness. You're numb to it. Who knows when your guard will be down and something terrible will happen. A bullet could zing right through here and blow your brains out."

"It won't."

I sipped coffee and dipped the corner of my toast in the yolk of one of the perfectly cooked dippy eggs on my plate. "You still make the best dippies, Mother."

She smiled and joined me at the table. "I'm starved. I waited until you got up so we could eat together. "Looks like a splendid day," she said, looking through the window. "Now that that man has gone home. Charlotte, he's a menace. One of these days he's going to kill somebody."

"Mother, please. Not now. I have to get ready for the game later."

"I understand, Charlotte. I really do. I'm just concerned for your well-being. To be perfectly honest, and you know I like to tell the truth whenever possible, I'm afraid that nasty Fergus Wrinkel is going to . . . oh, Charlotte. He could kill you. He has threatened you already."

I gave my mother a reassuring squeeze of her hand. "That won't happen."

We finished our meals in relative silence. I couldn't tell her how frightened I really felt.

Rose couldn't have prayed for better weather. The temperature hovered around seventy-five degrees all day with light clouds floating high in the sky. According to the channel two weather lady any rain would hold off until tomorrow. After supper, I got dressed in my uniform, which Mother had laundered and pressed for me. She had even washed my Keds, which didn't make me real happy, but I let it slide.

"Okay, Mom, the game starts at seven. I'll see you then." I hugged her and patted Lucky's head. "Now, don't make any plans to move to Florida with him, Mother."

She grinned. He grinned too, and I got the distinct impression that they were in cahoots.

I met Rose at her trailer about an hour before the Thunder were scheduled to arrive. We sat in the hand and Rose prayed for each and every Angel. She prayed for the Thunder and Cash Vangarten, and she prayed for me.

"And Lord God, be with Charlotte in a special way. Father, I'm just asking that you be Charlotte's coach and show her the way to victory if that be your will."

She signed off as usual.

"Do you really think we have a chance?" she asked after we climbed down.

"Sure. Why not? We have some good players, Rose. I'm banking on the fact that we didn't know what we were facing last time. But now, well, now we know, and we have two good incentives to win — baby Angel and Suzy."

"I sure would like to win," she said. "It would mean so much to everyone."

The team was at the field getting in some batting practice. Asa pitched while the others took turns smacking the ball. I watched Gwendolyn knock one three rows back into the cornfield.

"That ball is gone," Rose said.

"Now, if she could only do that when it counts," I said.

I saw Studebaker up on the scoreboard. He waved.

The Thunder's bus rolled in about ten minutes after six.

"They're early," Rose said.

"Just trying to psyche us out," I said. "Ignore them."

I gathered the team around and gave them a last-minute pep talk, but it wasn't needed. The Angels had pepped themselves up over the last few days and were eager to get started.

"We're gonna kill 'em," Gwendolyn said.

"I've been practicing a tricky pitch," Frankie said. "My version of a screwball."

"Just so it's legal," I said. "That umpire is a stickler for rules."

The Thunder unloaded their equipment and took the field for warm-ups. Cash Vangarten barked instructions like a seal, even clapping his hands in front of him. He seemed like such a nice guy, really nice, but he was sneaky, and I will admit that I felt nervous around him. I tried to stop the thoughts, but I just wasn't ready to trust any man.

Not wanting to appear too anxious, I deliberately didn't watch their practice. I wanted to give an air of confidence, even if my knees knocked like a car engine with

472

bad pistons. So I turned my attention to our side of the field. It seemed like everyone in Paradise turned out to watch. I saw Rube and Charlie and Jake on the sidelines already cheering the Angels on. There were lawn chairs, picnic baskets, and blankets set out, children running around and beer can flip tops popping everywhere. I thought the entire population of Paradise had turned out except Suzy and Fergus.

Even Fleur de Lee arrived with Jaster and the new baby. She walked up to me holding her tiny bundle in a blanket the color of a sunflower. "Look here, Miss Charlotte. I brought the littlest Angel." She opened her blanket and showed me. "And see that," Fleur de Lee said. "She's wearing a teeny, tiny Angels' shirt. That nice Hazel Crenshaw had it made special."

Jaster laughed. "She said if they could make one for Ginger, why not the baby?"

I reached my pinky into the blanket and Angel took hold of it. "That's quite a grip. She's gonna be a ballplayer, all right." That was when Mother startled me from behind. "She's beautiful. Just perfect."

Jaster gave Mother a funny look. "She is perfect. Not like Fleur de Lee or me."

"I didn't mean anything by it," Mother said.

"Sure you did," Jaster said. "But that's okay. Some of the normalest people I know are the most retarded."

I nearly busted out laughing and had to turn away, and, much to my surprise and glee, I saw Hazel sitting on our bench. I was so happy to see her I ran to her and kissed her warm cheek.

"You came. I am so glad."

"Course I did," she said. "I wouldn't miss this game."

I waved Mother over. "Why don't you sit with Hazel, Mother?"

"Hazel," Mother said. "I'm happy to see you. How are things at Willow Drive? Wasn't that what you called it?"

"Way," Hazel corrected. "It's Willow Way. And things are fine, but I do want to get back to Para —"

"Sorry," I interrupted. "The umpire has arrived. Time to play ball."

"Have a good game, dear," Mother said.

"Knock the stuffing out of them," Hazel said.

The umpire called the coaches and captains together. Cash and I exchanged smiles. He shook my hand. "Good luck, Charlotte. Hope you don't have any more pregnant women on your side."

"Nah, just the one."

Missy snarled at Frankie.

"Aw, put a sock in it," Frankie said.

"Now listen up," the umpire said. "We already have four innings played. Three to go. We pick up where we left off." He looked at a card. "The Thunder had Mulligan on second base. There are two outs, and Tyson was just coming to bat when . . . when the incident happened."

"It was a baby," I said. "Not an incident."

"Excuse me," the umpire said. "Baby."

The captains walked off. Cash caught my arm. "If you lose, we have dinner together."

My heart skipped a beat. The sudden action startled me, and I pulled away from him. My thumb instinctively found my empty ring finger. "Cash. What is this?"

"Whoa, whoa. I didn't mean to scare you."

"It's okay."

"I didn't know how else to ask. I want to take you to dinner."

"Can we discuss this later?"

"Please," he whispered. "Just say yes."

"I can't. Maybe later."

The Angels took the field to the applause of the Paradise fans.

"I have to get to the dugout." Then I looked into those sexy eyes of his. "Okay, maybe. If we win."

"No way. You'll never win."

"We'll see."

Studebaker had the score already in place. The scoreboard had looked a tiny bit wobbly since the storm; they'd shored it up best as they could with two-by-fours and chewing gum. We lost a number nine in the wind. The score stood at Thunder ten, Angels zero.

I took my spot near the bench. Lord have mercy.

Tyson walked to the batter's box. She grunted and smacked the plate twice.

Frankie wound up. She pitched. The ball took a nice, loping arch but dropped before home plate.

"Ball," called the ump.

Rose threw the ball back to Frankie. She took a deep breath.

"It's okay, Frankie," Ginger hollered. "You got it this time."

"No batter, no batter," hollered Clara Kaninsky.

Tyson smacked home plate and rested the bat on her shoulders. Then she got into her stance, bent at the knees, looking like she could send the ball to the moon.

Frankie wound up and pitched. Tyson swung an instant too early, and the bottom fell out of Frankie's pitch just at the right time. That must have been her screwball.

"Strike one," called the umpire.

Four pitches later the inning was over.

I had never seen a happier group of purple and white Angels run off the field.

"Good job, good job," I said.

"Ginger, you're up. Clara, you're next."

Ginger grabbed her bat and swung it a few times. We heard the laughter from the Thunder drifting over the infield. "Okay," I said. "Remember, whatever it takes."

Ginger took the plate. She held her tiny bat on her shoulder. Their pitcher pitched. Way high. Ball one. Ginger got into her stance. Ball two. I smiled. That woman couldn't pitch to her.

Ginger swung at the third pitch. She made contact. The ball dribbled down the third base line. Ginger took off running, her little legs moving as fast as they could. I saw horror in the eyes of the Thunder's first baseman. Ginger was headed right for her like a rogue torpedo. The third baseman threw the ball. It soared over the confused first baseman's head. Ginger rounded toward second. The throw was high again and soared into the outfield. Asa waved Ginger on to third. She was booking now. Asa put his hand up to stop her at third but she blew past him and was on a direct course for home and the Thunder's catcher. Ginger plowed right into the catcher, knocking her onto her back, where she lay like an upside-down turtle waving her arms and legs. Ginger had scored our first home run.

The Angels and the fans went nuts. Screaming and hollering. Ginger dusted herself off while the catcher complained to the ump. "She was like a bullet. She aimed right at me. That ain't fair."

The umpire waved her away. "No contest," he called. "Home run."

Cash Vangarten ripped off his cap and threw it on the ground. "Unsportsmanlike. Unsportsmanlike conduct," he hollered. But then he stopped, picked up his cap, and went back to his bench. He was close to being ejected, and he knew it.

The umpire shook his head, dusted off home plate, and hollered, "Play ball!"

I liked to think the umpire was on our side that day. Well, that umpire and the big umpire in the sky.

The game took on a decidedly vengeful air as both teams duked it out in one way or another.

But it was the top of the seventh now. The Thunder were up. They had a player in scoring position on third, and their big gun, Missy, was at the plate. All she needed was one good hit in Edwina's direction and it would be over.

I chewed my nails and called a meeting with Rose and Frankie, Gwendolyn and Marlabeth.

"Now, look," I said. "All she needs is a line drive into the outfield. Edwina can't field very well, and their batter will score for sure. We can't let that happen. Frankie, you pitch low and inside. Give her a hard time. And Rose, whatever you do, do not drop the ball."

I went back to the bench and stood next to Asa. "They'll do it," he said.

I sucked air. "I can't watch."

Asa pulled my hands from my eyes. "But you have to."

Frankie pitched. Their slugger swung at an inside pitch. She hit a slow roller right at Ginger. Ginger fielded the ball as their player on third took off toward home.

"Throw to home," I screamed. "Throw to home."

Ginger threw with all her might. She pulled the ball back with her little arm and heaved it toward Rose, and in all my days I had never seen anything like it. I could almost see flames on the ball. It was like a meteor hurtling toward Rose. It was like the hand of God carried it through the air.

"Catch it, Rose. Please, catch it."

Smack. I heard the ball land in Rose's glove, a millisecond before their base runner slid.

"She's out," called the umpire. "Game over. Angels win!"

The Angels leaped and hollered and congratulated each other. Marlabeth picked Ginger up on her shoulders and paraded her around the field to the cheers of the crowd. Even Hazel and Mother jumped from the bench. They held hands and jumped up and down like two little girls. Asa ran around with one sleeve flapping like a pelican wing, and I thought he was looking for an extra hand to clap. So I lent him mine.

"You did it, Charlotte. You won!" he said.

"We won," I said. "We won."

The celebration continued for five minutes before I sent the Angels over to the Thunder to shake hands. I didn't want to be criticized for being unsportsmanlike.

I offered Cash my hand.

"Good game," he said. "I never would have believed it."

"Well, you have size and power and experience on your side. But we have something you don't."

"I know, I know," he said. "Heart. You have heart."

I waved his word away. "Nah, heart shmart. What we have is a hell-on-wheels midget and a one-armed pitching coach. Not to mention a lactating mother with sore breasts, a tattooed lady, a group of house-wives who needed some fun in their lives, and two very special causes to spur us on."

Cash laughed. "Now that's dangerous," he said. "But you know what this means, don't you?"

"What?"

"Dinner. Friday night. I'll pick you up at seven."

"I can't, Cash. Not yet." I looked away from him and spied my mother coming near.

He grabbed my hand again, and this time I took it back. "I said I can't. Not yet."

"She said no." My mother glared at him.

"But why?"

"She has her reasons." Mother draped her arm around my shoulders. "Good game, dear. You really knocked 'em for a loop."

Hazel yakked it up with Asa and Rube. "Now, this is a team I am proud to spon-sor," she said loud enough for Cash to hear. He shook his head and loped toward the waiting school bus.

The Thunder rode off with their tails between their legs and the sun setting behind the mountains in ribbons of purple and white, orange and red. "Better luck next time, ladies," I said with a two-finger salute.

I gathered the team around. "That was amazing," I said. "I knew you had it in you."

Gwendolyn cried. "We did good, Charlotte. We did good."

"Well," Thomasina said. "We did well."

Edwina chuckled and said. "Well? Now that's a deep subject."

Asa patted her back. "You did. You all did good."

"Let's go home," I said. "And don't let this go to your heads. We still have eight games to play, but if you play every game like you did today, then I'd say we're headed for the championship of the Trailer Park League."

They held hands in a circle and cheered for themselves. A well-deserved moment of joy.

"Look," called Edwina. "I see smoke. It's coming from the trailer park."

"It is!" hollered Asa. "That's a fire." He took off.

"I smell something bad," Marlabeth said. "It's not wood smoke or trash."

I grabbed my mother's hand, and we ran through the woods toward the smoke, followed closely by Rose and Ginger. We stopped at the tree line just where the asphalt began.

"Something's on fire," Rose said. "I can see flames through the trees."

"O my Lord," I said. We moved closer.

"It's the Wrinkel trailer," Rose said, as she dropped to her knees and prayed.

38

Orange and yellow flames enveloped the Wrinkels's trailer. Black, billowing smoke rose from the roof and the windows.

"Suzy," I said. "Where's Suzy?"

I searched through the gathering crowd in the darkening light. I didn't see her or Fergus. I did notice that his truck was missing, and I hoped against hope that they were together.

"I can't believe my eyes," Mother said. She moved back from the intensifying heat. "Charlotte, come away from there. You'll burn up."

"Suzy! Suzy!" I called.

Just as the words left my mouth, Fergus pulled up in his truck. He stopped so fast the truck lurched forward and back. He dove out of the cab and headed for his front door.

Asa and Rube ran toward him. "No! Fergus. Don't!" they hollered. "Don't go in there!"

But it didn't matter. All we could do was watch. Fergus pulled open his front door, and BLAM! an explosion shook the ground and sent sparks and flames and debris hurtling toward us.

Asa grabbed Rose and flung her as far as he could. I scrambled toward them, my knees shook, my heart pounded. I could barely breathe from the heat and smell of the fire, burning wood and plastic that stung my nose and lungs. My ears rang from the sound.

"Fergus," I said. "Is he . . . dead?"

Asa swallowed and wiped perspiration and soot from his face. "There's no way he survived that."

Tears welled in my eyes, tears from the surging heat and the impossible emotions.

"Do they all explode like that?" I asked Asa. "Do all trailers just explode like a bomb?"

Asa helped Rose to her feet. He brushed off her back. "Propane. It was the propane tanks, I'm sure."

"Propane?" Mother said. "Charlotte, you are not staying here any longer. I demand that you move to Cocoa Reef with me.

Tonight!" And she marched off toward my trailer.

"Why did he do that?" Rose asked. "Why did he run back inside?"

"Suzy?" I said. "Do you think he went in after Suzy?"

I stared at the flames shooting into the sky.

"I don't want to think about that," Asa said. "But she . . . she was most likely in there."

Rose stood near the fountain area. She stared at the flames with fixed eyes.

"Come on, Rose. We have to find Suzy."

But she wouldn't move. She just stood there with a look of horror on her face. I knew in that moment she was remembering what had happened to her. She closed her arms tight against her chest. I looked for help, anyone to help Rose back to her trailer. Back to the hand of God.

Ginger appeared and then Marlabeth. "Please, Marlabeth," I said. "Take Rose home. She can't see this."

Marlabeth put her arm around Rose. "I have chamomile and valerian root in my Thermos," she said and led her away. Ginger followed.

All the men formed a line as near as they dared to the fire and chased the women and children home. I refused to go.

"Not until I find Suzy." The searing hot flames were loud like rushing wind as they spewed out of the trailer like huge tongues lapping at the air, drinking in the oxygen.

I heard sirens in the distance. "They're coming, but where is Suzy?"

I hollered as loud as I could for her. "Suzy! Suzy!"

A long fire truck pulled into Paradise, just barely missing the palm trees. The firemen went to work immediately. They uncoiled hoses and hooked into the fireplug on the road. Two men trained their hoses on the trailer, while another fireman kept a hose aimed between the Wrinkel trailer and the one on the other side. He kept a wide, steady mist flowing, almost like a spring shower. I could see color reflected in the water droplets, tiny, oily rainbows.

Asa and I stood with Rube until the flames were finally extinguished. There was still no sign of Suzy. "She must be inside," I told Rube.

Rube turned his head toward the trailer. "Maybe not. Maybe she got out. Maybe she got scared and ran off."

"Where? Where would she go?"

I wiped tears and perspiration from my face. I watched the firemen. They kept water on the wreckage for the better part of an hour until the last bit of smoke and embers died.

The crowd dispersed in eerie silence. I stayed with Asa and a couple of other men. We continued watching.

"I can't believe it," Asa said. "I wonder what happened."

"We'll know soon," Rube said. "The fire marshall will investigate. He'll get to the bottom of it."

"Good," I said. "But what about Fergus? What about the body?"

"What's left of it," Asa said.

A strange dark car with its high beams blaring and a blue light flashing on the roof pulled onto the scene.

"Who's that?" I asked.

"Medical examiner," a passing fireman said. "He needs to deal with the remains."

I swallowed. It was hard to imagine Fergus's charred body under all that blackened and smoking rubble. Even harder to imagine Suzy's.

A short but stocky man emerged from the driver's side and a taller man got out of the passenger side. They went straight to the fire chief. I watched them speaking, trying my best to overhear. But I didn't hear much except the name *Wrinkel* and the word *idiot.*

The two officials made their way to the wreckage and with the help of two firemen uncovered what I assumed was Fergus Wrinkel. I needed to turn my head as they removed the remains. The two men carried it in a black bag to the car, a station wagon. They opened the back and slid the body inside.

Asa tried to hold me back but couldn't, and I rushed to the car. "Is that all?" I asked. "Just one body? Was it a man's?"

The medical examiner stepped away from the car. "Just one body, Ma'am. And, yes. It's a male."

The smaller man, who sounded a little like Peter Lorre, said, "Was there someone else inside?" I half expected him to rub his hands together and drool at the possibility of another body.

"I'm not sure. A woman —"

The officers shook their heads in unison. "Just the one."

I went back to Asa, who was speaking with the fire marshall.

"Are you certain?" Asa said. "A gas can?"

The fire marshall nodded. "Yep. It will be evidence." And he walked away toward the still-volcanic carnage.

"What does that mean?" I asked. "So what? A gas can."

"Arson," Asa whispered. "It means the fire was deliberately set."

Shock wriggled through my body. "Arson. You mean Fergus or —"

"Shh," Asa said. "We have to find Suzy. Let's go."

"Where? Where would she go?"

"I don't know," Asa said. "But if she's in Paradise, I'll find her. You go check on Rose. She probably needs you now."

"I'm sure Ginger is with her."

"That's good. But she needs you, I think."

I had never felt so glum and helpless. There was absolutely nothing I could do but wait. It was almost like the day Herman died. But with him, well, it was easier, different somehow. I held him. I held his big head in my lap while I waited. But this time, this time I had nothing to hold on to.

The closer I got to Rose's trailer, the lower I felt. I could not begin to imagine the horror that Rose had endured, and now this — this fire was certain to bring it all roaring back.

I saw her up in the hand with Ginger.

"Rose," I called. "Are you okay?"

I waited a few seconds but heard no response.

Ginger came down the ladder. "She's okay. Been praying the whole time."

"I figured," I said.

Ginger grabbed my pant leg and shook it to get my attention. "She'll be okay, Charlotte. I imagine God will get her through better than we can."

"I guess. But I still want her to know I'm here. Sometimes you need help you can touch."

I climbed up the ladder. "Rose, it's me, Charlotte." I noticed a small lantern between the thumb and pinky. It cast eerie lights and shadows.

Tears streamed down her face. She blubbered and sobbed and reached out her arms. I fell into them and held her for a good long time. I petted the back of her head. I cried with her.

"The flames," she said. "It was the color of the flames. Orange and red and purple. That's what did it. For so long after what happened, I saw those colors whenever I closed my eyes. And now they're back."

"For now," I said. "The colors will go away, Rose. God will take them away."

She blubbered and wiped her nose on a tissue she pulled from her pants pocket. "Did you find Suzy?"

I took a breath. "No, Rose. We didn't. But Asa is out looking for her. He'll find her."

"Fergus?" she asked even though she

knew the answer.

"Dead."

Rose closed her eyes a moment. "No sign of Suzy?"

"Not in the trailer, Rose. Not in the trailer."

A look of relief passed over her face.

"Asa thinks she might have run off somewhere. Got scared and ran."

She nodded.

"There's something else, Rose."

Ginger started up the ladder again. "I heard that. Tell me too."

I waited until Ginger was sitting with us. "The fire marshall is calling it an act of arson."

"Arson," Rose said. "You mean, it was deliberate?"

"Uh-huh, they found a gasoline can, and apparently that leads them to believe it was arson."

"Fergus," Rose said. "It must have been Fergus."

"Then why did he run back inside?" Ginger asked.

"And Suzy wasn't in the trailer," I said. "It doesn't make any sense."

"Maybe he felt guilty after he did it," Rose said. "Maybe he ran back in for Suzy. Maybe he didn't count on the thing going off like the fourth of July."

"And Suzy got out in time," Ginger said.

"She could be hurt." Rose closed her eyes. "Dear Lord, help us find Suzy."

The three of us sat for a few more minutes, hoping against hope that Suzy would appear in the night.

"Rose. It's getting late," I said finally. "I should go check on my mother. Maybe you should get some sleep. You can stay at my house if you want."

She shook her head. "No. I think I'll stay here."

"In the hand?"

"Yep. Won't be the first time I spent the night up here."

"I'll stay with you," Ginger said.

"Thanks," said Rose.

"But it's getting chilly," I said. "Are you sure?"

"I'll go get blankets," said Ginger. "We'll be safe and sound."

I hugged them both. "I don't know what I can do. But I'm just up the road if you need me."

39

I heard Asa calling my name just as I reached my wooden path.

"Any sign of her?" I asked.

"No. Not a clue. I'm worried, Charlotte. I think Fergus did something to her and then set the trailer on fire to hide the evidence."

"But why would he run back?"

Asa scratched his head. "That's the part that makes no sense. Maybe he forgot one of his precious stamps."

"But to risk his life for a stamp?"

"Greed is powerful. And it's the only thing I can think of. There was something inside that he needed. And he thought he had time. He didn't count on the propane tanks going so fast."

I heaved a huge sigh. "Crazy."

"Yep. Look, Charlotte, I know this was a lousy way to end the day, what with the game and all."

I nodded. "That doesn't matter anymore.

Finding Suzy is most important."

"I'm gonna keep looking. But let's hope and pray that she comes wandering out of the woods with daylight and this was all an accident. That would be best."

We stood together a minute. Quiet.

"Good night," he said. Then he kissed my cheek. "We'll find her."

I watched until Asa disappeared into the darkness. About a million stars were visible through the trees. "God," I whispered, "I suppose if you know where every single one of those stars belongs, then you must know where Suzy is. Help us find her."

It was weird walking up to my front door that night. The little path lights were not turned on, and for some reason I didn't see Lucky bouncing at the kitchen window. It was eerie, but it might have just been the mood. I stood a moment before turning the key. The smell from the fire still lingered. It probably would for a while.

I gave the door its usual hip action, expecting to see Lucky bound through the door. But he didn't. I saw my mother standing there looking about as awful as she did the day Daddy died.

My heart pounded so hard I could feel it in my ears.

"Mom, what is it? Did they find Suzy? Is

she . . . is she dead?"

Mother shook her head. "Now, Charlotte. You need to settle down and not say a word. Just let me talk a minute."

"Where's Lucky?"

She took my hand and led me to the sofa. "Sit down, Charlotte."

"Lucky. Did something happen to Lucky?"

He barked. I heard his bluster loud and clear coming from my bedroom. I tried to get up, but Mother held my shoulders. "Charlotte. Stay. Let me say what I have to say. Lucky is fine."

I swallowed. Mother handed me a glass of water. "I had this ready. Figured you'd be parched from the smoke. Drink. It will help."

"Mother."

"Shh. Now listen. Suzy is here. She's in the bedroom with Lucky."

"Why didn't you tell me? Let me go see her."

"Not yet. I have to tell you something."

"Mother. This isn't right."

"Suzy started the fire, Charlotte."

"What? You're making that up."

"No, I'm not. I've been with her all night. She told me everything."

"I have to go see her."

Mother let me go this time. "Charlotte, I didn't tell her about Fergus."

Suzy sat on the floor with her back against my bed. She had her arms so tight around Lucky he could barely move. He barked once, but low and not with his usual bluster. He squirmed and wiggled and Suzy had no choice but to let him go. He bounded toward me and licked my face. "It's okay, boy. I'm home."

I knelt near Suzy.

"Are you all right?"

"I did it, Charlotte. I burned the trailer. I set the fire."

"But . . . but . . ." I didn't have a clue about what to say. I just pulled her close. "It's okay, Suzy. It's okay."

"I couldn't take it anymore, Charlotte. Fergus, he was real good for a while but then he started again. He wouldn't let up. Something snapped inside my brain and I set the fire. I just set it. I did it."

"But he wasn't in the trailer when you set the fire."

"No, no. I could never . . . I just . . . just thought I'd get rid of the trailer, you know. Burn the place and those stupid, lousy stamps of his. He cared more for them than me. That's why I did it, that's why. So I waited until I knew he'd be gone for a while.

Until he went into Cranston like he always does on Tuesday, you know. He was fooling around with some two-bit hussy."

I pulled her close again. "Come on, let's go into the living room."

"I'm scared, Charlotte."

"I know. Now look —" Mother and I helped her up. She seemed so stiff, like she had been in the same position for hours. "No one knows you're here. Let's just go get a cup of tea or something, a glass of water, and sit."

She nodded, and I led her into the living room.

I was going to have to tell her about Fergus. But this wasn't the time.

"That stamp collection was worth thousands of dollars, Charlotte," she said. "He told me he was getting ready to sell it and then run off with that Tuesday woman. And I snapped."

"But the whole trailer. Your home. Why would you destroy your home?" Mother asked.

I gave Suzy a glass of water.

"I got a little carried away, I suppose." She sipped. "I was just gonna burn the stamps, you know, take them outside and do it. But he hit me so hard —" She touched her swollen left eye. "I went berserk, I suppose, and dumped gasoline all over the place. Then I tossed in two matches, just two matches, and —"

"And then you came here."

She nodded. "I knew you'd all be at the softball game. And I hoped you didn't lock your door.

"I waited here with Lucky. I was happy about it for a little while, Charlotte, but when I heard the sirens I started to get scared and regret what I did, but I was so upset. Do you think they can find out I started it? Do you think they can put me in jail?"

My mother held Suzy's hand. "We'll get you a lawyer, Suzy. Don't you worry. You acted in self-defense."

For someone who barely spoke ten words in all the weeks I'd been living in Paradise, Suzy sure poured it on that night. It was almost as though setting the fire had opened a valve or something inside of her.

"Fergus will be coming home soon. He always gets back before two in the morning. He's gonna blow his ever-lovin' stack when he sees it. Does it look bad?"

"It's destroyed, Suzy. Completely and utterly gone."

She swallowed twice. "I am in so much trouble, but I just wanted to get back at him, that's all. Honest. I just wanted to get back at him."

"Well, that you accomplished," Mother said.

I raised my left eyebrow at her. "Mother."

I stood there a few minutes, hoping for the right words to drop out of my mouth, but I didn't know what to say to a woman who had just burned down her house and inadvertently caused the death of her husband — even if he was a rat.

The kitchen clock read one-thirty. I yawned. "You don't have to do anything right now, not this minute. Let's get some sleep and see what the light of day brings."

"Have you seen Asa?" Suzy asked.

"He's out looking for you. I should go try and find him."

"No," Mother said. "I won't let you go out in the dark under these circumstances. Asa will find his way home, and you can tell him in the morning."

The morning brought more rain to Paradise. I rose before Suzy and Mother. I peeked into Suzy's room just to make sure she hadn't run off. She was still asleep, snug under the covers like a caterpillar in a cocoon. I felt thankful she was able to sleep. Lucky spent the night on the floor nearby.

"Good dog," I said. I patted my thighs, and he came running. "You wouldn't have let her get away."

Lucky went outside. The acrid smell of charred metal and wood drifted inside the trailer. The rain made the smell even heavier as dark clouds rolled overhead.

Lillian woke next and padded into the kitchen.

"You have to tell her," she said over the rim of her coffee cup.

"I will. As soon as she wakes up."

"I imagine the police will want to talk to her," Mother said. "It'd be best coming from you."

Suzy woke around nine. She stood in the living room, still wearing the same thin dress she had worn the day before, and stared at me.

"Are you okay?" I asked. "Want some coffee?"

"I'm a little scared, Charlotte. My legs are shaking."

"I guess I'd be more concerned if you weren't scared."

She made her way to the sofa. "Wonder what happens now."

"I think we wait."

I could hear Herman hollering at me from the grave. "I told you if I ever left you on your own you'd get into a heap of trouble. You probably spurred that woman onto doing that heinous act. It was your fault, Charlotte."

I shook him from my brain and almost spoke out loud to him. I kept my thoughts to myself and poured coffee. "Suzy, do you take cream and sugar?"

"Just cream. But you don't have to give me coffee."

"It's okay. Are you hungry?"

She twisted her mouth. "Nah, not hungry. My stomach feels a little funny. I been worrying all night about Fergus coming home. I thought for sure we'd hear some kind of ruckus once he saw the trailer."

"Maybe he didn't come home this time," Mother said.

Suzy looked away and then back at me. "Maybe. It would make sense, since I didn't hear him tearing up Paradise trying to find me, unless he thinks I was inside the trailer and got killed in there. You think he could be thinking that, Charlotte? Maybe he went to the police to check on me."

"Charlotte, you need to tell her now, or I will."

"Tell me what?"

I had no choice but to tell her the truth. But I wasn't ready. I wanted to have the right words. "Breakfast?" I asked instead.

"Charlotte," Mother said. "I'll do it."

"Raisin toast, maybe, or how about a bacon and marmalade sandwich?" I called from halfway to the kitchen.

Suzy shook her head. "My stomach is funny. I better not."

"Suzy," I said, walking back to the sofa. "Do you have family?"

She sipped her coffee. "No. Just me. My mama died a few years back, and I never knew my daddy. I married Fergus in high school."

"Fergus," I said. I sat next to her on the sofa and patted her knee. "Suzy, I have to tell you something."

"It's about Fergus. He —"

"Hold on," Mother interrupted. "Here comes Asa."

"Asa?" Suzy said. "I can't let him see me. Not like this. He'll be so angry at me."

I patted Suzy's knee. "It's okay. He'll understand. He's been worried sick about you."

Asa stood on my stoop looking like a lost sheep. "I can't find her anywhere, Charlotte. I looked everywhere, been over every inch of Paradise, and I —"

"She's here, Asa. She's inside."

His eyes grew wide. "Really?"

I let him inside, and he went straight to Suzy.

"Suzy, honey, are you all right? What happened? Where you been?"

"Asa, oh, Asa." Suzy hid her face in her hands and sobbed. "I am so sorry. It — it just happened."

Asa pulled her hands from her face. "What happened, Suzy?"

Mother and I stood close together and listened.

"I did it, Asa, I started the fire. I —"

"You? But —"

"Asa," I said. "She doesn't know it all."

"Why, Suzy?" he asked. "Why?"

She explained to Asa what happened. "And that was all there was to it. I dropped two matches, just two matches, and then I ran. I ran as fast and as hard as I could, straight here, straight to Charlotte's."

"So you didn't see?" Asa sat next to her on the sofa. He took both her hands in his hand and looked into her eyes. "So you don't know about Fergus."

"Fergus?"

"He came back, Suzy. He came back minutes after the fire started. We saw him run into the trailer and it . . . it exploded. Fergus was killed."

Horror stretched across Suzy's face. "No,

he was supposed to be out all night, like he always is, you know, Asa, with his girlfriend."

"He came back. No one knows why he ran into the trailer. Maybe he thought you were in there."

Suzy shook her head. "No, no. Not me. His stamps. He went in for his stamps, I'm sure of it." Then she buried her face in Asa's shoulder and cried.

Lucky perked his ears and ran to the door.

"Now what?" I said.

I pulled open the door. "Charlotte Figg?"

Two men stood on my stoop. The shorter of the two men said, "I'm Lieutenant Dix, and this is Officer Pelka. We'd like to speak with you."

"Uh, certainly," I said as I backed away from the door. "What can I do for you? Would you like a nice slice of pie or is it too early for cherry? I'm sorry, but that's all I have at the moment. Maybe a cup of coffee?"

"No, thank you, Ma'am, that's very nice of you," Officer Pelka said. He had a nice, smooth baritone voice, and I wondered if he practiced it into a tape recorder.

Mother joined me at the door. The officers introduced themselves again.

"Pleased to meet you," she said.

"Mrs. Figg," Dix said. "Have you seen

Suzy Wrinkel?"

My mouth dropped open as my brain instantaneously rolled through every possible answer in this situation. I could have said no. I could have said I saw her yesterday but not since. But I knew I couldn't lie.

"Yes. She's in here." My mother and I answered in unison.

Dix eyed us suspiciously. The two men waited for us to step aside and then walked into my living room.

Asa stood.

"Who are you?" asked Dix.

"Asa Kowalski."

Dix looked past Asa at Suzy. "Are you Suzy Wrinkel?"

She nodded. Lucky growled and took a protective stance near Suzy. He knew Suzy was in trouble, and he was going to stay with her as long as he could.

"Ma'am," said Officer Dix, "where were you last night, during the fire?"

"I . . . I was here with Charlotte."

They looked at me. "Yes. She was here," I said. "All night. She spent the night in fact."

"She was," Mother said. "I can corroborate that."

Lillian always pulled out the twelve-dollar words when she felt nervous.

Lieutenant Dix cleared his throat. "A gas

506

can was found inside the trailer. It was arson. Do you know anyone who would have deliberately set fire to your home?"

Suzy swallowed. Asa grabbed her hand. I tried to will her not to speak, not to say a word until we could arrange for a lawyer. I learned that much from watching Perry Mason. Suzy kept shaking her head. I could feel her pulse in her wrist thrumming like hummingbird wings.

"The fire," Suzy said. "I —"

"I did it," Asa said. "I set the fire."

"What?" I said. "Asa, you —"

He put his hand up. "Didn't you just hear me? I did it. It was all my idea."

"I am so sorry, Suzy. I didn't intend for Fergus to die. I just wanted to get rid of that place, Suzy. I wanted to give you a new start. I thought —"

Officer Dix put his hand on Asa's shoulder. "Are you admitting to starting this fire?"

Mother and I looked at each other.

Asa stood. "Yes, sir. I am. I —"

"No," Suzy hollered. "I —"

I tightened my grip on her while my own head swirled with questions.

"Why, Asa?" I asked. He knew what I was really asking.

"It's the right thing," he said. "Fergus was a monster, and I wanted to scare him. I thought if I burned his trailer and got rid of that million-dollar stamp collection, then maybe he would leave Suzy alone." He looked at her with a deep, soulful stare. "Maybe he'd learn he can't treat her like he did."

Suzy clutched her stomach.

"You will want an attorney," Dix said. "But I need to tell you I am going to place you under arrest for arson and for the murder of Fergus Wrinkel."

"Murder?" Asa said. His voice squeaked. "But I didn't murder him. He did it. He ran into the trailer when it already was in flames. Ain't that right, Charlotte?"

"It's true. Fergus did it to himself. We were there. We saw him. He killed himself." I looked at my slippers and then at Suzy, who was still so stunned she could barely move.

Mother spoke up. "I saw him also. I saw Fergus Wrinkel run inside the trailer seconds before it exploded."

Dix shook his head. "Look, maybe he was a monster, like you said. Maybe he deserved what he got —" he looked at Suzy, "sorry Ma'am. But he still died as a result of your actions, sir."

Suzy finally moved. She took a step toward Asa. "But . . . but officer, Asa didn't —"

"It's okay, Suzy," Asa said. "I know what I'm doing."

Suzy swallowed and finally let go of Lucky's collar. He dashed to Asa. "It's okay, boy. I'll be back." Asa patted Lucky's head and rubbed his side. "You take care of Suzy and Charlotte."

"Place Mr. Kowalski under arrest," Dix said.

Officer Pelka removed handcuffs from his belt. He moved toward Asa. Stopped suddenly and said, "Jumpin' Jehosaphat! Hold on just a gosh-darn minute, Lieutenant, this man only has one arm. How do I handcuff a man with only one arm?"

I swallowed and held back a chuckle. Now, that was a good question. Mother put her hand to her mouth, and Suzy lunged toward Asa. "Please, don't take him. I —"

Asa grabbed onto Suzy and pulled her into his chest. He whispered into her ear. She backed away and fell into my arms.

Dix shook his head. "Pelka, sometimes your lack of brains astounds me. Just handcuff the one wrist and then cuff his belt."

"But I ain't wearing a belt," Asa said.

"Well, you got loops, don't you?" asked Dix. "You got belt loops in those jeans."

Asa lifted his tee shirt. "Well, looky there. So I do."

"How'd you lose that arm, anyway?" Pelka asked.

"I blew it off playing with dynamite."

Dix nodded. "So you like explosions, do you?"

"That does not bode well for Asa," Mother whispered.

Pelka cuffed Asa's left wrist, and then it took him a good couple of minutes to get the other cuff through one of Asa's belt loops. And when he finally finished, he looked proud, kind of like Lucky after he treed a squirrel.

"Come on," Dix said. He took Asa by the arm and led him out the door. Then he turned around and said, "Sorry for your loss, Ma'am."

Suzy looked at Asa. Asa smiled as wide as he could. "It's okay, Suzy. I'll be all right."

"I don't know about that," Pelka said. "The Commonwealth of Pennsylvania does not look kindly on murder."

I grabbed Suzy's hand to keep her from running after Asa. "Shh. Just wait."

We stood like pillars until I heard the car drive off down the street.

"Why did he do that?" Suzy asked. She sat in the rocker. "Why did he take the blame for what I did?"

40

I felt my mother's hands on my shoulders. "Come away from the door, Charlotte. We'll get this sorted out."

I dropped onto the sofa, stunned. "Mom, what have I done?"

"You?" Mother said. "You didn't do anything."

Lucky whimpered and put a paw on my knee. Mother patted his head. "She'll be okay, boy. She really will."

But I didn't see how. "If I hadn't come here, none of this would have happened," I said. Tears streamed down my cheeks. "I should have never moved to Paradise."

"Now, now, Charlotte. You can't blame yourself. I have a feeling this would have happened whether or not you bought this rickety old trailer."

"That's right," Suzy said. "This wasn't the first time I thought about burning down the trailer. I just got my nerve up this time."

I looked into her black-and-purple, swollen eyes. "Really, Suzy? But if you had the courage to do this, then how come you couldn't leave him?" She had no answer.

"I'm very surprised," Mother said, "that Rose and what's-her-name — Ginger — haven't come by yet."

"Me too," I said. "I'm sure they saw the police car drive in."

Mother went to the kitchen and grabbed a bag of birdseed from the refrigerator. "Of all the crazy things I've seen around here, this is the craziest. I need to give Tweety fresh seed."

Suzy fiddled with the fringe on one of my sofa pillows. "What do we do now?"

"Don't know. What can we do except hope and pray that Asa knows what he's doing?"

"Uh-oh," Mother called. "Here they come."

"Who?" Suzy asked. "The police again?"

"No, Ginger and Rose. They look — a little upset."

"Listen," I said. "I don't think we should tell them the truth."

"What?" Mother asked. "Why?"

"I just think the fewer people who know, the better. I don't want anyone else to get in trouble for withholding evidence or lying to police or whatever they can get into trouble for."

Mother nodded. "Good thinking, Charlotte. We'll just tell them the police arrested Asa. We'll say he confessed."

Suzy burst into tears.

"And you," Mother said turning to Suzy. "You have to be strongest of all until we get this figured out. Just don't say a word."

Suzy's head bobbed like a parakeet's. "All right. All right."

Lillian made the locking of the lips pantomime and then threw the key away.

Understandably upset, Rose barely spoke as Mother and I told her what had happened. Ginger, on the other hand, took the news well. "I always knew that man had it in him. I knew one of these days he was gonna go off and do something."

"But Fergus's dying was an accident," Rose said after a minute. "He didn't set out to kill him."

Suzy sat on the sofa with her arms clutched so tight around her chest I thought she might pop that cast right off.

"Mom," I said. "Take Suzy into the bedroom and give her a couple of aspirin. Maybe she can sleep."

"Good idea, Charlotte. Come on, Suzy."

"That poor girl," Rose said. "What's she

going to do now? No home. No husband."

"She'll be okay. We'll do something for her."

Rose asked a lot of questions, and several times I was on the verge of telling her the truth, but for once in my life I managed to keep a secret.

"What about Hazel?" Ginger said. "She probably has a bunch of fancy dancy lawyers who work for her. Maybe she can help Asa."

"Maybe," I said, "but don't forget, she doesn't believe Fergus is . . . was capable of hurting Suzy."

"Then we'll just have to convince her," I said.

That afternoon Rose, Mother, and I drove out to Willow Way. Rose left Ginger in charge of Suzy. I left Lucky in charge of Ginger.

Hazel's husband was correct; there were a lot of willow trees that lined the long, winding driveway to the house. And what a house it was, an old, flamboyant Victorian with miles and miles of lacy gingerbread arches and towers and turrets, sitting on a lawn about as green as Angel Field. It was almost as though the builder got started and couldn't stop. He kept adding more and more. But I will confess that seeing the house made me homesick for the Philadelphia suburb I left.

I rang the bell. "Now, remember, we have to convince her that Fergus was going to kill Suzy and possibly me. I'm gonna tell her that he threatened me at the barbecue."

"We'll tell her whatever we need to," Rose said. "I just still cannot believe we are even here. I cannot and will not believe that Asa did this. Something just doesn't smell right."

Fleur de Lee opened the door. She put her finger to her lips. "Shhh, Angel is sleeping."

"Okay," I whispered.

We stepped over the wide threshold.

"Do you need me to babysit again?" Fleur de Lee asked. "I will if you want."

"Not today. We're here to see Hazel," I said.

Fleur de Lee directed us into a spectacular room with wonderful overstuffed couches and chairs in chintz upholstery. A large portrait of an attractive man, which hung over the massive fireplace suspended from what looked like elastic suspenders, cracked us up for a second.

"Well, look there," Rose said. "That's the craziest picture hanger I have ever seen. I mean, who uses red suspenders like that?"

"That's Birdy," Fleur de Lee said. "Hazel's

husband."

"Of course," Rose said. "That explains it."

Fleur de Lee looked in the direction of the wide staircase. "I best be gettin' up to Angel."

Hazel padded out from a side room wearing a periwinkle cape, a small pillbox hat to match, and carrying a small orange kitten.

"Isn't she pretty?" Hazel asked. "I named her Peaches in honor of not only her color but also those pies I'm looking forward to. Remember, you promised me, Charlotte."

"Couple more months," I said, looking around the antique-filled room.

"My goodness gracious," Mother said. "Is that a George III mahogany bookcase?" she pointed toward the library.

"It is. You can go get a closer look if you want." Mother couldn't help herself. She liked pretty things, and unfortunately my trailer home had nothing to offer. And I will confess that standing in that room constructed of real wood and real plaster made me a tiny bit lonesome for a real house again.

Hazel put Peaches on a little round pillow near the fireplace. "Guess we need to get down to brass tacks," she said. "What in Sweet Fanny Apple's tarnation happened over there?"

She offered Rose and me a seat on a velvet sofa. Mother still ogled the décor.

"Oh, my, this is an Italian Renaissance revival table. It's spectacular."

"Just ignore her," I said. "I imagine you heard about the fire and all, Hazel."

"Well, of course I heard. Nothing can happen around here without Hazel Crenshaw either getting blamed for it or told about it. What I want to know is who and why."

"Asa confessed to setting the fire," I said.

I watched a look of surprise and then confusion fill the wrinkles in her face. "Asa? I don't believe it. Why, that boy couldn't even trap a raccoon for me, let alone set fire to a trailer and kill a man."

"I know, I know," I said. "I was as surprised as anyone when he confessed." I fought the urge to blurt the truth.

"But why? Why in the heck would Asa burn down the Wrinkels's trailer? This makes no sense, no sense at all."

Rose touched Hazel's hand. "There's more to the story. Asa had a good reason for doing what he did."

"It better be good or I'll see to it that he rots in jail, burning down Paradise and killing a man. It's outrageous."

"Hazel," I said. "You might know a lot about Paradise, but the one thing you didn't know is that Fergus was not who you think he was. He had been beating up Suzy for a long time. That's why she never came outside. Asa knew about it, and he tried to get Suzy to leave him but she wouldn't."

"Couldn't," Rose said.

"You're lying to me. Why would you want to lie to an old woman?"

"It's true," Mother said. She had returned to the room carrying a beautiful blue and white vase. "I saw the bruises. Suzy told us herself."

Hazel slapped her knees. "But they looked so happy at the barbecue. How can you say this?"

"This is a Boch Feres pottery vase," Lillian said. "It must be worth —"

"Keep it," Hazel said. "Now, go on with your story, Charlotte."

"It was just a show, Hazel. He even threatened to kill her if I told anyone. I wanted to tell you, but he said he'd kill her. Then he kidnapped Lucky and scared the bejeebers out of me. I had to keep it inside."

She put her palm over her heart. "This is almost too much for me. Maybe I should take one of them heart pills the doc gave me."

"Where are they?" Mother asked.

518

"Kitchen. On the counter. You'll see them."

"Sorry, Hazel," Rose said. "But it's all true. It seems like Asa just couldn't stand it anymore. I think that day we found Suzy in the woods all beaten black and blue is what tore it for him. But you have to know, Hazel, that Fergus wasn't supposed to be home. He ran into the trailer seconds before it exploded."

Mother returned with a glass of water and the pill, which Hazel took with no qualms. "So Asa didn't deliberately kill Fergus."

We talked about it for a few more minutes until Rose finally asked the question that was on all of our minds. "How come you have that painting hanging from suspenders?"

Hazel let go a relaxing chuckle that broke the tension in the room. "Because my husband was the elastic king. You won't find a better product. That painting has been hanging from those suspenders for fifty-five years. Not a weak spot on them."

"Elastic is important," Lillian said. "I remember conversations with the sales-people at John Wanamaker's about always looking for the best bands in our men's . . . well, our men's furnishings and women's unmentionables."

"Well, mention them," Hazel said. "We all got 'em, and unless they're made with Elsmere Elastic they won't last through a dozen washings."

I coughed. "Hazel. We still need to help Asa."

"Oh, pshaw. You are a worrywart. I'll have Asa home by suppertime if what you're telling me is true."

"How?" All three of us said it together.

"I got lawyers. The best lawyers. I'll call Cash Vangarten and get him on the case. Seems to be the only thing Asa is guilty of is what they call destruction of property, and as long as Suzy don't press charges, then —"

"But the cop called it murder."

Hazel took another sip of her water. "Well, that could be a bit of a sticky wicket, but I'll get my best people on it. I have a lady lawyer, they call her The Barracuda. You know the type. Wears dark pantsuits, has her hair in a tight bun, and carries a briefcase as big as my Aunt Freda's butt. How she does it in those high heels, I'll never know. She'll get him off on some lesser charge, I'm sure." She slapped her knees. "I hope. Rose, maybe you should offer up some of those prayers anyhoo."

"I already am," Rose said. "Been up in

the hand on a regular basis, Hazel."

"You and that hand," Hazel said. "Sometimes I think you are certifiable, woman. But whatever floats your boat, I reckon."

The mood in the car on the way home was odd. It was a mixture of relief and sorrow. "What do you think will happen to Suzy?" I asked. "She can't stay with me."

"I should think not," Mother said. "Especially since you will be moving back to Florida with me." She cradled the vase like a baby.

"What?" Rose asked. "You're serious, Charlotte? You're moving to Florida?"

I took a deep breath. "I . . . I'm not sure." And that was the truth. After seeing Hazel's house and all this commotion I had caused with Fergus and Asa and even the softball team, there was a part of me that wanted to go home.

"Please, Charlotte," Rose said. "Stay in Paradise. Things can only get better now. The Angels need you. We all need you."

"Oh, come now," Mother said. "Don't try and force her to stay. If she wants to come to Florida, you have to let her go."

We pulled up outside my trailer and were met by the Angels, some of the husbands, and a pack of children running amok. The instant I set foot out of the car, they bombarded with me questions. I raised my arms like I did at softball practice to call them to order.

"We heard they arrested Asa for murder and burning down the trailer," called Clara Kaninsky.

"Yeah," hollered Greta, "Ginger wouldn't tell us anything. What in blazes, um, excuse that, what the heck happened?"

"Okay, okay, simmer down and I'll tell you."

Mother tugged my sleeve. "Just tell them the facts. Nothing more."

Rose pushed through the crowd and disappeared inside the trailer. Mother stood right by me, and for the first time in my life I really believed she was with me. I looked into her eyes. "Thanks, Mom."

"For what?"

"For being here," I whispered.

"Okay, okay, simmer down. Greta, would you get Charlie off the hood of my car, please? He's jumping up and down and going to dent it." I took a breath. "Asa confessed to starting the fire. But not to killing Fergus. That was Fergus's own stupid fault."

A quiet, albeit relieved, cheer drifted through the crowd.

"That S.O.B had it coming," someone called.

I looked. It was Old Man Hawkins. "Fergus Wrinkel had it coming."

I felt my eyebrows rise, surprised at his moment of clarity. He wandered back to his trailer.

"Okay, anyhoo," I said. "We just got back from visiting with Hazel Crenshaw. She has her best lawyers on the job and promises that Asa will be home by suppertime. That's all there is to say on the subject. Now go on home, and you Angels out there, we have a game next week. Practice tomorrow."

After the crowd vanished, the trailer door opened and Lucky ran out. He leaped and greeted me with kisses. I rubbed his ears. "I'm so happy to see you too, Lucky."

Rose stepped out with Suzy and Ginger.

"Are you okay?" I called.

Suzy feigned a smile.

"She's good," Ginger said. "She heard what you said."

"So Asa won't need to go to jail?" she asked.

"Probably not, but we don't have the final answer yet. I have a feeling Hazel has a way of pulling bureaucratic strings."

Rose draped her arm around Suzy. "It's

over, Suzy. Everything is going to be all right now."

The dam broke, and Suzy stood in my yard for a full ten minutes and wailed like a banshee. The sound ricocheted down the street. Old Man Hawkins got back in touch with his more zany side and came out hollering that Paradise was being bombed and shouting orders to disperse and seek cover.

Mother, of all people, reassured him that we had it all under control and helped him back to his trailer. We gathered inside my trailer, and I made two pies while we talked about what would come next. No one really wanted to speak about it, but we would need to bury what was left of Fergus Wrinkel. Suzy had no clue about what to do.

"I didn't either," I said as I rolled out piecrust. "After Herman died, I worried until I found some insurance papers, and then I just went to my old church and the pastor did the rest. Course, I had to go the funeral home and pick out a casket and —"

"Insurance," Suzy said. "I don't think we have insurance."

"Well, you won't find any papers now," Rose said. "Even if there were any."

So we ruminated on the situation over a lattice-crust cherry pie and decided we'd ask everyone to pitch in and help pay for Fergus's funeral. Ginger suggested having him cremated, but that seemed a little redundant.

41

Asa arrived home that day a little after suppertime, just as Hazel had promised. He came to my trailer looking not too worse for wear, although he needed a shave and he smelled a bit gamey.

But that was okay. I hugged him anyway and welcomed him home. "Are you hungry, Asa? I made pearl onion and cucumber stuffed burgers."

"They're not as bad as they sound," Rose called from the kitchen. She was washing the dishes. "Pretty tasty. A surprise in every bite."

"I was hoping to see Suzy," he said.

"She's in the bathroom. She'll be right out. Now how about some supper?"

"Well," Asa said, "that jail food wasn't very good, and to tell the truth, I didn't have much of an appetite. A burger sounds good."

"So sit at the table. I'll get you set up."

Asa followed me into the kitchen. I poured him a glass of milk, which he downed in a second and a half. I left the jug on the table. There were two leftover burgers in the fridge, all stuffed and ready to fry. I dropped them in the pan.

Suzy came out of the bathroom. Asa stood and walked toward her.

"Asa," Suzy called. "You're home."

I expected her to run and leap into his arm, but she didn't. She stood, frozen. Asa kept his distance also, and the thought occurred to me that what he did could very possibly come between them.

Mother dried her hands on a blue terry towel. "Maybe true love isn't strong enough," she whispered.

Suzy didn't say a word. She slipped back down the hall and disappeared into her room. Asa took a step forward and stopped.

"Come on," I said. "Your burger will be ready in a minute."

"That's okay, Charlotte. I'm not hungry anymore."

A few days later I heard loud noises — crunching and twisting of metal. Workmen were at Hazel's, dismantling her trailer. A brand-new trailer, light blue with white windows, waited on the street, poised to take the old trailer's spot.

"Look at that, Mother," I called. She was watching TV. "Hazel's new trailer has arrived. Looks like they'll have it set up today."

She joined me at the window. "That's nice, dear. It's blue. At least that's a normal color."

"I said I'll have it painted as soon as I can."

"Well, that doesn't matter, since you'll be coming home with me as soon as softball season is over."

Suzy came out of the bathroom carrying a paper bag. "I guess I'm ready to go. I got my toothbrush and that new comb you bought me and the new panties in this bag."

"Good," I said. "We'll go shopping again, real soon."

"So," Mother said, "today's the day."

"Guess so," Suzy said. "I can't believe this is happening. It's like a dream sometimes."

Mother put her hands on Suzy's shoulder. "It's going to be okay. You'll see."

My mother continued to look into Suzy's eyes, and I knew she was imagining her in an alternate capacity — a confident woman in a John Wanamaker Young Miss Business Suit perhaps.

"Okay, here's the plan," I said as I pulled my keys from my purse. "We stop at the doctor and get that cast removed, and then it's off to Willow Way. Hazel said she gave you the best room. It's in the front with four windows and a closet so big you can walk right inside and have room to change your clothes."

"That's nice. But I . . . I don't deserve all this attention."

"Suzy," Mother said. "You are going to like it at Willow Way. And, remember, it's just until you get the insurance check and get settled someplace."

"I like it here," she said.

"But, but you said you couldn't stay here, remember? You said the memories were too strong. You won't even talk to Asa."

She turned her head away. "I know. I know."

I took her elbow. "Come on, the doctor is waiting with his trusty saw. It will feel good to get that plaster off your arm. It's been a long six weeks."

"I'll be back as soon as I can, Mom," I said.

I patted Lucky's back and side. "You take care of Grandmom."

When we got outside, Suzy saw the new trailer. "What's that?"

"It's Hazel's new place. She'll be coming back to Paradise just as soon as it's set up and furnished and everything's plugged in and hooked up and whatever else goes on with these buckets."

"It's pretty," Suzy said. "Kind of reminds me of Fergus and mine's trailer when we first moved here. It was all clean and shiny and almost brand-new."

I saw Asa walking down the street.

"He's come to see you off, Suzy. Are you going to talk to him?"

She shook her head and climbed into the Galaxy. "I can't. Not yet."

"Please. At least say good-bye."

She wouldn't even look out the window at him.

"Would you mind if I spoke with him for a minute before we go?"

"Free country."

I closed the car door and met Asa several yards away. "She still won't talk to you."

"But why? I don't understand."

"She feels guilty. She doesn't want you to take the blame for what she did. Last night she asked if there was anything she could do to make it up to you. I told her it was over. Finished."

"But it was to save her from being punished. She doesn't have to do anything but accept it. I love her, Charlotte."

"I know you do, Asa. Give her some time."

I kissed his cheek. "Hazel's trailer is going in today." I hoped to lighten his spirit. "She'll be home soon."

He looked at her property. "I know. She'll be back to her crotchety old self in no time."

"Oh, Asa, she's a good egg."

He pulled me in for a hug. "I know. She got me out of a deep jam. I'll always be grateful to her."

I drove away, and Suzy never even looked back.

"You'll need to talk to Asa," I said as I drove between the palm trees. "He put his life on the line for you. It could have turned out so much worse."

"I know that!" she shouted. "I never said I wasn't grateful for what he did, but I still did it, Charlotte. I still was responsible for killing Fergus, and I'm letting Asa take the blame."

I jammed on the brakes, causing the car behind me to swerve onto the shoulder. He beeped like crazy.

"Suzy," I said as I steered the Galaxy onto the side of the road. "You did not cause Fergus's death. He ran inside because he was greedy. He thought he could save his beloved stamps. You didn't make him do it."

"I know, I know. But it was still my fault."

"Okay, you think about it. But you also

think about how much Asa loves you, so much so that he —" I couldn't go on. Tears welled in my eyes and ran down my cheek.

"Charlotte," Suzy said. "What's wrong?"

I swiped at the tears and looked at their wetness on my hand. "I just thought of something that Rose has been trying to get across to me. Don't you see? That's why she put up that giant hand statue — to remind us all, every day, all the time, in living color, that Jesus loves us and carries us in his palm. There's just no better, safer place to be."

"What does that have to do with Asa?"

"Fergus gave his life for money — stamps. Asa was willing and happy to sacrifice whatever was necessary for you to be spared. Don't slip through Asa's hand."

Our ride to Willow Way was quiet. Suzy barely even looked at me, but I could tell her wheels were turning. I only hoped she would see the situation the way the rest of us did.

Fleur de Lee greeted us at the door. She held a wailing Angel in her arms. The baby sounded like she was in some kind of pain.

"Is she okay?" I asked.

"Well, she ain't sick, if that's what you mean, Charlotte. But I can't seem to get her to quiet down. She just cries and cries and I been walking the floors since early this morning. I changed her diaper. I fed her. I rocked her and sang to her and nothing, no, nothing is gonna make this baby be quiet."

Suzy dropped her paper bag on the floor. "Give her to me."

Fleur de Lee seemed happy to hand the baby over. Suzy looked in the baby's eyes. "Where's the bathroom?"

"Bathroom," I said.

Fleur de Lee pointed upstairs. "Jaster and mine's is connected to our bedroom."

We followed Fleur de Lee up the long, grand staircase. "Turn the shower on. It's a trick I learned. Just turn the water on full force."

Fleur de Lee followed Suzy's instructions. Suzy sat with the baby on the toilet seat and rocked her. Every so often she seemed to whisper something in the baby's ear, and after a few minutes Angel fell fast asleep.

"How'd you do that?" Fleur de Lee asked.

Suzy placed the baby in her crib. "Babies like the sound of the water, and sometimes, well, who knows, rocking gentle in someone else's hands does the trick."

Hazel wandered into the bedroom. "Goodness gracious," she whispered. "The baby is finally quiet."

"It was Suzy," Fleur de Lee said. "She did it."

Hazel put her finger to her lips and then called us into the hallway. "Suzy, I think you just got yourself a job."

"What? Doing what?"

"Well, I can't stay here. I want to get back to Paradise. But you can stay here and be in charge — sort of. The folks need someone to help them with things from time to time — like Fleur de Lee here with the baby. I'll pay you a good salary."

"What about the woman who ran Haven House?" I asked. "I just assumed —"

Hazel clicked her tongue. "Now, you know what they say about assuming anything. That windbag quit right after the storm. She didn't want to be bothered anymore."

"She never really liked us anyway," Fleur de Lee said.

Suzy swallowed and then looked in at Angel. "Maybe. If you'll have me." She looked around. "I always wanted to live in a real house with a real porch."

I smiled into Suzy's eyes. "I think you belong here. It's a good place, and you're not far from Paradise."

"Heck, no," Hazel said. "You'll be coming by all the time. I'm sure Charlotte has another barbecue to plan."

"And you can come to all the softball games," I said. "You can even play."

"I do have a pretty good arm."

The next week passed quickly. Hazel had moved into her spanking-new trailer, what was left of the Wrinkel trailer had been removed, Hazel named Asa as the new manager of the Paradise Trailer Park, and The Angels were set to play The Hop Bottom Hooligans.

The Angels were relaxed and ready to play.

Two strange station wagons pulled into the Frost sisters' driveway.

"That must be the Hooligans," Lillian said. "What a dumb name for a team."

"Must be," I said. "Now, Mom, you go sit with Hazel and watch. I have a feeling we're going to chalk up another check in the wins column."

"I do too, dear."

I watched until she joined Hazel, who sat on the players' bench holding Angel. Fleur de Lee, of course, stood right behind her, keeping a watchful eye. Suzy stood right behind Fleur de Lee, keeping a watchful eye.

The umpire arrived and called the team captains and coaches. He went through the usual routine, and the Angels took the field.

Ginger, who now had her regulation uniform, looked great at shortstop, and Gwendolyn was ready for anything. I moved her to the lead-off batter spot, and you'd think I had just crowned her Queen of the Universe. Rose looked almost comfortable behind home plate, and Edwina promised the hole in her glove had been repaired, to which Thomasina replied, "Just catch the dang ball, Edwina. Make Daddy proud."

Greta, who had been complaining about her leaking breasts, solved her dilemma by wearing two Kotex napkins under her Angels' jersey. All in all the team had worked it out, as my former Canaries coach used to say.

"Play ball!" hollered the ump, and off we went.

Frankie had no problem striking out their side, except for one slow grounder to Ginger, who tossed it nicely to Gwendolyn for the third out.

"This is going to be a piece of cake," Clara said as they came off the field.

Asa hurried over to give some pointers. "Just make contact. Don't kill the ball." He spoke directly to Gwendolyn. But she didn't listen, and the next thing I knew the Hooligan's center fielder fell into the cornfield trying to chase down a fly ball that landed six rows back.

"Oh, yeah," called Mother. "We got this one. Go, Angels."

And we did. Seven innings later the score was Angels 19, Hooligans 6.

The team enjoyed a few minutes of celebration before shaking the Hooligans' hands. We watched them climb back into their cars and drive off.

Rose made a check mark in the air. "That's two for the Angels."

But the most exciting part of the evening was when Suzy talked to Asa. It was during the fifth inning. He was standing along the third base line, when I saw her sidle up next to him. Of course, I couldn't hear a darn thing, but I knew, I knew in my heart that she had made peace with what he did for her. I knew it for certain when I saw her reach up and kiss his cheek.

Asa and Studebaker gathered up the equipment as the fans made for home and the team joined their families. Mother, Hazel, and I had started back through the woods when I felt a tap on my shoulder. I turned with a start.

"Cash," I said. "You've got to stop startling me."

"Sorry. I didn't mean to scare you."

"Cash Vangarten," said Hazel. "What are you doing here?"

"I came to watch the Angels play."

"You did?" I said. "You've been here the whole time?"

"From the first pitch. I was hoping you'd agree to that dinner now."

I took a few more steps. "Not now, Cash. Not yet."

"Then when?"

"Can't say."

"Mr. Vangarten," Mother said. "You seem like a nice man. But you can understand my daughter's situation. She just isn't ready to begin dating. Why, her husband, Herman — he was a salesman for the Fuller Brush Company — has only been dead for" — she counted on her fingers — "less than six months. You understand."

"I do," he said. "My wife has been gone three years now. Three years, seven months, and two days."

"I'm sorry," I said. "I didn't know."

Hazel slapped her knee. "All this maudlin talk. Yeah, yeah, and my Birdy's been dead for twenty-five years."

Lillian sniffled. "And my Henry ten."

We all looked at each other and then suddenly burst into laughter.

Cash took my hand after a minute or so.

538

"Okay, Charlotte. You let me know when you're ready."

"Might be a while."

"I can wait."

Then he looked at Hazel. "So, Mrs. Crenshaw, how much longer do I need to coach that team before you'll see I've repented? I've changed. I haven't touched a drop in three years."

Hazel twisted her mouth and considered his question. "Okay. You're done. This can be your last year."

"Thank you," he said. And he took off back toward the field.

Later that night after Mother and I ate a celebratory fried zucchini omelet and she was settled in front of the TV with tea and Lorna Doone cookies, I decided to take a walk with Lucky.

"I'll be back, Mom. I might go visit Rose. We haven't talked much over the last couple of weeks."

"You go right ahead, dear. Enjoy yourself."

"I'll take Lucky."

"That's fine. I'm sure I'll turn in early, or I was thinking I might go over to Hazel's and swap stories about elastic underwear bands."

Sad to say though, Rose wasn't home. I

said, "I bet she's at Ginger's." It was one of the only places she went. Lucky made himself comfortable under the hand near the petunias.

"Come on, Lucky, time to go home. Rose isn't here."

He wouldn't budge.

"Lucky, now. I said Rose isn't home."

He straggled to his feet and grabbed my pant leg and pulled me toward the hand.

"What are you doing? Home is that way."

He barked and circled himself into a comfortable spot.

"What, you want me to go up there?"

He blustered.

"Okay, okay."

I climbed the ladder and sat with my back against God's thumb, under the vastness and the miracle of a million stars. I thought God must have called the entire team onto the field because I never remembered seeing that many stars before.

"So, God," I said. "You know I've never really been comfortable up here. Always seemed just a teeny bit weird. You know, grownups sitting in a cement hand. But I just want you to know that I get it now. I also want you to know that I might not be very good when it comes to keeping secrets, but I am good at keeping my promises, and

I promised Suzy and Asa I would never tell. And I won't."

The street light blinked a couple of times, and I thought maybe God was winking at me, but that's silly. "So I guess this makes me an accessory to the crime. Learned that on Perry Mason. So I'm guilty. I confess, Lord."

Labor Day arrived, and the Angels finished the season with four wins and six losses, so we didn't make it to the playoffs. We were all a little disappointed; Gwendolyn cried worse than baby Angel. But, to be honest, I was pretty tired by then and wasn't too keen on coaching anymore that season after so much had happened. And the women, the Angels? Well, they looked plum tuckered out also.

Asa said he and Studebaker needed to close up the field for the season. I wasn't sure exactly what that meant, so before he had time to do it I took one last walk over there with Lucky. I looked out at the pretty brown and green field. The air was still warm as I watched the sun set behind the trees. "You know, Lucky, I never told you this, but I'm glad you stole the mail that day." I kicked at the dirt, and a small wispy beige cloud blew up around our ankles. I patted Lucky's head. "I still need to give Mother our answer about moving to Florida, though."

Lucky blustered.

"Don't worry, we're not going anywhere. We're staying right here in Paradise." I looked down. The tips of my Keds touched home plate. "See that, Lucky? Now this is what I call coming home."

DISCUSSION QUESTIONS

1. Early in the novel Charlotte says she was filled with a sudden burst of wanderlust. Has this ever happened to you? Did you ever want to make a huge change, maybe even run away and start over?

2. How would you describe Charlotte and Herman's marriage? Was she happy? If not, what kept her tied to him?

3. Several times Charlotte mentions phantom pain. An amputee will sometimes say she can still feel pain even though the injured limb is gone. Life is like that. From time to time past hurts and emotional injuries surface. Discuss this.

4. The theme of sacrifice is important in *Charlotte Figg Takes Over Paradise.* What does it mean to you to sacrifice for your family, friends, God?

5. Rose Tattoo worked hard to cover her scars, even going so far as to hide them under tattoos. What does this say to you?

Do you walk around with hidden scars? Why?

6. Rose has a giant concrete hand in her yard. She likes to sit in it and pray. She painted the Paradise residents' names on it as a way of lifting them to God. What does it mean to you to know that your name is written on God's hand and nothing can erase it — ever?

7. At first glance Paradise seems to be populated by misfits and oddballs. Is it really? Or do the people of Paradise have something the rest of the world is missing?

8. Charlotte played softball in her youth, but the joy of it was taken away from her. When she moved to Paradise, she got softball back. What does this tell you about redemption, about how God delights in giving us the desires of our heart?

9. The Paradise Angels started out rough, but in the end they became a team. The concept of being a team player is bandied about a lot in the corporate world, even in our PTOs and churches. Are you a team player? Are you comfortable in your position? Or are you more of a loner, going your way? Is there room for both?

10. Pie is always available in Paradise. Why is pie important? What does it represent?

ABOUT THE AUTHOR

Joyce Magnin is the author of *The Prayers of Agnes Sparrow,* which was chosen as one of Library Journal's Best Christian Fiction Books of 2009. Joyce attended Bryn Mawr College and is a member of the Greater Philadelphia Christian Writers Fellowship. She is a frequent workshop leader at various writers' conferences and women's church groups. She has three children, Rebekah, Emily, and Adam; two grandsons, Lemuel and Cedar; one son-in-law, Joshua; and a neurotic parakeet. Joyce leads a small fiction group called StoryCrafters. She enjoys baseball, football, cream soda, video games, and needle arts but not elevators. Joyce lives in Havertown, Pennsylvania.

The employees of Thorndike Press hope you have enjoyed this Large Print book. All our Thorndike, Wheeler, and Kennebec Large Print titles are designed for easy reading, and all our books are made to last. Other Thorndike Press Large Print books are available at your library, through selected bookstores, or directly from us.

For information about titles, please call:
  (800) 223-1244

or visit our Web site at:
  http://gale.cengage.com/thorndike

To share your comments, please write:
  Publisher
  Thorndike Press
  10 Water St., Suite 310
  Waterville, ME 04901